THIS IS ME

Also by Shari Low

The Story of Our Life
A Life Without You
The Other Wives Club
With or Without You

The Winter Day Series

One Day in Winter
Another Day in Winter

Non-Fiction

Because Mummy Said So!

THIS IS ME

Shari Low

First published in the United Kingdom in 2019 by Aria, an imprint of Head of Zeus Ltd

Copyright © Shari Low, 2019

The moral right of Shari Low to be identified as the author of this work has been asserted in accordance with the Copyright, Designs and Patents Act of 1988.

All rights reserved. No part of this publication may be reproduced, stored in a retrieval system, or transmitted, in any form or by any means, electronic, mechanical, photocopying, recording, or otherwise, without the prior permission of both the copyright owner and the above publisher of this book.

This is a work of fiction. All characters, organizations, and events portrayed in this novel are either products of the author's imagination or are used fictitiously.

A CIP catalogue record for this book is available from the British Library.

ISBN 9781788541435

Aria
c/o Head of Zeus
First Floor East
5–8 Hardwick Street
London EC1R 4RG

www.ariafiction.com

To my menfolk,
J, C and B
Who are everything and more…

...and This Is Them...

Claire Bradley (née Harrow), 39 – eldest child of Ray and Denise, mum to Max and Jordy.

Sam Bradley, 41 – dad to Max and Jordy, Claire's ex-husband. Currently living with his new partner, Nicola.

Max Bradley, 19 – kicked off Claire's empty nest syndrome when he left home at 17 to join the navy.

Jordy Bradley, 18 – just followed his brother out of the door, gone to take up a football scholarship at an American university.

Denise (McAlee) Harrow, 55 – Claire and Doug's mother. Martyrdom a specialty.

Ray Harrow, 56 – Claire and Doug's father. Obnoxious git.

Doug Harrow, 38 – Claire's brother. The only maths teacher in Scotland who looks like Ricky Martin. Wife

Fiona, a lawyer.

Jeanna McCallan, 39 – Claire's best friend since childhood. Superpower is brutal honesty.

Agnes and Fred McAlee – Denise's parents, Claire's grandparents. Also mum and dad to twins, Rachel and Ronnie, and Donna.

Jenny and Pete Harrow – Ray's parents.

Tom and Sandie Bradley – Sam's parents, also have sons Des, Jason and John.

Josie and Val, 70-something and 60-something (they refuse to confirm the exact numbers) – Claire's pals and support system, two towers of strength who have been through the wars but are still standing.

Prologue

Denise and Claire – August 2019

The fog was dense and chilling, but it was on the inside of Denise's skull. The sun shone through the window, reflecting against the mirror in front of her, but the heat couldn't permeate her body or her mind. Her movements were slow, fumbling, frustrating. The buttons on the black jacket that she couldn't make fasten. The hairbrush that she could barely raise to her head. The eyelids that she could hardly lift because she didn't want to view a world without him.

Ray was gone.

A visceral reaction to that thought forced the air out of her chest, causing her to buckle forward.

He was gone.

Her whole life wiped out in the seconds it took for his brain to stop functioning, then his heart to fail and stop. No warning. No second chances. No hope. Fifty-six years old and he was just gone, leaving a soulless vacuum behind.

She'd given up everything for him, willingly and without question. Now waves of grief were dragging the shifting sands of her life back into the water, sucking her down with them.

But she had to do this last thing for him today.

The crematorium was only a few miles away, on the south side of Glasgow. He was there already. Waiting for her. She was wearing the gorgeous Gina Bacconi black dress and jacket he'd bought her from House of Fraser last year, she'd done her make-up just how he liked it, and she was going to walk into that crematorium with her head held high.

Today she would say a last goodbye to the man who had been her world and she knew, without hesitation, that, despite everything, she would love him until the end of time.

A few miles away, her daughter, Claire, sat on the end of her bed, back straight so as not to put creases in the black dress she'd just peeled from the dry-cleaning bag. A loose strand escaped from the chignon at the nape of her neck and she pushed it back behind her ear with shaking hands, her fingertips gliding over the jaw that was set in defiance of her emotions. She wouldn't crumble. She wouldn't falter.

Her father was gone.

She exhaled, trying desperately to banish the knot that was twisting her gut.

He was gone.

For thirty-nine years, he'd been an undeniable force in her life, his actions and her reactions determining so much of who she was and what she'd become.

A vision of her mother flashed before her. Losing the love of her life would have left her heartbroken, but Claire was sure to her core that Denise would hold it together, put on one last show for her husband. She had never let him down, never faltered in her adoration for a man who was so much more than flawed.

It went against the laws of nature, the ways of humanity, but all she felt for her parents was disgust.

And that's why she too, was going to walk into that crematorium with her head held high.

Today she would say a last goodbye to the man who had treated her like she was nothing and she knew, without hesitation, that she would despise him until the end of time.

One

Claire – 2019 – One Week Earlier

'I've laced it with arsenic to put you out of your misery,' Jeanna said, as she put a steaming cup of coffee down in front of Claire. She hadn't bothered topping it up with cold water to cool it down and avoid scorching of the lips, because she figured Claire was so focused on staring at her phone it would take at least ten minutes for her to realise it was there.

'Yeah, lovely, thanks,' Claire replied distractedly, as predicted, the jokey threat of imminent poisoning failing to register.

Jeanna sat in her usual chair, directly across from her distracted friend, in the distracted friend's kitchen. It was only a few miles away from her home in Glasgow's city centre, so she dropped by at least a couple of times a week for dinner, and these Sunday cuppas were weekly events. They'd been best mates for over twenty-five years and stuck together through thick, thin, and opposing views on their favourite member of Take That (Jeanna – Robbie, Claire – Howard). Today, however, was more of an emergency visitation situation. Jeanna was here to provide emotional support and consolation in her friend's time of need. Unfortunately, as always, that came out like brutal honesty and flippant disregard for the gravity of the situation. 'Stop staring at the phone. He isn't going to call. Caramel wafer?'

Claire still didn't look up. 'No. I haven't been to Zumba for a fortnight. My arse is the size of a beanbag.'

Claire paused, her eyes finally leaving the phone to dart to the biscuit tin that was now silently shouting to her from the middle of the table. She tugged on the sleeve of her standard comfy jumper, then assessed the tightness of the waistband on her equally standard jeans. It wasn't cutting off the blood supply to her extremities, so there was room for indulgence.

'Sod it, I'll have one. Big arses are in fashion these days.'

As always, Jeanna resisted temptation. A dedicated gym goer with buttocks like melons, she hadn't willingly consumed a non-alcoholic carb since the nineties. Her daily dress code of trainers, Lycra running tights, a tiny vest and a clingy hoodie was a constant reminder that her body was a temple that could not be violated by Claire's stash of high calorie snacks. She took a sip of her green tea and spotted that Claire's eyes had strayed back to her phone. 'Dear God, will you give it up? He isn't going to call.'

Claire swallowed the heady combination of caramel, chocolate and wafer before replying with as much indignation as she could muster. 'He is.'

'No he isn't. You're wasting your life waiting around for him and he ISN'T GOING TO CALL. You realise this is an exact replica of a conversation we had when we were fifteen and you were madly in love with the bloke who played the bass guitar in that crap band that assaulted our ears down the youth club disco.'

Claire tried to be offended, but the twenty-four year old memory made her react with something between a laugh and a cringe. 'Bobby Wright! I wrote my telephone number on the towel he used to wipe the sweat off his brow between sets. I was sure he was the next Jon Bon Jovi. He works in the butchers in the High Street now and I can't buy pork chops with a straight face.'

Jeanna giggled. 'Go vegetarian. It'll save the embarrassment. But the point is… back then, Bobby Bon Jovi didn't call and Jordy isn't going to call either.'

Claire knew she was right, but she couldn't bring herself to give up hope. Back in 1994, her eighteen year old heart could take the rejection, but this was different. It wasn't some teenage crush she was waiting to hear from. All she wanted to see on the screen was an incoming call from her youngest child, Jordan Samuel Bradley. Age eighteen. Her son. The one who'd gone off to university last week without an ounce of hesitation. It wasn't even as if it was somewhere in Scotland, and he'd be popping home every weekend with his washing. Nope, a soccer scholarship had taken him to a university in Tennessee, just outside Nashville. Getting there had been a long, arduous process, sacrificing normal teenage life to train, work, graft, make himself the best player he could be. She was beyond proud and thrilled that it had paid off and he'd achieved the goal he'd set himself when he first went to high school, yet every time she thought of him being away for four years she had an urge to break into full Whitney Houston mode and deliver a tearful yet dramatic rendition of 'I Will Always Love You'.

His independence was nothing new. Hadn't she taught both her children to be that way? But that didn't make it any easier. When she took Jordy along to the school gates for his very first day at primary school, he might have been a little shy but only one of them had suffered acute separation anxiety and it wasn't the short one with the Power Rangers backpack.

Twelve years later, when she'd waved him off in the car park of a Tennessee university, it was a different backpack, same story.

'You know, it wasn't supposed to be like this. I thought when I had my kids I'd signed up for thirty years of love and devotion, with them by my side. Because, you know, no one was going to prise my little darlings away. And what happens?' Claire asked, then steamed on and answered herself. 'First, Max joins the flipping navy – I get seasick on the Gourock to Dunoon ferry and yet someone who shares my genes has decided to live underwater. And now Jordy has moved to the other side of the world. I mean, it's enough to give anyone a complex. I'm barely thirty-bloody-nine and I'm home alone already!'

'Is this the point when I'm supposed to step in with pearls of wisdom and sympathy?' Jeanna asked, slightly alarmed. Emotional consolations and expressions of comfort fell outwith her range of personality skills.

Claire sighed. 'Nope, I know your limitations. Just pass me another biscuit. Make it a Wagon Wheel this time.'

'No, I'm not doing it,' Jeanna replied, with unwavering defiance. 'Look, I'll give you today to wallow, and then that's it. You need to look at the positives. For the first time in nearly twenty years, you have your whole life back. You don't need to do anything for anyone, be anywhere because someone needs a lift, or be organising your life around other people. You're completely free.'

'Are you trying to make me cry?'

'No! I'm trying to say stop being pathetic and instead start thinking about all the brilliant things you can do now.'

Ignoring Jeanna was never an option, so Claire had no choice but to ask the question and brace herself for a slew of suggestions. 'Like?'

'Like read books. Find a hobby. Go to the gym. Get fit. Lose weight.'

'I'd rather knock myself out trying to get a large box of Wagon Wheels off a high shelf,' Claire replied, deadpan.

'OK. But you could travel. Meet someone. Have sex.'

'Make that two large boxes of Wagon Wheels.'

Jeanna wasn't letting her off the hook. 'You could just try putting yourself first.'

Claire tried to come up with a witty retort, but her heart wasn't in it. It would be 9 a.m. in Nashville now. She'd sent a text asking Jordy to call her as soon as he was awake and he'd have been up for at least an hour by now. She couldn't argue on the fact that she was being pathetic. She knew it was true. But this was day three without speaking to him and she just felt… lost. And slightly stressed. He could have been kidnapped. Had his drink spiked. Fallen down a mine shaft.

Note to self – check if there are many disused mines in a ten mile radius of Nashville.

She just wasn't equipped to deal with this situation. She'd been a mother for two decades and she'd pretty much sussed out everything except where to find the off switch.

'You're right,' she finally admitted. 'I know you are. And I know this is a perfect opportunity to get my chunky arse in gear. But I just… just…' She reached out for the Wagon Wheel, using the wrapper to stem the tears that were threatening to fall.

'Oh Jesus…' Jeanna sighed, rolling her eyes.

Claire took no notice of the lack of sympathy. 'I just miss them,' she wailed. 'And I know it's a total cliché, but I've been their mum for so long, I've no idea what to do without them.' It was true. Before the boys deserted her, her days had followed a set pattern. Get up, have breakfast with them, tackle the school run, go to work, collect them afterwards, take them to the gym or to Max's swimming practice or Jody's football training, or one of their mate's houses, or to a party, or – if they graced her with their presence – to a family night out at the cinema or the local Nandos.

Now? Nothing but bleak emptiness.

Jeanna's voice was barely audible over the noise of a loud sniff from her pal. 'You definitely need to have sex. Or get your jaws clamped.'

Claire fired the wrapper at her. 'And get a new friend,' she retorted, holding her own. They both knew she didn't mean it. This heady combination of brutal honesty, intolerance and underlying care was a very familiar dynamic. They'd been inseparable since high school, when Jeanna had lured her into the netball team with the promise that the football squad came to all their games and they'd find her irresistible. All Claire got was a new best friend who made her laugh, chafed thighs and a knock-back from the footie team's star striker.

Over two decades later, their dynamic hadn't changed much. Claire was the warm ying to Jeanna's incredibly dry, frequently bitchy yang. Through the years, they'd survived everything that the world had thrown at them. Jeanna's two divorces, followed by her enthusiastic embrace of the online dating scene. Health issues. Make ups. Break ups. A difference of opinion on almost every subject they'd ever discussed. Several career changes for Jeanna, until she had found her calling as a life coach – someone who lit fires under the buttocks of people who weren't reaching their personal and career goals. Then there was Claire's one failed marriage. The traumatic split at a time when she was at her most vulnerable. And her life as a single mother to two teenagers.

They'd weathered every storm together, triumphed over every crisis, right up to the point where one of them was sporting a disappointed duck face (Jeanna had overdone the fillers again) and the other was comfort eating retro, circle shaped chocolate biscuits.

Jeanna was still dwelling on Claire's comment about getting a new best friend. 'Good luck finding one as irresistible as me,' she retorted, her Botoxed eyebrows trying their best to form an indignant arch.

'You're right. I'd miss the DEFCON level one bitchiness and judgement.'

Jeanna laughed, the pressure of pushing her cheeks outwards almost, but not quite, causing the abomination of a crow's foot. 'And my unlimited, but understated, adoration.'

Claire's crows' feet appeared as soon as she chuckled, 'Yep, I'd be lost without that too.'

Her phone suddenly burst into life.

'Oh thank G…' she started, snatching it up, before her words drifted off and she was left open mouthed, just staring at the screen.

Jeanna leaned forward, curious. 'Aren't you going to answer it?'

'No.'

'Why not? Is this some maternal lesson you're trying to teach him? Only, you're cutting off your nose to spite your face there.'

'It's not Jordy.' Claire's words were low and could barely be heard over the repetitive ringtone.

'Who is it?'

'It's my… my mother.'

Her mother. It had been many years since she'd seen that name flashing on the screen and even the thought of that woman made Claire's throat tighten. It had been Claire's choice to remove her mum from her life, but there had been no argument from the other side.

Her gaze returned to the phone for a few more seconds. Then Claire pressed the red button and rejected the call.

Two

Denise – 2019

Denise hadn't expected her to answer. In truth, she knew Claire had no reason to pick up the phone to her, but contacting her had just seemed like the right thing to do. She could picture her daughter now – all bloody sanctimonious and defiant. Ray would say he was right all along, that Denise should have known better than to even bother trying to contact her.

She tossed the phone on to the silver silk duvet and spoke to him in her mind. 'I know, my love. I know,' she whispered.

The urge to climb off their bed became impossible to ignore as the longing to reach over and touch him became so overwhelming that she couldn't bear to look at the space beside her. For forty years, he'd been next to her. Not every night, of course. For many years now his work as the boss of his own construction company took him away, sometimes for a few days at a time, and on every single trip she'd count the hours until he came home.

The feel of the carpet under her toes was no comfort either. He'd picked it. Said the wooden floor they used to have there was too cold. Now the carpet was thick, grey, as dark as the hole he'd left behind.

On the black glass dressing table, there was a bottle of red wine, the last one they'd shared. She opened it and poured the last drops from the bottle into the glass he'd used, then pressed it to her lips. Inhaled. Exhaled. Then tipped the glass and drained the intoxicating red liquid.

She should eat something, but she couldn't face the kitchen, the fridge, the pantry, his favourite foods, the cheese he'd opened the day before he'd passed, the bread that she'd travelled to a French baker on the other side of the city to buy for him because he said it was the best.

It had been so sudden. He was there, then he was gone. An aneurism. Brain bleed. Caused by a slip in the shower, a fall, a bang to the head. A twisted episode of misfortune. If he'd just put his hand out, broken the fall, slid the other way, moved his head at the last minute, done any one of a hundred things that would have made a difference to the outcome, he'd still be here. But no. One moment he was there, singing in the shower while she drank coffee in bed. Then there was a crash and he was gone. They told her later that it was likely that his brain had been irreparably damaged almost instantly, before the paramedics she called had arrived, before the towels on the floor had dried, before her screaming had stopped.

Now, she was in the same room she'd been in when she'd heard him fall, the window was wide open and yet she could barely find the oxygen to breath.

She pulled another bottle of wine from the rack above the mini-bar in the lounge area of the bedroom. His idea too. They'd knocked the wall down that used to separate their room from Claire's childhood bedroom, and made it into a luxurious master suite, modelled on a hotel they'd stayed in on a weekend in Las Vegas. Ray had loved his five-star hotels, his upmarket restaurants, his expensive suits, his first-class travels, his luxury holidays.

She realised she'd lost her train of thought. The mini-bar. The suite at the Aria. As soon as they'd returned, he'd brought in a squad of his builders and taken the wall down. 'I want you to wake up in a beautiful room every day,' he'd told her.

And then he did what he was good at, took charge, made his vision into reality. Denise didn't have to give any input at all as he got to work creating a master bedroom and lounge in stunning shades of silver and greys, with glass and chrome furniture and lighting that cost more than the Vegas weekend. It had a seating area, a stunning, oversized, overstuffed chenille sofa, a huge television on the wood-panelled wall, a fireplace, a coffee maker, the wine rack and the mini-bar for soft drinks and water. After it was finished to perfection, they rarely used the downstairs lounge, preferring to come upstairs to relax, to talk, to watch movies, to make love.

On the outside, their house looked like any other three bedroom house in Giffnock, the Glasgow suburb that they'd lived in since just before the kids started school. Claire would have been about five, and Doug close to four. It had originally been Ray's grandfather's house, left when the old man died, with only a small mortgage still to pay off. Not that it bore any resemblance to the dilapidated, dingy place they'd moved into way back then. Over the years, as Ray's business grew and they could afford it, they'd converted it, room by room, into a family house. It helped that Ray was in the trade, so he got everything at cost and mates rates from everyone who worked on it.

Of course, back in the early days, he didn't have the team that he had now. He'd started out as an electrician in the same power plant as his father, before going out on his own and diversifying into general construction, bringing in mates to help on bigger extensions or kitchen installations. Denise had worked with him, answering the phone, booking appointments, sending out invoices, chasing up planning departments and building control. Along with bringing up the kids and taking care of this house, it had kept her busy, especially as Ray had gradually accrued a team of self-employed sub-contractors and moved on to bigger jobs, sometimes several renovations or builds at the same time.

After a few years, with the small mortgage paid off and good money coming in, they'd developed a taste for the nicer things in life. First-class travel. Expensive holidays. Great clothes. Fancy dinners. Ray liked to splash the cash and Denise wasn't complaining because she'd enjoyed it all right by his side, especially after the kids, Claire and Doug, had left. That's when they'd made the final alterations, changing the house into the perfect home for just the two of them. Ray always said that was all that mattered – the two of them.

On the back wall of the master suite there was a door to a walk-in closet. They'd converted Doug's old bedroom and made it into a 'his and hers' storage space, with Denise's clothes on one side, Ray's on the other, and a set of back-to-back drawers, topped with a large slab of granite, making an island in the middle.

Opening the mirrored door of one of his wardrobes, the scent of him immediately enveloped her. She held on to the door to steady herself, overcome once again with the pain of his absence.

How would she function without him? He was her everything. Her world. There was, and never had been, anyone else. Every decision, every thought, every action had been for them both. How would she ever adjust to a world in which he wasn't by her side, making her happy, filling every need she'd ever had? She was part of a pair, not a solo act. Without him there was nothing and nobody. What would be the point of waking up every day to a life of solitude? Yet, no one and nothing could ever replace him.

A quicksand of loneliness threatened to pull her down, but she struggled against it, taking large gulps of air until she could return to the task in front of her.

Tell me, she said silently. *Tell me what you want.*

She began to flick through his suits, all of them grouped by colour, shade, occasion, all perfectly pressed on padded velvet hangers. Eventually, she paused at a deep navy single-breasted jacket, the matching trousers tucked under it. She remembered when he'd bought that one. Last year, his birthday, a weekend trip to London. They'd gone to shows, shopped on Oxford Street, eaten in restaurants that Denise had only seen on the pages of celebrity magazines. Ray had absolutely belonged there. Denise wasn't sure she did, but she'd learned not to show her self-consciousness because it upset him. She deserved the best, he'd tell her.

They were two council house kids and look how far they'd come, he'd say.

She took the suit out of the wardrobe and placed it on the hook on the back of the door, then added a white shirt and the tie she'd bought him last Christmas. Socks. Shoes.

When the outfit was complete, she took it all into the main room and laid it on the bed, then opened another bottle of wine and filled her glass, not sure what to do next.

Of course she'd lost people before. Her parents. Ray's parents. But in those cases, their houses had filled with family and friends who came to offer sympathies, to share the loss, to bring casseroles and bread and tales of the times they'd had with the person who'd passed. Mourning was a time for gathering, for coming together to celebrate a life and share the sorrow of a passing.

No one was knocking on her door.

No one had come in the week since she'd returned home from the hospital, bereft, clutching only his bloodstained clothes, his watch and his wedding ring.

She snatched up her phone again, the second glass of red wine making her bold, pushing her to take action, to find someone – anyone – to share this grief. She scrolled through her contacts. When was the last time she'd talked to her siblings? Five years ago? Ten? Had she really not spoken to anyone else in her family in all that time? Of course, they had so little in common, and hadn't been close for years before that anyway.

No, she couldn't call them now. What would be the point? So they'd feel obliged to come, to sit awkwardly in her kitchen, giving fake sympathy and platitudes about a guy they'd never particularly liked in the first place? No.

Ray would hate that. He hadn't liked them when he was alive, so he wasn't going to want them there in death.

She flicked through more numbers on the screen, then stopped when one name brought on another flash of pain. Doug. Her son. She could hear Ray's roar of rage if she called that number. It had been many years since she'd heard his voice, seen his face, but that was his loss. She knew that. Hadn't she and Ray discussed it so many times? Claire and Doug had walked out of their lives for the same reasons. She didn't even want to think about that now. Hadn't Ray told her again and again that they weren't worthy of her? Only Ray deserved her time and her love.

Numbers exhausted, she threw the handset on the bed, her eyes drawn to Ray's mobile phone, which had been sitting on the charging dock on his bedside table since the morning she'd called the ambulance.

Reaching over, she picked it up, switched it on, then watched as the screen came to life with the image of the two of them, toasting each other with champagne on the deck of the Queen Mary 2 as it set sail from Southampton en route to New York just a few months ago. Their fortieth wedding anniversary. The captain hadn't believed them, said she looked far too young to have been married that long.

She punched in the code to open the phone, realising it was the first time she'd ever done that. She'd seen Ray doing it so many times that she knew the code by heart, but he'd have been furious if she'd ever looked through his phone, so she never had.

She went to contacts, the names coming up in alphabetical order. Restaurants. Hotels. Car valet. Architects. The tradesmen who sub-contracted for him on bigger jobs. Joiners. Landscapers. Painters. Plumbers. X. Y. Z. The end.

Or not.

The 'Z' category was empty, but there was one number in the preceding group, identified with only a Y. That was it. Just Y. It was all Denise needed to identify who it belonged to. That woman. Her.

He'd kept that bitch's number.

A guttural sob escaped her. A whole fucking set of contacts and there was not a single person she could call for comfort, for help, to listen to her pain, until the very last contact in his phone. Y. It was a cruel bastard irony. The only person who might have just a glimmer of understanding about how she was feeling right now. And it would be a cold day in hell before she made that call.

She quickly searched his messages and past calls for any contact with Y, but there was nothing. Small consolation. He still shouldn't have saved that bloody number.

She tossed the phone across the bed, the thud as it hit the duvet breaking through her red mist of anger, then she picked up her wine again and climbed into bed, still fully clothed, hoping that the warmth of the duvet would make the shivering stop.

She reached over to Ray's side and picked up the tie that she'd left there, wrapping it around her neck, desperate to have a part of him touching her.

How was she to live? What was she to actually do with her days? Her dreams had been *their* dreams. Her plans had been *their* plans. How was she to move forward on her own, to have a purpose in a life without him in it?

Ray Harrow had been her world from the moment she'd met him at fifteen years old, utterly clueless about life. Now the dark shadows of emptiness and loss were creeping in around the sides of her peripheral vision and she didn't know how to make them stop.

Three

Denise & Ray – 1978

The disco at the local youth club was a full house, with every teenager under the age of seventeen who lived within a five mile radius in attendance. Denise was in the toilets, topping up her Avon lipstick. She'd worked two nights in the cafe after school that week so she'd have the cash for her make-up order, because there was no way her mother would pay for it. The twins had just started high school and her mum was still bemoaning the cost of the uniforms. In the last couple of months, her wages had also stretched to the bell bottom jeans and the off-white cheesecloth shirt she was wearing now.

The sound of David Soul singing 'Silver Lady' permeated the walls from the main hall next door. He was her favourite in *Starsky and Hutch* too – when she was actually allowed to watch it. It depended on whether her dad was watching snooker or something on the other side.

Denise loved that song, but she wouldn't dance. No way. Although she knew what was coming because, beside her, her best friend, Alice, was already singing along.

'Oh, come on, let's go dance! I love this song!'

'No, you know I don't da—' Denise knew it was futile. They were best friends, neighbours and shared the bus to school every morning too, and in all that time, Alice, gregarious and always up for fun, had never taken no for an answer. Not once. Now wasn't any different. Before Denise could even finish the sentence, Alice grabbed her hand and pulled her out of the toilets and into the dark hall, illuminated only by two banks of flashing red and green lights that sat on top of the speakers on the stage, one on either side of the DJ. Actually not so much a DJ as the janitor who fancied himself as a bit of a star on the mixing desk.

The only consolation was that in the darkness, no one could see the burning flames of embarrassment that were creeping up her neck and onto her cheeks. Not for the first time, she wished she had Alice's wild side, the ability to let loose and not give a damn about what anyone thought about her.

The song changed. 'I Only Want to Be With You' by the Bay City Rollers. Crap. There was no way she was getting Alice off the dance floor now – this was one of their favourites, although Denise much preferred dancing in the privacy of her own bedroom, using a can of her mum's Elnett hairspray as a microphone.

Glancing up, she saw a reprieve in sight. Billy Jones was coming right up behind Alice, his hand raising to tap her on the shoulder. Brilliant. She could escape back to the sidelines where the pressure was off. The tap on her own shoulder confused her for a second. Just as Alice turned to see Billy, Ray Harrow appeared from behind Denise's left side.

'Wanna dance?'

Cue full body paralysis.

Ray Harrow. One of the best looking boys in school, he was in the year above her, although, like half the boys in his class, he'd be leaving soon to take up an apprenticeship at the power plant that was the biggest employer in the town. No way did he want to dance with her. This must be a joke. Or a bet.

Thankfully, he didn't wait for an answer, just started dancing three feet in front of her, his eyes not leaving her face, the grin on his face just making him even better looking.

Somehow, she forced her feet to shuffle so that she wasn't standing there looking like a plank, wondering if her face was now giving more illumination to the room than the disco lights.

He must be doing this as a favour to Billy. Yeah, that was it. Billy had fancied Alice for months, and Ray was one of his mates, so he was obviously just helping his pal out. Oh well. In a couple of minutes it would be done, and in the meantime, she got to look at him from under her thick blonde fringe. His dark hair was longer than the neckline of his jumper and she'd always thought he looked a bit like David Cassidy, especially in those denim flares he was wearing.

The music ended and she decided to make the first move away, to save the embarrassment of having him walk off and leave her there. Out of the corner of her eye, she could see that Billy had taken Alice's hand and he was leading her off the dance floor. Crap. It distracted her for a few seconds, long enough for Ray to step forward and say something in her ear. She couldn't hear him over the noise of Boney M's 'Ma Baker', so she shrugged, then came close to fainting when she felt his hand take hers and give it a gentle tug in the same direction as their departing friends.

Oh God.

Out in the foyer, Ray turned to her and she realised that this was the first time she'd been close enough to see how white and perfect his teeth were. He gestured to the snack stall set up in the corner.

'Wanna can of Coke?'

'Sure,' she replied, managing not to stutter the word out. Her heart was racing, her stomach flipping.

Why was he talking to her? Alice was always telling her how pretty she was, like a young Goldie Hawn, she always said, but still, he could have anyone. And besides, Denise was pretty sure Alice was biased because they were pals. After all, she'd never had a proper boyfriend, so she couldn't be that gorgeous. Although, she had snogged a couple of boys, but that didn't count because it was usually at parties after they'd had a few cans of cider, and she was always much too embarrassed to talk to them at school the following Monday, so she'd avoided them at all costs.

He was back a few seconds later with a can in his hand, not in the least fazed by having to walk around Alice and Billy, who were snogging against the wall next to the snack stall.

'Here you go. So we're heading over to Billy's house because his parents are away. Fancy coming?'

'I don't think I—'

'Yes!' It came from behind him, from Alice, who had finally come up for air. 'My mum will already be sleeping. She'll never notice if we come home a bit late.'

Denise flushed again. Go back to a boy's house? Her mother would kill her – and then pray to God for her soul to be forgiven. Her stomach began to twist into a knot. Alice's expression of defiance and giddy joy, and the fact that she was wound around Billy and showing no signs of letting go, told Denise there was no way she could make her friend change her mind. But she was supposed to be staying with Alice tonight and if she went home instead, her mother would immediately phone Alice's mum to tell her why.

'OK then,' she conceded, her stomach flipping once more when Ray grinned at her and took her hand again with a confidence that said he'd known all along that she'd agree. Ray Harrow wasn't the kind of guy that anyone ever said no to.

Shelley Cavenagh walked past right at that moment and when she saw them together her jaw nearly hit the linoleum floor, before her face set in a glare of complete fury. She'd been Ray's steady girlfriend for the last year and everyone knew they were sleeping together. It had been the talk of the school when they'd split up last month. Shelley was now seeing someone else, but the rumour mill had decided it was just to make Ray jealous. It clearly wasn't working.

'Let's get out of here,' he said, summoning Billy and Alice, who were back in full scale snog mode.

They reluctantly unlocked their lips and headed for the door, Alice giggling the whole way there. Outside, she pulled Denise to one side.

'Ray Harrow!' she giggled. 'Well, if you're going to lose it to someone it's as well being him.'

Denise nearly fainted. 'I'm not going to lose it to anyone! At least... not yet.'

The swinging sixties might have heralded an age of free love that had lingered into the seventies, but it had never swung into this working class town on the outskirts of Glasgow. Even Alice hadn't had full sex yet and she'd had four boyfriends.

Again, the prospect of her mother raging at her made her consider fleeing the scene. She'd be marched up to the priest first thing in the morning and then grounded until the end of time if she so much as entertained the idea of having sex before marriage. Not that she was going to wait until then, but at the very least, if she was going to sleep with someone, then they'd have to be engaged. Or maybe even just in a long term relationship. And it would have to be a total secret that no one – especially her mother – could ever find out.

Nope there was no way. Absolutely not. Besides, Ray Harrow was the coolest, sexiest guy in the school. If he wanted to sleep with someone, there were plenty of girls out there to choose from, and he wouldn't go for someone as shy and completely inexperienced as she was. Eyes glancing at him from under her fringe as they walked along the High Street towards Billy's housing estate, she was surer than ever that he was just doing this as a favour to his pal. He's couldn't be interested in her, but if he did try to kiss her, then she was going to let him, she decided. Shelley Cavenagh was going to make her life miserable next week anyway, so she might as well make it worth it.

But as for anything more than that? Even if he asked her, she was absolutely, definitely, 100 per cent positive that she was going to say no.

Four

Claire – 2019

Nine a.m. Monday morning. The first thing Claire did when she arrived at her bridal salon every day was head to the office area and check the appointment book. This morning was no different. The thick red leather planner, a Christmas present from Jeanna, told her there were no new clients today so that would give her a chance to work on her outstanding orders and prepare for the rest of the week, while fielding texts from Jeanna with suggestions of new ways she could fill her time. And no, she didn't care if pole dancing would give her the buttocks of a Kardashian.

In the hours since she and Jeanna had sat at her kitchen table waiting for Jordy to call yesterday, she'd ricocheted from sadness (she missed him!), to despair (was he missing?), to excitement about the future, to wondering if stalking someone that once lived inside your body was a criminal offence. Jeanna said it was – and that Claire would know for sure if she decided to get a life and go to the criminology night classes that were on after the pole dancing at the local community centre. Claire was sticking to her guns (also covered in the criminology class) and making her own plans. She'd spent the rest of the day and night yesterday trying and failing to sit down and tackle her reading pile, writing texts to the boys and deleting them before she sent them and cleaning and organising the house. Her linen cupboard could now feature in architectural magazines.

Now, her bones ached, she was weary, but at least work would keep her mind busy for the rest of the week.

As always, she got a surge of pleasure when she switched on the lights in the showroom area of Everlasting Bridal Design, her wedding dress creation service. She'd dreamt about making a living this way since her grandad, Fred, passed down her granny's old Singer sewing machine when she was barely a teenager. For the next few years, she'd made all her own clothes, before going on to study Fashion Design at college. Afterwards, she'd juggled her professional dreams with bringing up the boys, doing more with every year that passed, until she'd finally realised her dream of opening her own bridal salon last year.

Business had been thriving since she moved to the new premises, a small, two room and bathroom, first floor space in the Merchant City area of Glasgow. This was where she met clients, where they told her their vision, where she designed their dress and where they came for fittings the whole way through the process. The front door opened into a hallway, which fed off to the bathroom and another room that served as an office and small kitchen. The one large main room was the showroom area, simple but sumptuous with a gloss wooden floor, white panelled walls, six huge, almost floor to ceiling windows that flooded the room with loads of natural light, and a gloriously high ceiling from which hung a stunning chandelier she'd found in an old antiques warehouse and restored with some imagination and lots of polishing. There was a velvet pedestal in the middle of the room for the brides to stand on while she worked, two changing rooms, a rack with samples, a display cabinet with tiaras and other accessories, and two throne-like chairs and a chaise longue that had been discarded, battered and tatty, in the corner of the same place she'd found the chandelier. Claire had taken them home, sanded and painted the woodwork in pale gold, and re-upholstered the seating in dark red velvet. They now looked stunning. She loved this place. Every inch of it had been decorated and thought through with love and it showed.

Moving her work out of her home and into a city centre premises had been a big risk, but so far it was paying off even more than she could have hoped. The footfall and shopping demographic in the area really helped as the addition of her salon made the street something of a one-stop area for wedding preparations.

Downstairs was CAMDEN, an upmarket menswear boutique owned by a lovely guy called Cammy and his soon-to-be wife, Caro. Next along in the Victorian terrace was Sun, Sea, Ski – a holiday shop owned by the adorable Jen, helped out by an absolute sweetheart called Chrissie. And the third shop in the mini plaza was Pluckers, a legendary hairdressing and beauty salon that attracted everyone from the city's fashionista set to the local senior citizens who popped in for their weekly blow-dry, all under the watchful eye of Suze, a force of nature who could give Jeanna a run for her money in the sarcasm stakes. It was the perfect location for Everlasting Bridal Design, and the most heart warming thing of all was that the neighbouring owners had all swept in, supported her and sent clients her way, so much so that she was considering taking on a new member of staff. But was that what she really wanted?

At the moment, the business was run in a very intimate way, with Claire giving each bride a one-to-one service and seeing each dress through from conception to the dum-dum-da-dum bit. In the brides-to-be would come, with pictures torn from magazines, snaps on their phones, even – if they were full scale bridezillas – vision boards and swatches, and they'd begin the process of creating the gown of their dreams.

There was no escaping the irony. She was divorced, as were her brother and best friend, and her parents had the most dysfunctional marriage she'd ever encountered, yet here she was making other people's romantic dreams come true. Happy ever after by proxy. It was better than nothing.

Claire's bespoke creations weren't cheap and with rent, rates and materials she wasn't going to be buying a yacht anytime soon, but it was enough to clear a decent living and she'd never had a disappointed customer. Another seamstress would be a big help though. That had always been the next step in the strategy entitled Expand The Business To Take The Mind Off The Impending Empty Nest. She'd drawn the plan up the year before when Max left home and Jordy started his search for a scholarship. It was all very good in theory, but the flat feeling in the bottom of her stomach suggested it might not quite be working now that the reality of her empty nest had well and truly kicked in.

Back in the compact office slash kitchen slash staffroom off the main showroom, she'd just switched on the Dolce Gusto coffee machine, when the doorbell rang. Claire had barely opened it when two women stormed in, one a seventy something with grey spiky hair, red lips, wearing an all black, militaryesque outfit that clearly came from the House of SWAT, the other topped by a platinum blonde bob and the bluest eyeshadow in the history of cosmetics.

'Morning, Vera Wang,' the older of the two sang, as she barged past her.

'Aright love,' chirped the blonde bringing up the rear.

Not for the first time, Claire realised it was ridiculous – she was thirty-nine years old, and true, she was a couple of stone over her recommended weight, her make-up was a five minute exercise in the mornings and her hair was normally pulled up in a fairly nondescript ponytail, but still – she was being utterly out-glamoured and out-sexied by Val, who was pushing sixty and Josie, who'd been eligible for a pension for nearly a decade. Not that her friends' advancing years or pensions were ever up for discussion. Josie maintained that she was far too fabulous to acknowledge or comment on either subject. She was right.

'Morning, ladies,' Claire said, her voice oozing amusement. Josie and Val were two of her favourite perks of the new premises. Val's adopted daughter, Jen, owned Sun, Sea, Ski, and they were close friends of Cammy, Caro and Suze from the other shops downstairs too. They were the kind of women who believed you could never have too many friends and who took in waifs and strays, pulling them into their family circle. Hallelujah to that, Claire decided, the first time they'd popped up for a nosy and to introduce themselves. Since then, they'd made a point of dropping by a couple of times a week to ooh and aah at her latest creations, catch up on any gossip and work their way through her generous stock of chocolate biscuits.

She was just about to close the door behind them, when another force pushed it back open. Jeanna. Carrying a large tray of Danish pastries.

'So I decided, fuck it. If ever there was a day to blow the diet, this is it,' she announced, her perfectly white veneers glinting so much they could cause blindness to anyone who didn't have the sense to look away.

Claire followed her into the showroom and stood, hands on hips, trying not to smile at the scene in front of her. Val and Josie had liberated two tiaras from her headwear display and they were both sitting like royalty on the ornate chaise longue that was generally reserved for the mothers, grannies, sisters and friends of her clients. And, unlike any of those women ever, they had both brought flasks of tea and were now waiting expectantly for Jeanna to dole out the apple pastries.

'What's going on?' Claire asked warily. With this group it could be anything from a quick social chat to delivering earth shattering news.

'It's an interval,' Val blurted, earning a roll of the eyes and a swift elbow nudge from Josie.

'An intervention, Val,' Josie corrected her. 'Dear God. Here we are trying to be all modern day touchy-feely and you're messing up the terminology.' It wasn't the first time she'd failed to grasp the current lingo. Val thought a mansplainer was a DIY tool and a catfish could be purchased at the seafood counter in ASDA.

Unruffled, Val shrugged her shoulders, the action not even stirring her blonde bob, which was, as always, hairsprayed to the consistency of steel. 'Could be worse. I could just have said we're here to make sure she doesn't lie on the floor wailing into the shagpile all day. Which, let's face it, is the truth of the matter.'

Despite still trying to maintain an air of disapproval, Claire couldn't help but be touched. There was a chink in her DNA that made her endlessly surprised when people went out of their way to be concerned about her. She'd never get used to it.

Still, she wasn't giving in that easily to being railroaded, especially when she had no idea what the conspirators had planned for her.

'An intervention,' she repeated, deadpan, before rounding on Jeanna. 'I suppose this was your idea?'

'Nope, it was all Josie.'

Josie nodded, accepting the blame. 'I was looking for an excuse to sit on my backside all day and wallow in someone else's pain while eating free pastries. Those handsome boys of yours deserting you at this time was a happy convenience for me.'

The edges of Claire's lips turned upwards. It was impossible to be pissed off with this lot. And the truth was, most of what she was going to do today could wait, so hey, a morning with pals and comfort food suddenly sounded like a damn good idea.

'I give in,' she said, plonking herself down on one of the lush red velvet reproduction chairs.

Josie took charge. 'Good. So here's the deal. You get to talk about it all today. To reminisce about the good times, swear about the bad, and you can cry your eyes out over this chapter closing if you want. Val, you'll need to handle that bit, because you know I don't do tears and snot.' She grimaced at the thought, before continuing, 'And then, after that, we're going to talk about all the ways you can make life happier going forward, because it'll be an absolute beamer if you keep stalking those boys and they have to take out a restraining order.'

'Are you doing criminology classes down the community centre?' Claire asked, giggling.

'Nope, lifetime addiction to *Prime Suspect*,' Josie retorted.

'Excellent. You'll come in handy for legal queries then,' Claire shot back. 'Although, in my defence, I wasn't aware that I couldn't just drop by the Navy base and visit him whenever I pleased. Archaic rules if you ask me.'

'I'm sure the Ministry of Defence have their reasons,' Jeanna interjected dryly, 'You know, trifling things like national security and prevention of espionage.'

'I only wanted to take him my lemon drizzle, not commandeer a nuclear warhead,' Claire argued, her defiance disintegrating into amusement. 'Anyway, I don't want to wallow…'

'Of course you do,' Josie countered. 'And, like we said, this is it. Your one and only day to do it. After that, we reserve the right to tell you that you're pathetic and start sprinting across the street when we see you coming. And we can't have Val running, not with her hips.'

'Understood,' Claire said solemnly.

A buzz from her phone interrupted the conversation, and she lurched for it and snatched it up with such speed she got a head rush.

Jordy's name flashed on the screen. Yes! But... bloody hell, it was after 2 a.m. in Nashville. Making the most of Freshers week then.

She opened the text.

Hey mum, sorry I missed your 11 calls. I'm not dead, injured, in jail or in the boot of a kidnapper's car so you can stand down. Love ya, miss ya, and stop stalking me. PS: dad only called once this weekend, so you're winning the overprotective parent award so far.

A bellow of laughter was swept up from her gut on a wave of relief, followed by an immediate and even more ferocious flood of longing. She missed him so much. He made her laugh, would chat all night, and who was she going to dance with in the kitchen now?

She read it out to the others, that one text completely eliminating the pit that had been weighing down her stomach for days. Suddenly, all was right with the world.

'Thank God,' Jeanna said, drily.

Val was more sympathetic. 'I get how you're feeling, love. I was the same with our Dee and Mark when they were teenagers. But you're going to have to find a way to live without your entire happiness depending on your kids. You need your own life and your own joy too.'

Claire took a large bite out of an apple Danish, nodding in agreement as she did so. 'I know, Val. I'm just not sure where to start.' When it came to parenting, Claire had learned to listen to every word Val said. Josie might be the louder, more brutally candid of the two friends, but Val's wisdom and compassion hit the mark every time.

'How's Sam handling it? Have you spoken to him?' Josie wondered.

Sam. Claire's husband of nine years, ex-husband for another nine, and Max and Jordy's dad. Despite splitting when the boys were young, they'd managed to both co-parent and maintain a friendship, even when he'd moved in with Nicola – five years younger, two stone lighter, far more glamorous, far less neurotic. Not that she was comparing. Much.

It hadn't been without occasional flashpoints and differences of opinion, but they'd made their situation work. And Claire had managed not to resent the fact that he'd moved on and got a whole new happy ever after.

She'd thought about dating, about looking for someone else. Then – much to Jeanna's disgust – swiftly filed it under 'can't be arsed'. Where would she find the time? Between building the business and bringing up the boys with only her brother Doug and Jeanna on hand to help, she barely found time to shave her legs, never mind all the other palaver that went with the whole 'meeting someone new' saga. So, instead, she'd settled for happy parenthood and maintaining an amicable relationship with her ex, which had been enough – most of the time.

Claire shrugged. 'Not in the last couple of days. To be honest, I can't face him telling me that I need to pull myself together. I've already got you three doing that.' He'd say it nicely of course, but there was always that underlying history there. There was no getting away from the fact that

Sam had felt sidelined during their marriage. Looking back, she could see that he'd been absolutely justified, but in the midst of raising the boys, working to pay the bills, juggling a million everyday things, she hadn't seen it. Then, one day, it was too late.

It was inevitable, and yet, even now she found it hard to believe it had happened. Maybe because she'd been so sure they'd go the distance, that they'd make it. He was truly the only man she'd ever loved, and she'd felt that way from the first moment she set eyes on him…

Five

Claire & Sam – Millennium Eve 1999

'This seemed like a much better idea when we were planning it,' Jeanna hissed into Claire's ear. 'I hadn't factored in that I'd be freezing my tits off, squashed to a pulp and this bloke next to me would be intoxicating me with Diamond White cider breath and a cloud of Benson & Hedges every time the wind blows in this direction. And you look like a tangerine. Just saying.'

Claire took another swig from her hip flask. It contained vodka and Coke and she now understood why Russians partook of that particular alcoholic beverage as she was fairly sure that the booze, and her shiny new bright orange Puffa jacket (Topshop, £19.99 in the Boxing Day sale), were the only things insulating her extremities and fending off frostbite in the sub-zero temperatures. Either that or it was just making her a little too drunk to care.

'Stop being a downer! You couldn't buy an atmosphere like this!'

The enthusiasm in her voice was so contagious even Jeanna's face defrosted a little. She was right. Even the cold and the frequent blasts of biting wind couldn't detract from the joyous, electric buzz in the air.

They'd thought about going to one of their local bars to welcome the new century – all student hangouts frequented by the rest of the gang from college – but they'd decided they could do that any time. The standard Hogmanay celebrations in Glasgow were rambunctious, over the top and went on for days. However, the Millennium party in Glasgow's George Square, with nine stages around the area and live music headlined by the Human League, was a once-in-a-lifetime event. Couldn't beat a bit of retro pop. A group of ten of them, all mates from school or pals she'd made in her first year at the Glasgow School of Art, were here with 100,000 others and there was absolutely nowhere else Claire would rather be. Sure, it was crowded, and yes, penguins would consider this a chilly environment, but by God, the crowds, the music, the revelry, the relief that she was wearing two pairs of thermal knickers, the anticipation and now the sheer excitement of 100,000 people shouting in unison made it worth it.

Ten! Nine! Eight! Seven! Six! Five! Four!

She gripped Jeanna's arm, as, like buoys on an ocean, a sea of people started bobbing up and down in synchronicity.

Sod the cold. She would never forget this moment for as long as she lived.

Three! Two! One!

ROAR!!!!!

'Happy New Year!' she bellowed, throwing her arms around Jeanna and squeezing her tightly, before they both gazed upwards as a riot of fireworks began to fill the skies. And then more hugging: the rest of her friends, Mr Diamond White/Benson & Hedges, then every other person within a five foot radius, all the while laughing until her jaws hurt.

When the explosions of colour finally ceased, the mesmerising sound of a lone piper playing 'Auld Lang Syne' filled the cold night air, with nothing else but the smell of fireworks, love and optimism and sheer bloody joy. This was everything. Whether it was the occasion, the party or the vodka, Claire wasn't sure, but she absolutely knew she was having the best night of her life.

As she sang along, a voice she didn't recognise blasted in her ear.

'You're on fire!'

She gave the stranger – actually, the pretty handsome, easy-on-the-eye stranger – her widest grin. 'I know!' She'd never been complimented on her singing before, but she'd take it.

Her happiness was rudely interrupted by a thump on her back. Then another. Then another…

'I mean you're actually on fire!' the voice said, urgently this time, accompanied by more slapping on the back.

Jeanna joined in, screeching profanities while she did so.

A small space started to form around her as everyone, Claire included, realised that the acrid aroma wasn't the afterburn of the fireworks, but smoke coming from the bright orange Puffa jacket. She yanked the zip down, then the stranger pulled at the neck and managed to somehow get the whole jacket off her in one smooth motion. He tossed it to the ground and began stamping on what was left of the smouldering fabric – £19.99 up in flames. Literally. She was just glad that her hair had been tucked under her hat or she'd now be contemplating a whole new look.

'Oh my God! Thank you! Thank you so much,' she blurted, noticing out of the corner of her eye that Mr Diamond White/Benson and Hedges was slinking off into the crowd, cigarette still dangling from his lips. It must have come into contact with her jacket when she ambushed him in a bear hug.

'You nearly killed my pal, ya no-good tosser!' Jeanna yelled after him, but was thankfully prevented from chasing him by the crowd, which had ebbed back in their direction, surrounding them again and forcing them closer together.

Somehow, and Claire would forever swear it wasn't deliberate, she ended up body-to-body with the bloke who had shown a brave talent for extinguishing burning padded outerwear.

She had to look up to meet his gaze. 'No problem,' he replied, his grin making his eyes crinkle and his face flush a little. And that was it. Right there. Claire, in a radical departure from her usual laid back, ambivalent, go-with-the-flow personality, decided in that second that he was hers. And no, it had nothing to do with the vodka.

'I'm Claire,' she said, going up onto her tiptoes so that she could get closer to his ear. 'And that was my brand new jacket. May it rest in peace.'

'I'm Sam. And I'm sorry for your loss,' he said, laughing, and Claire decided it was the best sound she'd ever heard.

Even better than Prince singing about partying like it was 1999.

She kept eye contact, but paused, not sure what to say next. She was rubbish at this kind of stuff. Every relationship she'd had so far had been with someone she knew from school or college, so she had never done the whole 'meet a stranger, chat him up' thing. If only she had a pause button so she could press it, ask Jeanna what to say, then kick back into action.

'Happy New Year,' he said, filling the silence, and Claire realised they were both still grinning at each other like fools.

'Happy New Year,' she replied, as she realised he was leaning down to give her a hug. It was all the opportunity that Claire needed. Just as he was about to give her the customary kiss on the cheek, she turned her head, her lips found his and the next thing they were locked in a slow, mesmerising, utterly magnificent snog.

Claire heard Jeanna's shocked, 'Holy shit, how did that happen?' but she ignored her, only coming up for air when her lungs were somewhere close to collapse. So far, the year 2000 was full of surprises and they were only ten minutes in.

When she recovered her power of speech, she blustered, 'Sorry, I don't normally snog random men…'

'She does,' Jeanna interjected. 'Two postmen and the bloke that empties our wheelie bin so far this week.'

Claire ignored her, and Sam… Well, he was just standing there, staring at her, with that amused grin still splitting his face.

'But you did save me from melting and…'

She didn't even get the words out before he was leaning down, kissing her again.

'Christ, she's going to have lips like a sink plunger if we don't save her soon,' Jeanna said to Carrie, another one of their gang. The music had stopped now and people were slowly making their way out of the square, giving a bit of breathing room to those still there. 'Come on, let's go. Claire, are you bringing Romeo?'

Reluctantly, Claire stopped kissing him again. 'Are you here with anyone?' She really hoped he said yes, otherwise she'd start to worry that she was kissing the face off a bit of a weirdo who wandered around on his own on milestone occasions, putting out jacket fires.

Thankfully, he nodded in the direction of two other blokes who were standing a few feet away. 'That's my brother, Des, and my mate, Gary.'

'Oh. Good. We're all heading back to our flat for a party. You're welcome to come if you… you know… you don't have plans. Or more lives to save.'

'Des, do we have plans, mate?' he shouted over.

Claire could see the family resemblance. Same height, same dark hair, same squarish jawline, just as handsome. 'Yeah, we're going to—'

Sam stopped listening and turned back to Claire. 'We don't have plans,' he said, completely blanking his brother's reply.

His reaction gave Claire the giggles. 'Good. Then you're welcome to come to our place. Just to make sure I don't stand too close to a candle, or electrocute myself with the toaster.'

In the end, Des and Gary blew off whatever other plans they had and joined them. By the time they'd walked back to the flat that Jeanna, Claire and three of the other girls shared on the south side of the city, the hip flasks were empty and they were singing Deacon Blue songs, interspersed with a bit of Proclaimers. Sam had held on to her hand the whole way, but there had been no chatting, just a whole lot of singing, laughing and shouting New Year greetings to everyone who passed. It was like the whole city was carried away on the excitement of the new century. Or, as in their case, just using it as an excuse to sing, dance and snog strangers.

Halfway down their street, they could hear 'We Like To Party' by the Vengaboys thundering from their flat. About two dozen other people were already packed in with Joyce, the one flatmate who hadn't come along to George Square, and there was a mass cheer when the new arrivals joined the revelry.

The first person Claire saw was her brother Doug. A year younger than her, they'd always been close, especially since he grew up to be so good looking that every one of her pals inevitably fancied him. Claire gave him a tight hug.

'Happy New Year, ugly,' she whispered.

His laugh was low and loud. Jeanna had observed many times that it was also 'so fucking sexy it made your knickers melt', but the only effect it had on Claire was to give her an irresistible urge to ruffle up his impeccably groomed Ricky Martin hair. She loved her brother. They might have lucked out on the parent stakes, but at least they had each other.

She introduced him to Sam, then gestured that they were going to grab a drink. Taking hold of Sam's hand again, she led him through to the kitchen, where they got a couple of bottles of beer from the fridge, then handed another two back to Des and Gary, who were now being dragged into the living room to dance by Jeanna and Carrie. They didn't look like they were complaining.

'I'll be back in a second – I just need to make a quick phone call.' She caught his puzzled expression, but it was too noisy in here to explain. Instead, she ducked out and fought her way back through the crowd to the phone on the wall by the front door. She quickly dialled a number. 'Grandad, it's me! Happy New Year!' She could hear the TV in the background and knew he would be watching an old movie.

'Och, it's yourself,' he bellowed back jovially. 'Your brother's just off the phone too. Sounds like quite the party over there.'

Yep, definitely quite the party, Claire thought. 'Did you go down to the social club?'

The power plant Fred worked in had its own club attached to it for the workers. Fred had been going there for over forty years on Hogmanay and tonight was no different. He was happy there, alongside the men he'd worked with for most of his life. Like him, many of them had raised their families and were close to retiring. Some still had their wives by their sides, but others were on their own, so it was the perfect place for them to get together.

'Aye, I did, lass. There was a ceilidh on and Harry Colquhoun's missus near danced my feet off 'cause that old bugger was too busy moaning about his varicose veins.' That made Claire giggle, but she didn't have time to reply before he went on, 'Now away back to yer party, lass, and don't be worrying about being on the phone to an old git like me.'

'I'm pretty fond of old gits,' she joked, 'except the ones that moan about their veins.'

Fred was laughing now. 'Aye, well I'm glad about that. I'll see you tomorrow for your steak pie, ma darlin'.' It was a Scottish tradition – steak pie either just before midnight on Hogmanay, or at dinner time on the first of January. Fred had always done the latter.

'See you then, Grandad. Doug and I will bring pudding and beer.'

'That's all we need for a right good night. See you later, lass,' he added and she could hear the warmth in his gruff voice.

Her grandfather was an old-school, working man and she adored him. Now that she knew he'd had a good night and was happy, she could relax and enjoy the rest of the celebrations.

Back in the kitchen, Sam looked at her searchingly. 'Look, if this is a bad time…'

'It's not,' she said, slightly puzzled.

'Or if there's someone else you'd rather be with…'

'Why would you think that?'

He shrugged. 'The phone call? If there's a guy…'

She cut him off right there. 'I was calling my grandad!'

'Your grandad?'

'Yes! To wish him a happy New Year.'

He visibly sagged with relief. 'Oh, thank God. I had visions of some bloke charging in here and declaring his undying love for you, then punching me in the face.'

'Grandad's not the violent type,' she giggled. 'At least, not since he gave up bare-knuckle boxing.'

He flinched, then immediately grinned when he clicked that she was kidding.

OK, time to get back to the flirting stuff they were doing earlier. 'Do you want to dance?' Claire asked, really hoping he'd say no. She'd had enough of being jostled for one night. And besides, she was now feeling like this guy was a little bit into her, and if he realised that she danced like a malfunctioning robot on coke, he might change his opinion.

'Are there any other options?' he asked, and she could see he was teasing her now.

'That depends,' she answered. She could play this game too. Actually, usually she was rubbish at it – she had no dating game whatsoever, but something about him made her insides turn to mush and it made her bolder than she'd ever been in her life. She had no idea how to be seductive or coy, but for the first time ever she was managing to pull off something close to sexy.

'On?' he asked.

She leaned back against the kitchen worktop and took a swig from her bottle. 'Are you married, engaged, going out with someone or a serial killer on the loose?'

It struck her that she should probably have asked at least a couple of those questions before she snogged the face off him. It also struck her that it was now heading towards 3 a.m., she'd consumed a considerable bucket of alcohol, and yet she had never felt more clear headed in her life.

He feigned contemplation for a few seconds. 'No to the first three and hell no to the last one. I hate the sight of blood.'

'Then there are definitely a couple of other options.'

Who was saying this stuff? Who? The words were coming out of her mouth, but her gob appeared to have been hijacked by someone whose inhibitions had gone up in flames with their Puffa jacket.

This was crazy. She'd met this guy tonight. They'd barely spoken half a dozen sentences to each other. She absolutely did not buy into casual sex. Usually she'd be self-conscious about her flatmates hearing anything, about what to say in the throes of passion, showing her body to a stranger, but yet…

'Come right this way,' she said, her grin as wide as his, as she grabbed another couple of beers and then led him to her bedroom.

Six

Denise – 2019

The windowless room was silent, except for the gentle hum of some kind of electrical machine coming from somewhere outside. The walls were cream, a warm contrast to the navy carpet, with a bank of flowers on a pedestal in one corner. She had no inclination to sit on any of the four chairs that surrounded a grey marble coffee table in the centre of the room. She'd sat there already, a few days before, on her first visit.

'Mrs Harrow?' The undertaker's voice was steeped in sincerity.

Denise turned, holding the suit bag firmly by her side as she as she did so. She'd spent an hour that morning polishing his shoes until they gleamed, just as he did before and after every time he wore them. His commitment to looking smart was one of the things she loved about him. Always had been, even in the early days when they didn't have two pennies to rub together. She wasn't going to let him down now. She'd picked the casket, the order of service and music on her previous visit the day after he died and informed the funeral director that they'd be having a cremation. Solid rosewood coffin. Top quality. Fifty copies of the Order of Service, although she doubted there would be that many people there. They'd deliberately kept their world small. They didn't need anyone else. And the music… That had been the toughest decision, but she settled on Maria McKee's 'Show Me Heaven' and Sinatra's 'My Way'. The first captured her wish that she could be with him eternally and the second… well, he'd like that. The boss in life and death.

'Mr Steele…' her words trailed off. What did one say in these circumstances? Lovely to see you again? It wasn't. Thank you for seeing me? She was paying him to cremate her husband, so seeing her was part of his job.

'Mrs Harrow,' he replied, simply but kindly. Perhaps in his profession, he'd realised that pleasantries and inane questions like 'Good to see you' or 'How are you?' were both unnecessary and a minefield that should be avoided for fear of offence or irritation.

They both stood for a moment, a silence hanging between them, before Mr Steele took charge like a man who was skilled at dealing with people at the most vulnerable times of their life.

'Ah, thank you for bringing these along,' he said softly, reaching across to take the items from Denise's hands. For a moment, she held them, unwilling to let them go, before relinquishing them to him. She watched as his long, almost elegant fingers curled around the metal hook, while his other hand folded effortlessly around the shoebox. 'Is there anything else I can do for you today, Mrs Harrow? Or would you like a cup of tea? Some water?'

Was there anything else he could do? No. Nothing else mattered. There was nothing anyone could do for her now.

'No, thank you. If there's anything else you need for my husband, please let me know.'

His smile was kind as he walked her out, shook her hand and then opened the heavy oak door to let her go.

She stepped out into the August sunshine but felt no heat from the sun's rays. Just like yesterday, a sweeping feeling of loneliness engulfed her. She couldn't do this on her own.

She pulled out her phone and searched for Claire's number again. Her thumb hovered over the green button for several seconds, her hesitation reinforced by the sound of Ray's voice in her head. '*She won't come,*' he said. '*That's why we always had to stick together, because you can't trust anyone else. Just us. The two of us. That's all we need.*'

Denise put the phone back in her pocket and walked on, wishing more than anything that she could hear the familiar sound of his steps beside her.

Just the two of them. But he'd never told her what she should do if only one was left.

Seven

Denise & Ray – 1979

Denise pulled a load of washing out of the spin section of the twin tub and dumped it into the basket at her feet. Her back was killing her, but there was no way she was complaining to her mother. Agnes worked two cleaning jobs, brought up three kids (the twins were twelve now and had a list of chores of their own), ran the house and was from the 'get on with it' school of motherhood. She would make absolutely no concessions to her daughter's aching muscles and complaints were more likely to set her mum off on a rant about all the things she needed to get done that day before her dad came home from his shift at the power plant. Most of the men who lived in the town worked there – over 5000 of them. Her dad, Fred, worked in a completely different area from Ray, so they'd never met, although their parents knew each other to nod to. That was how it worked in this town – everyone knew everyone, and if they didn't, they definitely knew someone who knew them. Whole families lived in the same street, went on holidays together, socialised together at weekends.

Ray's family were a slight exception because his grandparents lived in somewhere called Giffnock, which was over the other side of Glasgow. Denise had never been. In fact, she'd only ever been to Ray's parents' house twice and that was on Boxing Day and again on Hogmanay.

His parents seemed nice enough. She'd helped his mum, Jenny, in the kitchen preparing the Boxing Day lunch and then on the next visit, she made the sandwiches and sausage rolls for the first-footers – the traditional name for the first guests to come knocking on the door after midnight. It was her first Hogmanay out of the house, and she was surprised that her parents had let her go, but Agnes said she was so knackered she'd be going to bed early anyway. She'd been tired a lot lately, which wasn't like her, but she'd still never missed a day of work. Bills to pay, she said.

'Denise, can you make sure you get that hung up in the next five minutes – I've got another load to go on and I need to get that lot dry pronto.'

'I'm just doing it now,' Denise replied, trying to add a smile that turned to a wince as a shooting pain caused an excruciating spasm in her back. Gingerly, trying to manage the pain, she bent down and picked up the basket, then turned away from her mother and headed for the back door.

She'd barely taken two steps when her mum let out a gasp of, 'Oh, dear Christ.'

Denise stopped, turned, fear immediately sending her nerve endings to the outside of her skin.

'Put that down, right now,' Agnes hissed, crossing the room to her, not for one second taking her eyes off her daughter.

Denise dropped the basket just in time for her mother to grab her arm and turn her to the side, then run her hand over her daughter's stomach.

'Denise Margaret McAlee…' She only used her full name when she was really, really furious and Denise knew, without any sliver of doubt, that her mother was about to kill her. 'Are you pregnant?'

Not one part of Denise's body was willing to work. She couldn't speak, because her throat was being strangled by a sob. She couldn't breathe because she was too terrified. She couldn't even cry, because, God knows, she'd cried every tear she had to shed in the last month.

She'd suspected for a few weeks, but she hadn't told anyone. Not Ray, not her mother, not even Alice. Instead, she'd decided to ignore it, hoping beyond hope that it would just go away. People had miscarriages. It had happened to a few of Agnes's friends and even to Agnes twice over the years, so she'd just been praying that would happen here too. She couldn't believe that her mother had spotted it. She was barely showing at all.

Agnes was so close now, Denise could feel her breath on her cheek as she nodded. She expected rage, fury, screams, but instead Agnes staggered back until she was leaning against the yellow Formica on top of the units beside them.

'Jesus wept, Denise. How could you be so stupid?'

Denise stared at the floor. She'd asked herself that so many times too. The truth was that she'd held out for seven months, never let Ray go the full way, but then at New Year they'd nipped up to his room for a cuddle while everyone partied downstairs and he'd persuaded her. His hand had flicked open the top button of her jeans and pulled down her zip. She'd instinctively put her hand on his to stop him.

'Come on, Denise, we've been going out for bloody ages and I love you, you know I do.'

Every time he said that, something inside her melted. He was the only person who had ever said that to her. Her mum and dad weren't mean to her, but they didn't do all that 'mushy' stuff, as they called it.

Still, something – probably the worry that as soon as they'd had sex he'd lose interest in her – had always stopped her from giving in. She had no idea why that night was different, but it was. She'd taken her hand away, and they'd had sex that night, and many times afterwards – every time they could get a private moment at a pal's house, at a party, even – a few times – in the staffroom at the cafe when she was left to lock up after an evening shift.

She'd started to feel different by Easter. Her boobs were sore, and she was getting waves of nausea in the mornings. Still she refused to believe it until one morning before school, when she could no longer fasten the button on her skirt. Since then she'd been in baggy jumpers and stayed out of the house as much as possible, either at school or working at the cafe, where the very smell of the fryers made her want to hurl. Which was a good thing, because that, combined with the fact that she could barely face food, had kept her naturally skinny frame from changing too much. Even Ray hadn't spotted anything, although he was getting a bit irritated that she had made excuses not to have sex on the few occasions they'd been together over the last couple of weeks. He was so knackered after work that instead of seeing each other every day or so, it had tailed off to once or twice a week.

'How far along are you? If it's not too long...' there was a glimmer of hope in Agnes's voice, which Denise soon extinguished.

'About five months.'

Another guttural wail from Agnes, followed by a babbling outburst of, 'How the hell did I not see it before now? Why didn't you tell me? Jesus Christ, Denise, we could have... Oh, bloody hell, your father will go mental. And what's that boyfriend of yours saying to it then?'

Denise finally found the ability to speak.

'He doesn't know either.'

Agnes snorted. 'Christ Almighty, you're as daft as each other.'

Denise waited, unsure what to say next, waiting for the next outburst. It didn't take long.

'Right, get your coat,' her mum demanded.

They were out of the door and down the street before Denise realised she hadn't asked where they were going. The doctor? One of her aunts' houses? The hospital?

Her steps got faster and faster as she tried to keep up with Agnes, going left, right, crossing roads, until... Oh, shit.

They turned into Ray's street.

Agnes ignored the bell and battered on the door, while Denise tried not to pass out with panic.

'Keep yer knickers on, I'm coming,' yelled a voice from inside, before Ray's mum, Jenny, finally answered. Her hair, dark like Ray's, was pulled back in a ponytail and she still had on her brown uniform from the supermarket where she worked on the checkout. 'Hello, love,' she said, clearly puzzled. 'Ray's not here and—'

'It's you I've come to see,' Agnes spoke up, while Denise, face burning, lowered her gaze to her shoes. 'I'm Agnes McAlee, Denise's mum.'

Jenny's face gave away the fact that she immediately realised that this wasn't a social call.

Agnes steamrollered on. 'This one's pregnant and your boy's the father.'

To her credit, Jenny didn't go for drama. She simply opened the door wider and let them pass through, before ushering them into the kitchen.

'You'd better sit down.'

Agnes didn't need to be told twice, and Denise thought again how exhausted her mum looked. Or maybe it was the shock of this afternoon's discovery.

Jenny sat down opposite them. 'Are you sure?'

'Sure it's your boy's?' Agnes asked, ready for battle.

'No,' Jenny clarified, maintaining her calm. 'Sure that you're pregnant.'

Denise managed to meet her eyes, before nodding.

'How far along?'

'Nearly six months.'

Jenny's eyebrows furrowed. 'But you're not showing.'

Agnes smoothed down Denise's sweatshirt so that a gentle bump was visible. 'I was the same when I was pregnant with her. Didn't show at all until I was six months gone and then barely went up two sizes before she was born. It was different with the twins though. Bloody huge with them.'

'I need a cup of tea,' Jenny suddenly announced, getting up from the table.

No one said a word until she put the teapot between them, added three mugs, then took a bottle of milk from the fridge and placed it next to the sugar bowl on the teak veneer table.

She poured as she spoke. 'I don't know what to say, Mrs McAlee.'

'Well I've got plenty to say, so maybe I should start,' Agnes retorted.

Denise wanted to die. She actually wanted to end it all, right here and now.

'I can't keep her and the baby in my house. We're overcrowded as it is, with myself and Fred, and the twins and Denise already squashed into a two bedroom terrace. And I can't be looking after a baby, especially not in the next few months.'

Jenny looked at her quizzically, making Agnes sigh.

'I've got one on the way myself.'

Denise nearly fainted. Oh God. Her mum was pregnant too. No wonder she looked knackered. The embarrassment level just took another step towards unbearable. She was actually pregnant at the same time as her mother! This was a nightmare. A complete and utter nightmare.

The two women continued to talk, but Denise zoned out. She couldn't bear it. Her heart was racing, her palms were sweating, she was faint with hunger but couldn't face putting a morsel of food in her mouth.

It was almost a relief when they heard the front door open and Ray and his dad, Pete, came in from work. Both in the standard plant uniform of work trousers, steel toecapped boots and sweatshirts, they brought with them a sticky aroma of dust and oil.

Denise could hear them in the hall, laughing over some story Pete was telling, but Ray's smile faded when he stepped into the kitchen and saw the committee of women before him.

'Denise? What's going on?'

Of course, she couldn't speak, so his mum stepped in.

'You'd better sit down, both of you,' she said, then waited until they'd done as she asked, before getting straight to the point. 'Denise and her mum came to tell us that Denise is pregnant.'

'No!' Ray blurted, eyes wide. Denise couldn't keep looking at the shock and horror on his face, so she stared down at the table instead.

His dad said nothing, just sat there, his expression giving away nothing.

'So we've decided that she's going to move in here,' Jenny went on calmly. 'She can have the box room for now and then we can see how it goes when the baby is born.'

'Aye, but they'll be married by then, so one room will be fine for them,' Agnes piped up, in a tone that made it absolutely certain it wasn't up for discussion.

Marriage? It hadn't even been discussed. This morning she'd told no-one and now, suddenly she was moving out of her house, coming to live with Ray's family, and her mother was marching them up the aisle. The room started to spin. This was too much. She felt sick. Glancing up, Denise met Ray's glance and saw nothing but fury and horror in his eyes.

The last thing Denise heard before she fainted was the screeching sound of Ray's chair as he leapt up and stormed out of the room.

Eight

Claire – 2019

Claire was sitting cross legged on the floor on a thick padded red cushion she'd liberated from the chaise longue Val and Josie were perched on. Jeanna was now lounging one of the red velvet thrones that were usually reserved for brides, a lopsided, two foot wide pink mother-of-the-bride hat on her grey-free, expensively cut, shiny and extended russet hair, cackling into her second coffee of the day.

'What's so funny?' Claire asked, puzzled.

Jeanna immediately caught herself, stopped laughing and assumed an expression of innocence. 'Nothing. Just enjoying the stories and reminiscing about those days. What a way to spend the millennium. We had some great parties in that flat until they threw us out for noise pollution.'

After almost thirty years of friendship, Claire could spot a lie at a hundred paces. 'No, no, no, Jeanna McCallan, what are you not saying? Come on, spill.'

Josie and Val immediately cottoned on to what was happening. 'Val, you hold her down and I'll get the flashlight from the boiler cupboard. We'll have the truth out of her in no time.'

That made Jeanna cackle even more, before she got a grip and pulled herself together. Claire was beginning to wonder if she'd added a little something of the alcoholic variety to her morning coffee. Hair done to perfection. Flawless make-up applied. Designer leisurewear on. Wee nip of tequila in her soya latte macchiato. Nothing would surprise her.

Jeanna finally composed herself enough to speak, albeit reluctantly and under pressure. 'OK, OK. So, first of all, it might have been me who set you on fire.'

'What?' Claire gasped.

'I'd cadged the cigarette off that bloke and it was in my hand when I hugged you. I'd given it back by the time we realised you were going up in smoke.'

Claire was dumbfounded. 'Why didn't you tell me? All these years, I've been looking for that guy in crowds, ready to punch him for almost killing me.'

'I know!' Jeanna blurted. 'That's why I couldn't tell you! I'm so sorry! I didn't want you to hate me. Or to get some kind of complex that I was trying to bump you off.'

Claire narrowly missed the target with the croissant she shot in Jeanna's direction. 'And what else?'

'What?' Jeanna asked, feigning innocence.

Val piped up. 'You said "First of all". So what else do you have to add about that night? Did you also hatch a conspiracy to nick all her worldly goods? Steal her identity? Shag her boyfriend?'

Jeanna was outraged. 'Indeed I did not! I'd never do something so low. No, I shagged her brother instead.'

'You did not!' Claire squealed, unable to stop herself laughing at the same time. 'You slept with Doug? How do I not know this? How?' Claire had lost count over the years of how many of her friends had had a crush on Doug. He was seriously handsome back then, still had it now. On top of that, he was one of those people who had no interest in how he looked so that made him even more attractive.

'Because you were so obsessed with Sam the world could have exploded at any point in the weeks after the millennium and you wouldn't have noticed as long as you were with him and naked. And anyway, we decided to keep it quiet because he was going out with that Fiona chick…'

Claire interrupted her. 'She wasn't just some chick. He married her a few years later!'

There was a sharp, disapproving intake of breath from Val, while Josie muttered, 'Slapper. Just sayin'.'

Jeanna ignored her. 'And how did that work out? They ended up divorced anyway. At least he had a bit of fun and brought in the new century with a bang. Quite literally.' That set her off with the cackles again. There was definitely tequila in that coffee.

Although, when it came to Doug's relationship, she was right. Doug and Fiona's marriage had fallen apart when they realised they wanted very different things. He was a maths teacher at a high school in Bearsden, but Fiona had higher aspirations. When she was headhunted to a new law firm in the capital with the promise of a partnership, she'd traded in her old job, life and husband for a swanky flat in Edinburgh, a high flying career and a relationship with a government advisor at Holyrood. It came out later that they'd been having an affair for years. Claire had expected Doug to be crushed, but he was surprisingly pragmatic about it.

In terms of possessions, it was a marriage that was easy to dissolve. They'd never had children – Fiona hadn't wanted a family and Doug didn't want one enough to make it a deal breaker – so they'd simply halved their bank accounts and gone their separate ways. He'd ended up living at Claire's house for a few months, helping out with the boys, and in some ways it had been a blessing because it made them closer than ever. At least, she'd thought they were close. They obviously weren't tight enough that he coughed up deep dark secrets about having sex with her best friend!

Claire wasn't letting Jeanna off the hook. 'You are shameless. And I'll be speaking to my brother about this. It'll be worth it to make him squirm. I can't believe I'm finding this out almost twenty years later. You're a crap pal. I really need to get a new best friend. And a new brother.'

'I'm sorry I didn't tell you,' Jeanna said, feigning remorse.

Claire wasn't buying it for a second, but she decided to let it go. In three decades of friendship, there was bound to be the occasional secret.

Jeanna was obviously on the same wavelength. 'Anyway, you haven't always been candid and truthful with me either, Ms Bradley.'

Claire knew what was coming before Jeanna said another word.

'Oh, my God, this is like an episode of *Emmerdale*,' Val said, refilling her teacup from her flask.

It was Claire's turn to deflect the inevitable. 'I've no idea what you're talking about.'

'Of course you do. Did you even bother to tell your very best friend in the whole wide world that you thought you were pregnant?'

Nine

Claire & Sam – 2000

It was the usual Sunday afternoon threesome. Sam. Claire. And Robbie Williams on the CD player. Claire was lounging on the bed, reference book in hand, while Sam was lying with his head on her stomach, reading something to do with demographics and… Actually, Claire had no idea. What she knew about marketing could be written on the back of a baked beans label.

'Your head is extraordinarily heavy. And big. Has anyone ever told you that?' Claire asked, shifting her hips so that the full weight of his outsized napper wasn't on her hips.

Sam helped her out by raising himself up on one elbow and turning to face her, finding the comments on his physicality highly amusing. 'No, no one has ever pointed that out. I'm thinking that even if they thought it, they'd keep it to themselves so they weren't perceived as a cheeky cow.'

He leaned down and pushed up her long T-shirt so he could kiss her thighs, her stomach, the appendix scar she'd had since she was a kid. Eventually, he pulled himself up on top of her and planked on her torso, making her squeal, her giggling only subsiding when he put his mouth on hers and kissed her, then swept their books aside and slipped his hand under the top of her T-shirt.

Only then did she realise that had been her subliminal plan all along. In fact, it had pretty much been her plan on every single day of the five months they'd been dating. By the end of January, barely four weeks after they'd met, they'd known this was love. Quick love, but definitely huge, undeniable, couldn't-get-enough-of-each-other love. Sam had more or less moved into her room at the flat and, since then, he'd stayed over almost every night, only going back to his family home in the suburb of Bearsden to pick stuff up or see his parents. Even then Claire usually went with him. Thankfully his parents didn't seem to mind. They were happy for him. Supportive. Interested. It was all a bit of an alien concept for Claire, who still hadn't introduced Sam to anyone in the family except Doug. She had consistently used the excuse that she didn't have time, and there was some truth there. Between the cleaning shift she did every morning at the college and the four night shifts she did in a local restaurant, supporting herself took up much of the time that she should be socialising with her boyfriend. Or lying here snogging him. It certainly didn't leave time for taking Sam to meet her parents. Actually, she preferred the term gene donors, since they wouldn't understand the concept of parenting if it came with a manual and someone shouting instructions on a megaphone.

His kisses were trailing back down her neck now, giving her the chance to reach for his belt and unhook it.

'You did this deliberately,' he whispered between kisses.

Claire laughed. 'Definitely beats studying on a Sunday afternoon.'

She chose not to ponder on the fact that it would be a different matter the following week when Sam was sitting his marketing degree finals and she had a 10,000 word dissertation due in on the evolution of textiles through the last hundred years. Sod it. This was a distraction she'd take all day long.

'You are such a bad influence. I'm going to end up flunking out of college and earning money to eat by busking in Buchanan Street,' he told her while he slipped off her bra.

'You can't play any musical instruments or sing,' she teased him, her hand pushing down the waistband of his jeans.

'So I'll live off you instead,' he joked. 'God, I love you,' he murmured, his fingers working their way around to…

'Fuck!' Claire blurted, as she pushed him away and leapt up off the bed.

'What the…?' Sam gasped, confused.

Claire didn't stop to explain. She dived out of the room and into the bathroom next door, only just getting there in time to throw up with mortifyingly undignified sound effects.

Sam came in behind her, just as she flushed, then slumped to the floor, the back of her head pressed against the ceramic tiles on the wall.

'Again?' he asked, concerned. 'I thought you were going to see the doctor about this?'

Claire shook her head. 'I didn't go because I was feeling better the last couple of days. I thought it was just one of those mad bugs that hangs around for a while and that I'd got over it.'

There was a silence as he reached over and pushed her hair back off her face. Eventually, he was the first to speak. 'So, which one of us is going to say it first?'

They'd never discussed it, never mentioned it. It was the very anxious, full of dread and fear, convinced it was wrong, elephant in the room. The one that had been vomiting for two weeks and had taken a violent aversion to the smell of coffee, petrol and Toilet Duck. Which was unfortunate given her current location.

'You say it,' she said, dreading the inevitable. Denial was a much better place to be.

'I think you might be pregnant.'

'Noooooooo. Don't make it real,' she groaned. 'I'm on the pill. How could I be pregnant?'

They both knew the answer. For the first couple of months after they got together, they'd used condoms, then – being completely sensible and utterly unsexy – they'd both nipped to the sexual health clinic at their local health centre for check-ups. When all was clear, they'd scrapped the condoms and Claire had switched to the pill. All they'd had to do was wait seven days before having sex to give the pills time to take effect and they'd be fine. They'd managed five.

What were the chances of becoming pregnant in that tiny window, with the pills already in her system?

Possibly high enough to have her lying on a bathroom floor vomiting her guts out two months later.

She knew pregnancy was a possibility. Of course it was. She hadn't had a period for a couple of months, but she'd put that down to going on the pill. Her boobs were sore. Again, maybe a pill thing. But the vomiting? Maybe one coincidence too many.

'Stay here. I'll be back in ten minutes. I love you,' Sam blurted. He reached over, kissed her, then darted out of the room. Claire knew exactly where he was going. The row of shops across the road from the flat had an 'open 7 days a week' chemist's that they occasionally frequented for aspirin, hair removal products, razors and the sun cream they'd bought for the cheap deal to Palma they'd managed to land at Easter.

She couldn't be pregnant. Just couldn't. She still had two years of her degree left to do. Two years older and further along in his career path than her, Sam had just landed a job in a city centre marketing agency and would start there in July. They were skint, lived in student digs and their idea of a balanced meal was pakora in one hand and a bottle of beer in the other.

It wasn't that she had any doubts about how she felt about Sam. She had never believed that love at first sight was a real thing, but she'd been head over heels from the very first time he tried to clap out a living flame from her Puffa jacket. And, thank God, he felt the same. He'd told her he loved her a week later, while they were sharing a bath to ease his bones after a uni football game. It was the perfect setting. Intimate. Bubbles. Two people squashed in an avocado bathtub. Cheap wine that came with a screw top. And Jeanna shouting outside that she was going to call the fire brigade to break down the door if they didn't let her in, because she needed to shave her legs in case she decided to sleep with the guy she was seeing that night. 'My calves are like fucking Brillo pads. I could do him an injury,' she'd yelled.

'You're everything, do you know that?' Sam had said, grinning at her as he took a slug from the wine bottle, then passed it over.

Claire had laughed as she'd reached for it. 'I think you may only be saying that because I'm doing things to your penis with my toes,' she'd teased. 'It's called coercion.'

'You could be right,' he'd agreed. 'But I prefer to call it falling in love with you.'

The bottle had frozen in mid-air and her foot had frozen in mid-fondle. 'You're in love with me?' she'd asked, eyes wide, smile beaming. 'Definitely?'

'Definitely,' he'd confirmed, grinning. 'Just be careful what you do next with that foot.'

In one water-splashing moment, Claire was on top of him and Jeanna never did get in to shave her legs.

Now, with another wave of nausea assaulting her, she wished unshaved legs were her only problem in life. She couldn't be pregnant. Just couldn't. Not now. She had to finish college, travel a bit, get a real job in her chosen field. She had to live life first.

She had a sudden longing to have Jeanna sitting on the floor here beside her, just as they'd done at countless parties over the years. Claire adored her best pal beyond words, but she hadn't even told her about the sickness and the missed periods because she couldn't face making this a reality. She also couldn't face the inevitable bollocking that

Jeanna would dish out. The whole street would be left in absolutely no doubt as to how stupid Claire had been.

Sam burst back in the door, face flushed from running up the stairs to their second floor flat. There was no way she was getting a pram up all those stairs! She couldn't be pregnant. No way.

He thrust a white box at her. 'Do you want me to stay here with you?'

Claire shook her head. 'You've already seen me vomit today. If you have to watch me pee on a stick, I'm fairly sure you'll never want to have sex with me again. Actually, I'm so fricking terrified right now, I never want to have sex again anyway.'

Sam squatted down, put a hand on either side of her face and kissed the top of her head. 'Whatever it is, we'll deal with it, OK? We'll work it out.'

It was just one of the many things she adored about him. He was strong, decent and he had a confidence about him that everything would always come good. Claire sometimes wondered if that came from having loving, supportive parents, whom he knew would stand by him no matter what.

'Aren't you scared?' she asked.

'Fucking terrified,' he replied. 'But I'm trying to do that stoic thing for you. Is it working?'

'No, but thanks,' Claire said, so grateful he wasn't freaking out. If she wasn't so absolutely gripped with fear, she'd be falling in love with him just a little bit more.

He went back to the bedroom, and after brushing her teeth, taking several deep breaths, plucking up every bit of courage she possessed and then running out of ways to delay the inevitable, Claire peed on the stick.

When she'd shuffled back through to the room, he was already lying on the bed, so she sat down beside him.

'How long?' he asked, gently pulling her head down on to his shoulder.

The words 'Three minutes' got stuck in her throat.

They didn't even need three. Barely two had passed when the blue line appeared very clearly and absolutely undeniably in the second box.

She was pregnant.

She looked up at Sam and saw his eyes close, his head fall back. It was all very well saying all the right things, and being madly in love when it was all about fun and frivolous stuff. But she was about to find out if he was the kind of guy she could count on when things got tough.

And history had already taught her, time and time again, that when it came right down to it, the people who were supposed to be there for her, to stand behind her when she was about to fall, were the ones who let her down the most.

Ten

Denise – 2019

The coffee shop was busy, but Denise spotted a little table for two in the back corner. That very thought made her heart flip. Her whole life, she'd looked for tables for two. Now she would only need one. She should just have gone home, but she couldn't face the four walls that encompassed a lifetime of memories. Here was better. She didn't need to speak to anyone, but she was surrounded with people. It was enough to make the loneliness that seeped from every pore almost bearable. No one gave her a second glance, not even a flicker of curiosity. When had that started happening? When she was younger, Ray had loved the fact that she drew appreciative glances wherever she went. When had people – especially men – stopped looking at her with interest as she passed by? And when had she stopped caring? Someone once said to her that they'd been heartbroken when they realised that they no longer turned heads in this ageist society. Denise could honestly say that it didn't bother her in the least. The only opinion she had ever cared about came from the man who was no longer here to give it.

She made her way across the shabby chic, organic cafe, weaving in and out of prams, bikes and oversized bags that were thrown over the back of chairs by women in yoga pants. Didn't anyone actually wear real clothes any more? Ray would have been horrified if she'd left the house like that. He liked her to be smart, stylish, and she did too. She'd rather stay home until the end of time than leave the house in a pair of leggings.

'What can I get for you, dear?'

The waitress interrupted her thoughts and she realised that she'd been staring at the menu for several minutes but hadn't read a word. 'Just a tea please. Earl Grey.'

The waitress bustled off, almost falling over a tiny toy pram belonging to a little girl at the next table. A memory flicked to the front of her mind. She'd had one like that when she was a little girl. Not that her mum had bought it for her. Agnes didn't have the money for lavish presents. No, the family next door had given it to her when their daughter had grown out of it and Denise had adored it with all her heart. It was a different story, far too soon afterwards, when she was barely out of her childhood and facing real life motherhood.

The waitress returned and placed a china cup with a blue pattern on it in front of her, then a matching teapot, milk jug and sugar bowl. Denise thanked her but made no effort to strike up conversation.

A sudden burst of laughter from the table of yoga women made her glance over, and as she did, one of the women put her arm around another and hugged her. It was a simple gesture and Denise longed to know what had brought it on. Sometimes people-watching was a wonderful distraction, sometimes it was like seeing a movie play out in front of you, set in a world in which you didn't belong. Today it was the latter and it wasn't the first time in her life that she'd had that feeling.

She was rescued from slipping into the past by the ding of the cafe doorbell. The door opened and a woman with a stressed expression and harassed demeanour came in holding a baby on one hip, a toddler's hand on the other side and two large bags over her shoulder, so bulky they threatened to clear every table she passed. Hair escaping from her ponytail, face flushed with exertion, brows furrowed, she stopped in front of a man sitting on his own at a table for four, just a few feet away against the left hand wall. He glanced up at her expectantly, a look of hope on his face. It was soon dashed when the woman promptly plonked the baby down on his lap, then lifted the toddler on to the seat beside him.

'There you go, Oli. Daddy's going to do lots of fun things with you today, so be a good boy.' She kissed the toddler's head and then finally spoke to the man. 'Daisy isn't due another feed until two o'clock and she's just been changed. I'll pick them up here tomorrow.'

'Babe, can we talk…?' the guy asked, hope back in the equation.

'No,' she said simply, before repeating firmly, 'I'll pick them up tomorrow.'

'Lucy, please…'

She completely ignored him. 'Bye Oli. Love you.' And with that she was gone.

Denise watched it all with interest, glad to have something to take her thoughts off her own life. Who knew what their story was? It certainly looked like they were a couple, probably married, because he was still wearing a wedding ring. They'd obviously split up and were acting out a scene that played out in every town and city in the country. Parents sharing custody, swapping the kids between houses at the weekend. Since these two were doing it on neutral territory, it was obviously acrimonious. What had happened? The fact that she wouldn't even look at him meant she was either disinterested or too hurt and pained to even contemplate a dialogue. Poor girl. Poor guy. Who knew?

Denise would never offer an opinion, but if she were asked, she'd tell them to really think about what they were doing. It was much easier to split than to stay together. But 'easy' was never the best route to take in the long run. That was the problem with young people these days. They gave up too soon on marriage. They fell at the first hurdle, as soon as something went wrong, the minute they felt slighted or disrespected. Didn't they realise that people had to grow? Had to change? Had to find their way in a partnership.

As she lifted the china cup to her lips, a thought made her smile. If she had walked away from Ray as soon as it got tough, they wouldn't have made it past their wedding day.

Eleven

Denise & Ray – 1978

'Make sure all the photographs get taken from the front,' Agnes demanded, as she fussed around Denise's dress. Both women were very visibly pregnant now, Denise with only two weeks to go. The wedding had been arranged at top speed by the mothers, with neither the bride nor groom being given much say in the matter. In fact, they'd only discussed it once, the night after the kitchen showdown, when Denise had arrived back at Ray's house with her entire worldly goods packed into a suitcase.

She'd expected his mum to be furious and to hate her for trapping her son, but actually Jenny was nothing but nice to her. Ray was a different story. He barely spoke a word as she unpacked her things, then sat on the single bed in the box room, next to where Ray was lying, staring at the ceiling.

'We don't have to do this, you know,' Denise told him, knowing full well that she didn't have any other options up her sleeve. Still, much as she wanted to be with him, she wasn't going to force any guy to marry her, not even one she loved with all her heart.

'We do. My mother will kill me if I don't. My dad still hasn't spoken to me, but Mum says he'll thaw out once we're married. Besides, I love ya.'

She wasn't sure if he was trying to convince her or himself.

Agnes had helped her to pack everything she owned into that one case and had her round at Ray's before the Harrows had a chance to change their minds. 'You've made your bed, Denise,' she said, making it clear there was no room for negotiation, 'so you'll just have to make the best of it.'

And make the best of it, they had. In the three months since then, they'd hastily booked the wedding with a wholly disapproving priest down at the chapel, who gave them a toe curling lecture about the evils of temptation. They were both too young to drink alcohol, but the local pub agreed to let them use their function suite as long as everyone under eighteen – bride and groom included – were out by 11 p.m. Agnes, Jenny and some pals had rustled together a spread of the usual soup, sandwiches and sausage rolls to greet the guests on arrival at the reception. Ray's best man, Billy, had borrowed a disco set from his uncle and would be DJ for the night. And Agnes had used her Singer sewing machine, bought on tick from the Co-op, to run up a plain, mint green, A-line bridesmaid dress for Alice and a cream dress in the same style for Denise, adding lace sleeves and a lace hem to make it look more bridal. It was a rush job, for sure, but it had all come good in the end.

Denise hadn't had a hen do (in her state it would be shameful, her mother had informed her), but Billy had organised a stag do for Ray, and he'd come home at nine o'clock the next morning smelling like a pub carpet. She hadn't asked questions, just grateful that he was in one piece and home.

Over the last few weeks, Ray had seemed a bit happier, especially when his mother relented and let them sleep together. They'd still been able to have sex and that – combined with the fact that Denise had taken over his washing, ironing and making his lunch for work every day – had helped him to see that this could be a good thing.

As her Uncle Joe, nominated official photographer for the big day, clicked photos of them standing outside the church, with her groom at her side, Denise absolutely knew that she was the talk of the town, but she didn't care. Now that it was all out in the open and they'd made their relationship official, there was a big part of her that was truly, absolutely thrilled about today. Yes, they were young, but she'd just married the boy that she adored and they were going to have a baby and be set for life.

Her thick layer of black false eyelashes swept up as she gazed at him, and he responded by leaning down and kissing her, earning a rousing cheer from the spectators.

'Och, they look like movie stars,' Ray's auntie Dorothy sighed. Denise liked to think so too. Ray agreed with Alice that Denise looked like that American actress Goldie Hawn, and as for him… he could be John Travolta's brother. With his black hair and that gorgeous smile, no wonder she melted every time she looked at him. Especially when, like now, he was being lovely to her.

'We'll make this OK, you know,' he told her, and she loved him even more for trying to reassure her.

She didn't even care that his smile didn't quite meet his eyes. She knew that this wasn't what he'd have chosen for them just yet, but she had to believe they could make it work. Nothing was going to make her give up on this, even if times got tough. What was the option? Go back to her house with a baby and bunk up with her mum and dad, the twins and the new addition? She heard her mother's voice in her head. 'You've made your bed, Denise.' Yes, she had. And she would be lying next to Ray in it. That thought brought a flip of happiness to her stomach.

At the reception, the male guests congregated at the bar and completely ignored the fact that the groom wasn't of legal drinking age by plying him with lager.

The women took their places at the long trestle tables, each one putting their bags on the seat beside them to save it for their man. Only an hour or so later, when the music started, did their partners finally make their way over to join them.

Billy, the makeshift DJ, kicked off with 'Hopelessly Devoted To You,' calling for the bride and groom to start the first dance. There were cheers as they made their way to the dance floor. Denise had picked the song. *Grease* was her favourite movie ever, and she'd seen it three times since it came out the month before.

Ray's touch was all she needed to feel like the luckiest girl in the room, but her smile faded as she waited for his gaze to meet hers, for some kind of loving connection to pass between them. It didn't come. Ray didn't so much as look down at her, no less whisper words of love. She told herself it didn't matter. It would come.

As was tradition, the bridesmaid, Alice, and best man, Billy, joined them on the floor halfway through the song. They looked even more awkward than the bride and groom. No wonder. They'd split up around the same time as Ray's stag night and hadn't spoken since. Alice shrugged it off every time Denise asked about it. Now, she saw that her best friend was watching them over Billy's shoulder and Denise gave her a smile. That was a true pal. A broken romance, yet she was here and keeping her eye on Denise to make sure she was OK.

Denise was distracted from that thought as both sets of parents were next on to the dance floor, her father, Fred, having to stretch his arms as far as possible to get around her mother's seven months pregnant bump. Her dad had been typically low key about the shotgun wedding, with just a muttered, 'I knew I should have kept you locked up, with you looking like that.' There was a compliment in there somewhere. Her dad wasn't one for sentimentality. He always stayed in the background, went to work, came home, read his paper, watched a bit of telly, left the discipline and the problem handling to her mum, so at least he didn't give her a bollocking or cast her aside when she'd got pregnant. On the other hand, Ray's dad, Pete, still couldn't look at them, but at least tonight he was taking part – mostly thanks to the four or five whiskies he'd already sunk at the bar.

As the song began to fade out, Billy switched seamlessly into 'You're The One That I Want,' making at least a dozen more guests get out of their seats and shuffle to the dance floor. Despite the circumstances, the next couple of hours passed in a whirl of dancing, singing and ignoring the pursed lips of the one clique of aunties and neighbours who were determined to make their disapproval of the circumstances clear, thinking this gave them some kind of moral high ground. If they didn't drop the glares soon, Denise was fairly sure Agnes, who was getting increasingly irritated by them, would wipe the smirks off their faces.

After tea and cake was served at 9 p.m., Billy got everyone back on the dance floor by playing 'Knock Three Times' by Tony Orlando and Dawn – a mating call to the entire female population to get to a dance floor and do the Slosh, the unofficial national dance of Scotland, a synchronised mass movement performed at every gathering Denise had ever been to.

Traditionally, the men didn't join in and tonight was no different. Denise could see Ray swaying over at the bar. She had seen him drunk a few times before, but tonight he was getting more and more wasted.

'Can you believe you're married!' Alice screeched, diverting her attention from her concern over her inebriated groom. 'You know, I think you'll be so happy together. I mean, I'd rather stab myself with a fork than get married at our age, but I think it will be the perfect life for you.'

There were so many loaded comments in there that all Denise could do was laugh as she – and every woman lined up beside her – did three steps to the side, a kick, then three steps back the other way.

'But promise me things won't change and we'll still see each other,' Alice went on, and the more she spoke, the more Denise could tell that she'd had a couple of Babychams too.

'Of course things won't change,' Denise assured her. 'Well, maybe a little bit, because I'll have the baby and I won't be able to get out as much, but I promise I'll make sure we still do stuff. Ray will watch the baby sometimes too.'

At that they both glanced over to see that Ray was knocking back what looked like a whisky, egged on by the men he was standing with. Glass drained, he didn't seem to have the faculties to get his head back up to a normal position. Like a lamp post keeling over in the wind, his whole body suddenly fell backwards as he collapsed on the floor, earning a cheer from his drinking buddies.

The outraged aunts and neighbours over at the judgemental table in the corner now added wide eyes to the pursed lips. They would be discussing this over the garden fences for weeks.

Agnes, completely sober due to her advanced state of pregnancy, sussed out every aspect of the situation. She stormed over to a table by the door, where Ray's dad was sitting on his own, grabbed the man by the collar and hissed something in his ear. Denise had no idea what it was, but he immediately got up, went over to the bar and picked up his son, half carrying, half dragging him outside. Ray's mum, Jenny, was too busy dancing to notice.

Denise felt the tears well up in her eyes as she realised this wasn't going to be the romantic night that she'd hoped for. Agnes, meanwhile, was heading back in her direction, stopping momentarily at the table of disapproving faces. Denise couldn't hear what she said, but the shocked reactions were enough to tell her that it wasn't anything good. Bugger. Her mother was a force to be reckoned with when someone crossed her.

Agnes pulled her shoulders back, chin out, head high, as she continued her march to the dance floor and slotted in right next to Denise.

'What did you say to Ray's dad, Mum?'

Agnes rolled her eyes. 'I told him that he'd better get his son sorted or Ray was going to be the first bridegroom in the town to be physically dragged out of his own wedding by his pregnant mother-in-law.'

'Mum!' Agnes ignored her rebuke and Denise didn't take it any further. There was no point. She'd never been able to stand up to her mother and that wasn't going to change now. 'And what did you say to them over at that table?'

Agnes took three steps to the right, kicked, three steps back, kicked…

'I just said, "And as for you lot, you can sit there all night with faces like a wet weekend or you can piss off home because, quite frankly, none of us give a toss about your opinions."'

Denise said nothing. Heart thudding louder than the jaunty tune coming from the speakers, she just walked off the dance floor, through the spaces between tables and out of the door. She'd be lucky if Ray's family would let him stay married to her after that performance by her mother. She pushed open the swing doors of the function suite and scanned the street. No sign of Ray or his dad. She was about to go back inside when she heard voices coming from the right hand side, from the alley that ran along the side of the door.

It was Ray's that she recognised first, although it was slurred by the alcohol.

'What have I done, Dad? How the fuck did I end up in this mess?'

'You don't need me to answer that, son,' his dad spat. 'But let me tell you... you've got a wife and a baby due any day now. So it's time to drop the self-pity and make the best of a bad lot.'

The best of a bad lot. So that's what she was?

Denise turned to run back inside and bumped straight into Alice. Her best friend. She'd come looking for her. Gratitude almost made her weep.

'Denise, I need to tell you something.' Alice was slurring now, her eyes brimming with tears. 'About Ray. I'm so sorry, Den. It was a mistake. I shouldn't have done it, but...'

'What are you talking about?' Denise challenged, her father-in-law's words now the least of her worries.

Alice barrelled on, tears falling now. 'On his stag night... I... Oh god, I'm sorry, Denise, but you need to know. He stayed with me and we...' She didn't finish the sentence. Instead she jumped to another strand of confession. 'It's why I chucked Billy. Couldn't look at him after it. And you... I'm so sorry. Say you'll forgive me. Please, Denise. Please,' she begged.

A sound behind her. Denise turned to see Ray, his dad next to him, staring at Alice with pure hatred in his gaze.

'She's lying. She tried it on and I knocked her back. I stayed with one of the boys from the football team. She's lying,' he repeated, his words slowed by the alcohol he'd sank.

'I'm not bloody lying!' Alice screeched, indignant.

'Aye, she is,' Ray countered, his full attention on Denise now. 'She's sick with jealousy. Billy told me that she's desperate to get married and she can't stand that you got there first. She's always had a thing for me too. That's why he chucked her.' Ray's tone was vicious now, and the throbbing pulse in the side of his jaw was a visible beat of his anger. 'Who do you believe? Her or your husband?'

Denise didn't get the answer out.

The pain was excruciating, so much so that she buckled forward, putting her hands on her knees to steady herself.

It took her a few moments to realise that the pain wasn't being caused by his words but by a searing tightness that was ripping across her swollen belly.

Twelve

Claire – 2019

Jeanna threw her hands up in the air, in mock outrage. 'Exactly! I was completely ignored! Who doesn't tell their best friend that they think they might be pregnant? That's at the top of the list on Girl Conversation Code.'

Claire laughed. 'You're right. I'm repentant. I fully intend to tell you should I ever find myself with child in the future.'

'Don't think we're due an immaculate conception anytime soon,' Jeanna jibed with a wink as she stood up, stretched and then headed out of the door with a, 'Back in a min. Just going to grab a drink.'

It took Claire a moment to shrug off the emotions she'd felt retelling the story about being back there, in that student bedroom, in the moment the little blue line appeared and their lives were changed forever.

Val snapped her back to the present with a sigh. 'Och, that must have been so hard for you, love. What is it they say? Life happens when you're making plans.'

Josie let out her twenty-cigs-a-day, low cackle of a laugh. 'Christ, Val, you're starting to sound like one of those notepads with deep and meaningful quotes.'

'Well, it beats "Let's have a gin" being the answer to everything in life,' Val retorted pointedly, her right eyebrow arched in indignation

Josie shrugged. 'Never done me any harm.'

Claire smiled, wishing that she'd known these women back then. Val would have swept in, taken care of all the practicalities, lavished her with affection and made sure she was coping, while Josie would have made her laugh through the pain.

And plenty of pain there was. How naïve they'd been to think that they'd figure it all out and everyone in their lives would climb on board the baby bus and support them.

As if Val read her mind, the next question out of her mouth was, 'So what did your parents make of it all then?'

Before Claire could answer, Jeanna came back into the room, holding a tray containing four glasses of Prosecco and an iced ginger cake, already cut into thick slices. 'It's wine o'clock.'

'It's not even mid-morning. I'll be wasted by lunchtime if I drink that,' Claire countered with a giggle.

Jeanna gave her a dismissive wave. 'It's eleven o'clock. And when it comes to times of emotional stress, this is required for medicinal purposes. You three can eat the cake. If I have another carb this morning, I'll have to donate my whole wardrobe to charity and buy trousers with elasticated waists.'

Despite the token protestation, Claire happily took the glass, completely surrendering to this day, knowing how lucky she was to have this. If these women – these bloody magnificent women – hadn't ambushed her today, she'd have been dealing with all these feelings of loss on her own. How tough would that be? She'd be sitting in here on her lonesome, pathetically weeping into a pile of tulle. Instead, she was surrounded by love, enjoying herself more than she had in ages. Yes, the boys had gone and she was going to have to adjust her life and her mindset, but at least she wouldn't be doing it alone. She would, however, require a liver transplant and a bankruptcy lawyer if she continued to pop open a bottle of wine every morning. But sod it. Today was for just being in the moment with her pals.

'Anyway, where were we?' Val attempted to get them back on track. 'The whole point of today is to listen to Claire pour her heart out, so she'll get everything off her chest. It soothes the soul to talk about heartache, I promise you, love,' she said, directing the last comment at Claire. They all knew that Val had more experience of heartache than any of them. Her daughter Dee had been killed in a hit-and-run by a drugged-up driver a few years before and they knew how Val had struggled to get over it. It had taken her a long time to find a way to accept happiness again, but she'd managed it somehow, although she still missed Dee every single day.

Josie spoke up. 'You just asked how her mum and dad took the news that she was up the duff. See! I do listen to you. Even though you sound like the Dalai Lama with all that profound stuff. You can be the Valai Lama,' she said, before inserting a chunk of ginger cake in her mouth and dusting the crumbs off her lap.

Claire felt her happy buzz fizzle just a little at the very thought of her parents. They weren't people she ever talked about. How could she explain their relationship in a way that let people really understand what they were like and how much they'd hurt her? Weren't you supposed to love your parents unconditionally? How many times had she heard glib comments like, 'You've only got one mum and dad,' implying that no matter what they did or how they behaved, she should suck it up and continue to love them, care for them, respect them. It just didn't work like that. When she'd been growing up, she'd been left in no doubt about where she stood in their affections. By the time she found out she was pregnant, she was an adult, one who was going to her parents with news that would absolutely change the course of her life and her future.

And how they reacted that day was the beginning of the end for them.

Thirteen

Claire – 2000

'You ready for this?' Sam asked, before swigging the last drops from his bottle of beer. It was her brother Doug who'd persuaded her to stop off for some Dutch courage on the way to their parents' house. Claire was dreading it.

'Absolutely not,' she replied truthfully.

Doug grinned, as he placed his pool cue against the wall of the bar and lifted his beer. 'Look, it could be worse…'

'How?' Claire pleaded.

Doug shrugged. 'I've absolutely no idea. I was just throwing that out there to cheer you up.'

Claire rolled her eyes at him, so wishing she was clutching a vodka and Coke instead of a glass of fresh orange juice. Apparently the vitamin C was good for the baby. Sarcastic brothers who thought they were funny, however, were not good for this situation at all.

In fairness to Doug, though, he'd been great since she'd told him. It was the night after they'd found out, and he'd stopped by to see Jeanna about an album she'd borrowed, or something like that – Claire couldn't remember the specifics given that her brain cells were being battered into a coma by the dual blows of fear and panic.

He'd come into her room and flopped on the end of the bed. 'Nice togs, sis,' he'd offered, teasing sarcasm dripping from every word. She could understand his amusement, given that she was wearing an old pair of ripped up jeans and one of Sam's beat up LA Lakers sweatshirts, which hung halfway to her knees.

'So, where's big Romeo tonight then?' he'd asked, with his trademark cheeky grin, using his nickname for Sam.

A year younger than her, Doug was definitely boyband material, if you overlooked the fact that he was asked to mime in the school nativity plays because the music teacher said he had all the tonal ability of a birthing frog. Still, with his cute square jawline, deep brown eyes and a faint resemblance to the bloke who sang Livin' la Vida Loca, Claire could absolutely see why her friends all fancied him. Except Jeanna. She always said he was way too pretty for her – she preferred her blokes to be a bit more rough and rugged.

'He's gone to talk to his parents,' Claire had said, trying for nonchalance because she didn't want to think about what Sam had gone to tell them.

'That sounds serious,' he'd replied, not being serious at all. 'Don't tell me, let me guess. He's been arrested. He's flunked out of college. He's got you pregnant.'

Her face had said it all and he'd realised it immediately. 'He's been arrested?' he'd blurted, shocked.

'No, you tit,' Claire had groaned. She hadn't planned to tell him tonight, but since he'd pretty much got there on his own… 'I'm pregnant.'

'Holy shit. I mean, congratulations? Yes? No? Fuck, I've no idea what you want me to say.' It took him a moment before he'd added. 'How do you feel?'

She'd shrugged. 'I honestly don't know. Happy, I think. We were gobsmacked to start with, but we're getting used to the idea now. It's just… unexpected. I didn't think I'd end up pregnant at nineteen. It's going to change everything, but I love Sam and we're going to keep it.'

'Shit,' he'd said, that grin flashing again. 'I'm going to be an uncle.'

His enthusiasm was infectious, made her giggle as she replied, 'You definitely are,'

In one move, he threw himself up the bed and gave her a hug, making her shriek with laughter and squashing all her doubts, worries and insecurities. That was how they'd always been with each other. Inseparable. Mutually supportive. If there was anything positive to come out of their family dynamic, her relationship with her brother was definitely top of the list.

She was so busy smacking Doug with a pillow that she hadn't heard the door opening.

'I take it you've told him then?' Sam had said, laughing.

'Big Romeo!' Doug had exclaimed, jumping off the bed and giving him a man hug with several thumps on the back. 'Congratulations, man. You two have just made me look like the responsible one in the family, so I'm chuffed for ya.'

Sam took it all in the humour it was meant. 'Cheers. But if you could screw up some time soon and take the heat back off us, that would be great.'

While he'd been messing with her brother, Claire had searched Sam's face for clues as to how it had gone, then decided she couldn't stand the suspense.

'So how was it? Are you OK? Am I banned from their home forever for ruining their son's life?' she'd asked, dreading the answer. They'd talked about whether she should go with him to break the news, but he'd decided it would be better if he talked to them on his own first. Claire hoped it was the right decision.

Releasing Doug, he'd slid onto the bed beside her. Doug had sunk into the armchair in the corner, clearly interested in the reply.

'My mum cried,' Sam had admitted.

Claire couldn't help the groan that escaped her. 'Oh, God. She must hate me.'

Sam had carried on. 'But then I told her how happy I was, how happy we were, and that we were going to figure it all out and make it work and she was great. She honestly was. My dad said what we knew he'd say – that he was disappointed it had happened and hadn't he given me enough talks about the whole condom thing, but then he said they'll help us out where they can. It was probably the most stressed-out hour of my life, but it was OK in the end. They want us both to come over for dinner this weekend. Mum says she needs to get to know the mother of her grandchild much, much better.'

Claire had opened her mouth to speak and then promptly burst into tears. 'God, they're so lovely.' She'd met them half a dozen times and they'd been so welcoming and friendly. They had four sons and great relationships with all of them.

It was the kind of family that Claire had dreamt of being part of when she was growing up.

Sam had wrapped his arms around her and hugged her tightly. 'Hey, it's OK, I promise.'

'I'm sorry, it's the bloody hormones,' Claire had sobbed. 'And you can stop bloody looking at me like that,' she'd snapped at Doug.

'No wonder. I don't think I've seen you cry since you were about twelve. Not a bad thing. You're really not attractive with the whole snot situation going on.'

'Piss off,' Claire had shot back, with a wail that was somewhere between a laugh and a cry. Bloody hell, she had no idea how she was feeling. If this was what it was going to be like until the baby came, she was going to be an emotional wreck.

It had taken her all week to stop swinging between elation that Sam's parents were being so supportive, terror over what was in front of them, and sheer dread at breaking the news to her own mum and dad. She'd woken up that morning with puffy eyes, a banging headache and a firm resolution. 'I think I should go and tell my parents today, before we go to your house for dinner,' she'd announced, before Sam had even opened his eyes. He'd managed a nod, then rolled over and went back to sleep.

She'd called Doug to tell him the plan and he'd offered to meet for a beer before she went. That's why they were now sitting in a pub, on a Saturday afternoon, absolutely dreading what was in front of them.

'Right, I'm going. If I don't do this now, I'll just keep putting it off and they'll find out they're grandparents when the kid knocks on their door on its eighteenth birthday,' Claire said, trying to muster up some courage.

'Are you sure you don't want me to come with you?' Sam asked, for the twentieth time.

She shook her head. 'No, honestly, it'll be better if I do it on my own. I don't want the first time they meet you to be when you rock up and tell them you're going to be a daddy.'

Putting off letting Sam meet her parents had seemed like a good idea in the months that they'd been together. She'd only seen them once since the millennium herself and that was at her Grandad Fred's birthday dinner, when her parents had stopped by for twenty minutes to drop in a cheap bottle of whisky. She'd refrained from commenting, having learned long ago that there was no point. They were who they were and nothing would change them.

Fred was a different story though. Sam had come with her to her grandad's house for dinner almost every week since they'd met and the two of them had struck up an easy friendship. Fred's approval meant everything. Her parents' thoughts, not so much. Still, telling them had to be done, and it was definitely something she'd rather do alone.

'And you don't want me to come with you either? Please say no,' Doug asked her, not even trying to hide his reluctance.

Doug rarely visited his parents and called them even less. The truth was that while she would occasionally touch base with her parents out of some kind of dysfunctional loyalty, Doug had no time for the manipulation and fakeness, so he just stayed well away. He had never had any kind of relationship with a father who made it quite clear he had no interest in his kids whatsoever. He'd never gone to Doug's football games as a child. Never attended a parents' night at school. Had no clue what they were doing at college and uni and made it quite clear he wouldn't support them.

When she was fourteen, and Doug was thirteen, there had been an almighty and irreparable rift that had forced them to leave home and go to live with their Grandad Fred. It suited everyone. Fred was alone after his wife, Agnes, had passed away and his other children had moved out. Claire and Doug finally had a home that they felt loved in. And Ray was delighted that he was shot of the kids earlier than he'd expected and he and Denise could get on with living the unencumbered life he'd always dreamt of. And, of course, Denise bought right into everything her husband said. Ray was top of her importance list. Her kids didn't even make the top five. That's why Doug kept his distance and refused to be a part of the charade and Claire respected him for it.

She flicked him on the side of his head. 'No, you coward. You stay here and stop Sam from fleeing the country to escape his hormonal pregnant girlfriend. Ply him with beer until he can't run.'

'Tough job, but I'll do my best,' Doug fired back.

God, she loved these men. She was so lucky to have them. And that thought was going to get her through the next hour of her life.

Make that two hours. She was about to jump on the bus that would take her to her parents' house when fate intervened. A different bus came first, one that she caught at least once a week, one that stopped right outside the house her grandad had lived in all his life. Before she gave it a conscious thought, she climbed on, instinctively knowing that she had to tell Fred first. Emotionally, her grandad was about as different from his daughter as it was possible to be. He showed he cared – not in a gushy, sentimental way, but in that West of Scotland, old school, slightly gruff but there at the first sign of trouble, way. Her mother had often moaned that he was an invisible presence when she was growing up, but Claire's experience of her grandad was completely different. She loved Fred. He'd taken her and Doug in as teenagers and he had been their rock ever since.

He was in the living room, watching the horse racing on TV when she let herself in. The house hadn't changed a single bit for as long as she'd known it. The electric bar fire sat against the far wall, with a tiled fireplace around it. There was a mirror above it, brass edges, suspended on a chain. On the back wall was a teak sideboard, with a couple of ornaments on the top, strategically placed on lace doilies. A picture of a sunset with a boat silhouette disappearing over the horizon was on another wall, just along from a clock with wood spokes coming out of it in a starburst fashion. The two couches, dark brown Dralon and at right angles, faced the TV, their arms protected by covers made by Agnes from remnants more than a decade before. This could have been a scene from any time she'd walked in here since she was a child. Only Fred was showing the signs of age. Almost sixty now, he was slower to turn than he used to be, thanks to a lifetime in the power plant that had left him with a bad back and an aching neck.

'Claire, love!'

His delight at seeing her immediately made her feel better. Fred was food for her soul. Always had been. If he noticed that her hug lasted longer than normal, he didn't comment.

'Sit yourself down, lass – I'll put the kettle on.'

'Thanks, Grandad, but don't worry about the tea. It's a flying visit. I'm on the way to see my mother.'

Fred's expression changed in a heartbeat. 'You're either a glutton for punishment or something's wrong.' There was a hint of a joke in there, but it was balanced by the fact that they both realised that was the reality of the situation.

Still, she put up a show of brushing it off, buying time before she landed the bombshell. 'What makes you think—'

She didn't even get the rest of the sentence out before he interrupted.

'Come on, lass, out with it,' he said, the directness of the words diluted by the tenderness and care in his voice. 'Whatever it is, we'll get it sorted.'

Seeing the worry written all over his face, Claire decided to go with direct and straight to the point too. 'I'm pregnant, Grandad. I'm so sorry.'

For the longest moment, he said nothing, and the panic began to wrap its way around her throat, stealing any hope of saying more.

'Well, I didn't expect that,' he finally said, with a weary sigh.

Another pause, and she just managed to blink back tears before he spoke again.

'Bugger, Claire, I'm not doing very well here, am I?' he said, tone lighter now, reaching over and taking her hand. 'And that Sam lad is the father?'

She nodded, still unable to speak.

Fred's brow furrowed, two deep lines forming above the bridge of his nose, and she could see that he was thinking this over and trying to choose his next words carefully.

'Well, lass, you don't need me telling you all the reasons that this is a shock…'

Claire realised she wasn't breathing. More than anyone else on earth, she couldn't bear the thought of disappointing Fred.

He went on, 'But worse things have happened in life. How do you feel about it?'

Claire felt the tears prick her lids. 'Shocked. Surprised. We were horrified to start with, because it wasn't planned, but now… well, we're… kind of happy,' she finished, realising as she said it that it was true.

Fred thought some more. 'Well, lass, if I've learned one thing over the course of my life, it's that you can never have too many people to love, or too many people loving you back. So it looks like we're going to have another wee thing to love. And I don't reckon that's something we should be unhappy about.' The sincerity in his eyes and the kindness in his tone told Claire that he meant every word.

She lurched at him and threw her arms around him, knowing full well that the physical affection would have this big gruff man turning bright red in the face, but right now all Claire cared about was showing him how much she loved him.

'Thanks, Grandad.' She almost told him just how much she loved him, but that would mortify him even more, so she stopped herself. It was enough that they both knew exactly how much they cared without having to actually say it.

'Aye, well...' he blustered. 'It's changed days now, lass. Just as well yer gran is long gone – she nearly had a hairy fit when yer mother announced she was pregnant.'

Claire had heard the story many times, about how Agnes had marched her mum right round to her dad's house and insisted they took her in.

'Bit rich since she'd been in the same situation herself.'

'No!' Claire blurted, shocked. 'Gran was pregnant when you got married?'

How come this was the first that she'd heard of it?

'Aye, she was,' Fred admitted with a deep sigh. 'We'd only been courting a few months. Big ideas Agnes had, and she ended up with a bairn and a husband she didn't love.'

'Grandad! Of course she loved you.' Claire was reeling with the shock of it.

'No, lass – we made the best of it, but the truth was we were never suited. She was a bit of a giggler when I met her. Och, she had a temper on her, but she loved to have a good time and she could fair kick up her heels. That all changed when there was another mouth to feed and little money coming in. Stuck, she was, and she was furious about it – she was pretty much in a permanent foul mood for the rest of her life.'

'But why didn't you leave?' Claire asked.

He shrugged. 'Because it was my mess too. What kind of man would I be to leave a wife and a bairn? Especially in those days. I just kept my head down, went through the motions, while Agnes simmered. That's probably why her old ticker didn't go the distance. Och, the rages she'd fly into. Let's hope this wee one doesn't inherit her temper.'

Claire grinned, loving that he was already talking about his great-grandchild's personality traits and sharing his hopes. But she couldn't shake off what her grandad had just told her – it explained so much. She remembered her Granny Agnes as a fierce and ferocious woman. When Claire was eleven or twelve, Agnes had dropped dead of a heart attack, right in the middle of a bawling match with her neighbour over some disgruntlement. That wasn't an unusual event in Agnes's life. She wasn't the kind of granny who handed out Mint Imperials and wiped runny noses. The words that came first to mind when Claire thought of her were irritated, combative, argumentative. The only thing Claire ever saw her enjoying was her cigarettes, her sherry and her sewing. She'd bustle away on the old Singer machine that Claire inherited when she died, making clothes for herself, her family, and even for Claire and Doug, although, of course, behind her back, Denise would turn her nose up at them and refuse to let the kids wear them. Only shop bought stuff for her children, Denise would say. They had an image to keep up. Those pleasures aside, Agnes was a woman who never seemed happy, while Denise was a woman who was utterly self-consumed and devoid of empathy.

Thinking now about the gene pool this child was coming from, Claire just hoped that the baby would be 50 per cent Fred and 50 per cent Sam's side.

Talking of which…

Giving Fred's hand a final squeeze, she pushed herself up off the couch. 'I'll come back later, Grandad – but if I don't go and tell my parents now, I'll lose my nerve, so I'm going to go and get it over with. God, three generations of women in our family, all knocked up by accident. Not a great track record, is it?'

'It'll be fine, lass,' he reassured her. The two deep ridges between his eyebrows returned. 'But when you tell your mother… you know what to expect, don't you?'

Claire nodded, no words necessary, causing Fred to sigh again.

'You know, Claire, I wasn't much of a father to her. There was only room for one parent when it was someone with as big a personality as Agnes. And with the hours I was working at the plant, and the way things were with your gran… well, like I said, I didn't have the energy or the inclination to do much other than take the route of an easy life and say nothing. It's something I'll always regret, but I hope I've done better by you and our Douglas. And I promise you I'll do everything to help with this little one too.'

Claire threw caution to the wind and threw her arms around him again. 'Thank you. You're an amazing grandad and we're lucky to have you. And I'm going to go now before I cry and get you all flustered,' she added with a grin. Tears were up there on the scale of emotions that made Fred pull at his collar and hope for a large hole to appear and swallow him.

With one last hug, she headed back to the bus stop, the weight significantly lifted from one shoulder. Just the other one to clear now.

Alighting twenty minutes later, she walked the ten minutes to her parents' house, a knot growing in size in her stomach with every step. She hated confrontation, antagonistic situations and awkwardness at the best of times. Hated having to have serious discussions with her parents too. There was a pretty good chance this was going to tick all of those boxes.

Taking a deep breath, she let herself in the back door. Her mum was already in the white glossy kitchen, making coffee. Denise wore her hair in a trendy bob, her make-up was flawless and in her jeans and white T-shirt she absolutely did not look thirty-five, or old enough to have a nineteen year old daughter.

'Hey, Mum,' Claire said, giving her an awkward kiss on the cheek.

'Hello there,' Denise replied breezily. 'Do you want a coffee?' She gestured to the hi-tech machine that was built into the glossy kitchen units. Claire was fairly sure a masters in engineering was required to operate it.

'No, I'll just have water thanks.'

She helped herself to a glass and water from the tap, while her mum shouted her dad through. He didn't appear, so she immediately explained, 'He's watching the football. You know that's what he likes to do on a Saturday.'

There it was. The first dig. She shouldn't have come around during Dad's football hours. God forbid, he should miss a split second of twenty-two blokes chasing a ball, even for the daughter he'd barely seen in six months.

It was hard to describe her parents to people because they simply didn't believe the stories. Not just because Ray and Denise were a mere sixteen and seventeen years older than her. But because it was difficult to fully paint a picture of the mother who spent her whole life dedicated to the man she adored beyond question. Or the father who demanded 100 per cent of his wife's attention, even to the exclusion of her own children – offspring for whom he could barely hide his disdain. But it was the manipulation that drove Claire crazy. Her mum was absolutely under his control, not because she was scared of him, but because she loved him so much she was willing to sacrifice everything for him. Claire had no idea why her mother put him on such a pedestal. He was a shit father, had no friends to speak of and was only a big bollocks in his own twisted world. Sure, he was relatively wealthy and his business afforded them a bit of high living, but that was because they lived in a house that had been handed to them with a tiny mortgage that they'd soon paid off. It was all show, him acting like a big shot, because he could afford to splash his cash on self-indulgence – an aspect of their lives that Denise adored to the extent that she was blind to his failings. Claire just wished her mum could see the reality of how he was pulling her strings, but no. They had a twisted, co-dependent relationship that Claire and Doug had long since stopped trying to connect with.

It was another half an hour before her dad graced them with his presence. Must be half-time in the game.

He pulled out a chair and took the beer that Denise had jumped up to fetch for him. God forbid he should get his own beverage.

He opened with, 'Have you seen that brother of yours?'

Hackles immediately upright, Claire went right back at him, her tone challenging. 'Of course. I see him all the time, Dad. Most days. Why?'

'Bloody ridiculous that he hasn't called his mother. After everything she's done for him.'

Ding ding, round one. There it was. As always, he encouraged his wife's martyrdom by appearing to be defending her. The compliment on the top gave a little boost to Denise's ego. And the net result was that she gazed at him adoringly.

Claire wanted to retch. And it wasn't down to her pregnancy.

'You know, you could always call him if you want to speak to him, Mum. Or me.'

'I know, Claire, but I'm just so...' She had that pinched look and Claire knew what was coming. '... Busy. I never seem to have a minute these days.'

Busy. Yes, it was a hectic life, between working as her husband's home based secretary and pandering to said husband's every need. Definitely no spare minutes in there for communication with people you actually gave birth to.

It was her mother's dichotomy: the attention seeking martyrdom over the fact that her children didn't keep in touch, versus the fact that she made it perfectly clear she had no time for them anyway.

Claire wasn't going to get into the argument – she'd had it way too many times before and she never won. Nothing would change.

'Anyway, that's all beside the point, and not what I came to talk to you about.'

OK, here goes.

She took a deep breath. She could do this. Her hands were sweating, her heart was racing, and she suddenly felt like her mouth was full of cotton wool. But she had this. Didn't she?

'You're pregnant,' her dad said, scorn all over his face.

'Well, there's my thunder stolen,' Claire quipped, defaulting to using humour to diffuse difficult situations.

'You're pregnant?' her mum gasped, and Claire could see her glance at Ray. As always, her mum's response would depend completely on what her dad thought.

Unfortunately, he didn't waste time telling her.

His face twisted into a sneer. 'Seriously? You're pregnant. At nineteen. So I'm going to be a grandfather at thirty-six? Jesus Christ.'

Claire knew that would absolutely set his vanity into overdrive. She also decided now wasn't the time to point out that her mother had her at sixteen.

She opened her mouth to explain the situation, but she didn't get the words out because her father was in full flow.

'Well, let me tell you, that's your problem. Your mother and I did our bit, we brought up you and your brother and we won't be watching grandchildren and paying for bloody nursery fees. This is our time to enjoy our lives and we won't be giving any of that up because you made a stupid decision.'

'I didn't ask you to,' Claire responded calmly, somehow managing to ignore the hormonal surge inside her that wanted to punch him in the face.

'What was it your mother said to you, Denise, when you were pregnant?'

Denise switched into full scale drama and self-pity mode. 'That I'd made my bed and I could lie in it.'

'Exactly,' her dad said, as if it proved some point he was making. He went on, 'It wasn't often that old bag was right, but she was that time. And now, you've gone and done exactly the same thing. Well, you've made your bed too. Good luck with that.' The cruel curl of his lip told Claire he was being facetious, but before she could comment, he cut the conversation off with, 'So we all know where we stand? Good. I'm away to watch the second half of the game. Denise, I've booked a table for half past eight tonight, darling. I'll have a cab pick us up.'

And with that, he sauntered out of the room, without another word in Claire's direction.

That was that then. Parents told.

'You know, Claire…' her mother began, quietly.

For just a glimmer of a second, Claire thought she might be about to offer some maternal comfort. A little support. A kind word even.

'… I really don't know how you can do this to us,' she added haughtily.

Claire opened her mouth to fight back, but weariness and disappointment got there first. She didn't say a word. Instead, she simply stood up, picked up her bag, opened the back door and walked out.

There were some battles in life that just weren't worth fighting.

For now, this was one of them.

Before she'd taken half a dozen steps, her hormones changed her mind and she marched back inside.

'You know, Mother, I just don't get you. You live in this bubble where only you and Dad exist and you don't give a damn about anyone else. Where do you get off treating people like that? And do you even have a clue what you're missing? Grandad is getting on and he's such a good man, and Doug is the kind of son anyone would be proud of. Meanwhile, you ignore all of us for that arrogant, uncaring tosser because you think the sun shines out of his arse. I've no idea what kind of mother I'm going to be, but I tell you what I do know... I'll be one that always puts her kids before anything or anyone else.'

With that, she turned and stomped out, taking her hormones and her dignity with her. She also took enough self-awareness to know that Denise wouldn't give a toss what she thought because no one's opinion except Ray's actually mattered to her. It was pathetic. Baffling.

As she marched back to the bus stop, fighting a sudden urge to pee, Claire realised that the visit had gone exactly how she'd expected. They'd been true to form. Totally in character. She just wished she knew what had happened to make her parents into the utterly self-centred people they were.

Fourteen

Denise – 2019

Denise threw three pound coins onto the saucer holding the bill the waitress had brought over for the tea. Fifty pence tip was quite sufficient given that the waitress barely had to do anything for her. Back when she worked in that grubby little cafe after school, it was a miracle if anyone left a tip, much less a decent one.

That was something else that Ray's death had taken away – her job. And she wouldn't be getting another one. The thought that she'd be dropped into in a new environment where she'd be forced to interact with other people filled her with horror. She shuddered. That wasn't for her. She and Ray had been blissful in their own world with just the two of them and she had absolutely no desire to start all over again at almost fifty-six. This was the age when people were starting to think about retirement. Thank God she didn't need the income. They had no mortgage and Ray had a substantial life insurance policy that he always said would make her a rich woman when he died. Not that she cared about the money, but at least she wasn't going to have to worry about where she'd live or how she'd support herself. He'd taken care of everything. Just as he always had.

Besides, she wasn't qualified to go back into the workplace. For over twenty five years, she'd worked as Ray's assistant, making bookings for his building company. It had given them a very nice life and a gorgeous house. Denise knew how lucky she was. Past tense.

The yoga women were laughing again now and it was beginning to seriously get on her nerves. Her heart was shredded, she'd just been to a place where her husband lay dead and they were cackling like they didn't have a care in the world. Time to leave.

Just as when she entered, she had to weave through the tables, this time to get to the door. Outside, she inhaled, trying to ease the tightness in her chest. She tried to analyse why she suddenly felt like she couldn't breathe. Anger. That's what it was. Blind fucking fury that her life had been snatched from her the moment he took his last breath. She just wanted him back, would give anything to be walking home right now, with him waiting there for her, ready with his next plan for doing something fabulous. A holiday. A new restaurant. A gift he thought she'd love. He was the happiness in her life. How could she survive without that?

Her feet automatically started heading towards home, people coming in the opposite direction pointedly turning away so they weren't caught staring at the tears that were sliding down her cheeks.

She had no idea how long it took, but she eventually stumbled up the gravel path to her house and somehow managed to get the key in the lock. She burst through the door, slamming it behind her like she was being chased for her life.

Legs giving way beneath her, she slumped against the hallway wall, then slid down it to the floor, put her head on her knees and howled, each tear and roar desperately trying to cast the physical pain out of her body.

When the noise and the trembling finally eased, her head fell back against the wall, her glance going to the mail under the letter box on the floor beside her. Desperate for a distraction, she kicked off her shoes, pulled off her jacket and lifted the pile of envelopes from the floor. As she sifted through it, she saw they were all addressed to Ray.

In almost forty years, she'd never opened a letter addressed to him. Today didn't feel like the day she wanted to start, but what choice did she have? There were people to be notified, accounts to be closed, legalities to be sorted.

The letter on the top had the crest of his bank on the front. They had three accounts. One was his business account, one was his personal account, then they had a joint account that all the bills and expenses were paid from. That was the only one that Denise used. Not that she'd ever been a spender. Ray treated her so well and bought her so much that she didn't need to splash out on her own.

Opening the mail was going to be her job now – one of the many that she was inheriting. She succumbed, only because it would give her something to do.

Sighing, she ripped open the envelope and unfolded the statement that was tucked inside. At the top was the bank's logo, then below that was the account name: R.H. Construction. He'd always said it was all about perception, and the title gave the impression that it was a company of considerable size, as opposed to just Ray and a team of ad hoc sub-contractors. Smoke and mirrors.

Her eyes scanned the rest of the document. Transactions in. Transactions out. The final line was the one that she settled on: £106,000.

It was more than she expected. She'd had no idea he kept that volume of cash in the business account. She handled enquiries, typed estimates, arranged sub-contractors, basically everything Ray didn't have time for, but she didn't touch anything to do with the finance. Now she wished she had – and that she'd persuaded him to go on that Caribbean cruise he'd had his eye on.

Her groan was involuntary. Who was she going to go on holiday with now? She was going to be one of those sad old people, sitting alone on a sun lounger on a SAGA holiday, trying to make conversation with everyone who passed. She'd seen so many travellers like that over the years. Not that she ever spoke to them. Ray wasn't keen on meeting new people when they were away. He said he just wanted to focus 100 per cent of his attention on her and vice versa. He always said he didn't want to go home having spent half his holiday making small talk with Bert and Edna from Skegness.

Another sigh. Was this how it was going to be now? Just a constant chain of realisations of all the things that would be missing from her life now that her soulmate was gone? Love, companionship, conversations that mattered, laughter, luxury and great sex. Oh yes, that side of their relationship had never diminished in all these years. The thought caused a pang of longing to twist around her heart until she couldn't bear another second of it.

Sleep. Perhaps if she went to sleep then it would be a reprieve from the pain, the fear, the devastation. Yes. Sleep.

She was tempted to pull a coat down from the row of outerwear on the pegs above where she was sitting. Another thing to do. She could see Ray's favourite Barbour there and she knew she had to pack that – and every other coat and jacket – away.

Tomorrow's problem.

Right now, she needed to get off the floor and go up to bed for a nap.

Pushing herself up the wall, she felt the ache in her back from the sobbing.

Deep breath. All she had to do was walk upstairs, climb under the duvet and she'd feel at least a little better than she did right now.

She tossed the pile of unopened envelopes on the hall table, then placed the opened bank statement on the top. It was only when it caught her eye again that something stopped her.

She turned, picked it up again, reread it.

The bank name. The company name. Transactions in. Transactions out. Then the figure at the bottom: £106,000.

She stared. That couldn't be right. It was exhaustion that was making her brain foggy.

She squeezed her eyes shut, then opened them. Looked again.

No, there was no mistaking what she was seeing.

There must be some kind of error. Some mistake.

The £106,000 was definitely there. But it was typed in red, with the word 'Overdrawn' written next to it.

Fifteen

Denise – 1978

Denise pushed herself up in the bed and stared straight ahead. She would never get used to the house being completely silent. She'd grown up with the twins causing riots in her house, with Agnes shouting, the telly blaring, but here at the Harrows', Ray and his dad were out at work all day and his mum was in and out from her job at the supermarket. Sometimes she didn't speak to anyone for hours at a time.

Today was Saturday, so the men were out at the football and Jenny was doing an eight hour shift. Her own family never visited because they said it was awkward, sitting in someone else's house. The relationship between the families was civil, but they weren't exactly bosom buddies. And as for Alice? She hadn't seen her since she'd said those terrible things about Ray at the wedding. How could she? Ray had brought Billy to the hospital that night and his mate had backed up everything Ray had said. He'd looked absolutely mortified. Red faced and squirming, like he didn't want to be there. Hadn't seen so much of a glimpse of him since either. Ray hadn't been hanging around with him so much – he said it was natural that they'd see each other less because Billy was still a single man on the pull. Alice had called, but Denise wouldn't speak to her. She wasn't going to listen to any more of her lies. Friends like that she could do without. All that mattered was that Ray loved her and they had their whole lives in front of them.

The book she was reading slid off the bed and fell to the floor with a thump. She didn't care. Jenny had been bringing six books a week home from the library, but Denise had never been much of a reader and, much as she tried, she couldn't make the words hold her attention for a whole day. Another whole endless bloody day. For four weeks now, this was all she'd done – lie, sit, read, stare. Complete bed rest, the doctor had said. They'd rushed her from the wedding to the hospital, but she wasn't in labour. False contractions, they'd told her. But her blood pressure was so high that they'd ordered her to stay on her back until the baby came. She was so grateful to Ray's family for taking her in, but the boredom was driving her crazy.

Jenny would bring her a cup of tea and maybe sit for a little while after her shift. Then Ray would come home, chat for a little while, eat his dinner on the bed next to her, then he'd go back off out again, to football training or to meet his mates or go down the pub. He looked over eighteen, so he had no trouble getting into the local now. They never checked. She wished he'd stay in more with her, but she understood that wasn't a life for a seventeen year old guy and she didn't want him stuck here with her and miserable.

She groaned as a twinge of pain shot from the side of her swollen belly. That happened sometimes.

Another came shooting in. Then another. Suddenly, her whole stomach tightened in a ferocious cramp.

Oh dear God. She needed Ray. Where was he?

It passed after what was probably less than a minute but felt like an hour. Sweat buds were popping out all over her skin and her jaws were clenched together. She had to get up, had to get help.

Groaning, she pushed herself off the bed, but right at that moment, another dagger of pain made her scream, taking the legs out from under her. She fell to the floor, then managed to get on her hands and knees and crawl out to the hall, where the white telephone sat on a wooden table with a side seat. She was suddenly grateful that the ground floor tenement flat was all on one level because stairs would have been impossible to tackle.

Reaching up, she yanked at the cable, and brought the handset tumbling towards her. Voices. She heard voices.

'Hello?' she gasped.

'Whit have ah bloody telt you aboot listening in on ma conversations?' came an indignant screech.

The party line. It was a common thing in this area. You shared a phone line with someone else in the town, so when you picked up the phone and heard them, you could either listen in or hang up and keep trying again until they were done. It did nothing for privacy, but it was much cheaper than having your own line, and the only way many people could afford a phone in the house.

'I'm sorry,' Denise panted, 'But I'm having a baby.'

'I don't care if yer having a hippopotamus, love, get aff the phone. I'm talking to ma sister.'

Denise's response was a blood-curdling scream.

Another voice, more uncertain this time. 'Are you actually havin' the wean right noo, hen?'

'Yes. Need. An. Ambulance,' Denise panted.

'Aw jeez, Betty, she's no' joking. Whit's yer address, hen?'

The first voice again, all business now. 'It's that Jenny from the supermarket's hoose. Her boy knocked up some young lassie. I ken where they live. Right, hang up Isa, and I'll get the ambulance noo.'

The receiver suddenly felt unbearably heavy, but Denise somehow managed to get it back on the phone. She then crawled over to the door, reached up and took it off the latch so the ambulance medics could get in.

This baby was coming. It was actually coming, ripping itself out of her and she had never felt so terrified in her life.

Don't let me die. Please don't let me die. Please don't let me die.

Her mantra was interrupted only by her screams as another contraction came tearing through her body.

Why wasn't her mum here? Or Jenny? Most of all, why wasn't Ray here? She was going to die here alone, and her baby would die too. Terror shot even further up the scale than the pain.

The second hand on the clock on the hall wall ticked round and round and she tried to focus on that. Every minute was closer to someone getting here. Every minute she could hold on would help her, help the baby.

Another contraction. Another scream. Another contraction. Another scream. The minute hand had moved twenty times when she felt the need to open her legs, to push…

A bang on the front door. She answered with a guttural roar and the ambulance staff took that as a cue to come right on in.

Two men. 'Right, love, I'm Barry and this is Gavin. Let's see what we've got here then, shall we?'

She was mortified when they immediately got down on the floor and peered between her legs, but she didn't have much choice. They were talking to each other, urgent tones, all a blur, then one was right in there, his shoulders between her knees, shouting at her to push.

She did as he said, a sound that she barely recognised as human coming from her gut, then another feeling, a release, a slipping sensation… and then a cry.

A baby's cry.

Her head fell forward, a giddy mix of relief and adrenaline charging through her, until one of the medics lifted a purple faced baby onto her lap. The relief was replaced with pure fear. This was her responsibility now, this baby. She was sixteen years old and another life depended on her.

Barry and Gavin were still clearing up around her when the door burst open again and Jenny ran in.

'Oh, holy mother of God!' she cried, her hand over her mouth, before sinking to the floor beside her.

'It's a girl,' Denise told her. Jenny wasn't one for tears, but Denise could see she was emotional.

'Och, she's beautiful,' Jenny whispered. Then, talking to the baby, she changed her tone to a more playful, 'What are you like, little one? Coming early and scaring us like that? I think you're going to keep us all on our toes.'

'We're going to take them in just to get them checked over,' Barry said. 'Do you want to come too?'

Jenny nodded. 'Aye, but I'll follow on. I'll go track down my boy and let him know what's happened first.' She switched her gaze to Denise. 'And I'll phone your mum and let her know. Only reason I got here was because that old bint we share a party line with came charging into the supermarket, desperate to tell me. Only time I've ever been grateful that she can't keep her mouth shut.'

Denise nodded gratefully. She wanted more than anything to have Ray with her, so she just hoped Jenny found him quickly.

Denise held the sleeping baby, now wrapped in a white blanket knitted by Ray's granny, while Barry and Gavin helped her onto a wheeled seat and took her out to the ambulance.

Within an hour, she was on a ward with four other women and their babies, with a lovely nurse who helped clean them both up and then showed Denise how to latch the baby on. It hurt so much it made her toes actually curl up, but everyone insisted it was the best thing for the baby, so she couldn't refuse to do it.

'Cabbage leaves,' the woman in the next bed told her. 'Get them in yer bra and they'll help with the pain. No' that I need them. This is ma sixth. I've got nipples like rubber noo.'

The clock on the wall said five o'clock. Six o'clock. Seven o'clock. Then a bell rang to signal visiting hours and in came her mum, pregnant belly leading the way, her dad and the twins. Her mum immediately lifted the baby from the cot next to them.

'She looks just like you when you were a baby,' she said, with a softness that Denise barely recognised. Agnes definitely wasn't one for gushy declarations of affection. 'Have you got a name for her yet?'

'We were going to call her Claire if it was a girl. It's Ray's favourite too.' They'd found the name in a baby book from the library and Denise had loved it immediately. In a world full of Traceys and Sharons, she didn't know a single person called Claire. Her baby would be unique.

'Claire,' Agnes repeated, before giving tacit approval with, 'That suits her just fine.'

The twins, completely disinterested, sat in the corner with the magazines they got every Saturday as their one weekly treat. To Denise's surprise it was her dad, Fred, normally so reserved and detached, who gave her the first words of kindness as he took the baby and rocked her in his arms. Denise thought it was such a strange sight, this big hulk of a man, reduced to mush by such a tiny bundle.

'You did good, Den,' he said. 'I'm only sorry you were on your own, pet.'

'That's OK, Dad,' Denise replied, suddenly fighting the urge to weep. She was sore. Exhausted. Overwhelmed. And all she wanted was for Ray to walk in that door and tell her it was all going to be fine.

Right on cue the door opened and Denise's spirits soared… and then immediately crashed as she saw it was Jenny, a bunch of lupins from the garden in her hand.

There was a moment of awkwardness as she greeted everyone – a group of people who had only spoken half a dozen times yet were inextricably tied together in such a fundamental way. Politeness was getting them through so far.

Jenny laid the flowers on the bedside table, then asked for the baby. Fred gingerly handed her over.

'She's your spitting image, Denise,' she cooed.

'Aye, I was just saying that too,' Agnes said, before getting straight to the point as always and asking the question that was screaming in Denise's brain. 'And where's Ray then? Is he on his way?'

An expression of embarrassment crossed Jenny's face. 'Well, the thing is…'

Denise's heart clenched in her chest and tears immediately shot to the inside of her bottom lids. She blinked them back. There was no way she was going to cry in front of everyone.

'It took me a while to find them because they'd headed to the pub after the game. By the time I got to Ray and his dad, they'd had a few pints and when I explained what had happened…' She paused, hesitant to deliver whatever was coming next. 'They decided to stay and wet the baby's head.'

There was a lull as everyone took a moment to assimilate the conflicting thoughts in their minds. It wasn't Jenny's fault. Wetting the baby's head was a long held tradition in these parts, and it was customary for the men to celebrate the birth on the night the baby arrived. Although usually they had actually seen the baby before the first pint was downed.

Agnes cut right to the point. 'So what you mean is that he was on the piss and wasn't for having his night out interrupted, so he decided to just carry on drinking, as if my daughter wasn't lying here after giving birth to his baby?'

Jenny gave a defeated shrug, and Denise could see that she was as upset as her own mum about this, but loyalty to her son and husband meant she'd never admit it. Women stood by their husbands in this world, right or wrong – it was just the way it was.

'Aye, well, you can give him a message from me…'

'Don't, Mum,' Denise interrupted, barely able to speak because of the lump that was lodged in her throat. She appreciated her mum sticking up for her, but when they let her out of this hospital she had to go back and live with Ray's family, so she didn't want there to be any bad feelings or problems. Besides, Ray had every right to be happy and celebrate his new baby. Of course he did. And if he didn't love them so much he wouldn't be out raising a toast to them, would he?

Her mum saw it differently and just carried on speaking as if Denise hadn't said a word. 'You tell him that he's not some seventeen year old lad with not a care in the world any more. He's my daughter's husband and this bairn's father, and it's high time he started bloody acting like it.'

Jenny's face flushed and her voice dropped, while on the bed, Denise's stomach churned. These were both strong, working class women who wouldn't let anyone or anything interfere with their lives, their families or their opinions. It was like watching two gladiators, with home perms and their best coats on, square up for a fight to the death.

In the end, it was Jenny who took the high road and replied in a low, firm voice, 'You don't need to tell me what I've to do to keep my family in order, Agnes McAlee.

You rest assured they'll do what's expected of them. And rest assured too, that I'll take mighty good care of *your* daughter and *our* grandchild.'

The emphasis was subtle but it made the point – don't lecture me when you're not taking care of your own.

Denise clenched her teeth together, terrified that her mum would kick off and make a huge scene, but Agnes merely stared at the opposing mother, eyes narrow, before deciding to retreat. Although, of course, she had to get the last word in.

'Aye, well I hope yer right,' she said, claiming back some of her righteous indignation.

It was only when the bell rang to signal the end of visiting that Denise realised that no one had asked what she thought about Ray not visiting, or how she was feeling, or whether she was OK about spending her first ever night in hospital with a baby she didn't know how to look after.

The truth was, she'd never felt more alone in her life. That would change soon though, she told herself. She had a baby now. Ray would instantly fall in love with the wee thing when he saw her. And she knew, just absolutely knew, that they were going to be a proper family now.

Sixteen

Claire – 2019

The ear splitting door buzzer cut right through their conversation, making Josie jump. 'For the love of God!' she exclaimed. 'You can't have sudden bloody noises like that when you're a woman with my bladder control.'

Val hooted with laughter, but Claire eyed Jeanna nervously.

'If you've arranged male strippers, I'll kill you,' she warned, as she got up off the floor and headed across the room in the direction of the door.

Jeanna tutted, rolling her eyes. 'Damn it. I knew there was something I forgot to do.' She picked up her phone, pressed voice notes, then spoke into the handset. 'Reminder. Call naked men with baby oil.'

Claire ignored her. She adored her friend beyond words, but she was very aware that dealing with Jeanna was very similar to dealing with a wild teenager – the more she rose to the bait, the more Jeanna took great delight in shocking the crap out of her. At the very slightest encouragement, Jeanna would have a troop of greased up, muscle pulsing Chippendales swaggering in that door singing 'You Can Take Your Hat Off.' In the hall, she listened for any sign of a stripper tune. Thankfully, there was none.

There was more than a little relief when she pulled open the door and saw Caro standing there, beaming smile and arms out ready for a hug.

Claire gladly welcomed the affection. Caro was the fiancée of Cammy, who owned the very trendy menswear boutique, CAMDEN, downstairs. They'd been together for almost two years and they were the loveliest couple. Not that it mattered, but they looked great together too. Caro definitely went for the natural look – make-up free face, twinkling eyes, her caramel hair pulled back in a messy ponytail, yet with her perfect bone structure and beaming white smile, she looked as stunning as any fully made-up model.

'Come in, come in. It's like *The Witches Of Eastwick* in there, but you're welcome to join us.'

'Yeah, I heard there was some kind of intervention going on this morning,' Caro said, grinning. 'How are you holding up?'

To her surprise, Claire felt tears spring to her eyes again. 'Sorry! Don't be kind, it makes me pathetic,' she wailed, wiping her eyes with the cuff of her jumper. 'Who knew empty nest syndrome was a real thing?'

'You're not being pathetic,' Caro assured her. 'It's just an adjustment. You'll be absolutely fine when you get used to it.'

Claire nodded. 'I know you're right. You are. It's just been so long since I didn't have other people to organise and take care of that I feel a bit lost. Although – and I'll deny this if you tell them – I really appreciate having this lot here this morning. It's really cheered me up.'

Caro put her arm around her as they headed down the hall. 'Good. We'll keep you busy and you'll be used to this new life in no time.'

'Hurray!' a cheer went up from the other three women in the room as Caro entered.

She responded with a bow.

'Caro, love!' Val exclaimed. 'We thought you couldn't make it?'

Claire knew that Val and Josie absolutely adored this woman. They'd been friends with Cammy for years – in fact, before Josie retired, she worked with Cammy in a his and hers lingerie boutique – and they were absolutely thrilled that he'd found his perfect love. Val and Josie had immediately welcomed Caro into their merry band of extended family and friends, just as they'd welcomed Claire and Jeanna too.

Caro gave them all a hug before she responded to Val. 'I know, but it's quiet down there right now, so I just thought I'd nip up for half an hour and leave Cammy to it. I'm sure he'll cope,' she joked.

Jeanna stood up. 'Wine or coffee?'

'Would love wine, but definitely coffee because I need to go back to work. There's no telling what carnage I could wreak if I went back down there full of vino.'

'It would be fun to watch though,' Josie said, before turning uncharacteristically serious. 'Although, I once fell into a changing room after too much port at a Christmas lunch and caught some bloke shoving three pairs of socks down the front of a pair of Armani boxers. That mental image will stay with me forever.'

Her mock gravity had the others in stitches.

'I think I might have dated him,' Jeanna added as she disappeared out of the door, leaving them chuckling in her wake.

With all the seats taken, Caro perched on the red velvet covered box in the centre of the room, the pedestal that brides stood on so they could see the full effect of their dress in the mirrors that were on every wall.

'So have you heard from Jordy then?' she asked.

Claire read out his text and Caro feigned outrage. 'That's despicable. How dare he be having a good time when he doesn't have us lot there?'

'Exactly!' Claire agreed, giggling.

Jeanna reappeared with Caro's coffee.

'Thanks,' she said, taking the white and gold mug from her. 'Right, so…' she began, catching everyone's attention with her uncharacteristically business-like tone. 'I popped up to see if I could give you something to take your mind off your empty nest.'

'Have you got Gerard Butler stashed downstairs?' Jeanna asked hopefully.

Caro grinned. 'Unfortunately not. And if I did, I wouldn't be sharing him.'

'Our Cammy beats him hands down any day of the week,' Josie snorted, indignant.

'He does,' Caro admitted. 'And that's why I was wondering…' she was looking at Claire again, '… if you would design my wedding dress for me?'

There was a resounding cheer from the other women – except Claire, who promptly burst into tears again.

'Of course!' she wailed. 'Oh, Caro, I'd be delighted to.'

She'd secretly been hoping this lovely lady would ask her to make the dress since the first time she'd met Caro and Cammy. They'd been engaged for a while, but both seemed completely laid back about the whole 'getting to the altar' bit.

'Hang on, let me grab my pad.' She jumped up and reached for the notebook that was never far from her side. 'Do you have a date?'

'That's the thing, it's quite soon... We're looking at December.'

'Oh God, that's brilliant!' Claire exclaimed. 'It'll give me the perfect excuse not to do anything Jeanna is planning to keep me busy.'

Jeanna pursed her lips, unamused.

'Are you sure?' Caro checked. 'I promise I won't be offended if you can't do it.'

'I'm absolutely positive,' Claire assured her, before turning to Jeanna. 'And you can get that look off your face, madam. While you're at it, get me off Tinder. Don't think I don't know you've signed me up.'

Jeanna couldn't keep up the stony facade. 'Tinder will be great for you! You need a few wild nights to remind you how good it can be.'

'I am so not ready to be dating,' Claire reminded her. 'My confidence is shot. Tinder is all looks based shallow stuff. It's got ego crushing all over it. I'm thirty-nine. I'm knackered. The last time I did glamour, Britney Spears was still in the charts. Oh, and I've put on so much weight none of my half-decent clothes fit me. And please don't give me all that "beauty is on the inside" stuff. If that's the case, then to get to mine you'd have to dig your way under a decade of pickled onion crisps.' She turned to Caro again, 'Anyway, my darling, back to you. We'll make you the most beautiful dress you've ever seen.'

'I know you will.' Caro took a sip of her coffee. 'To be honest, I want something fairly simple as the wedding's going to be pretty small.'

Claire nodded, making a couple of notes on her pad. 'That's no problem. Why don't we get started tomorrow? Or the next day? Bugger, I want to get sketching right now, but we can't get to work with all this lot piping in with their opinions.'

'Thanks, Claire,' Caro said, leaning over and giving her a hug. 'I feel so much better now. I've kept putting it off because I can't stand the thought of being the centre of attention. I'd suggested eloping, but Cammy said—'

'I'd be wounded to my mortal soul if you two did a runner,' Josie interrupted, outraged. 'I've got a hat like a manhole cover that's ready and waiting for a day out.'

Caro burst into giggles, then carried on, 'Yep, Cammy said that Josie would be totally dramatic and devastated if we did that.'

'You just ignore her and have exactly the kind of wedding that you want,' Claire said, her glare putting Josie right in her place. 'I felt exactly the same as you. That's why Sam and I got married the way that we did.'

Caro took another sip of her coffee. 'Really? What did you do?'

Seventeen

Claire – 2001

Claire had never felt pain like it. So much for the bloody drugs and meditation. She'd been too late for the epidural and every time she tried to go to her mental place of bliss and tranquillity, she got another searing pain that had her convinced she was currently trying to push an elephant out of her vagina.

'One more push, babe. You've got this,' Sam pleaded, his hand so tightly wrapped around hers that she was sure her knuckles were being displaced.

'I. Don't. Bloody. Have. This,' she panted. 'I. Really. Really. Fucking. Don't.'

She'd always thought those reports of women punching their partners or swearing off sex for life during childbirth were exaggerated and a tad dramatic. Right now, she'd happily do either, if it would just make this stop.

One last push. She could do it.

Come on baby, she told the elephant inside her, *come on*.

Steeling herself, sweat running down her face, absolutely no care that there was a very nice midwife, who'd introduced herself as Rita, grappling with her nether regions, she took a deep breath and then pushed with everything she had.

A movement. A sensation. A wonderful feeling of release. And…

The baby's cry ripped through the air. Rita scooped it up and in one well practised movement, wiped its face and body with a towel, then immediately placed it on her chest.

'Here's your gorgeous boy,' she announced. 'Congratulations.'

Tears streaming down her face, all pain forgotten, Claire looked into the eyes of her son. 'Hey, gorgeous,' she whispered. 'I'm your mamma. And this…' Sam's cheek was pressed against hers now, '… this is your daddy.'

The little boy immediately stopped crying and nuzzled into her chest, eyes closing again, as if he was satisfied that he'd sufficiently expressed his outrage at his sleep being interrupted.

'Hey, little guy,' Sam whispered softly, gently stroking his face with the back of his finger.

'Do you have a name for him yet?' Rita asked.

Claire nodded. 'Max Frederick. After Sam's grandad and mine.'

'Ah, that's lovely,' she said. 'He's an absolute cracker. I'm so happy for you all.' With a kind smile, she finished up whatever she was doing down at the other end and pulled a blanket up over Claire's legs. Claire marvelled at the fact that this lovely woman must have seen hundreds of births, yet she had made them feel like they were the most special people she'd ever nursed. 'Right then,' Rita said, 'I'll leave you to it for a wee while. I'll put the kettle on and get you a cuppa and some toast just as soon as I get a chance.'

'We can't thank you enough, Rita,' Claire told her truthfully. 'And sorry about the swearing.'

'Och, you're fine, love. Had one mum who knocked her boyfriend out last week. A bit of swearing is nothing.' And with that she was off, leaving the three of them.

The three of them.

They were no longer a couple. Claire wasn't sure when that thought would stop being terrifying, but right now she was too high on hormones and gas and air to worry about it.

'I can't believe he's ours.' Sam's words were choked with emotion, a surprise to Claire because he was usually so calm and impossible to ruffle. 'I have absolutely no idea how we're going to do this, but I know we'll be fine. I love you,' he said, kissing her. He then bent down and kissed his son's head. 'And I love you. I'm going to take such good care of you.'

Claire felt like she was going to burst with love for this man and the son that they'd made.

He went on, 'I'll teach you stuff. And I'll play with you. And I'll cook, because your mother can only make spaghetti and even then it's barely recognisable.'

Her laughter came with more tears of joy, on top of another feeling of such overwhelming protectiveness that she struggled to put it into words. Her whole life, she'd felt like an inconvenience to her parents, something to be tolerated. This little guy was never going to feel that way. Not for a single second. She made a silent vow that she was going to love and cherish and protect him every minute of every day, above everything else and no matter what or who stood in her way. Over the last few months, she'd wondered if becoming a mum herself would help her find any kind of mutual ground with her mother. Now, with this instant maternal bond and overwhelming love she felt for her boy, she knew that they had never been further apart.

After the tea and toast, Rita moved them up to the ward that would be home for the next two days. Thankfully, the nurses were flexible on the 'two visitors to a bed' rule, because Sam pretty much took up permanent residence beside her, Jeanna and Doug were there for every visiting session and they were joined by a steady succession of family and friends. The girls from her old flat came. Her grandad stopped by. Sam's parents and brothers were next to descend on them. They'd been brilliant right from the moment they'd found out. Claire had taken the rest of the term off college, but his mum, Sandie, had agreed to look after the baby until he was old enough to stay in the college crèche. They'd also helped them out with a deposit on a two bedroom flat near the marketing agency Sam was now working in. Their own home. A year ago, she didn't know this guy, now she had a house, a child and a lifelong connection to him.

Every time she looked at him, sitting in the chair next to her hospital bed, holding their son, she was sure she wouldn't change a thing. This was the absolute best time of Claire's life, no regrets, no hesitation, just pure love, happiness and really sore boobs, but she was slowly getting the hang of breastfeeding.

Of course, it was Doug and Jeanna who were there, waiting for them, when they were finally discharged two days later.

'Is it wrong that I'm fairly terrified to be leaving the nurses and doctors?' Claire asked Sam, as the doors at the hospital exit slid open. She couldn't help it. She had zero experience of babies, no idea what she was doing and all she knew was what she'd learned from reading every single book on the parenthood shelf in the library.

'Nope, I'm right there with you,' he admitted, and she could see there was a tiny brow furrow of anxiety there. He quickly recovered. 'We'll be fine, babe, I promise. There's nothing we can't cope with. And if there is, we'll just hot-tail it over to my mum's and beg for help.'

'I like your thinking,' she told him, feeling a little better that they had a semblance of a backup plan. 'Did you bring all the paperwork?' she asked him, as they carried the little one in a car seat outside. Her steps were still slightly tentative thanks to the stitches Rita had inserted after the birth.

Sam nodded, taking her arm with his free hand. 'I did.'

'Great. Can we stop at the registry office on the way home?' she asked Doug as they climbed into his car. He'd saved up and bought it with the proceeds of his part-time job as a personal trainer. Her brother was in the second year of the course that would ultimately qualify him as a maths teacher, and supporting himself entirely. No parental handouts for either of them, but at least he'd chosen to work in a gym in an affluent area of the city and was making great money.

'Sure,' he replied. 'Anything you need.'

Jeanna raised an eyebrow. 'We just need you to drive carefully and get us there without killing us. Honest to God, Claire, he's fucking terrifying. I've no idea how he passed his test. I thought I was going to meet my end in a Ford Fiesta all the way here.'

'You're welcome to walk,' Doug said breezily. 'And I was only driving like that because listening to your constant moaning gives me a death wish.'

'Well, you could at least end us all in a BMW or a Merc. Have a bit of class,' Jeanna shot back.

Claire ignored them, too busy making sure the baby was strapped in properly. She and Sam then squeezed in next to the car seat, put their seat belts on and both sat gazing adoringly at their boy the whole way to the registry office, ignoring the bitching in the front.

'Don't listen to them, Max,' she said quietly. 'They're always like that. They love each other really.'

'No, we don't,' Jeanna quipped.

Claire hoped that wasn't true. Those two bickered constantly, but she chose to believe it came from a place of affection.

At the registry office, they all trooped in and queued together at the window for birth registrations. When it was their turn, they handed over the relevant documents to a completely unimpressed woman at the desk. No ooohs and aaahs over the baby. Barely a smile.

She read the name aloud, checking it. 'Max Frederick Bradley.'

'That's right,' Claire agreed.

Doug's beaming smile was instant. 'Aw, you gave him grandad's name too? He'll love that.'

'I know.' They'd both wanted to name the baby Max after Sam's late grandad, but it meant everything to her that Fred be honoured too.

The registrar completed the paperwork, stamped a few documents, then handed a sheaf of papers back to them. 'There you go,' she said, in the manner of someone who did this fifty times a day and just wanted a break with a cup of tea and a packet of custard creams.

'While we're here…' Sam began, and the registrar let out an impatient sigh. She really should consider a new career in something more suitable – preferably a role with no public contact whatsoever. '… Can you tell us what we have to do to get married?'

Claire's eyebrows shot up. 'Married?'

Of course, they'd talked about getting married eventually, and they both wanted that to happen, but they just hadn't had a chance to think about it with the baby, and college, searching for a new flat and all the other stuff that had consumed every waking moment for the last few months. They weren't even engaged and had no plans to do so. Claire had warned Sam not to ask, telling him she didn't need some fancy ring to prove they loved each other. Besides, they needed every penny to support their new family. But now… A quick wedding was cheaper and far more meaningful than a bit of jewellery on her finger.

'That's if… if that's OK with you?' he asked Claire, his eyes full of mischief and his voice full of laughter.

Everyone waited for her reaction and, bearing in mind she was in the middle of a hormonal swirl, it was a risky move.

She paused, contemplated, processed, then, 'Can we do it today?' she asked the registrar. 'I just need to go and collect my grandad, but then we'd be good to go.'

The other three's cheers were rapidly stifled by the bureaucratic response.

Mrs Chirpy regarded them with something close to disdain. 'Of course not. You have to register bans. There's a process.'

'And how long does this process take?' Sam asked patiently.

'Three weeks.'

'OK then,' he replied, brimming with happiness, his arm around his new fiancée, squeezing her tight. 'Then we'd like to book in for three weeks today.'

'Really?' the woman asked. There was a hint of a smile around her mouth now. Maybe this was something a bit unusual and unexpected to brighten up her day and thaw out her frostiness.

'Really,' Claire repeated, very definitely, absolutely sure that this was exactly what she wanted and, if truth be told, a little disappointed that they couldn't do it today. Big fancy weddings with posh cars, a meringue frock and monogrammed napkins gave her the kind of anxiety that made her want to jump on a bus and flee the scene. She wanted to marry Sam. That was all that mattered. Whether their wedding cost a hundred quid or ten thousand, all she cared about was that she would wake up the next morning and be his wife. She'd be happy to do it right here with the five people she loved most in the world by her side. Sam. Doug. Jeanna. Max. And they'd have nipped to Fred's house to collect him. They were her family, blood relatives or not, and the people she could count on, the ones who had never wavered in their support – apart from Jeanna's repeated assertions that she was a daft cow for not abiding by the instructions on the contraception pills. The digs had completely stopped the minute she'd clapped eyes on Max, and even cynical and bitchy Jeanna had blinked back the tears as she instantly fell in love with him.

Two arms came around her shoulders and she realised they belonged to Doug. 'Congratulations, sis.'

'This is way too mushy for me. I need a drink,' Jeanna hissed, but she couldn't help the beaming grin that had overtaken her face. Claire knew she was delighted for her – it just wasn't Jeanna's style to be giddy with delight in times of romantic events.

'OK. Hang on…' The registrar went off and came back with a big, slightly battered diary, then proceeded to flick through the pages. 'We can fit you in on the eighteenth.'

'I'm free that day,' Claire said, looking up at her new fiancé. 'You free?'

'Think I can make it,' Sam confirmed, laughing.

Three weeks later, the four of them stood back in the same building, on the floor above, accompanied by slightly more people than would have been there if they'd done it on the day they left the hospital. There was still Doug, Jeanna, and a sleeping Max in his car seat, but they'd been joined by Sam's parents, Tom and Sandie, his three brothers, Doug's girlfriend, Fiona, and, of course, her grandad, Fred. Her mum and dad were going on holiday that day and had declined the invitation. That was fine by Claire. Fred walked her up the aisle, his craggy face glowing with pride as he told her she was beautiful. According to Sam, her grandad wasn't wrong. When she met him at the top of the aisle, in a long white floaty dress that she'd run up from a spare bolt of satin backed crêpe on her gran's old Singer machine, and a pair of white Reebok trainers and a tiara she'd borrowed from the college drama department's costume store, he'd whispered that she'd never looked more stunning.

An elderly registrar with a florid face and a booming voice conducted the ceremony. They promised to care for each other, to protect each other, to honour and love each other, to the exclusion of all others, until the end of time.

And when Sam took her face in his hands and kissed her, she knew, without a speck of doubt, that she would spend the rest of her life with him.

She would never have believed that, just a few years later, she would discover she was wrong.

Eighteen

Denise – 2019

Denise peered at the piece of paper in her hand for the longest time, like she was staring at some kind of abstract image, trying desperately to make sense of it.

£106,000 overdrawn.

This didn't make any sense at all. It had to be a mistake.

The intense thudding in her chest began to make her feel light headed, so she leant against the wall. Stared a little longer.

Nope, she still didn't understand. They couldn't be overdrawn. It just wasn't possible. Ray had been grafting his socks off over the last few years, sometimes having to work away on jobs for a fortnight at a time, constantly telling her that this was a last blast to get the money in before he started winding down to retirement.

No. They'd got it wrong. He was always saying that the folk at the bank were incompetents. This just proved it.

That said, she had to get it rectified, but how did she even begin to do that?

Heart still pounding, she made her way into the room Ray had converted into an office many years before, furnishing it with an antique mahogany director's desk and leather chair, matching sideboard and display cabinet and an eye wateringly expensive reclining lounger that faced a sixty-five inch LCD HD state of the art TV with surround sound on the opposite wall. It was his man cave. His place of work and solitude. The only time she ever came in here was to run round it with a Dyson, so just being in the room felt strange.

Denise pulled out the huge black chair that was tucked under the desk and sat in it. The smell of the leather, the smell of him, combined with the panic to make her stomach twist.

Why was this happening to her? Why? How could he leave her? How was she meant to deal with all this stuff on her own?

Her fist slammed on the top of the desk, the noise startling her. He didn't like her to swear, but for fuck's sake! This was a living nightmare.

Fingers trembling, she switched on the computer and watched as the screen burst to life. Password. No idea. She tried a few of the obvious ones – his date of birth, the football team he supported, a dozen more, but nothing let her in. She even tried her name and her birthday, and felt a physical stab of pain when neither worked. Damn it. Why would he even have a password on there? He knew that she would never pry or have any reason to switch his computer on. Until now.

Frustrated, she sat back, unsure of what to do next. First things first. She pulled out her phone and checked the app for the one account that she had access to – £360 in there. OK. That was normal. Ray always transferred cash into that account at the beginning of every month, and any ad hoc bills, expenses and money she needed came out of there.

If she couldn't get on to the bank accounts online, then she'd have to search for the paper statements for the other two accounts – his personal and the business ones.

Leaning down to her right, she tried to open the bottom drawer. Locked.

Her nerve endings bristled like spikes across the outside of her skin. Why would he lock it? None of this was making any sense at all.

She pulled open the middle drawer that spanned both pedestals and searched it for the key. Nothing. She tipped the pen holder out. Nothing there either. The other drawers drew a blank too.

She slumped back in the chair, her eyes roaming the room. He didn't have it on him when he... he... The flashback to the frantic ambulance ride to the hospital with her dying husband next to her made her wince. She forced herself back to the present. The key wasn't on him, so it must be here. She just wasn't looking in the right place.

Scanning the room again, from left to right, her gaze stopped on the display cabinet. In the centre was a brass trophy cup, one of his most prized possessions. He'd won it when he was twenty-one and the star striker for the local football team. He'd loved being one of the lads and had played football every Sunday until the business got busy and he started working weekends. The vision of him walking in the door with the trophy over thirty-five years ago was one that she would never forget.

The realisation dawned. Slowly, she rose up, crossed the room, felt inside the cold of the brass cup and wrapped her fingers around the key that lay inside. She told herself he left it there because he knew she'd look there. Yes, that must be it.

Hands still shaking, she inserted it in the bottom right hand drawer and slid it open. She flicked through the files that were suspended on two steel rods down either side of the drawer. Quotes, instruction manuals, correspondence, invoices and, right at the back, she saw the familiar logo of their bank.

Pulling out the cardboard folder, she let it fall open on the desk, revealing a sheaf of statements about an inch thick. Without even looking, she knew they'd be organised in date order. Ray didn't do sloppy organisation.

Taking a deep breath, fearful but anxious to get whatever she needed to sort out the issue with the bank, she scanned the statement on the top. It was for last month. Company name: RH Construction. Transactions in. Transactions out. Balance £104,500. Overdrawn.

The oxygen was sucked right out of the room.

So there had been an issue last month too that Ray had missed? That wasn't like him.

She checked the one below. The month before. £103,250. Overdrawn.

This couldn't be right.

But, hang on, this was the business account, not his personal one. Perhaps this was down to some kind of financial juggling that minimised tax or was of some other kind of benefit to a small company. God knows, his mood was utterly foul every time he had to send money to the VAT department or HMRC.

Back in the drawer, she flicked through the files again, until she spotted another sheaf of statements that had been tucked into a second banking folder, behind the business one. He obviously had one for the company and one for personal accounts.

Pulling it out, she tried to steady her breathing. This was all going to be OK. There was a simple explanation. If there were problems, he would have told her. They'd always been a team, told each other everything, shared good and bad. There was nothing to worry about here. Nothing at all.

Opening the folder, she saw that, once again, the statements were in date order, the most recent at the top. This time, it was his name at the top of the page. Ray Harrow. Her husband. Her lover. Her best friend.

Transactions In. Transactions Out. Balance £636.00.

Her gaze remained on the numbers, trying to work out if the full stop was in the wrong place, if she was reading it incorrectly.

No.

£636.00.

That was all he had in his personal account.

The net effect of Ray Harrow's financial situation, the result of a lifetime of work for them both, was that he'd died leaving them with less than a thousand pounds in savings and over one hundred thousand pounds in debt. That just couldn't be right. Ray would never do that. He was successful. Sharp. Brilliant. He'd never leave her destitute. He… The thoughts dried up as a long, slow howl filled the room. It took her a dazed moment to realise it was coming from her. Arms around her stomach, she buckled over, trying desperately to make her lungs work.

Breathe. Breathe. Breathe.

For a long minute she stayed like that, collapsed in two, head on knees, rocking back and forward.

This couldn't be happening. Where had all the money gone?

Sure, they lived a nice life, took great holidays, bought quality clothes, but other than that they had minimal expenses. If any work needed doing in the house, Ray did it himself or brought in the guys he worked with. They hadn't had a mortgage for decades, because after Ray's grandad had died, they'd taken over his mortgage payments and cleared it off in a few years. Denise clearly remembered heading off to Marbella for a week to celebrate the fact that they were barely out of their twenties and they were already mortgage free.

Bolts of confusion were ricocheting around in her mind. She forced herself to sit upright, tried desperately to regain some kind of composure.

The answers to all her questions had to be in this paperwork. She just had to find them.

OK, start at the beginning.

Her eyes went back to the pile of documents.

Company name. Transactions In. Transactions out.

She picked up a highlighter from the desk and began to mark up every outgoing payment.

If the money had disappeared, this would tell her where it had gone to.

Nineteen

Denise – 1984

The wail was so loud it could shatter windows. In the kitchen, Denise put the iron up on its side on the ironing board and trudged through into the living room to see what the problem was now. She immediately saw the issue, even before four year old Doug gave her the update.

'She. Switched. Off. Music!' he yelled, his little face red with outrage as he pointed at Claire.

'Didn't,' Claire replied petulantly, her thumbs hooked into the straps on her little dungarees. Jenny had bought them for her granddaughter, and when Claire grew out of them Denise would give them to her mum for her wee sister, Donna, who was born just two months after Claire. It was strange having a little sister sixteen years younger than her, but Denise only saw her every second Saturday when she took the kids to visit Agnes and Fred, so she'd never really built up a relationship with her. Nothing unusual there.

None of her family were particularly close. Agnes was permanently irritated, while Fred wasn't the kind of man to express his feelings. A hug on her birthday and at Christmas was about as far as it went. He absolutely doted on the kids though. He was like a completely different man, interested in them and full of the joys when they were around. That was the only reason she went back time after time, because he played with them for hours and gave her a break.

Bedlam was still breaking out in the living room.

'Did!' Doug argued. He'd come along only ten months after Claire and he'd been making his voice heard ever since.

'I didn't.' Claire shouted back.

Dear God, they could go on like this all day.

Denise left the room without even trying to intervene. She knew exactly what had happened. The radio had run out of batteries again – and it would just have to stay silent because she didn't have the money to buy new ones until Ray got paid next week.

Back in the kitchen, she ironed the last of the name tags onto Claire's new school shirts. First day tomorrow. Ray had even – because his mother strongly suggested it – told his work he had a dentist's appointment so he could come with her on her first day. He'd lose an hour's pay, and God knows they needed it, but her mother-in-law had insisted that this was one of the milestones that shouldn't be missed.

She glanced up at the clock on the kitchen wall. Six o'clock. Jenny would be back home soon from her shift at the supermarket – it was time and a half on a Sunday, so she took it whenever she could. The shop wasn't open, but she restocked the shelves and did some cleaning to get it ready for Monday morning. Ray was out playing football for his team and his dad had gone along to watch. It was their regular routine every weekend. On a Saturday they'd go and watch whatever teams were playing locally, then head to the pub for a few pints, and on a Sunday, Ray would play for his pub team and his dad would go along to support them. Over the summer, she'd enjoyed having him home at weekends, but she could see he was chomping at the bit to get back to playing. Today was the first game of the new season and when he was heading out he'd looked happier than he had in weeks.

'You've got to remember he's still a young lad,' his mum would say, if Denise ever dared to give the impression that she resented him leaving. It wasn't that she minded, not really. It was just that… well, she missed him when he wasn't around. There weren't many other people in her life. The last close friend she'd had was Alice, and look how that ended. Last she heard, Alice had got some secretarial job in Glasgow and moved into a flat with a couple of other girls in the west end. Not that Denise would ever have done that. Alice had been pretty smart at school, but Denise didn't have the same grades. Typing and home economics were her best subjects, but she'd left to have Claire before she'd sat her exams. Probably just as well.

Anyway, she could see now that even if Alice hadn't lied to her face, they'd have nothing in common. Her former pal was twenty-one, single, working and no doubt out to have fun. Denise was also twenty-one, but she was a married mother of two, who lived with her husband's parents and couldn't remember the last time she'd been out to a bar or gone shopping for new clothes. None of that was a priority any more.

No, the only people in her life now were Ray, the children, his parents, and those visits back to her family every fortnight. And sometimes she felt that neither the relationship with his parents or hers was real, because she was always watching what she was saying. She would never say anything negative about Ray or his family to her mother, because Agnes would pounce on it and milk it for all it was worth. Or worse, threaten to march round and sort them out. And on the other hand, she never discussed her own family with the Harrows, because she didn't want them to think badly of the people she came from. It felt like she was absolutely stuck in the middle. Not that she was complaining. Like Agnes said, she'd made her bed.

Besides, it was worth it to have Ray in her life. It was difficult to explain, but it was like when he walked into a room, she immediately felt alive. He made her laugh, he was sexy, he was the one with the ideas and big plans. They were going to get a house of their own soon, he promised. He was planning to leave the power plant and he was going to set up on his own, doing commercial and domestic electrical work. He was going to be someone, do something with his life. Denise had no doubt he'd achieve that – and he'd give them a great life in the process.

They just had to be patient, put up with the current situation for a while longer, and it would all come good, he said, as long as they didn't have any more bloody kids. Denise didn't argue on that one. They were already falling over each other and the thought of starting all over again with nappies and bottles... Nope, it wasn't for her. She'd come to realise that she wanted to be out with Ray, not stuck in the house with her life passing her by. Claire and

Doug had both been accidents, both of them conceived because Ray was too horny or drunk to wait until they had a condom, but she wasn't going to get caught out again. She was on the pill now and she made sure she took it religiously. Jenny kept telling her that motherhood was the greatest experience in life. Denise would never admit it, but she sometimes wondered why she didn't feel the same. It wasn't exactly bringing her boundless joy.

Ray's picture of their future was the dream that she hung on to when things got tough at home. Her mother-in-law was lovely, but she made it very clear that it was Denise's job to look after the kids and Ray, and since her in-laws were out at work, it had become her job to clean the house too. And the kids… Being cooped up in this house every day or trailing them to the shops or the park was exhausting. Sometimes she felt like she was fifty-one instead of twenty-one. If she was being really honest, sometimes she was jealous of girls like Alice who were out having a great time. Not that she'd swap her life for theirs – not if it meant giving up Ray.

She stirred the mince on the stove, then went back to the ironing, ignoring the arguing next door. The kids were still at it. It was a relief when she heard Jenny come in ten minutes later, brandishing their weekly bag of sweets, and stopped them whinging.

'There's mince on the stove and potatoes in the oven,' she told Jenny, who responded with a smile.

'God, yer a lifesaver, so you are. I'm absolutely famished. Any sign of the menfolk?'

Denise shook her head. 'Not a word. I'm sure they'll be back soon.'

Her confidence was misplaced. By nine o'clock there was still no sign of them. The kids had been bathed and put to bed, Claire's uniform hanging on the bars of the bunk beds in the box room that they shared.

Denise knew better than to be worried. When Ray and his dad were out, they could come home at six o'clock or they could come home at midnight. It was just the way it was. Jenny didn't bat an eyelid and Denise was working on accepting it too. It would have been nice to have spent some time with him this weekend though.

At 11 p.m. she took herself off to bed. She was no sooner under the covers when the door flew opened and her grinning husband stood there, a jubilant expression on his face. He punched the air, clearly chuffed with himself.

'Ask me who the top scorer was today then? Go on, ask me,' he said, laughing his head off. He was drunk. He was happy. Even standing there in his muddy strip – thanks to the Scottish weather taking no heed of the fact that August was supposed to be summer – not even changed or washed after the game, he was the most attractive man she'd ever seen. And that's why every moan, every worry, every moment of irritation she'd had that day simply faded into the background the minute he entered the room. It was the effect he'd had on her since the day they met.

'Who was top scorer today?' she asked, giggling, so happy to play the game.

'That would be your absolutely fucking sexy husband!' With that, he threw himself on the bed, forcing her to muffle her own shrieks of laughter in case Jenny and Pete heard.

There was no apology for staying out late or missing dinner. No enquiry as to how the kids were or how her day had been. Just laughter and kisses and now his hand was under her nightdress and she felt happy for the first time in days. This was what she lived for. This man, right here.

She reached out and pressed the play button on the tape recorder on her bedside table. It was left there precisely for this purpose. She'd be mortified if she thought Jenny and Pete heard them having sex, so she made sure the only sound they heard was the mixtape of Culture Club, Wham and Lionel Ritchie songs she'd recorded off the radio.

Denise closed her eyes and surrendered completely to his touch and the words he was murmuring in her ear. 'You are so fucking gorgeous.' 'I get hard just thinking about you.' 'I've been waiting to do this all night.'

It lasted longer than usual, probably due to the dozen or so beers he'd downed at the pub, but she wasn't complaining. He was the very best bit of her life, and she'd take every second of him that she could get.

Eventually he came, just as Kajagoogoo were singing about being too shy. The motion of him exploding inside her made her come too, and she was still feeling the aftershocks and tingling of ecstasy when he kissed her, rolled off, and his muffled snoring told her that he was already asleep. She didn't mind. He'd had a long day.

Still buzzed up on the passion and happiness, it took her a while to follow suit, so she was already exhausted when the alarm woke her at 7 a.m. the next morning.

Ray was usually up and out on the way to work by then, so it was a real treat to wake and feel his arms around her.

'Man, I feel like shit,' he groaned. 'Thank Christ I didn't need to get up for work this morning.'

Denise laughed, kissing him a dozen times on the face and neck. 'No, but you need to get up now and get ready. It's Claire's first day of school, remember?'

Of course he did – it was why he'd taken the morning off.

'Ah bollocks, I'm going to give it a miss,' he murmured.

Her heart sank as she turned and raised herself on one elbow. 'Come on, babe, she'll be so disappointed if you're not there.' It was true. Perhaps because he could be a little disinterested in her sometimes, Claire clung to him constantly and always seemed to want his attention and affection.

'She won't even notice,' he argued, yawning. 'Just tell her I'm not feeling great. A tummy bug,' he added with a cheeky grin.

Denise knew there was no way to change his mind. When Ray Harrow decided something, that was it. There was no point moaning or nagging, so instead she got up as she heard Jenny leaving for her 7.30 a.m. start, got the kids fed, washed and ready and it was only when they headed to the door that Claire realised someone was missing.

'Isn't Daddy coming?' she asked, anxiously.

'He's not, pet. He's not feeling very well today, so he has to stay in bed so you two don't catch his tummy bug.'

Tears immediately filled her daughter's eyes and, sensing an excuse for sympathy and attention, Doug got in on the act too. Soon, they were both crying at the top of their voices. Denise thought the noise might bring Ray out of the room, but it didn't. Instead, the bedroom door that had been very slightly ajar was pushed shut from the other side. There was the definitive answer as to whether or not he would change his mind.

Holding the hand of one crying child on one side and another on the opposite side, Denise walked the twenty minutes to Claire's school, then forced herself to smile as all the parents were welcomed into the classroom with their children. They saw the little desk and chair their child would sit at, met the teacher for the first time and smiled at the other mums and dads. Mums and dads. And in some cases, grannies and grandads. As far as she could see, she was the only one there on her own.

Denise was relieved when people began to drift towards the door, and joined the departing parents straight away.

Only when she was crossing the playground, her hand holding on to Doug so he didn't run back to join his sister, did she realise why she was feeling deflated and like the whole morning wasn't as great as she expected it to be.

It just wasn't the same without Ray there. It was one of the rare occasions that she could feel herself becoming irritated with her husband, but she shrugged it off immediately. He worked so hard that he deserved the odd day off. He was going to give her a great life, and although it was tough, it was already ten times better than living with her parents in an overcrowded house, with no clue how she was ever going to escape it.

She was at one end of the tunnel. And Ray was going to get them to the light at the other end of it.

Twenty

Claire – 2019

Caro may have been intending to pop up for half an hour, but it was way over an hour before she even made a move to leave.

'I so wish I'd got in another member of staff so I could spend the day up here with you lot. Keep me a glass of Prosecco and I'll pop up when the shop closes if you're still here.'

Claire shook her head. 'There's no way these three are keeping me here until then,' she replied playfully. 'I think that crosses the line to a hostage situation.'

'Anything that could bring a big, muscly SWAT team charging in here is fine by me,' Josie quipped. They knew she meant it.

Caro hugged them all and headed off, leaving the four of them with their topped up wine glasses.

'What were we talking about before Caro came in?' Val asked. 'Honest to God, I can't remember what I did an hour ago. This getting old is a frigging nightmare. I was up for a pee twice last night and I'm in Pluckers every month, begging Suze to cover the grey,' she said, talking about the salon on the street below. 'I only hang about with Josie because she makes me look younger,' she added, digging her pal in the side.

Josie didn't waste a minute. 'I only hang about with you because you make me look thinner,' she shot back, before the two of them dissolved into giggles. Claire loved their relationship. It was like watching a premonition of her and Jeanna in thirty years' time.

Claire stepped in to answer Val's question. 'We were talking about my parents,' she said. 'And how they wanted nothing to do with me being pregnant and didn't come to my wedding.'

'I shagged Doug that night too,' Jeanna said wistfully, almost to herself.

The other three stopped and slowly turned to look at her, eyebrows raised in curiosity.

'What?' she feigned innocence. 'Did I mention he looked like Ricky Martin back then? Anyway, he still wasn't married.'

'No, but he was still seeing Fiona!' Claire exclaimed. 'In fact, she was with him!'

Jeanna nodded, remembering. 'You're right. She was. It was a quickie in the restaurant cleaning cupboard. That Boris Becker didn't start that trend, you know. I've had several passionate moments with the heady aroma of Mr Sheen and those circle things they put in men's loos.'

Claire could see Jeanna found this all hilarious, but she wasn't quite having the same reaction.

'Have you been shagging my brother my whole life and I've been completely clueless to it?'

'Absolutely not! Just back then. Before he was married.'

Val asked the obvious question. 'So why didn't you ever give it a go with him?'

Jeanna shrugged. 'Because he was seeing someone and then Brian came along and swept me off my feet. And that's not easy to do when you're called Brian.'

Claire smiled at the memory of Jeanna's first husband. He'd been a lovely guy, but five years into the marriage, Jeanna had met Giles, and their affair led to a messy divorce, and Giles becoming husband number two for a relatively short period of time until Jeanna was back at the lawyer's office. Claire wasn't going to bring that up because she knew that had been the very worst time of Jeanna's life and she didn't want to drag her back there.

Jeanna obviously felt the same. 'Anyway, we're not here to talk about what my bits got up to in a cupboard. Or my zero-for-two marriage record. I much prefer it when it's you who's wallowing in your failures.'

'It's a wonder either of us made it to marriage at all after what we grew up with,' Claire mused. 'That could have put us off for life.'

It was true. When they were growing up, Jeanna's mum had a succession of live-in partners, and as for her own parents...

'But your mum and dad are still married, aren't they?' Val asked.

Claire nodded. 'Honestly, though, Val, it's not a marriage I'd have in a million years. My parents met at a youth club disco when my mum was fifteen and my dad was sixteen. Sometimes I think their emotional development ended right there. She's been like a lovestruck teenager her whole life, like she's only truly happy when she's with him. Doug and I were always afterthoughts. Didn't really matter. She kinda tolerated life, just went through the motions until he walked in the door and made her come alive. Meanwhile, he's like a spoiled, demanding, arrogant brat. He didn't give a toss about us. In fact, he resented it when we took my mother's attention from him.'

Val was listening intently. 'Because he loved her?'

Claire shrugged. 'Because he couldn't stand it if she wasn't focusing 100 per cent on him. That's who he is. And my mum went along with it every time.'

'Sounds like he controls her,' Josie said, her face pinched with disapproval. 'Was he abusive?'

'No,' Claire replied honestly. 'He was never violent or nasty to her – the opposite actually. You're right though, he does control her.' Claire paused. 'But it's not through fear or intimidation – she willingly goes along with it because she worships the ground he walks on. She adores him above everything and everyone else, and truly believes he's the perfect man and they have the perfect marriage.'

Val couldn't grasp this. 'She loves him more than her kids?'

'Definitely more than her kids. And it didn't matter to her how he treated us. Still doesn't. We've always been way down the priority list. He doesn't even pretend to want anything to do with us any more and she goes along with that. Everything he says is right, and she takes his side every time. For her, it was all about him. Still is.'

'Well, let me tell you. I love the bones of my Don, but he knows the kids have always come first. And it's the same for him. If it wasn't, he'd be out on his ear,' Val said.

Claire knocked back a slug of Prosecco. Talking about her parents was killing her happy buzz. They always had that effect on her. 'Me too, Val. I think that's why I went so far the other way with my two. They were the centre of my world from the minute they were born.'

'I thought I was the centre of your world?' Jeanna teased.

'Nope, you were the centre of my kitchen. For the first few years that Sam and I were together, he thought you lived with us. Now I know you were just hanging out there, waiting for my brother to pop in so you could shag him in the utility room.'

'The spare bedroom wardrobe,' Jeanna corrected her.

'Noooooooo, don't say that! You're scarring me for life here! I really need to drink more.'

'I'm joking,' Jeanna said, finding this hilarious.

'Oh, thank God,' Claire blurted.

'It wasn't the wardrobe. It was the bath.'

'Right, that's it. I'm not even going to speak to you any more,' Claire replied, deadpan. If Jeanna knew she was getting shock value, this would go on all day. Much better to ignore her.

Josie came to the rescue, switching back to the topic of Claire's parents. 'That's no way to live. What do your mum's friends think?'

'She doesn't have any. Not because my dad doesn't let her, but because she genuinely doesn't want any. She would rather save every moment of free time for him. It's twisted, Josie, it really is, but I gave up trying to work it out a long time ago.

There's no reasoning with her. I've just had to accept that's how she's chosen to live her life, and she's genuinely happy. It's just not my version of happiness, thank God.'

The beep of an incoming text message interrupted the conversation. 'That'll be yours, Jeanna. It's Doug asking if you fancy a quickie,' Josie joked.

'Nope, not mine,' Jeanna replied, before scanning the room. 'And there's nowhere big enough in here anyway,' she teased.

'I swear to God, I'm going to tape your gob shut,' Claire said, exasperated.

Jeanna was on a roll and couldn't be stopped. 'Yep, Doug did that one time too. It was an S&M thing.'

It was so ludicrous, a gale of laughter derailed Claire's disapproval.

Val and Josie had both fished their mobile phones out of their bags and checked. Nope, not them either.

Claire reached out and grabbed her phone from the desk.

Yep, there was the message.

Sam.

She opened it up.

> So it sounds like our boy enjoyed his first weekend at college… On a scale of 1–10, how frantic are you?

She typed back.

> 10. Jeanna and I are planning his retrieval right now

Claire smiled as she pressed 'send' then replayed the conversation to the others. The one thing that she was most proud of was that she and Sam had managed to stay friends throughout everything. Sure, there had been a few stumbling blocks along the way. It had taken her a moment or ten to recover when he'd moved in with Nicola, a colleague from work. Especially as Nicola was five years younger than her, stunning and the kind of organised, switched on, perfectly groomed career woman that Claire couldn't be if her life depended on it. Getting out of the house with a matching bra and knickers proved to be a challenge most days.

He replied instantly.

Thought so. Seem to remember that happening on his first day of school too.

'What's funny?' Jeanna asked, seeing her expression.

'Just Sam,' Claire replied. 'He's talking about Jordy's first day of school. Remember that?'

'Yup. It's a miracle we didn't get arrested.'

'Nope, what happened was much worse than getting arrested.'

There was a pang of sadness in the midst of the memory. That was in the days when she and Sam were good. In hindsight, she should have seen the clues. But back then she didn't have an inkling about what was to come.

Twenty-One

Claire – 2007

'Right! Spiderman backpack?' Claire asked.
'Yup,' Jordy replied.
'Spiderman lunchbox?'
'Yup.'
'Spiderman pants?'
That made Jordy giggle. 'Yup.'
'Spiderman trainers?'
'Yup.'
'School uniform?'
Jordy's brown eyes glanced down at his grey shorts, grey socks, navy jumper with the school crest and pale blue polo shirt underneath. 'Yup.'
'Superpowers?'
'Don't have any.'
'Oh. That's a disappointment,' she teased. 'I wonder if I could trade you in for Iron Man. Anyway, tell me then, what must you do at all times?'

'Put my hand up when I want to speak to the teacher, ask if I can go to the toilet before I'm bursting and try not to fart in class.'

'I think my work here is done,' she told him, tickling him and making him shriek with giggles. It sounded glib, but she was so far from nonchalant that she'd struggle to spell it. When Max had gone to school the year before, there had been tears and fears. But none of them belonged to the little guy who wandered in without a care in the world or a backward glance at his overwrought mother. Even then, though, she knew that Max would be fine. He was her bold one. Her sociable one. Her little guy who could round up five pals at a moment's notice and turn any occasion into an opportunity to play 'Duck, Duck, Goose' and have a right good giggle.

Jordy, though? He was her baby. Her little, sweet, shy guy, who was perfectly content in his own company and kept his feelings to himself. He was happy just to wander about with a football at his feet and ignore the rest of the world. For the last year, it had been just her and him, every day. Now he was going off to school and it was the end of an era – no more kids at home. She'd just lost her excuse for afternoon double bills of Avenger movies and weekly cupcakes.

Jeanna groaned as she put her coffee down on the table. 'Tell me you're not crying. If you are, I'm calling Pathetic Parents Anonymous. You need help.'

'Jordy, tell Auntie Jeanna to stop being mean or she'll spend the next hour on the naughty step.'

Jordy chuckled. 'Auntie Jeanna, Mum says you've to…'

He didn't get any further before Jeanna scooped him up and performed a second bout of tickling, with the same ear piercing results.

'Hey, put my nephew down right now,' Doug demanded, as he swung in the back door. 'Don't worry, Jordy, I'll save you from evil,' he said, before grabbing Jeanna in a hug and giving her a big sloppy kiss on the cheek.

Jeanna dropped the five year old with a disgusted, 'Eeeeeeew.' It was absolutely the best tactic, given that her aversion to public displays of affection were legendary.

Not for the first time, Claire thought how lucky she was to have them. Jeanna was like a sister, both to Doug and to her, and the three of them had gone through life as a team since they were fourteen years old.

Jeanna gave Doug a twister on his arm in revenge, his howls prompting Claire to step in. 'Eh, any chance you two could act like adults? I mean, I know it's a long shot…'

They all knew she didn't mean it. On the contrary, she was beyond grateful that they'd both showed up for Jordy's first day of school. Her parents were hopeless and completely disinterested in the boys. Sam's parents had decided to up sticks and move to Spain to enjoy their early retirement, while his brothers had scattered to New York, London and Edinburgh. Doug and Jeanna, and her grandad Fred, were the only family they had left who were actively involved in the kids' lives and she appreciated them beyond words. Her grandparents on her dad's side had both passed away a few years before, Grampa Pete of a stroke and Granny Jenny of bowel cancer just a few months later. Both of them were gone much too young and she was sad about that, but she'd had little relationship with them. They'd barely spoken since she was a teenager and her gran had castigated her and Doug for moving in with Fred, telling them what a wonderful father Ray was and how he'd sacrificed so much for them. Such bullshit. But it didn't take a psychologist to work out where Ray's demand for 100 per cent devotion and unfailing adoration came from.

Thank God Fred was still with them, although he was riddled with emphysema, a consequence of a twenty a day fag habit since he was about twelve. He loved to have them all over to visit twice a week and would read to the boys for hours. Fred still had a twinkle in his eye, the same one that his grandson Doug was trying to deploy now to get himself out of trouble.

He also flashed that way too good looking smile of his. 'Sorry, sis. It's her – she's a bad influence.'

Jeanna's response was cut short by Sam, who darted into the room in full suit, briefcase in one hand, mobile phone in the other, harassed look on his face.

'My navy and silver tie,' he blurted. 'I can't find it…'

Claire cut him off by picking the missing tie up off the back of a kitchen chair where Sam had left it the night before and dangling it in front of him.

Sam tried to smile, but she could see how flustered he was.

Despite that, he high-fived Jordy. 'Okay, tiger, are you ready?'

'Ready,' his son answered seriously.

Claire's heart squeezed just a little bit more. He was so small. So sweet. How could she throw him out into the big bad world?

'Right, let's go,' Sam prompted and Claire's hackles rose just a little. Here she was, trying to find ways of delaying the inevitable and all Sam wanted to do was get the show on the road. Traitor.

Sam didn't even notice her furrowed brow as he turned to her, 'You've got the address and you'll definitely be there at one o'clock?' he asked.

She nodded. 'Of course. I'll pick Jordy up from school and then Jeanna is going to watch him until we get back. I wouldn't miss it.'

It was just typical. On the same day as Jordy was starting school, Sam was getting an award from his company for the most successful advertising campaign they'd ever had. It was at a posh lunch in a swanky hotel and it was for… for… She couldn't remember. He worked on so many projects and – much as she was embarrassed to admit it – she regularly tuned out when he was talking about work. It wasn't entirely her fault. He'd come home every night around seven, when she was right in the middle of bath and story time. He'd join in and help, always happy to spend the last hour of their day with the kids, but by the time they got downstairs to make dinner and have a bit of adult only time, she was too knackered, or too busy planning the next day, to really give it her full attention.

This happened to all couples with young kids though, didn't it? Things got so busy that the time they had for each other dwindled to nothing. They'd survive. It was all just part of this time of their lives. It didn't help that they were both busy with work too. Sam spent twelve hours a day at the office and Claire worked from home, her alterations and dressmaking service being the perfect role for her because she could combine it with bringing up the kids and work when they were in bed. An old pal, Carrie, from the flat she'd lived in when she was a student, had even asked her to create her wedding dress. Bridal wear had been her favourite area of design at college so she'd been thrilled to take on the job and Carrie had been delighted with the beautiful gown she'd made for her.

'Can we speed it up a bit?' Sam asked, leading the way.

Claire took a couple more photographs to add to the 100 she'd already taken, then the four of them, plus Jordy and Max, walked the ten minutes to the school gate. As soon as they got there, Max galloped off to join his pals. Jordy stood next to her, Spiderman trainers flashing, arms around her leg.

Decision time. Scoop him up and run off home with him, and keep him by her side until he was at least forty, or get a grip and ease him in gently. Reluctantly she went for the latter. 'Right, tiger, there's Mrs Minns over there. On you go and join her line.'

The kids and parents had already visited the school for a one hour induction the week before, where they got to see the classroom and the desk the child would be sitting at. To avoid teary goodbyes inside, the procedure on the first day was that they line up with their teacher, who took them inside with a quick wave back to the parents. In theory. Spiderman wasn't for budging.

'Right, buddy, on you go,' Sam prompted, and Claire could see that much as he was trying to disguise it, he was keen to get off to the office. He'd usually been at his desk for two hours by now.

It took much cajoling, gentle prising of the fingers and a beckoning from the teacher before Jordy – reluctantly and with tear filled eyes – slowly trudged the across the playground to join the rest of his class.

Claire's heart disintegrated into tiny pieces.

'You're not going over there to get him back,' Jeanna hissed, reading her mind as always. 'He'll be fine.'

'I won't, though,' Claire whimpered. 'Look at him. He's miserable. What kind of mother am I, sending him in there?'

'One that knows that there's this pesky thing called education?' Doug offered.

These two weren't helping. Sam, on the other hand, wasn't even engaged in the moment.

'Right, I'm off,' he said, giving her a quick kiss on the cheek and darting towards his car. He'd brought it here earlier this morning, when Claire made the point that they were all going to walk to school with Jordy, because they'd done the same with Max. Sam had driven the car to school, parked it and then jogged the ten minutes back to the house.

Now, he was climbing into the front seat before she even had a chance to object.

At the school doors, Jordy turned and gave a last wave, and that's when Claire spotted one solitary tear running down his cheek. Her heart shattered yet again.

Jeanna gently put her hand on Claire's arm. 'Steady there. You're not going to be that mother who races over and snatches him back. He'll never live it down and he'll still be getting slagged for it in high school.'

Claire glanced up again and saw he was gone.

'Right, sis, I'm off.' Doug said, giving her a hug.

'Thanks for coming,' she told him, voice still choked with emotion.

He scrunched up her hair, like he'd done since they were kids. 'I've no idea where you got this maternal side from. Grampa Fred took me to school on my first day because Mum and Dad were in Torremolinos.'

'Dad didn't bother showing up to mine. Mum was miserable because he wasn't there and barely said a word."

'Just another normal day then,' Doug said, grinning. 'It's a miracle we turned out so fabulous.'

'Completely fabulous,' Claire parroted in her best posh voice, grateful that he was trying to divert her attention from the emotion of the occasion.

Laughing, Doug hugged Jeanna, then he headed off at brisk walking pace to his own work. The high school started a day after the primary school, but this was an in-service day to help with preparations. He'd been teaching maths for four years now and loved it.

'Right, come on then, hairdresser's, make-up and then home to try on all the dazzling outfits I've brought for you,' Jeanna said. 'I've taken the whole day off…'

'You got fired!' Claire reminded her. It was true. Jeanna had been diplomatically 'let go' from her fourth job in the fashion department of a very upmarket store, for telling a customer – quite truthfully – that an outfit made her look like she was heading to the bingo on a cruise ship. She was now on the hunt for a role that required no tact whatsoever.

'OK, so I've taken the whole day off from writing out job applications and dodging the scary woman at the job centre. So let's go.'

Claire had the same reluctance as Jordy trudging to that classroom line, but she went along with it. They headed to the salon Jeanna frequented on a weekly basis and Claire was immediately swarmed by a hairdresser, a junior assistant, a make-up artist and a nail technician. They pampered her, they preened her and they applied more make-up than she'd worn since her over-affection for eyeliner in the nineties.

By eleven o'clock, Jeanna was perusing the results like a proud mama at a pageant. 'Ah, it's a miracle what make-up and a good hair cut can do. You're stunning!'

She clearly didn't get the reaction to those comments that she expected. She reached over with her foot and spun Claire's salon chair round to face her, causing Girt, the stylist, to eject setting spray into mid-air. He recovered, then after a flourish of mirror action and a promise that Claire would return monthly for a trim, bustled off to his next client.

Like all good interrogators, Jeanna got straight to the point. 'OK, so what's with the doleful expression? You look better than you've done in years and yet you're moping and putting a damper on my sunny disposition.'

'I'm not moping, I'm fine. Great.'

Jeanna wasn't convinced. 'Well, you'd better tell your face that because it appears to be under the impression that someone stole your last biscuit.'

Claire spoke with minimal mouth movements so as not to crack her newly applied lip liner. 'Nothing's wrong. I'm just a bit preoccupied because I'm worried about Jordy. Do you think he's OK?'

Jeanna rolled her eyes. 'I think he's having a blast! He's probably on top of a desk leading the whole class in a rap sing-off.'

'He doesn't know any rap songs.' Claire countered, labelling the notion as ridiculous.

'Eh, I might have taught him one,' Jeanna confessed. 'But don't worry – it only mentions tits once and if he says it fast the teacher will never notice.'

Despite herself, Claire cackled with hilarity. 'Oh God, expelled on his first day. I'm going to have to make the kids wear earmuffs when they're around you. Right, come on, let's head back to the house before you tell me you also taught him to shoplift and operate a can of spray paint.'

She quickly checked herself one last time in the mirror. They'd done a great job, making her look more polished and pretty much unrecognisable as the knackered, anxious mother of two infants who'd walked in less than two hours ago.

Stretching out of the chair, she hugged Jeanna. 'Thanks, luvly. I feel so much better and Sam is going to love the new me.' She checked her watch. 'Right, if we jump on the bus, we'll be home in ten minutes and that gives me over an hour to throw on a dress and get back out the door.'

Jeanna went along with it, although Claire knew her friend was more of a taxi than a bus kind of chick. To her credit, she didn't moan once. Or if she did, Claire was too preoccupied to notice. Was he OK? Was he sad? Missing her?

They were one stop from the house when Claire realised they were round the corner from the school. In a flash, she was up and off the bus.

Jeanna came staggering after her. 'Fuck! Could you give me some warning when you need me to run in heels? I nearly ended myself there.'

Claire wasn't paying attention. She moved like an Olympic speed walker, reaching the school gate in about a minute and a half. Jeanna was ten feet behind her the whole time, only catching up when Claire finally stopped.

'What are we doing here, you mad woman?' Jeanna panted.

'I just need to know that he's OK. That's all. I don't even need to speak to him, but I just can't stand the thought of him in there, breaking his heart, and I'm not there for him.'

Jeanna shook her head. 'You've lost the plot. Seriously. So what, you're going to go in there and ask if your primary one son is settling in and happy? They won't put a big "neurotic" tick against your name. Nope, not at all.'

'I don't care,' Claire retorted, in response to the sarcasm. She didn't. She'd spent her whole childhood feeling like – apart from Doug – she was on her own. There was never anyone there to talk to, to comfort her, to give her a hug when she was worried. She'd be damned if her sons would feel that fear or loneliness for a single second. 'Sod it,' she said, before taking off through the gate.

'Oh bollocks,' Jeanna cursed, limping after her.

Claire didn't head to the front door. She knew what class Jordy was in, the one to the left of reception. If she could just glimpse him through the window, see that he was OK, then she'd be fine. She'd go home, have a cup of tea and listen to Jeanna casting this up until the end of time.

She crept towards the building, touched the wall, pressed her face was against the window, her eyes scanning the room, until… There he was! He was sitting at a table of four, drawing a picture. No tears. No snot. No visible signs of trauma.

'Mrs Bradley?'

To quote Jeanna, 'Oh bollocks.'

She slowly turned to see Mrs Thompson, the headmistress, hanging out of the next window along. She must have seen her doing her sprint across the playground. And by the looks of things, she wasn't hanging out of her window to invite her to join the mums' race on sports day.

'Would you like to come round to my office?' The words formed a question, but her tone made it clear that there was only one answer.

'I preferred it when it was me who got us in trouble with the headmistress,' Jeanna whispered, walking with her to the door. Jeanna spent most of high school in detention for something, often landing Claire in it too.

Now the roles were reversed, Jeanna seemed to find this hilarious. Claire not so much.

An hour later, after a firm lecture from the headmistress about boundaries, policies and acceptable (or non-acceptable) standards of behaviour, Claire and Jeanna were back out at the school gate. The primary one kids finished at twelve for the first week, while the rest of the school, Max included, stayed until three. Seconds after the shrill of the bell, they watched Jordy and his classmates run towards them.

'Well, Spiderman, how was it?' she asked, trying desperately to mask the tension in her voice.

Her beautiful little guy shrugged. 'It was OK. I wanted to come home, but the teacher said I couldn't.'

For the third time that morning, her heart crumbled.

'Hold it together, pal,' Jeanna warned her.

Claire forced a smile on to her face. 'Och, that's just because it's the first day,' she said jovially. 'I promise you'll love it more and more each day until you won't even want to come home when the bell rings!'

He didn't look convinced.

The whole way home, Claire tried to engage him in sunny chat about his day, and he gave her doleful one word answers. By the time she reached the house, a decision she hadn't even realised she was making was already cast in stone. She dug her phone out of her bag and texted Sam.

> Really sorry – won't make the lunch. Going to stay home with Jordy. He's fine but just think he needs some love. See you later. Xx

He didn't text back and she didn't give it a second thought.

Her children would always be her priority. And if it came down to choosing who needed her most, they would win every time.

Twenty-Two

Denise – 2019

Denise put the highlighter pen down and closed her eyes. She couldn't look at bank statements any more. She needed a break from this before her head exploded, needed to centre herself, to do something that would unravel the twist of panic and fury that was consuming her.

Ray. The only thing that would break this pain for even a few moments was to remind herself of who he was, what they'd been.

Years of meditation had taught her how to focus her mind and block out the rest of the world. That's what she did now.

Ray. The synapses of her brain worked together to pull up a memory of a night only a few weeks ago. He'd been working away all week on a job in Edinburgh, and she'd missed him every second he was gone.

He'd walked in the door on the Friday night with a huge bouquet of her favourite lilies. Stargazers. Of course, she'd been expecting him, so she'd done her hair, her make-up was perfect and she was wearing a Diane Von Furstenburg wrap dress that he'd bought her for Christmas a few years before. He'd said all the celebrities were wearing them so she deserved to have one too. It was still one of his favourites and he clearly appreciated it because, with his free arm, he'd picked her up, swung her around and kissed her hard on the lips.

'God, I missed you, gorgeous,' he told her, his breath hot on her cheek. 'Come on, let's go out.'

Her arms tightened around his neck as tingles of excitement flooded her body. Forty years and he could still make her feel like she was fifteen again. 'Are we celebrating something?' she asked, giggling.

'We're celebrating that I absolutely...' He kissed her. 'Love...' He kissed her again. 'My wife.'

'I like that kind of celebration,' she murmured, utterly swept away by her adoration of this man.

'Go put something stunning on,' he told her.

She took a step back. 'Not dressy enough?'

He pulled her back towards him, tugged on the strap that held the dress closed, allowing it to fall open. She smiled, knowing that he liked what he saw. Sure, her boobs were a bit lower than they once were, but the La Perla lingerie he'd bought her for her birthday took care of that. At fifty-five, the rest of her body was still tight and toned, thanks to daily workouts at the gym. She wanted her body to please her man. The look on his face told her that it still did.

He tossed the flowers on to the granite worktop, then they made love right there on the kitchen table. It was the perfect Friday, the perfect moment, the perfect man.

Reluctantly, Denise let the delicious feeling of his touch dissipate as she brought her mind back to the present, calmer now, the memory restoring her faith and trust in the love that they'd shared. Those weren't the actions of a man who kept secrets from his wife. Or a businessman in crippling financial difficulties. Ray Harrow was a man who had made a success of his life, built a thriving company, lived with a wife he adored, had no worries to keep him awake at night.

Sitting forward, she returned to the sea of highlighted lines in the business bank statements. The easy ones to cross off were payments to contractors that she had booked to help him on jobs. She knew them all by name, either individually or the companies that they worked for. Next were the transfers to the credit card he used to buy supplies and equipment for his jobs, and petrol and diesel for the vehicles. Cross checking them with the credit card statements that were at the back of the file, they looked to be completely in order. VAT debits were what she'd expect. As were the lease payments for his company van, his Mercedes and her BMW, both of which were arranged via the business for tax reasons that she didn't particularly understand. Phone bills paid – mobile and landline. Electricity and gas bills – also through the business books. The only other regular debit was a transfer to his personal account for... wow, £6,000 a month. Was that how much it cost to maintain their lifestyle?

She mentally totted up their other outgoings – holidays, nights out, groceries. That was it. And sure, their travel was expensive, but that was only a couple of times a year, yet the £6,000 was moved to the personal account every month. Strange, for sure.

She was about to close the folder when she realised that she'd only looked at half of the picture. If the account was so deep in the red, then obviously there wasn't enough cash going into it. She scanned the credits, mentally tying up the payments with the jobs she had helped him to arrange. There was Mr & Mrs Lemon's conservatory. Paid in full. The refit of the chip shop in the high street. Paid over three months, as agreed, to help the owner with his cash flow. The construction of the new forecourt for the independent garage in Paisley. The emergency jobs caused by the torrential storms at the beginning of the year. All paid in full. So what wasn't there?

The Edinburgh job, two months of regular travel through there for up to four days at a time. That one finished weeks ago. Then there was the loft conversion in Stirling. The kitchen extension in Falkirk. The summer house construction in Ayr. And those were just the ones she remembered off the top of her head.

Fury bubbled inside her. Bad debts. Was that what had caused this? A sudden thought... These were also all jobs that he'd arranged himself. She hadn't booked contractors to work with him because he said he'd contacted them personally and arranged it all. At the time, she thought he was just trying to take some tasks off her plate, but now... None of this made sense.

As she closed the file on the business account, she'd learned two things. He hadn't been paid for half of the jobs he'd done in the last year – and the ones he hadn't been paid for were all jobs that he told her he'd organised. And he was transferring six thousand pounds a month to his personal account – the one that currently had a balance of £636.00.

She'd spent two hours digging through this web of confusion and she was no further forward in understanding the situation.

Opening the second folder, the one with his personal statements, she just hoped the answers were in there.

Twenty-Three

Denise – 1986

The lights on the Christmas tree in the corner were flickering, the angel on the top a little lopsided. Not that the kids had cared. Now that Claire was seven and Doug was six, they were beyond excited about Santa's visit tonight, and so hyper before they went to bed that they were practically swinging from the paper chains that draped from every corner of the room.

Kneeling on the floor, Denise sat back on her heels and rubbed the base of her back. She'd been bending over, wrapping these presents for the last hour and her festive cheer had well and truly disappeared.

She'd been hoping beyond hope that Ray would get home in time to help, but in truth, she'd known it was a long shot. The plant shut at lunchtime, so it was normal for the men to head to the pub for a pint on the way home. In Ray's case, that invariably meant ten pints once he got going. He couldn't help himself, she knew that. He just loved being sociable and having a good time with the other guys. It was one of the things she loved about him, so she rarely complained. Besides, how many times had his mum told her that the worst thing Denise could do was put demands on him? He had a lot on his plate, Jenny said, between working and supporting a family with two kids. Denise had to make allowances.

If she were being honest, though, she just wished those allowances didn't need to be made at 9 p.m. on Christmas Eve, when she still had to finish sorting the presents and get the preparations done for her first time hosting a Christmas lunch tomorrow.

Her own family weren't coming – Agnes said she wasn't traipsing across the city on Christmas Day – but Ray's mum and dad were definitely going to be here. Ray had said that offering to do it was the least they could do now that they were in their own house. She got a tingling in the pit of her stomach just thinking about that. Her own house. And it was a bought one too, not one off the council. No one in her family had ever owned their own house before, and much as her mum would die before she admitted it, Denise knew Agnes was a tiny bit impressed.

It was just a shame they'd got it under such sad circumstances. Situated in Giffnock, a lovely suburb in the south of the city, it had been Ray's grandad's house, until he'd passed away a couple of months before. The house had been left to his only son, Ray's dad, Pete, although there was still an outstanding mortgage on it. Pete had decided that he was too late on in life to be taking on a mortgage and a house that needed complete modernisation.

He and Jenny were happy in their tenement flat and had no desire to move. 'They'll take me out of here in a box,' Pete always said. Jenny was in agreement for three reasons – first, she was deeply wary of any financial commitments. She was paid in cash every week by the supermarket and she had her savings club for Christmas. They had no credit cards, no loans and no interest in having them. And secondly, well, what did they need to move and leave their friends and neighbours for? She was perfectly happy in the council home she'd lived in since she married Pete. Most importantly, her Ray and the kids (yep, Denise noted she didn't figure in the equation) were just starting out in life and this would be a fabulous move for them. It would give them a lifetime of security and it would get them out from under her and Pete's feet. Not that she didn't love having them close, but four adults and two children in a two bed, one box room flat was definitely a challenge.

Ray had jumped at the chance. The important thing was that it was in a posh area, he said. They could do it up over time and they'd be set for life. Not that he'd had much time to work on it yet, right enough. Between work and football, sometimes it felt like he was barely home.

Claire and Doug had settled fine into their new school though. Maybe one of these days she'd get round to talking to some people, maybe at the school gate. Sometimes it felt like she went days without speaking to another soul.

She was on the lookout for a part-time job too because Ray said they needed the money for the house improvements. Just the mornings, because she had to pick the kids up every day at three o'clock. She was two buses away from her mum and Jenny now, so there was no one nearby to help.

Stretching, she loosened her muscles off and then went back to wrapping presents again. Just after ten o'clock now. The opening bars of a familiar theme song on the telly made her look up. *Dallas*. JR Ewing was strutting about with that smug grin on his face. It was one of her favourite shows, but Ray reckoned it was nonsense. She'd seen an advert that Larry Hagman and Linda Gray were going to be on a Wogan Late Night Christmas Special tonight as well, so she could watch that while she was getting things sorted, at least until her husband came home.

It was after midnight when she heard the door open. Presents wrapped, Wogan watched, veg and potatoes for tomorrow's lunch peeled, she was dozing in the armchair by the dying embers of the coal fire.

He burst in the door, Christmas hat on his head, still in the work clothes he'd left in that morning.

'Merry Christmas, ma darling,' he crooned.

'Sssssshhhh,' she said, giggling. 'Don't you dare wake those kids up.'

He ignored her, bursting into a chorus of 'I Wish It Could Be Christmas Every Day.'

Laughing, she decided to stop objecting and just enjoy the show. Even now that they'd been together for seven years, she still thought he was the best looking man she'd ever seen. She'd seen loads of posters for that new *Top Gun* movie and she really thought Ray was much better looking than that Tom Cruise bloke.

Second verse and another chorus sung, he glanced around the room, seeing the cookies and milk by the fireplace and the pile of presents already wrapped and under the tree. If he remembered that he'd promised to come home early enough to help her wrap them, he wasn't saying. Not that it mattered. All she cared about was that he was home now.

'You've done a grand job here, Den,' he told her. 'Christ, yer a fab wife. Do you know that?'

She grinned. 'Yeah, but you can keep telling me,' she teased.

'Oh, I will,' he said, enjoying the joke. 'Come here so I can tell you just how great a wife you really are.'

He leant down to kiss her and she reached up to curl her arms around his neck. Her lips were almost on his when she recoiled. What was that smell? It was…

'Perfume?' she blurted, anxiety ripping through her.

'What? Naw,' he tried to shrug her comment off. 'Don't be crazy. Of course it's not perfume.'

She bit her bottom lip, not sure what to say. She was sure it was perfume. Positive. However, challenging Ray was something she rarely did because it never ended well. She'd learned growing up with Agnes, that on almost every occasion, it was much easier to back down, keep your mouth shut and let the issue pass.

For once, she didn't take her own advice. 'But it smells like…'

'It's not fucking perfume,' he argued. 'Or if it is, it came from being in the pub on Christmas Eve, with a hundred folk, half of which were women who were drowned in the stuff. Why are you giving me grief? I came home to see my wife, ready to cuddle up and bring in Christmas, and you're giving me a hard time. I should have stayed in the bloody pub.'

And she should have kept her mouth shut, she decided. What had she been thinking? All night she'd been waiting for him and now she'd completely ruined everything the minute he walked in the door. How stupid was that?

Her first reaction was to try desperately to make it right. 'I'm sorry, it's just that it took me a bit by surprise because it was so strong. Anyway, don't get annoyed. I'm just glad you're home now.'

It took a moment to determine how that was going to go. If he was really annoyed, he'd kick off and storm to bed, but maybe she'd apologised quickly enough that it would be OK. She loved him so much, she didn't want to be fighting with him on any night, but especially tonight.

'OK, but enough of the third degree. Stop being mental.'

Still a bit hostile, so she wasn't forgiven yet. The knot in her stomach tightened a little, but then he grinned and kissed her again and she began to relax.

'Quite like it when you're a wee bit jealous though,' he said, nuzzling her neck now.

All was fine again.

She pushed his chest playfully. 'Oh yeah? Well, don't be making me jealous too often. Never know what I'll do,' she said, and it was funny because they both knew that she didn't have an aggressive bone in her body.

'Poison me with one of those Brussels sprouts?' he teased, gesturing to the pot in the centre of the coffee table, where two pounds of sprouts sat in water. She'd brought them in to the living room to peel them while she was watching Wogan.

She didn't get a chance to answer because his lips were hard on hers now and she felt that familiar thrill of his touch. They made love, then they fell asleep, right there on the floor in front of the fire.

'Mummmmmmm!' It was still dark, sometime around 7 a.m., when Doug was their early-morning alarm call. 'Santa has been!'

Shit. His bellows snapped her awake. Thankfully, Ray had pulled a rug over them at some point last night, so at least the kid wasn't looking at them lying naked on the floor.

'You go and get your sister, and then Mummy and Daddy will help you open them.'

'Claire! Claire!' he yelled, running back up the stairs.

This wasn't how she'd planned this morning. Reaching out, she grabbed her clothes from the night before and pulled them on, shaking Ray awake.

'Babe! Ray! The kids are up.'

'Tell them to go back to bed,' he groaned.

'We can't! It's Christmas morning!'

'So?' he asked, not quite jumping on board.

'Quick, throw these on,' she said, tossing his jeans to him. He'd only just got them on when Doug appeared back, with his sister trailing behind him.

'Merry Christmas, you two!' Denise chirped.

'The milk!' Claire squealed, pointing to the fireplace behind Denise.

Crap. She'd meant to throw it and the cookies away last night and she'd completely forgotten. How was she going to explain why Santa and Rudolph hadn't eaten and drank them?

'It's gone!' Claire added, her second squeal just as loud as the first.

Denise turned around to see… Yep, it was gone. She caught Ray's gaze and he winked at her.

'I think maybe Santa was hungry and thirsty during the night,' he said, grinning, and she immediately caught on to what had happened. She leaned over, threw her arms around him and kissed him, even though he had hair that was going in fourteen directions and smelled like a pub carpet. God, she loved this man.

She made the two of them tea, and they sat on the floor, his arm around her, watching the kids opening their presents. She only had to nudge him awake twice.

'Look, Daddy, look!' Claire said when she opened the Care Bear she had been desperate for since she'd fallen in love with the new TV show. The same when she unwrapped the box containing a bright pink skateboard. That little one just adored her dad. It was so sweet to see. And every time she thrust another toy in his face, he managed to fend off the hangover and raise a smile for her.

When all the gifts were opened – Doug screeched with excitement over every one of his Transformers and his Pogo ball – Denise pulled a box from behind the armchair and handed it to Ray.

'What's this?' he asked, clearly pleased as punch.

'Just a wee something,' she replied coyly. He didn't need to know that she'd been saving a couple of pounds a week for the last six months for this present.

He ripped open the paper, opened the box and pulled out a pair of Adidas football boots. 'Yes!' he exclaimed, smothering her face in kisses.

'Yuk,' Doug exclaimed, disgusted.

Ray took no notice. 'Just as well I got something for you too then.' He reached up for the jacket that had been tossed over the couch when he came in the night before, rummaged in the pocket and pulled out a tiny jewellery box. It wasn't gift wrapped, but Denise didn't care.

Cheeks sore from smiling, she popped it open to see two gold heart shaped earrings. 'Oh my God, I love them,' she gasped.

'Not as much as I love you,' he told her. 'Happy Christmas.'

Ray kissed her again, a full blown snog this time.

'Yuk!' Doug moaned again.

'Hey, that's enough, you,' Ray told him, in mock seriousness. He pushed his arms up in the air and stretched. 'Right, is that us done with the presents?' he asked, gesturing to the kids.

Denise nodded.

'Thank God. It was taking forever and I'm needing my bed.'

Denise tried not to show her disappointment. She was hoping they could spend every minute of the day together today.

'Come on, then,' he said, kissing her playfully.

'I can't, babe. It's Christmas Day.' It just didn't seem right. Besides, she had so much to do. The family would be arriving in… Shit, four hours.

He nuzzled her again. 'Who's the most important person in your world?' he asked, laughing.

Her smile was automatic. She just couldn't resist this man. And she loved that whenever he was with her, he wanted all of her attention. How many times had he told her how he just couldn't get enough of her because he loved her so much?

'You are,' she murmured, kissing him. She didn't even care about the morning beer breath.

'I am,' he agreed. 'So come and pay some attention to your husband then. Call it an extra Christmas present.'

'But the kids…'

'They'll be fine,' he objected. 'Look at them!'

He had a point. They were so busy with their presents, they wouldn't even notice she was gone. Surrender. There was no way she could say no to him.

'Right you two, Mummy and Daddy are just going for a lie-down because we were helping Santa last night,' she said.

Claire looked up from her doll. 'But, Mummy, I want to play with you. I want to show you my—'

Ray cut her off. 'Later, Claire. We'll play with you in a while. Man, these kids are hard work.' With that, he tugged on Denise's hand and she willingly followed him upstairs to the bedroom.

He was right. They'd have plenty of time to play with the kids later. Quality time with her husband was top of her priority list.

On the way down the hall, she glanced in the mirror, her eyes immediately drawn to the new earrings in her ears. Two hearts. One his. One hers.

And she absolutely knew that as long as he loved her, there was nothing else she would ever need.

Twenty-Four

Claire – 2019

'Yeah, but tell them the rest of it,' Jeanna demanded as Claire finished the story about Jordy's first day at school.

Claire's face was the same colour as the red velvet pedestal in the middle of the room. 'I'm mortified just thinking about it,' she admitted. 'The headmistress sent a letter out to all parents expressly forbidding them from entering the playground during school hours. And I don't know how it got out, but everyone sussed what I'd done. Some mothers started crossing the road when they saw me coming.'

'Oh, my toes are curling,' Val hooted. 'And that's no mean feat with my bunions.'

'And…' Jeanna pressed, making it clear that there was more and forcing Claire to spill the details.

'And Sam was totally pissed off because it turned out that he'd arranged for his brother to come through from Edinburgh to take over from Jeanna and look after the kids, and he'd booked dinner and a night in that swanky hotel he got the award in. He'd planned this whole big surprise. Thankfully he phoned and cancelled his brother when he got my text, so at least he didn't come all that way for nothing.'

'You didn't know this? You couldn't have persuaded her to go?' Val rounded on Jeanna, who put her hands up in surrender.

'He didn't tell me! Knew I'd crack and spoil the surprise.'

Josie shrugged. 'Yep, I can understand that. Mouth like the Clyde tunnel.'

Jeanna laughed at the dig. As someone who dealt out brutal honesty, she'd long ago learned to take it when it was coming in her direction.

Claire carried on, cringing as she spoke. 'So, yep, it was the biggest achievement of his career and he wanted to celebrate it. Instead, I stood him up and he was home and in bed by nine o'clock. He didn't speak to me for days.'

Josie shook her head dolefully. 'Claire, my darling, you know I love you, but that might not have been one of your better days.'

'You don't have to tell me,' Claire conceded. 'But at the time, in the moment, I really thought I was doing the right thing. Like I said, if my parents were one end of the care spectrum, I needed to be at the other. I may have got slightly carried away, I can see that now.' It was true. Sort of. Even now, she knew she would probably still make the same decision and stay in with Jordy to cheer him up.

'Slightly?' Jeanna asked pointedly.

'OK, very. But you have to remember, I grew up with the kind of people who couldn't even be arsed staying with their kids on Christmas Day. They once pissed off for a snooze the minute Doug and I finished opening our presents. Thank God Doug and I had each other.'

Val couldn't comprehend this. 'What? They just left you to it? On Christmas Day?'

Claire nodded. 'I still hate chipolatas,' she said mournfully, making the others laugh.

'Was that the year your dad got your mum those cheap earrings down the pub?'

'Yep. They made her ears turn green by Hogmanay and she had to get TCP for the infection. But he spun her some story about how they represented their love, so she wore them anyway. That's what he's always done. He's so charismatic, one of those guys who is always the centre of the room. She's the opposite, so when he comes out with all the grand gestures, and a load of bullshit chat about how much he adores her, she falls for it every time. She's never sussed that none of it is real, that it's just his way of reeling her in so that she'll do whatever he wants.'

'What a pair,' Val whistled.

'They are,' Claire agreed. 'In hindsight, I can see how much he resented us. He had this big life planned for himself and he ended up getting tied down with a wife and kids at seventeen. I honestly think he never got over it. He hated Doug and me for changing his life, but he made the best of a bad situation by making sure my mother pandered to him at every turn.'

'But why have Doug if he was so unhappy when you came along?' Val asked, gobsmacked by the whole story.

'Ah, another accident. Contraception wasn't my mother's strong point. Apparently, he hit the roof when he found out, as if it wasn't his fault too. Same old story. Anyway, barmaid, my wine glass is empty. What kind of establishment is this?'

The door buzzer delayed Jeanna's answer and she went off to answer it, leaving Claire groaning, 'Oh God, who's there now? This is like one of those TV shows where they shock the crap out of some poor unsuspecting person. It had better not be Ant and Dec.'

Claire's warm and bubbly feeling of happiness was instantly restored when Suze marched in the door, pulling a cabin sized suitcase on wheels. 'Nope, I'm much better looking. And taller. And not in possession of a penis.'

Suze was the owner of Pluckers, the hair and beauty salon in the row of shops downstairs. She was so gregarious and outspoken that she made Josie, Val and Jeanna look introverted, but Claire – and everyone else who knew her – loved her for it. It was what made her salon so popular. Little old ladies who'd been her customers for ten years still popped in. The Glasgow glitterati loved to hang out there because Suze was the person who knew everyone yet was completely irreverent and unfazed by celebrity. And teenagers flocked to it because it was considered trendy and the place to be. That atmosphere and the young, edgy, anything goes culture was all down to Suze.

She was also absolutely stunning too. Her long red hair fell in waves from a side parting to her shoulder blades, her pale skin was flawless and a brilliant advert for the treatments that were available in the salon, her make-up was always impeccable and she wore her standard salon uniform of black trousers and a black T-shirt with the word 'BOSS' embroidered in gold on the back. Only when you were up close, could you see that it also – in smaller letters underneath – said, 'So don't piss me off.'

'I heard there was an intervention and I'm here to play my part,' she announced, eliciting a loud groan from Claire.

'I'm scared to ask, but your part is…'

Suze gazed upon her with something that sat between pity and exasperation. 'Doll, on the inside, you're truly beautiful.'

'Thanks,' Claire replied, touched.

'But, my God, the outside needs work.'

She didn't even give Claire time to be offended before she opened the zip of the cabin case in one smooth motion and flipped the top section over to reveal the contents. Claire saw brushes, make-up, scissors, tubs of hair dye, tin foil, straighteners, rollers, a hairdryer, towels and several implements that looked like they belonged on the equipment tray of an operating theatre.

'So, I'm giving you a makeover. And yes, it would be easier to take you down to the salon, but I know you've been indulging in the vino and the last time these two were pissed in my salon…' she gestured to Josie and Val, 'they started singing "Hi Ho Silver Lining", got everyone up to dance, then they told three of the cast of *River City* that they'd heard they were getting killed off by a rare bug after eating a dodgy kebab.'

'That was Josie,' Val said, trying to defend herself.

'I didn't think they'd believe me,' Josie exclaimed. 'Everyone knows I talk nonsense. Would be a great storyline though. Killed by a doner kebab.'

Suze rolled her eyes. 'One of them spent the next three hours in tears, trying to get a hold of her agent. She doesn't come in any more. Told the others that she still has flashbacks.'

'Josie, you are totally my bitch goal,' Jeanna told her, cackling into her wine.

'Also...' Suze went on. 'I wasn't going to work down there when you lot were having a riot up here. That would give me serious FOMO. By the way, Jeanna, that bag over there...' she pointed to a large brown paper bag she'd dropped at the door, 'has the food you asked me to pick up.'

Only then did Claire realise she could smell something delicious.

Jeanna pulled plastic cartons of buffet food out of the huge bag. Sausage rolls. Spring rolls. Chicken satay sticks. Cold meats. Crusty bread. A tub of salad. Claire suddenly noted how hungry she actually was. A glance at the clock told her that it was after two o'clock. The day had flown by.

'I'll swap you the food for a large glass of wine and a tiara. Looking at those two is making me jealous.' Suze said, gesturing to Josie and Val, who instinctively tapped their sparkly, diamanté-studded hair accessories, making sure they were still perfectly positioned.

Laughing, Claire removed another tiara from the headwear display and crowned Suze, just as Jeanna passed over the requested vino. Once again, a massive wave of gratitude flooded Claire's senses. How lucky was she to have this? Yes, she'd lost the company of her sons, and yes, she was going to be living alone for the first time in twenty years, but today was definitely showing her how she could fill that gap with a different kind of love and laughs.

Suze disappeared into the office, and came back with the black wheelie chair that usually sat at Claire's desk. 'OK, plonk yourself on here and I'll get started.'

'Do I get a say in this?' Claire asked.

Suze shook her head. 'Absolutely not. This is my job. God forbid, if Tom ever ditches me for a trophy wife, I'll come to you for my next wedding dress, but leave this stuff to me. I promise you'll love it. And I haven't killed anyone yet. Well, apart from that one client, but the post-mortem was inconclusive.'

Claire was 95 per cent sure she was joking. So, as she'd done since she'd walked through the Everlasting Bridal Design door this morning, she decided to roll with it.

The others dished up the food, refilled the glasses and then settled back down to eat, drink, watch and chat some more.

'I'm curious, Claire…' Val began. 'What you were saying about missing Sam's award thingy that day… Is that when you realised you two were in trouble?'

Claire tried to shake her head, but Suze had pulled a towel around her shoulders, inserted a clip in her hair and was brushing on some kind of disgusting smelling cream.

'No. Looking back, it was the beginning of the end, but I don't think I realised it until later.'

'I remember exactly when it was,' Jeanna interjected. 'It was Christmas 2010.'

Claire was shocked. 'How come you remember the details?'

'Because I shagged Doug that night too.'

Twenty-Five

Claire – 2010

'Babe, come to bed,' Sam pleaded. 'Every single thing is done, and I want to give my wife her present.'

'Is it an actual present or one of your body parts?' Claire asked, knowing the answer. It used to be their annual tradition – sex immediately after midnight on Christmas Eve, the perfect way to celebrate the festivities.

'Body part,' Sam admitted ruefully.

Claire leaned over and kissed him. 'Then, much as that would be very nice, I'll pass. I've still to put batteries in all the kids' toys and I want to check everything is working.'

'Of course everything is working. It's all brand new and in the boxes!' Sam argued.

Why couldn't he be reasonable about this? It wasn't like she was asking him to do it. She was perfectly happy to stay up and do it herself. She didn't want a single thing to spoil tomorrow. At ten and nine, the boys had stopped believing in the chunky bloke in the red suit, but that didn't mean she wasn't going to make Christmas absolutely magical.

Sam sighed as he saw that she wasn't budging. 'Want me to stay up and help you and then I can give you your present?'

She had a nagging feeling that she should be more into continuing the traditional sexy start to Christmas Day, but she didn't have time to worry about it right now. Too much to do. And besides, they could have sex any other day of the week, so it was no big deal.

'Tempting,' she said playfully, 'but no, it's fine.'

She realised she actually didn't want him to help. It was nothing personal, but she just wanted to do everything at her own pace, without worrying that he was rushing her or getting pissed off. There had been way too much of that lately.

Once upon a time, their arguments had been so insignificant she barely remembered them. Now it seemed like they spent most of the time getting on each other's nerves. They were both busier than ever at work, she popped over every day to check on her grandad and when she had downtime, all she wanted to do was cuddle with the boys on the sofa and enjoy their company. Sam was rarely home before 8 p.m. now, and at least two or three times a week he was out at client dinners or events. The boys had activities on every night of the week that needed drop-offs and pick-ups, so there was no time together Monday to Friday. And at weekends she and Sam split the duties, with one of them taking Max to his rugby, swimming and taekwondo and the other taking Jordy to three sessions of football and one of athletics. It was just unfortunate that her boys didn't participate in any of the same sports. They were completely opposite characters in so many ways, yet, just like her and Doug, there was a closeness there that she was eternally grateful for. They would always have each other. And she would always have them.

Sighing, Sam got up and headed to the door. 'Merry Christmas then, love,' he said, and Claire would have to have been incredibly naïve not to register the irritation in his tone. Instead of making her feel guilty though, it just annoyed her. For God's sake he was a grown man, throwing a sulk because he hadn't got what he wanted. Countless scenes from her childhood flashed into her head of her mother conceding to her dad on every single occasion. She pushed them all out of her mind before the memories robbed her of her excitement about tomorrow.

She heard Sam moving about upstairs and then the bed quietly creaking as he climbed into it. Why was he so hung up about having sex tonight anyway? It wasn't as if that was a regular occurrence these days anyway. It was a once-a-month event, if they were lucky. It wasn't that she didn't want to, it just seemed like they were never on the same naked page at the same naked time.

Somewhere along the last few years they'd stopped communicating on any kind of deep level. She absolutely knew it, but knowing about it and changing it were two different things. Juggling all the other stuff made it impossible to deal with, but they'd get around to it at some point. After the New Year, she'd make a conscious effort to spend more time focusing on Sam and try to relight that spark they'd always had until life, jobs and parent duties sucked up every minute of the day.

It was after 2 a.m. when she climbed in beside Sam and he was already snoring. She gently rolled him on his side. Still snoring. Sam had hit thirty last year and Claire wasn't far off it. Jeanna claimed it was all downhill after that. She might be right. She couldn't remember Sam snoring or sulking when he was twenty.

It felt like her eyes had only been closed for five minutes when Max and Jordy began jumping on the end of their bed.

'Merry Christmas, boys,' she chirped, immediately wide awake. As a teenager she'd always dreaded Christmas – it was the one day she was forced to stay at home and couldn't go and hang out somewhere else to get away from the Ray and Denise show. However, since she'd had the kids this was her favourite day of the year and she didn't want to miss a second of it. She cuddled Max, kissing him on the top of his head. 'Merry Christmas, son. Can't tell you how much I love you.'

Her eldest boy hadn't yet hit that age of being embarrassed about affection – she hoped he never would – and rewarded her with a tight hug. 'Love you too, Mum.'

His brother followed suit, then Sam sat up too, arms open and the boys immediately jumped into them.

'Merry Christmas, you two! I've asked Santa to bring loads of stuff just for me this year because you two don't need anything else.'

Max and Jordy thought this was hilarious and, of course, a wrestling match ensued.

Things with Sam might have gone off track, but nothing changed the fact that he was a great dad who adored his boys and they adored him right back.

They got up and headed downstairs together, all in the Christmas pyjamas that Claire had given them the day before. When the boys came along, she'd been determined to create loads of new festive traditions. New pyjamas on Christmas Eve was one of them. Listening to Christmas songs while they opened their presents was another.

The boys both cheered with delight when they spotted the two stockings hanging from the fireplace and the two sacks of presents below. Sam nipped into the kitchen and rustled up two quick coffees, while Claire got the fire and the music on. The boys, patient for five minutes, then descended on their gifts. As always, they opened them one by one, each of them taking turns so that everyone could see and appreciate what they got. The final present, a joint one for them both, got the biggest cheer.

'It's an Xbox!' Max yelled, his face beaming with joy. He then launched himself at Claire, and then Sam. 'Thank you, thank you, thank you, this is ace!'

'Ace,' Sam repeated to her, winking.

The boys immediately rushed their new Xbox to the TV to connect it up.

Claire decided to leave them to it, knowing that they played these at their friends' houses all the time, so they were far more likely to know how to set it up than she was. She was just happy she'd put the batteries in the extra controllers, as well as in all the other gifts that required power. Nothing worse than looking for a packet of double-A batteries on Christmas morning. Instead, this had been perfect. Just perfect.

'Erm, boys, have you forgotten something?'

The two of them turned around, caught Sam's eye and immediately realised what they'd omitted to do. They grabbed a large, gift wrapped rectangle from under the tree and presented it to her.

'This is from us, Mum,' Max told her proudly. 'We totally picked it and everything.'

Claire laughed as she began tearing open the paper, knowing full well that – as every year – it would be her favourite seashell chocolates and that – as every year – she would act surprised when she saw them.

'Yes! Oh, boys, thank you – I love them.' She smothered them both in kisses.

Jordy then retrieved another parcel from under the tree and presented Sam with it. 'We picked this one too, Dad,' he said with a cheeky grin. Shy since he was a baby, he'd absolutely come out of his shell in the last couple of years and now had a lovely, impish sense of humour that made Claire howl.

Sam made a big show about being delighted with his aftershave and socks too. Just as with the chocolates, they'd been buying the same gifts for the boys to give each other for years.

Claire was about to fetch a bin bag from the kitchen to start tidying up, when Sam reached under his chair and pulled out another box, a small one this time, and handed it to her.

'Merry Christmas, baby,' he said, leaning in to kiss her.

Claire tried and failed to hide her reaction as she realised to her horror that he was giving her a personal gift… and she'd completely forgot to wrap up his. In fact, she couldn't even quite remember where she'd put it because she'd been hiding presents all over the house for weeks.

Shit.

Bollocks.

Shit.

How could she have done that? She'd been so concerned about making it the perfect Christmas for the kids that she'd completely forgotten to think about Sam.

Shit.

Bollocks.

Shit.

She unwrapped the box, then lifted the lid to see a beautiful gold heart-shaped locket. Picking it up, she opened it to see a photo of Max and Jordy's smiling faces. It was perfect. The perfect present. Thoughtful. Kind. Generous.

She'd got him a jumper from Marks and Spencer, she hadn't even wrapped it and she had no bloody idea where it was.

Epic. Fail.

'I love it, Sam, thank you,' she said truthfully, as she leaned over to give him a kiss.

'Eeeeeeew,' Jordy exclaimed, as always. He'd inherited his Auntie Jeanna's aversion to PDAs.

'Where's your present to Dad, Mum?' Max asked.

'Erm, I'm going to give it to him later. I just need to get the lunch started first.'

The boys thought nothing of it, happy to get back to setting up their games.

Sam followed her through to the kitchen.

'I'm so sorry,' she said, feeling absolutely terrible about what had just happened. 'I've no idea where your present is. It's hidden somewhere, and I totally forgot to look it out and wrap it.'

The fleeting expression of hurt on his handsome face was swift but unmistakable.

'You know, Claire, I don't care about the present,' he began, his voice more sad than annoyed. 'But I care that you forgot about me. I think that says everything we need to know about where we are now.'

She didn't get a chance to say anything else, because, with a sad smile, he headed back into the living room to help the boys with their new games.

Over the next couple of hours, there was no chance to apologise again, or repair what she'd done, or even go and search for the bloody jumper. Giving it to him now would just rub salt in the wound anyway. Better to do it later when it was just the two of them and she could apologise once more. Perhaps while naked and that way she'd be making up for both her festive failings.

Instead, she got on with the lunch preparations, while Sam stayed in the living room with the boys, shouts and yells of excitement over some football game on the Xbox wafting through to her. The turkey was in the oven, she was working to schedule on the vegetables, and her best crockery and cutlery were out, ready to be set on the table. Christmas songs were playing on the radio in the corner and a huge box of crackers was waiting to be opened. It was all going according to plan – apart from the disgruntled husband, the gift wrapped guilt, and a woeful lack of seasonal joy.

Sam's parents called and lifted her mood for a little while. They were spending Christmas at home, in the gorgeous little casa on the beach in Andalucía they'd moved to after taking early retirement three years ago. Claire, Sam and the boys all missed them dreadfully, but Granny and Grampa

Bradley called twice a week and flew back to Scotland every couple of months to see their grandchildren. It was the way grandparents should be – as opposed to her own parents, who'd never shown the slightest interest in the boys. They'd gleefully announced that they'd be spending Christmas in a five star resort in Tenerife and they were delighted to be doing so. 'Just the two of us – it'll be perfect,' her mother had wittered. Claire eyed the turkey baster in her hand and had a sudden thought as to how it could be used in a violent act.

Thankfully, the back door being barged open distracted her and in walked Jeanna and Giles. Two years into their marriage, Claire still hadn't taken to Jeanna's husband number two. There was something about him that reminded her of her dad: good looking, always immaculately dressed, liked to be the centre of attention but with an edge of conceit. Jeanna certainly wasn't a woman like her mother, content to pander to him, so it invariably made for some bristly conversations between them at social gatherings.

'The boys are all in the living room,' Claire told him, after they'd exchanged Christmas greetings. He headed on in to join them.

Jeanna's troubled sigh of relief was loud and impossible to ignore.

'You OK?' Claire asked, basting the large turkey crown in the oven.

Jeanna shook her head, her expression not matching the joyous, sparkly red sequins of her figure hugging dress. 'You know that cliché about the excitement of the honeymoon period wearing off and people realising that they actually have little in common except mutual irritation?'

Claire nodded.

'Well,' Jeanna went on. 'I think we're there.'

'Oh, honey, I'm so sorry,' she said, hugging her friend.

Jeanna laughed. 'No you're not – you've thought he was a tosser from the start. You're a rubbish actress.'

After a shocked pause, Claire conceded the truth of that.

'OK, that may be true, but can I just point out that you're a life coach? You're supposed to be the person that makes a plan, takes action, solves problems and is always the best version of themself.'

It was a fair point. After years working in various jobs – she'd been everything from a restaurant manager, to a personal assistant, to a misguided stint as a nail technician that faltered because she 'couldn't listen to people telling her about their plans for the weekend every fucking day' – Jeanna had finally decided to capitalise on her naturally bossy and intolerant personality and apply them to a job in which they would be an asset. She'd trained as a life coach and built up a bank of professional clients, who paid her money to keep them in line when it came to their finances, their fitness and their future plans. It was the job she was born to do and she loved it.

Right now though, she folded her arms, unimpressed by this home truth.

'Yeah, well you're a dressmaker and you haven't worn anything flattering since 2002.'

Claire glanced down at her Rudolph jumper and Santa leggings and shrugged. 'Rudolph is the new black this year.'

The two of them were still laughing when Doug and Fred came in the back door. Doug and Fiona were having a trial separation and she'd headed to her folks in Inverness for the festivities. For the last three months, Doug had just been his usual self, not giving much away about how he felt about it, but Claire could sense that he wasn't happy. She hoped he would manage to enjoy the day regardless of what was happening with his marriage.

Claire gave her grandad a tight hug, setting off a coughing fit.

'Sorry, Grandad,' she yelped.

He waved away her apology. 'Don't worry about it, ma darlin. It's not you, it's ma fecking lungs.'

His laughter then set off another coughing fit.

Claire took his arm and supported him as she led him into the living room to join the others.

Jordy spotted him first. 'Grandad!' He ran over and threw his arms around his great-grandad and Claire had to blink back the tears. Max followed suit and Fred beamed as he gingerly lowered himself into the chair.

Choked with emotion, she hugged him again before she went back to the kitchen.

Jeanna and Doug were still in there, although they stopped talking when Claire entered.

'You OK?' Doug asked her.

She nodded. 'Just worried about grandad. He's getting frailer all the time.'

'He is,' Doug agreed.

Claire shook off the melancholy. 'Anyway, he's here today and that's all that's important. Right, what am I doing here?' she asked, turning her attention back to the food.

'How can we help?' Jeanna asked.

Claire ran through a checklist in her head. 'I just need all the stuff in from the freezer in the garage. Roast potatoes, croquettes, pigs in blankets, a cheesecake and a pavlova.'

'I'll get them,' Doug offered.

'I'll give you a hand,' Jeanna said.

The two of them trooped off to the garage at the end of the drive.

Busy with everything else, Claire lost track of time, but it was a good ten minutes before they were back, maybe longer.

'Thought you'd got lost out there,' she said. 'Was ready to round up some Sherpas to come and search for you.'

'The bloody things were right at the bottom of the freezer. Took us ages to find them,' Jeanna said.

Distracted, Claire didn't give her reply any thought.

Instead, she got busy preparing the best Christmas lunch she'd ever made, with her brother by her side, singing Christmas songs while they cooked. Her earlier worries about his happiness disappeared – he was definitely getting into the festive spirit. It was great that being here with them today was having such a cheery effect on him.

When they sat down to eat three hours later, she scanned the room, realising that every single person she loved was right here.

She had no idea that by the following Christmas, two would be gone and one would be changed forever.

Twenty-Six

Denise – 2019

Denise padded back out of the kitchen, holding a mug of coffee in her hand. She'd had to stop for a break before she delved into the next file of bank statements, because the pain in her head was crushing her temples and making her eyes hurt. She'd popped two paracetamol and brewed an Americano on her built in coffee machine. Almost five hundred pounds it had cost when Ray had bought it nearly five years ago, the last time they'd redone the kitchen. 'Can't put a price on quality,' he'd said, and he was right. The rest of the room was gorgeous too, as expected for a man in his trade. He'd taken loads of pictures of it and used it in his adverts, so it was tax deductible and brought in new clients at the same time. He was always so smart that way.

Denise loved the room. Oversized, cream quartz tiles gleamed on the floor, the perfect contrast against the white gloss cabinets. The coffee machine sat below an integrated microwave, and in the adjacent larder cabinet, there were two high-tech ovens, one above the other. Not that she ever used the two of them. She only ever cooked for her and Ray, so one oven was more than enough. The hob was ceramic and could do all sorts of things that she'd completely forgotten about too, because, at most, she only ever used two rings at a time. She knew she should eat something now. How long had it been? A day? Two? Three? Didn't matter. She wasn't hungry anyway.

Halfway down the hall, she stopped as she caught sight of her reflection in the mirror above the glass and gold console table. She barely recognised the person she saw there. Her cheeks were sunken into the side of her face, shadows forming underneath the side of her mouth. Her brow, only Botoxed a couple of months ago, was puckered into frown lines between her bloodshot, swollen eyes. There were dark circles under her lower lids and her mouth was so pinched and drained of colour that it was almost invisible. She bore absolutely no resemblance to the beautiful, vibrant, healthy woman she'd been only a week ago. Ray would be so disappointed in how she'd let herself go.

Sighing, depression oozing out of every pore, she slowly walked back into the office. The fear and panic had been joined by a lethargy, a detachment from reality and a dawning realisation that she had no energy left to fight whatever was happening to her. It had to be a dream. A nightmare. He was going to walk back in that door any minute and this would be over.

Sitting back in the office chair, she put the coffee down on the closed business file. Ray had loved this desk, so she had to ensure the mug didn't leave a ring mark on the wood.

Pulling the file with the personal statements towards her, she shook her head, trying to clear the fog from her mind. OK. Concentrate. There was a simple answer in here somewhere. She just had to find it.

She picked up the statement on the top of the pile and saw that it was the most recent one. The 'transactions in' column was straightforward. One transfer on the first of every month, from RH Construction, of £6,000. That was exactly what she expected. Good. It was making sense.

The temporary rise in her spirits rapidly plummeted to earth when she switched her focus to the 'transactions out' column.

There was a £1,000 monthly payment to Ray & Denise Harrow – his third account, the one that was in their joint names and that she used for all her outgoings. Everything from groceries and daily expenses, to her yoga, gym, nails, beauty and hairdressing costs. She also used it to buy the odd item of clothing, but that was pretty minimal because Ray treated her to gorgeous new outfits so often that she rarely shopped on her own. That absolutely tied up with what she knew. The last transfer had gone over a couple of weeks ago and there was still a few hundred pounds in her account.

Other than that there was…

She stopped, checked again. That couldn't be right, surely?

She snatched up the statement for the previous month. Then the one before that. Then every single sheet of paper that had been sent in the last year.

Yep, every one of them said the same thing.

One more debit. On the second of every month. For £5,000. Cash.

And it was too much to have been withdrawn from an ATM machine so that meant he'd gone into a branch every month and withdrawn the money himself.

A fleeting thought. Maybe it was scammers. Someone pretending to be him? You heard so much about identity theft these days and that was absolutely possible.

Or not.

She discounted the theory as quickly as it had come. Ray had been getting these statements every month for a year. He would absolutely have noticed the transactions, and if there was anything dodgy going on he'd have been straight down at the bank reading the riot act.

The panic was winning the battle of emotions again. What the hell was going on? What had Ray done with all that money? Had he been in trouble? Planning something spectacular for them? Moving it elsewhere for a reason?

Leaning down, she flicked through the hanging files in the drawer again. There was only one other one that could possibly give her answers. She pulled it out and opened it.

Pensions and insurances.

Maybe he'd put all the cash into some savings bond or pension to ring fence it from the taxman?

Of course, she'd worked for Ray since the kids were small, so she didn't have any pensions or savings of her own, but she knew he'd made provisions for that. How many times had he told her that if he went first, she'd be set up for life?

She could hear his voice in her head. 'I've made sure my girl will be taken care of,' he'd tell her, before joking, 'I'm worth much more to you dead than I am alive, but don't be slipping anything in my dinner.' She'd laugh, kiss him, tease him about how she just might, then she'd tell him in every way possible how she couldn't live without him. It was all just frivolous chat. She'd had no idea she'd be testing those words any time soon.

Her fingers began to flick through the paperwork. One pension, left over from a million years ago when he still worked in the power plant. It had a few hundred pounds in it. Not even enough to pay for his cremation, she thought bitterly. There was another one, a private pension that she knew about. They'd set it up over twenty years ago with a broker who had visited the house and the idea was that it would provide Ray with a basic monthly sum after he retired. 'No need for it to be huge,' he'd said, when he was deciding how much to pay monthly into the fund. 'After all, we'll have plenty in the bank. This is just a bit of extra security,' he'd assured her.

She flicked to the back page of the latest communication. The pension was worth less than £50,000. At current rates, it was estimated that it would pay out approximately £2500 a year. That might have seemed like a lot when they set it up, but it was nothing these days.

The next document was a surprise. Life insurance. In her name. She racked her brain but she couldn't even remember setting it up. Her sore eyes scanned the words that were swimming in front of her. Life Insurance for Denise Harrow. Age at commencement – thirty-five. Over twenty years ago. That must be why she couldn't remember it. Or perhaps Ray had organised it because he knew she couldn't be doing with paperwork and stuff like this.

She read on. Sum assured £500,000.

What? If she died, Ray stood to inherit £500,000? All these years she should have been worried about him slipping something in her dinner!

She chided herself for the bad joke. Ray adored her. No amount of money would have soothed her loss, just as no amount of money could ease the pain of him being gone now. It did sting a little though. If she'd died first, he'd have been rolling in it. Who knows what he'd have got up to with that kind of cash.

A strange blast of jealousy coursed through her and she pushed the document to one side. It was irrelevant, because she hadn't left Ray. He'd left her first.

Moving it aside revealed the final document, the one that he'd spoke about often. Ray's life insurance policy. She saw that she was named on the document as the sole beneficiary should he die before her – sum assured £150,000. Wow. Not exactly living in riches as he'd promised, but at least it would take care of things until she got the finances sorted out.

A dark thought tugged at her mind and she tried her best to fight it back. He'd insured her for far more than he'd insured himself. Why would he do that? There must be a good reason. Had to be.

Before she really thought it through, she picked up the desk phone and dialled the number at the top of the page. After answering a dozen questions by pressing countless buttons, she was left holding on an automatic queuing system, listening to some country music that made her want to scream.

Fifteen minutes later, just when she was about to give up and batter the handset off the desk, a human voice eventually came on the line.

'Winter Life Assurance, how can I help you?'

In the fifteen minutes she'd been waiting, she should really have thought the call through, but she hadn't. Her mind was suddenly blank, her throat constricted and she had absolutely no idea what to say.

'Hello?' the customer service agent on the other end of the line prompted her again. She sounded like she was barely out of her teens and yet here she was waiting to talk to Denise about a loss that had destroyed her life.

'My husband is dead,' was the best Denise could manage. At once, she realised it was the first time she'd actually said that sentence and punctuated the last word with a deafening sob.

The agent paused, then some kind of crisis training must have kicked in, because she came back with a tone that made her sound like she was sympathetically talking to a five year old.

'I'm so sorry to hear that. Please tell me how I can help you today.'

Denise fought for composure, knowing that she had to do this right because she didn't have it in her to call back. She cleared her throat.

'Sorry. I'm calling to let you know that my...' She hesitated, trying to keep it together. '... Husband has passed away. He has a life insurance policy and I'm the named beneficiary.'

'I see. Can I ask, do you have a lawyer acting on your behalf?'

'No. At least, not yet.' They did have a lawyer, but she'd only met him a few times over the years. He'd drawn up their wills for them, but she hadn't even thought to contact him before now. She and Ray had always been very clear that all their worldly goods would pass directly to each other if one of them died. There was no one else to factor into the equation.

'The normal process is that the lawyer who is handling the estate forwards on the death certificate to us and we then release the funds. Can you give me the policy number please and I will arrange to send you our handbook, which clearly explains the process?'

This wasn't going to be as simple as she thought. Why couldn't anyone just help her? Everywhere she turned it felt like she was hitting a brick wall.

'Yes, it's SDGEFV34562.'

'And the name?'

'Denise Harrow. The policy is in the name of my husband, Ray Harrow.'

The line went quiet apart from the tapping of a keyboard.

'Can I just check that number with you again please?'

Denise repeated it slowly and carefully, enunciating every letter and number.

More tapping. Then finally, the voice again. It sounded strange now – hesitant and tentative.

'Mrs Harrow, I'm afraid I'm having problems with my system right now and I can't actually access that account. Could you possibly ask your lawyer to contact us directly and we can move this forward?'

'Yes, ehm, sure.' Denise agreed, not even caring any more. She was done. Had enough of speaking to some twenty year old who knew nothing about life, about love, about the pain she was feeling. She hung up without even saying goodbye.

She lifted up the document and put it to one side. She'd call the lawyer tomorrow and sort it out, let him deal with it.

Only when she moved the policy did she see the other letter that had been tucked behind it.

Same insurance company. Same letterhead. Dated five years ago.

Dear Mr Harrow,

Thank you for your recent communication. I can confirm that, as per your request, your life insurance policy has now been cancelled and no further payments will be taken from your bank account. We would advise that you notify the beneficiaries of this policy of your decision to terminate it.

Should you wish to discuss this matter further, please call the number above.

Kind regards…

That was as far as she got before every bit of strength she had deserted her.

He'd cancelled the policy? But why?

And…

The thought was forming in her head and she couldn't stop it.

Had her husband, the man she'd loved her whole life, actually left her penniless?

Twenty-Seven

Denise – 1989

'How's that for you?' the hairdresser asked, holding a mirror up so Denise could see her new cut and highlights from the back.

Denise smiled. 'Perfect, thanks, Joanne. It's lovely.'

'Smashing. You have a lovely holiday, and I'll see you in eight weeks.'

On the way out, she paid and left a four pound tip. Four pounds! There was a time when she'd had to make four pounds stretch to buy dinner for the whole family. For two nights!

How things had changed now, she thought, as she pulled on her new pink leather jacket and jumped into her Mini. Ray had bought it for her the day she passed her test and she adored it. She'd put off taking driving lessons for years because they didn't have the money and she wasn't sure she had the confidence to try, but she'd finally done it last year and never looked back. Ray had been so encouraging. He said now that he was working more than ever, she needed to be able to get about on her own. He was right. He couldn't be coming off jobs to pick the kids up from activities, ferry them around or do the shopping, so it made much more sense for her to get herself on the road.

On the way home, she stopped off at Boots for some sun cream for their holiday. It was going to be their first time abroad and she couldn't be more excited. Majorca. Flying from Glasgow airport. They were leaving later that evening, but she was pretty sure she had everything organised. Her case had been packed and sitting in the hall for three days. She'd offered to pack Ray's case too, but he wanted to do it himself. He'd become so fastidious about his clothes in the last couple of years. He liked everything to be the latest fashion, and it all had to be perfectly pressed. Between that and the monthly haircut, he looked better than half the models she saw in the catalogue adverts.

'All part of being a businessman,' he'd tell her, when he came home with something new.

Yep, a businessman. A couple of years ago, he'd quit his job at the power plant, bought a van and set up his own business as an electrician and builder. Denise had been mildly terrified at the prospect of not having a steady income, but she'd been wrong to worry.

There was never any doubt he was going to make a success of it. So many people knew Ray – the guys from the football team, people from school, the folk that drank in the same pubs as him – that he was kept busy right from the start, so much so that she abandoned any idea of getting a part-time job and became his assistant instead.

She answered calls, made bookings, typed out quotes on a second-hand typewriter she'd found in a charity shop. He'd also teamed up with mates who were joiners, plasterers, and painters to work on big jobs. Every time another one came in, there would be a big purchase. Her car. A shopping spree. And now a holiday. They were living the life. She was happy, his mum and dad were beyond proud, and the kids were doing fine. Life was good.

Sun cream in her bag, Denise headed home. The kids would be getting back from school soon and she wanted them to get their rooms tidied before they left tonight. Sometimes she thought about picking them up from school if she was out, but Ray said it would turn them into spoiled brats if they got chauffeured around. Maybe he was right. Her parents didn't have a car, so they had never given her a lift anywhere in her life and it hadn't done her any harm.

For once, he was home on time and greeted her by snogging her in the kitchen. 'God I can't wait for tonight,' he said. 'I'm going to make this the best anniversary present you've ever had. I'm going to spoil you every single day and I'm going to do filthy things to you. We are going to have such a good time.'

She knew he would. Wasn't it already like that every weekend? Now that they could afford babysitters, they'd go out either Friday or Saturday night, to a nice restaurant, sometimes even a club for a bit of dancing. A couple of times, if Jenny was watching the kids, they'd even stayed overnight in a hotel in the city centre. It was so far from her old life, she found it hard to believe it. There had been many tough times in the early years, but her husband had always told her it would come good and it definitely had. Ray was all about enjoying his life, and to him that meant going out, having fun, partying whenever he could. Sometimes he still went AWOL – football team nights out, his mates' birthdays, stuff like that. But they had just as many nights out together.

Ray went upstairs to finish packing, and Denise was just clearing up the dinner dishes, when she realised that Claire and Doug were standing silently in the doorway.

'What's up, you two?' she asked warily. At ten and nine now, they always operated in a twosome. Apart from when they were bickering. Sometimes they were so noisy that she completely understood why Ray said he much preferred it when it was just the two of them.

'I don't feel well,' Claire announced.

Denise put her hand against her daughter's forehead. Yes, she did feel a bit warm. Bugger. Jenny and Pete were going to be here to collect them in five minutes. They were going to Gran and Grandad's for a week. Of course she would miss them – she could count on the fingers of one hand the number of days they'd spent apart – but they had school anyway and it would be worth it to spend a whole week alone with Ray, just being adults and enjoying themselves. They'd missed their teenage years because they'd had two babies by the time they were eighteen. 'This is our time now,' he'd tell her. 'Just you and me.'

Ray came downstairs and saw her concerned expression. 'What's up?'

'Claire's got a bit of a temperature.'

'Och, she'll be fine. When's my mum coming?' he asked.

'In five minutes.'

'Why can't we come with you?' Doug wailed. He wasn't usually one to show his feelings or make a fuss, preferring to let Claire do his talking for him.

'Because this is Mummy and Daddy's trip,' she told him, trying to be patient. She went back to Claire. 'Does anything hurt?'

'Look,' Ray said, getting exasperated. 'She just doesn't want us to go, so she's playing up. You know she's an attention seeking little madam.'

'I'm not,' Claire argued sullenly.

'Of course you are. Now get through there and make sure your bags are packed and get a smile on your face for your gran coming, OK?'

His tone made it clear that it wasn't up for discussion. Denise briefly wondered whether she should stall them and just make sure Claire was ok, but dismissed that idea. Ray was right. Claire just didn't want them to go so she was being difficult. Besides, Ray's mum knew how to deal with sick bugs and ailments far better than she did, so better that they just left them all to it.

The kids trooped off in the direction of the living room. Not for the first time, Denise thought how Claire's attitude to her father had changed. She used to be so desperate to get his attention. Now, it was as if she no longer cared. Must be the start of the pre-teenage hormones kicking in.

Ray slid his hand around her waist. 'Stop worrying right now,' he cajoled her. 'I know you only do it because you're such a great mum, but I promise you, she's fine. The minute she's out of the door, she'll be back to normal.'

'But...' she began.

He didn't let her finish. 'No buts. I'm not having my holiday spoiled by a ten year old who just wants a bit of attention.'

The vehemence of his tone startled her for a moment.

He must have realised that, because he immediately softened, kissing her on the lips. 'It's only because I want to spend time with you. Do you know how much I've been looking forward to a whole, uninterrupted week with my wife?'

Placated, she nodded, 'I know. I have too.'

'Then don't worry about Claire, she'll be fine.' Letting her go, he grabbed a beer from the fridge. 'I'm just going to go back up and finish packing.'

Denise felt her doubts diminish. He was right as always. And he had every right to want a stress free holiday without the kids to run after. He worked so hard, slogging away, long hours, week after week to support them and give them this lovely house and the life that they now had. If ever someone deserved a break, it was her brilliant husband.

Her thoughts were disturbed by the doorbell.

Denise heard footsteps and knew it was Doug, running down the hall to let his gran in.

Jenny immediately bent down to hug him. 'How's my boy?' she crooned.

'Claire's not even feeling well and they still won't take us with them,' he blurted.

Jenny looked up at Denise quizzically.

'She's fine,' Denise explained. 'She's just a bit warm. Ray says they're just playing up to get attention.'

She could see the conflict on Jenny's face. She loved her grandchildren, but there was absolutely no one on this planet who came before her son. Not even her husband. Ray had been the centre of her universe since the minute he was born and, as far as she was concerned, he could do no wrong. There was no way that she would criticise him or overrule him. In ten years, Denise had never seen her so much as chide him, even when he deserved it. Unlike her own mother, of course. Even now, Agnes seemed to want to make it her life's work to criticise and moan about her offspring. Ray had grown up feeling that the world was his kingdom. Denise had grown up feeling like she just wasn't good enough to belong.

Jenny decided which side of the fence she was coming down on and it wasn't a surprise. 'I'm sure he's probably right,' she said.

'He's not right,' Claire said, petulantly, and Denise realised she'd been standing just inside the living room doorway and had heard everything. 'Why does nobody even care about me?'

'Of course we do, pet,' Jenny argued. 'Look, go and get your stuff and we'll get out to the car and get you home. We can lie on the sofa and watch whatever you want and I'll take such good care of you that you'll forget all about feeling sick.'

Claire could see that she wasn't going to win this one, so she stomped off to get her bag and her jacket. Naturally, Doug followed right behind her.

'I'm sure she'll be fine,' Denise said again, hoping that she'd managed to hide the little edge of doubt in her voice.

'Don't you worry, hen. Between Ray and his dad, I've looked after a few bouts of imaginary sickness in my time. Ray used to claim he had food poisoning every Monday morning because he didn't want to go to school. Sometimes,

I just gave in and let him stay home with me. I think I enjoyed it every bit as much as he did,' she said, smiling at the memory.

'Hey, Ma,' Ray said, coming down the stairs.

Jenny's face immediately lit up, as it always did when her son entered a room. 'Don't you be worrying about us,' she reassured him. 'We'll be fine, won't we, you two?' she chirped to Claire and Doug, who'd just returned clutching coats and bags.

They both nodded sullenly.

Jenny rounded them up and bustled them towards the door.

Denise stepped forward and hugged them. 'You two be good for Gran and Grandad, OK? And we'll phone you every night.'

'That'll cost a fortune!' Jenny objected. 'Once every couple of days will be fine.'

'OK,' she conceded. Jenny was right. It was probably extortionate to call home.

Denise wished the kids would stop staring at their feet. They were just trying to make her feel bad, she knew it.

'Thanks, Jenny, we really appreciate you having them,' she said truthfully.

Jenny had been her absolute rock since the day Agnes had dragged her round there to announce that Ray had got her pregnant. They'd developed a relationship that was definitely more supportive than the one she had with her own mother.

She steered the kids out of the door, each of them picking up their holdalls on the way. 'Go on now. Grandad is waiting in the car.'

Claire and Doug did as they were told. If anyone noticed that neither of them said goodbye to their dad – or vice versa - they didn't mention it.

'Right, well, you two have a great time and I'll see you in a week,' Jenny said, opening her arms to give Ray a hug. Denise got a quick squeeze too, then she was off down the path.

Denise waved as the car turned out of the street, then closed the door, not quite sure how she was feeling. Excited. Sad. Relieved. Anxious. Happy.

Happy won the day when Ray pulled her towards him.

'Thank God that bit's done. Let's get going to the airport then, love, shall we? We can check in and then head to a restaurant for a bite to eat and a drink.'

Denise nodded. She'd never flown abroad before but she'd been to Glasgow Airport a few times to see Jenny and Pete off to Benidorm, so she knew there were several bars and restaurants there.

'Do you hear that?' Ray asked her suddenly.

She shook her head, brow furrowed. 'I can't hear anything.'

He laughed, his arms around her waist now. 'Exactly! It's only you and me now, baby. Just the way I like it.'

He wasn't laughing two nights later, when the ring of the hotel room phone woke them at 4 a.m.

Fighting against the fog of too many sangrias, Denise picked it up. 'Hello?'

'Denise, love, it's Jenny. Listen, I don't want you to worry, but we've had to bring Claire to the hospital.'

She was suddenly bolt upright and wide awake. 'Why? What's happened?'

Ray was up on one elbow now, facing her, and she tilted the phone at her ear so he could hear the conversation too.

'It's her appendix. She hasn't been feeling well since you left, but tonight she got really bad. Rolling on the carpet, the poor soul. My Pete just carried her into the car and brought her here. They reckon the appendix is burst and they're taking her in just now to whip it out.'

Denise's heart was racing. 'Oh God, Jenny, of all the times...'

Beside her, Ray flopped back on to the bed, face like stone.

'I know, love. But don't you worry – they're taking good care of her and I'm here. Pete took Doug back to the house to get him to bed because he's got school in the morning. We've got it all covered.'

'OK, well, look – I'll speak to the rep in the morning and we'll get home as soon as we can. But can you call me back and let me know how she is? It doesn't matter what time.'

'Aye, of course, love. Don't worry. I'll keep you posted.'

When Jenny hung up, Denise slumped back against the pillow. 'Oh God, Ray. Now I feel totally guilty for leaving them. Do you think we'll be able to get back tomorrow? I mean, surely it's an emergency and they'll—'

'Hang on,' he stopped her. He looked serious, his eyebrows low, jaw set. 'Let's think about this. By tomorrow the operation will be done and she'll be on the mend. Getting an appendix out is nothing these days. Do you really want to make her feel terrible, knowing that we had to cut our holiday short for her? And making my mum feel that we don't think she can deal with this?'

'Of course not! But...'

He leaned over, his mouth on hers. 'Then let's not go tearing back there just yet. Mum has her. She'll be fine. What we need to think about now is how much we need this holiday, this time, just you and me. You deserve this. It's the first proper holiday you've ever had and I'm not going to let anything take this away from you. I love you, babe. It's my job to look after you and that's what I'm going to do.'

When he put it like that… there was no point panicking. She'd speak to Jenny in the morning, and they could decide what to do then.

Between the warmth of his arms wrapped around her body, and the glow left by his words, she fell back asleep feeling more loved than ever before.

Twenty-Eight

Claire 2019

'Right, head up,' Suze ordered and Claire lifted her hair out of the sink.

She was scared to look in the silver gilt mirror in front of her, so she just wrapped her towel around her head and followed her personal hairdresser back into the showroom.

'Your grey was seriously out of control. When was the last time you dyed your hair?' Suze asked her as she sat back down on the chair in front of the gallery of Val, Josie and Jeanna.

'Twenty-five years ago,' Claire replied with a grin. 'I was fourteen, Jeanna did it, and my hair turned so yellow everyone called me Big Bird for months.'

'And you've had nothing done since then?'

Claire shook her head. 'I think I've had my hair cut in a salon maybe twice ever. Jordy or Max usually just cut it at the back with the kitchen scissors and I trim the fringe. One of the benefits of having a run-of-the-mill straight bob and fine hair. Maintenance is minimal.'

'But it's not just about the haircut!' Suze said, outraged. 'It's about taking time for you, pampering yourself a little bit. It's good for the soul.'

Claire couldn't argue, but she at least decided to give an explanation in her defence. 'I've been a single mum of two boys with the busiest sports schedules on the planet for the last decade – there was no time or money for pampering!'

'Well there is now,' Suze countered. 'I'm going to make you look like a fucking goddess, and we're going to keep you that way.'

'Think I might need to lose thirty pounds before I reach goddess level,' Claire joked, feeling the waistband of her jeans cutting into her skin after one too many of those spring rolls.

'Nope, love, you're perfect just the way you are,' Val assured her.

Claire wasn't so sure, but she appreciated the sentiment. Jordy was eighteen and she still hadn't lost the last two stone of her baby weight. It didn't help that she always seemed to be too busy, too tired, too focused on other things to worry about it, much less do anything about it.

'You know the problem here, pet?' Josie started, and Claire couldn't wait to hear the rest. You never knew what was going to come out of her mouth. 'You've got so used to putting yourself last that you don't even know how to change it,' she said.

Claire exhaled, relieved. For Josie, that wasn't too bad. Fairly sensible, even insightful advice. She didn't realise her chum hadn't finished.

'And you're not getting sex, so you've forgotten how fricking brilliant it is to feel sexy and loved and good about yourself. Jeanna is right – you need a shag.'

Yep, there it was. The real Josie, the seventy-something-year-old, live for today, bend the rules, have a bloody glorious time, was back in the building.

And she was still speaking. 'When was the last time you had sex?'

Claire didn't even have to think about it. She knew exactly when it was – she just didn't particularly want to admit it to the others because she knew what their reaction would be. In fact, if she were an outsider looking in, her reaction would be exactly the same. Bugger. They were all staring at her, waiting for a reply. The pressure made her crack and spill all.

'That Christmas. The one where I forgot Sam's present. We had sex the next day because I felt so bad and wanted to make it up to him. Clearly it didn't work.'

As expected, the other three stared at her in shocked silence. No wonder.

She'd thought about it over the years, of course. Jeanna was always nagging her to get out there, and a few times she'd set her up on blind dates that had inevitably ended with excuses and an early night. It just wasn't a priority. Besides, she honestly felt that she didn't need a bloke to make her happy. There was nothing about the last ten years with Max and Jordy that she would change, not a single thing. All that mattered was that she gave them a childhood that was nothing like the one she and Doug had known.

Her life? Parents who didn't even come home from their holiday when she was whipped into hospital for surgery to remove her appendix.

Max and Jordy's life? A mum who was there for every important moment, who was involved in their lives, shared their wins and cuddled them through their losses. When they were with her, her time was fully booked with lifts, organising and spending time with them. When the boys were with Sam, she used that time to sleep and to catch up with the work she needed to bring in to support them.

She'd absolutely dedicated the last decade to bringing them up – and she'd do it all over again in a heartbeat. Even if it did leave her with a hole in her heart when they left and stunned pals who were staring at her now in disbelief.

'You haven't had sex for nearly ten years?' Suze clarified, clearly so horrified by this revelation that she had to stop cutting her hair until the shock passed.

'Nine years,' Claire corrected her, then realised that it didn't change the point and shrugged. "It didn't seem important. And after Sam left…' To her surprise, tears shot to her bottom lids and she blinked them back. 'Oh my God, look what day drinking does! It turns me into an emotional wreck,' she spluttered, laughing through the tears. She hadn't cried about Sam since she cleared out what was left in his sock drawer six months after he left. It was much easier just to put her head down and get on with living life, with making sure the boys were okay and adjusting to the split – how she felt didn't really matter and there was no time to feel sorry for herself.

'Why did you split up then?' Suze asked, as she lifted up long sections of her hair and cut into them with concentrated precision.

'Och, so many reasons,' Claire replied, with no particular desire to hash them all out again.

'I always felt a bit responsible for that,' Jeanna chimed in, uncharacteristically regretful.

'No! Don't be crazy. It was absolutely nothing to do with you. It really wasn't.'

It was true. There had been many factors that had ultimately contributed to the split, but what had happened to someone she loved had taught Claire about priorities – and she had realised, back there, back then, that saving her marriage wasn't one of them.

Twenty-Nine

Claire – 2011

The family mourners flocked in to the front row of the crematorium. Her mum, wailing, despite the fact that Claire knew she'd barely acknowledged Fred in the last ten years and had visited him less than a handful of times. Of course, her dad was rubbing her mother's back, playing to the martyrdom. 'You're OK, Denise. Fred knew you loved him. You were such a good daughter and you have to remember that.'

Not for the first time in her life, Claire wanted to punch him in the face. It was all bullshit. Complete nonsense. But her mother lapped it all up, gazing up at her husband adoringly. His smug face told Claire that the manipulative prick knew he would get so much mileage out of this. Another padlock on the chain of his wife's devotion to him.

Next in the row were Fred's other children, twins Rachel and Ronnie and their families, and then Donna, who was almost the same age as Claire. It was weird having an aunt that was younger than you. Claire smiled at them all, but she barely knew them. Her mother had no relationship with them, said they had nothing whatsoever in common. Claire knew the truth was that Denise looked down her nose at them. In her mother's mind, she'd improved her life and they hadn't, so she wanted nothing to do with them. Not even Fred.

In fact, none of them were close. Ronnie, Rachel and Donna were dotted over different areas of the city and rarely travelled back to the housing scheme they grew up in. Fred had once told her that her gran, Agnes, was hard on the kids and he didn't blame them for taking off as soon as they could. Maybe that was the case, but Claire didn't understand how they could pay so little attention to their dad when they knew he was frail.

The emphysema, combined with pneumonia, had got him in the end. He'd got sick just after Christmas and he'd passed away on a cold, wet February, in Claire's spare room. She'd moved him into the house on the day before Hogmanay, when she could see he was struggling to take care of himself. She'd asked him to live with them countless times over the years, but he'd always been too proud to accept, even when she told him truthfully how much it would mean to the boys. They adored their grandad. He was their constant, their wisdom and their naughty sense of humour. Much as that argument had almost swayed him, Fred had held on to his independence for a while longer. It was telling that this time he hadn't refused.

She'd always be glad that he'd spent his last weeks with her, Sam and the boys, with Doug popping in every day and Jeanna always on hand to make the old man laugh. It didn't matter that they weren't related – they'd always had a special bond.

Next to her, she felt Jeanna take her hand, just as she appreciated Sam and Doug being on the other side of her, all of them acting as barriers against the pain of her loss and her disgust with her parents and their crocodile grief.

Somehow, she got through the service, then kept her composure through the small wake, finally succumbing to her grief when she got home later that night. She'd locked the bathroom door, run a bath, climbed in and then sobbed until the water was cold and there were no more tears left to cry. Fred had been her person. Her one blood relation – other than Doug – who still cared for her, loved her, was always there with his down-to-earth goodness and his unashamed affection for her. Now he was gone.

The next morning, she woke up, put a smile on her face, made the boys their breakfast and kept on going, determined that her gut wrenching sadness wasn't going to affect their lives. When Sam asked her how she was doing, she said she was fine, and off he went to the office, satisfied that she was OK.

She wasn't. But she wasn't going to be her mother, playing the martyr, making it all about her. Fred would have expected her to be strong and carry on, and she wouldn't let him down.

It was almost a week later when she realised that Jeanna hadn't been in touch for a few days. They normally spoke at least once a day, so it was unusual.

Christ, she suddenly felt like a crap pal. Why had it taken her this long to notice Jeanna's absence?

She gently placed the wedding dress she was working on down on the protective sheet that lined the floor of her sewing room. Over a thousand diamantes had already been applied to the train and there were a thousand more still to be done. Not that she was complaining. Her wedding dress design and creation service was now so busy she had a six month waiting list. She picked up her phone and called Jeanna. Straight to voicemail. She checked the time. Sod it. Jordy had football practice straight after school, Max had swimming, but that still gave her a couple of hours to nip over and see Jeanna, then get back to pick them up.

Grabbing her bag, she jumped in the car and pulled up outside Jeanna's flat ten minutes later. The curtains were closed, which was odd. Jeanna was always fastidious about being up and attacking the day early in the morning.

It took a full five minutes of pressing on the doorbell before Jeanna finally answered and it took every ounce of Claire's tact and discipline not to gasp when she did.

Jeanna was dishevelled, gaunt, had bags under her eyes and was wearing pyjamas that didn't look like they'd seen a washing machine in days.

Without speaking, her friend opened the door and let Claire pass her into the hallway, then followed her into the kitchen. It was a mess. Unwashed dishes, an overflowing bin and – most disturbing of all – a pizza box. Jeanna McCallan hadn't knowingly eaten a carb in ten years. Something – everything – was wrong.

Claire flicked on the kettle, washed out two mugs, put in two teabags, milk, then sat at the table, opposite her friend, while she waited for the kettle to boil.

'Tell me,' Claire said simply, hiding the fact that inside her stomach was churning and she was seriously scared. It had to be something pretty serious to make Jeanna fall apart like this.

There was a long pause before she got a reply. 'Remember that well-woman appointment we went for?'

Claire nodded. It had been Jeanna's idea, trying out a new service to see if she wanted to recommend it to her clients. They'd spent the whole day in a private hospital in the west end of the city and were checked for their general health and all types of female related cancers. The smear test had made her toes curl, the mammogram was admittedly uncomfortable and the results on the day told Claire everything she already knew. She was overweight, her triglyceride levels were too high (thanks to too much crap food in her diet), her blood sugar was thankfully still in the normal range and her blood pressure was a little high. The morning of Fred's funeral, the results of the smear test and mammogram had dropped through her door. All clear. After a moment of relief, she'd filed them away, then gone to bury her grandfather. It had completely slipped her mind since then.

Shit, she hadn't even checked with Jeanna on her results.

'I have breast cancer,' Jeanna said, her voice oddly detached, her face devoid of any emotion. 'Got called back last week for more tests. It's in my left boob.'

Claire was too stunned to speak for a moment.

'Oh God, I'm so sorry, Jeanna.'

She would not cry. She would not cry. This wasn't about her, it was about her friend, and she needed to be strong for her. She managed to keep it together until one silent tear ran down Jeanna's cheek. She'd seen Jeanna cry once in her life, when they were in college and her mother – her only relative – died. So the sight of this woman she loved shedding a tear was too much.

Claire crumbled, shot over to Jeanna's side, wrapped her arms around her and they cried until their chests hurt with the pain of it.

Eventually, throat hoarse, Jeanna found the words to talk.

'They're removing the lump next week and then I'll have radiation and chemo. And I know I'm crying, but I'm fine. I am. I've totally got this.'

Claire could see otherwise. She had a sudden flashback to that night when she'd found Jeanna in a similar state. When she'd calmed down enough to speak, she'd revealed that her mum had passed away. Cervical cancer. They'd known she was ill, but were so sure she would beat it because her mother had never admitted how advanced it was, choosing to play her illness down to her daughter, not wanting to worry her. She'd been stoic and tough as nails, insisting she was fine... Just as Jeanna was doing now. Claire knew better than to believe her.

'What can I do to help you?' she begged, devastated, willing to do anything to ease her friend's pain.

Jeanna smiled ruefully. 'Tidy my kitchen?'

'Done,' Claire replied, getting up and pulling on a pair of marigolds from the counter. 'We'll get through this, Jeanna. We will. I'll be with you every single day until this is done.'

'Just as well, because the other news is that Giles is gone too.'

'What? The bastard! He left you now? When this happens?'

'Nope, he doesn't know. I didn't tell him. We were done. To be honest, I've been seeing someone else – you don't know him – and I've no doubt Giles was too. I didn't want him staying here out of pity, so we called it a day. I think he was relieved.'

'And the other guy?'

Jeanna shrugged. 'That's over too. It was just a fling. Nothing serious.'

Normally Claire would press for details on the participant of the 'fling', but now wasn't the time. 'Bloody hell, Jeanna, I leave you alone for a few days…' she said, trying to copy Jeanna's pragmatic attitude.

'I know,' Jeanna agreed. 'And, er, I did fall apart a bit as you can see.'

Claire was loading the dishes into a sink of hot soapy water now. She'd have this place sorted out in no time, but she was furious with herself for allowing her friend to deal with this on her own. She should have been here, taking care of her.

Suddenly, she stopped soaping, the answer completely obvious. 'You know what, Jeanna, this is no good.'

'I know, it sucks.'

'No, I mean this situation. Go pack a bag, you're coming to stay with us until you're well again. No arguments.'

Jeanna automatically ignored the last part. 'But I'm—'

'Jeanna, no arguments! Look, Sam and the kids and you and Doug are the only family I have left. My mum and dad don't count, because they're fecking useless. I want to take care of you.' She could see Jeanna still wasn't on board, so she chose another tack. 'Do it for me. I've just lost Fred, and that's a huge hole. His room is lying empty and it makes me weep every time I pass it.'

'So you want me to fill your huge hole?' Jeanna asked archly.

Bloody hell. The worst time in her life and she was still going for inappropriate innuendo. This cancer didn't stand a chance, Claire decided.

'Absolutely. As soon as possible. Go pack a bag. Besides, my boys will be delighted to have you there. Just don't lead them to a gutter or a cell.' If Jeanna could use humour at this time, then so could she. She'd play this out on any terms that Jeanna wanted.

Jeanna sighed, rolled her eyes. 'OK then. I suppose so. It'll save me cooking. I phoned for a pizza last night, so I'm clearly on the road to ruin.'

Claire laughed, bringing on more tears, and threw her arms around her pal. Whatever Jeanna had to face, she would do it with her.

'We've got this, Jeanna McCallan. Don't you worry.'

Jeanna hugged her back, an unusual occurrence given her loathing of displays of affection.

Claire finished clearing up the house while Jeanna packed, and made sure the bins were empty and nothing electrical was left on.

Half an hour later, they were in the car when Jeanna reached over and took her hand.

'Thanks for this. I know I don't tell you, but I love you.'

'I know. And I love you back. More than you know.'

They drove on with red rimmed eyes.

They picked up Jordy and Max on the way, both of whom were delighted to see their favourite aunt.

'Right, you two, I'm going to be staying with you for a while…'

'Why?' Max asked. He was almost eleven and eternally curious.

'Cockroaches,' she replied. 'They've taken over my flat.'

'Eeeeeeew,' the boys recoiled.

It set the tone for them to drive the rest of the way talking about all things bug related and disgusting.

Claire had no idea how the next couple of months would play out, but she knew that the boys were going to be Jeanna's greatest distraction. She loved being around them and that had to be good for her. They'd manage the tough times, the fatigue, the sickness and the chemo on a day-by-day basis. But whatever came their way, they could deal with it better if they were together.

Back home, they had a quick bite to eat, before it was time to leave for their afterschool clubs, but Claire suddenly felt reluctant to go.

'We can skip their clubs tonight, it's no problem. Let's just stay in, watch a movie,' she suggested to Jeanna, who was having none of it.

'Absolutely not. Look, I can only do this if we try to keep things normal. I'm not having the kids miss stuff because I'm here. To be honest, I could do with unpacking and having a sleep, so I'd be grateful if you all buggered off.'

'You're sure?'

'Positive,' Jeanna assured her.

Claire decided to go with it. If she tried to smother Jeanna, her pal would get pissed off and hightail it back to her own house. Better to play it out exactly as she wanted.

'OK, well, I'll be back at nine o'clock. Sam should be in about then too. Max's rugby is over near Grandad's house, so I'd planned to meet Doug there to help him clear it out. I can make it another night…'

'Noooooooo,' Jeanna blurted, exasperated. 'Do exactly as you planned. If I'm bored before you get back, I'll shag your husband to keep me amused.'

Yep, they were back in the gutter.

'Good to know you've got a backup plan,' Claire quipped, laughing. She hugged her friend, rounded up the boys and took off, dropping Jordy at football, then Max at rugby.

When she pulled up outside Fred's house, her first reaction was devastating sadness. She'd been coming here since she was a kid. She'd even lived here for a couple of years as a teenager, when she couldn't stomach her parents any longer. This was her and Doug's place of safety and comfort. It was where she felt more at home than anywhere else she'd ever lived. Now Fred was gone and she'd miss that feeling, just as she'd miss him every single day.

Her second reaction was confusion when she saw her father's Mercedes parked outside, next to Doug's ancient jeep.

What the hell were her parents doing here? Dear God, hadn't there been enough turmoil today?

Worry about Jeanna rose from her gut and closed her throat. None of this petty stuff mattered. All that was important was that she sorted out Fred's house, then got back home to look after her friend.

She tried to use her front door key, but it wouldn't work. Doug must have heard her because, the next minute, it swung open. Claire's first thought was that she'd never seen him look so flushed and flustered. And that was before she even told him about Jeanna. The two of them had been so close their whole lives, she knew he'd be devastated.

'Hey,' she greeted him, kissing him on the cheek and hugging him as she always did. 'What's up? Are you OK?'

'Run now,' he said, sounding desperately weary. 'Save yourself. If this turns into a crime scene, tell the police you knew nothing about it.'

Oh Jesus. This couldn't be good. Doug was the most laid back guy she'd ever known. If he was stressed, it must be really bad. But then, their parents did have that effect on them.

Instead of fleeing, she followed him into the kitchen to see her mum and dad standing there, leaning on the worktop, holding hands. Of course they fucking were.

'What are you two doing here?' she asked. She was still sickened after their display of hypocrisy at the funeral.

'Don't speak to your mother like that,' her dad chided her like she was six and had just answered back.

'Dad, I've had a long, tough day. I can't be doing with this just now, I really can't. Doug and I need to get Grandad's house cleared so we can give it back to the council. So whatever it is, whatever you want, just take it and leave us to it.'

Her father came right back at her, his usual sneer on his face. 'Yeah, well, we were just telling Doug you don't need to worry about that, because we'll take care of it.'

That news almost floored her. They would take care of it? They were finally stepping up and helping? They'd wanted nothing to do with him when he was alive, but they were going to help now that he was dead? If this was what guilt did, she was happy to take it, especially now when she had other priorities.

Her expression must have shown that she viewed this as a positive thing, because Doug jumped in before she could reply.

'And go on, tell her why you're suddenly being so fucking magnanimous.'

'Don't you dare speak—' their dad started.

'Aw, fuck off,' Doug cut him dead.

'Douglas!' her mother shrieked.

Claire finally found her voice. 'What the hell is going on?'

'We own this house,' her mother said sniffily, 'so we'll take care of everything from here on in.'

'You what?'

Claire didn't understand. This was a council house. Fred had been insistent that he would never buy it because he wanted it to go to a family that needed it after he was gone. How could they own it? And then it dawned on her.

'You bought it? Is that why my key wouldn't work? You've already changed the locks because you've bought this house? Grandad wouldn't have wanted that and he'd never have allowed you to do it.'

Her dad shrugged. 'Well, sometimes he didn't know what was best for everyone concerned. This house is worth something. No point letting that go to strangers.'

Doug spoke up. 'How did you make him sign it over to you?'

'You don't need to worry about the ins and outs of it,' Ray shut the question down. 'All you need to know is that it's ours now.'

Claire challenged them, her voice raised now. 'How could you? How the fuck could you do that?'

Her mother came right back at her. 'He was my father. Who are you to tell me what I can and can't do?' she sneered. 'Your dad is right. It was the smart thing to do. The old fool just couldn't see that.'

'The old fool?' Her voice was rising to a level that could crack Fred's old windows. 'Don't you bloody dare call him that. He was the most loving, the most decent man we ever knew and he was no fool.'

She took a deep breath, trying desperately to calm herself and dispel the urge to slap her mother's smug, arrogant face. There was a pause before she could continue.

'So what are you going to do with it?' she demanded.

'Fix it up, sell it on,' her dad said, completely unashamedly. 'Make a tidy profit. That's what life's about, isn't it?'

Claire's fingers tightened into a fist. Her heart was pounding so loudly it sounded like a bass drum in her head and she couldn't remember ever being angrier in her life.

These two had been crap parents her whole life, but this was an all time low. They'd absolutely betrayed Fred. They'd somehow conned him into signing this house over when he was alive and now they were going to make money from him in death. It was about as despicable as it got and there was no coming back from it. Ranting and raving about it wouldn't change things and it definitely wouldn't bring Fred back. In truth, he was the only important person in all of this. These two truly, absolutely did not matter.

Her gaze met Doug's and there was a telepathic exchange in which they both instinctively knew what the other was thinking.

She pulled up her shoulders, stared her father square in the eye.

'You two are scum,' she said, her voice low and unrelenting. 'And Doug and I don't associate with scum. We're done. Not that you ever cared, but don't call us, don't text us, don't contact us ever again. And good luck with the profits from this sale – I hope they choke you.'

'Who the fuck do you think you are, Miss High and Bloody Mighty?' He was going red in the face now, spittle flying from his mouth as he spoke.

'Ray, don't let her upset you,' her mother wittered.

'Upset him? Oh Christ. I can't tell you how much I hope that I am absolutely nothing like you.' She turned back to her dad. 'And as for who I think I am? I'm Fred McAlee's granddaughter. I'm sure as hell not related to you two.'

And with that, Claire turned around and she and Doug walked out of their parents' lives.

She just hoped that one day this abhorrent behaviour, this absolutely repulsive lack of loyalty and decency, would come right back and destroy them. The sooner, the better.

Thirty

Denise 2019

Staring at the ceiling wasn't working. Denise had hoped that it would still her mind, centre her soul, but all it was doing was sending her brain into overdrive and allowing the pain to spread until it was permeating every sinew and crevice of her body.

This bedroom had always been her haven, her sanctuary, but now, with the afternoon sun forcing its way in around the edges of the blinds, the quiet solitude was allowing her to replay the morning over and over again in her head. Looking out Ray's clothes, taking them to the funeral home, then returning home and all the financial stuff. This morning she was aching with loss. Now she was drowning in fear.

She just didn't understand. It was like some kind of bad movie playing out, with the man she loved in the central role.

Why was she dealing with all this alone? She had never been one of those women who had a gaggle of girlfriends like the yoga chicks in the cafe. If she had spare time, or worries, or things to plan, the only person she wanted to share that with was her husband. He'd been her best friend since she was fifteen years old and she honestly didn't regret that for a single second. He had always been everything she needed, but now he wasn't here, she didn't know where to turn. Again, she thought about calling Claire and Doug, but decided against it. Neither of them could make this any better, so what was the point? The only person she wanted here was Ray.

Sleep wouldn't come, no matter how tightly she squeezed her eyes shut. Instead she rolled over, pulled his pillow towards her and hugged it, like she could pretend for just a moment that it was him. It still carried his scent. A week after he'd passed, she hadn't been able to bring herself to change the bed linen because she didn't want to lose that smell. Sometimes it was a comfort, other times it was like a vivid reminder, tormenting her, reinforcing her loss.

She couldn't lie here any longer. Not on the sheets they'd shared, in the bed that Ray had picked himself, in the room he'd designed. This was all him and she'd adored every corner of it. Not now.

Mind racing again. There was nothing she could do to change the fact that he was gone, but the practicalities were weighing on her. She'd planned to leave everything to one side for today, but now that sleep wasn't coming, she decided she needed the distraction. Anything to stop her mind spiralling into ever darker places.

With a defeated groan, she pushed herself up from the bed and headed to the shower, dropping her clothes on the way. She'd never have done that before, but right now she didn't care – she just wanted to be rid of the outer shell she'd had when she stood in that undertaker's room, when she walked back, when she opened that bank statement and when she discovered a whole heap of questions about the man she'd been married to.

The shower belched steam when she put it on the highest heat and stepped in, desperate to wash away every trace of the day. Her pain receptors screamed as her skin turned scarlet, but she didn't care. At least for a few minutes, the physical pain masked the hurt on the inside.

When her body could stand it no more, she shut the shower off, grabbed the robe from the back of the bathroom door and swaddled herself in it. Too late, she realised it was Ray's, one of the matching silver-grey pair he'd bought them before their skiing holiday a few winters ago. The last time she saw him wearing it was on his way to the shower on the morning he died. He'd hung that robe on the back of the door and less than five minutes later he was dying. The memory slayed her, forcing her to the floor for the second time today. She curled up on the marble tiles, her whole body shaking with the violence of her sobs.

Time passed – she had no idea how long – before she could finally control the crying. Her wet hair was clapped to her head, and the robe so big it fell from her shoulders, secured only by the tight knot on the belt around her waist.

Out in the dressing room, she went to open one of her wardrobe doors and then froze for a second and turned to face Ray's wall of storage instead. Once again, the aroma of his aftershave, his skin, his breath assailed her, but she had no tears left to cry.

She had no idea what she was looking for, but she had to start somewhere to find answers. Perhaps he had cash stashed in the house somewhere? If he did, then it would be in this room, she was sure of it. His wardrobes and drawers were the only places she didn't clean or use, so if there was something to be hidden, this was where it would be. Cash. Cheques. Gold fucking bars. She didn't care what it was, she just wanted something to explain everything she'd seen today.

She started with the drawers that were in the centre of the space, between his wardrobes and hers, pulling everything out, not caring that within minutes the room began to look like it had been ransacked. His underwear, his socks, his T-shirts... all of them perfectly ordered, grouped together by size and colour, now in one tangled mess on the floor. But there was nothing unusual to be found.

On a roll of adrenaline now, she turned to the three double wardrobes that stood side by side. Each wardrobe had the same layout. In the bottom were two shelves of shoes, then midway up was a pull-out rack that had individual hangers for a dozen pairs of trousers, then above that, a row of jackets in one, shirts in the next, and polo shirts and jumpers in the one that was furthest to the left. In the very top of each was a shelf with miscellaneous stuff. Ski wear. His gym bags. A weekend travel holdall. Sweatshirts. His painting clothes. His gardening clothes. An old briefcase she'd bought him in the eighties when he first started up his own business. Starting at the bottom, she pulled out every pair of shoes, searching in the crevices at the back for anything that would give her a clue as to what was going on.

Nothing. Damn it.

Frustrated, she pulled over the library style stepladders that were tucked in at the end of the row of wardrobes, then used them to reach the top shelf. All restraint pushed aside, she simply pulled everything towards her, then let it fall to the floor. Shelves cleared, she climbed back down and started sorting through the mess, checking inside bags, in the compartments of the briefcase, between the layers of the clothes.

Nothing.

Weary, exhausted, defeated, she slumped to her knees in the middle of the pile of chaos. Ray would be furious if he could see this. He liked order, efficiency, he prided himself on taking impeccable care of his possessions, and in the space of an hour she'd managed to turn his prized room into something resembling a landfill site.

The three wardrobes stood wide open in front of her, top and bottom shelves completely empty. It was no use. There was nothing there. She should concede defeat, give up, speak to the lawyer as soon as she could face it and then spend the rest of the week clearing up this mess.

Climbing to her feet, she stepped forward to close the doors of the middle wardrobe, when one of his favourite suits caught her eye. A deep charcoal Zegna single breasted jacket with straight leg trousers, they'd bought it in Macy's in New York, and the store had tailored it to fit him perfectly. He looked amazing in it. So much so, he planned to buy another on their next trip to the Big Apple. That wouldn't happen now.

A sense of longing made her reach out and touch it, stroke the faintly textured surface of the exquisitely cut jacket. Her hand slipped inside, against the cool silk of the silver lining. Ironic. There was no silver lining to any of this. Her fingers grazed the labels, the inside pockets, moving upwards...

She stopped. Retraced the path her hand had just taken. The inside pocket. There was something hard tucked inside.

Reaching in, she pulled out a mobile phone. Not Ray's iPhone – she knew that was in the other room where she'd left it. This was an older one, maybe the model he'd used before he upgraded last time. She tried to compute.

That must be it. He got his new phone and must have left the old one in his pocket.

The screen was black and it wouldn't switch on. Battery must be dead. Curiosity suddenly consumed her. There would be texts on this phone, old conversations between them, photos of years gone by. The thought of them made her smile as she felt a need to step back in time, to connect with the man he was back then.

Taking the handset into the other room, she plugged it into the charger by his bedside table, and left it there to power up.

She looked at the clock. Just after five. Daytime drinking had never appealed to her, but today, for the third or fourth time this week (but who was counting?), she made an exception. There was a bottle of red wine on the counter over at the minibar and she uncorked it, poured a glass and downed half of it in one go, desperate to feel the numbing effects of the alcohol. They didn't come. She took a second slug, then lay down on the bed again, ready to make another attempt to sleep.

Her eyes had been closed for a few moments when the phone sprang into life beside her, making her sit bolt upright and lurch for it. Notification after notification flickered on the screen. That was strange. She was sure this would have been superseded by his new phone, so it wouldn't be active. Ray must have put a different SIM card in it. Why would he do that?

The phone finally stopped beeping, leaving just one message on the screen.

You have 23 missed calls from...

She let that sink in. Twenty-three missed calls. How? From who? And when?

Pressing her thumb against the home button proved futile – it wouldn't open. She entered the same code as his current handset. Incorrect. Now her heart was beginning to pound again. How many tries did she have before the phone locked her out?

She had to think about this. Really think about it. That's when she noticed all the missed calls were from the same number. There was no contact name, just a row of digits. She stared at it for the longest time.

The number wasn't one she was familiar with.

A supplier? A contractor? Maybe. It could even be a wrong number.

She was about to give up, to consign it to the long list of things that she didn't understand today, when a devastating thought struck her.

It couldn't be.

Yet...

She picked up Ray's other handset from where she'd tossed it on the bed that morning, searched for the initial she'd seen earlier. Y. There it was. Just one letter. She pressed on it and revealed the contact info behind it, then held the two handsets side by side to compare the entry. The two numbers were the same.

Her stomach lurched, sending her racing to the bathroom, where she vomited every drop of the red wine back up into the sink.

Noooooo. How could this be happening? This was amputation of the heart, without an anaesthetic.

When she was sure her legs could carry her, she staggered back into the bedroom and over to the bed. She picked up the old handset again, and with a thumb that was shaking uncontrollably, she pressed the home button, then watched as the passcode box appeared.

Terror and utter fear that she was right almost stopped her, but she had to know.

She pressed the first letter, then the next, then the next…
Y V O N N E

Then she pressed the blue box in the bottom right hand corner.

Please don't work. Please, please don't work, she begged silently.

The Gods weren't listening. The phone kicked into action, the lock screen changing to a home screen picture of her husband, next to woman she'd met only once, but whom she felt she knew inside out.

Devastated beyond pain, she opened the call history. There was only one telephone number there, the same one the missed calls came from. And it was repeated hundreds of times, going back years. The history showed there were both incoming and outgoing calls, and the most recent one was a week ago, the morning of the day he died. Outgoing. He'd called her.

Numb now, almost robotic, she pressed the text message symbol and the screen filled with messages. She started to read them and the first few were pretty innocuous.

How are you today?

What time will you be back?

Her chest almost unclenched enough for her to breathe, and then wham – a whole conversation that left her doubled over, retching her empty guts up.

I miss you so much. Not long now. See you tomorrow baby.

Wear the outfit I bought you last weekend. Nothing underneath.

My cock is hard just thinking about you.

Oh baby I'm so wet.

Find a way to get out – come to me right now.

I'm thinking about you and my fingers are slipping inside…

Denise screamed like someone had pierced her skin with a knife and was plunging it in and out, time after time after time. She screamed until she had no voice left, until she collapsed on the bed, her legs kicking everything within reach. The bedside lamps. The tables they were sitting on. The glass of wine went flying across the room.

When she finally felt spent, she lay back gasping for breath. No. This couldn't be happening. Not again. Just couldn't be. It was done. She'd made sure it ended last time. Ray had been unfailingly devoted to her for all these years so there was no way he was still messing around.

Or had she been kidding herself on all along, a deluded fool, unwilling to see what was really happening?

Rage now. Uncontrollable, blind fury.

And in the haze of frenzied temper, she picked up the concealed phone, opened it again, then typed in a message to the only number in the memory.

My husband is dead. You fucking bitch.

Send.

Thirty-One

Denise – 1993

Sometimes it really did feel like her daughter hated her. Denise knew Claire would never say that, of course. Claire preferred to do that sullen teenage thing and just avoid coming home. But then, Ray always said that all teenagers avoided their parents. Just a fact of life.

Every single night Claire had something on after school, then she'd usually go to a friend's house or to her Grandad Fred's home for dinner, or maybe just pick up something from the chip shop, then she'd wander in, bang on her 9 p.m. curfew.

Claire wasn't the type of girl to argue or look for confrontation. Thank God she didn't seem to have inherited any of Agnes's genes. But this staying out all the time was no use, especially when she had chores to do.

Denise took a deep breath. Ray was always reminding her that too much stressing about things would give her wrinkles and she wasn't having that. She'd turned thirty last month and she was determined that she was going to hang on to her looks and not let herself go like some women did. That's why she got her hair done every week and tried every new beauty product on the market. Ray told her all the time that she'd barely changed since the moment he clapped eyes on her back at that youth club disco. She'd once asked him why he'd asked her to dance. 'Because you were the most beautiful girl I'd ever seen and I knew we'd look great together. All the guys in the football team fancied you, too.' This had surprised her – she'd genuinely had no idea that anyone had even noticed her back then, much less found her attractive. That same lack of confidence had made her wonder sometimes if they'd have stayed together if she hadn't fallen pregnant. During a drunken argument shortly after their wedding, Ray said he'd never have stuck around if she hadn't trapped him, but Denise knew he hadn't meant it. How many times over the years had he said she was the best thing that ever happened to him? And if it took a baby to get them together in the first place, well, it was worth it for the bliss they'd found together.

The clock in the hall chimed 9 p.m. and, right on cue, she heard the door slam shut, and in Claire came. It was like looking in a mirror sometimes. Or a throwback to when she too, was fourteen. Claire was taller than her, and her hair was a darker blonde, but there was no doubt they were related. Although, Denise liked to think they looked more like sisters than mother and daughter.

'Where have you been?' were the first words out of Denise's mouth.

'Netball practice, then Grampa Fred's house for tea, then I went to Jeanna's to do my homework,' Claire replied, still standing in the doorway.

'I told you I don't like that girl,' Denise replied. 'Your dad says she doesn't come from a nice area and I'm not having you turn into some kid that's wandering the streets at night with a rough crowd. I've worked far too hard to bring you up better than that.'

Claire rolled her eyes and adopted that defiant look that Denise had seen one too many times lately. 'You've worked far too hard?' she said, her voice dripping with audacity.

Denise put her hands on her hips, furious at the implied challenge. 'Yes, I have. How many times has your dad told you how I've given up my life to bring up you and your brother? And your dad too, out working all hours of the day and night to support us.' Denise could feel her temper and her volume rising. They'd had far too many of these fights recently and they escalated so quickly. It was that girl's attitude. She had no gratitude at all for everything she and Ray had done for her and that pressed Denise's buttons every time.

She knew what would happen now. Claire would turn around, walk away, slam the door and stay in her room for the rest of the night. And that's exactly what would have happened if Doug hadn't walked in.

At thirteen, he was already taller than them both. Just as there was no mistaking that Claire was related to her, there was no doubt that this was Ray Harrow's son. The same black hair, same cheeky grin, same ability to charm his way into, or out of, anything. He had a lovely, caring side too, though, especially where his sister was concerned.

To Denise's surprise, and she'd never admit it, she'd had the odd tug of jealousy over how close Doug was to Claire. They'd been thick as thieves since they were little, and nothing had changed now that they were older.

'Don't shout at her, Mum,' he said to Denise, his voice quiet but firm.

How bloody dare he?

'Don't you dare speak to me like that, young man,' she spat, refusing to take any of his nonsense.

'Leave it, Doug,' Claire said tensely. 'I don't need you to fight my battles. Won't make any difference anyway.'

Denise was getting seriously sick of this girl's cheek now. 'What's that supposed to mean?'

She should have noticed that Claire's face was more flushed than normal. Her voice a little higher.

'I said, what's that supposed to mean?' Denise pushed, knowing that Claire would back down, walk away, avoid the challenge.

She was wrong.

For the first time ever, Claire didn't turn her back on confrontation.

'It means you're absolutely deluded, Mum. You believe every single thing he tells you, even when it's a pile of crap.'

'Don't you dare…!'

'Why? What are you going to do? Tell him? Good luck with that, because… Oh, that's right, as usual he's not here.'

Denise thought her head would explode with fury. 'Your dad is out working to—'

'Don't say "support us". Or "give us a good life". We don't want to hear it. He's a prick, Mum. That's the truth. A self-centred prick, who doesn't give a toss about us and who fills your head with complete crap so that you'll worship at his feet. And you fall for it every time!'

The sound of the slap was as loud as it was violent. Consumed with rage, Denise hadn't even realised that she'd stepped forward and struck Claire across the face until she saw her daughter's blazing expression.

The girl stood there, chin jutted high, absolutely defiant.

'Mum!' Doug stepped forward, aiming to get between them, but Claire put her arm out to stop him.

'It's fine, I'm OK,' she said, her voice an ice-cold calm that Denise had never heard before. 'But let me do you a favour and be the one person who tells you the truth for a change. He isn't out working to support us. He's out shagging that woman whose house he's working on. She lives round the corner from Jeanna and it's the talk of the scheme. So next time you're worried about my pals being the wrong kind of people, maybe you should think about the fact that the real scumbag here is your lying bastard of a husband.'

With that, she turned, walked back down the hall, opened the door and walked out of the house.

Doug stared at his mother for a few minutes, disgust all over his face, then stepped back, and followed his sister, running to catch up with her.

Denise gasped as she slid against the wall. Not because she'd hit her daughter for the first time since she was a young kid who needed the occasional smack for naughty behaviour, but because of the words that had come out of Claire's mouth.

How dare she? How dare she speak to her like that? How dare she have no gratitude at all for the lives they'd given those kids?

But it was the lies... the lies about Ray. How dare she say those horrible, awful things about her father? Denise's throat closed as she re-ran the words in her head. 'He's out shagging that woman whose house he's working on.' It was ridiculous. He worked long hours because he wanted to squeeze in more jobs, to get the project finished quicker so he could get paid and move on to the next one. And yes, it was after 9 p.m. now, and dark outside, but he'd told her before that he organised his day so that he was doing external work in the daytime, and then internal work at night when daylight had faded. Made perfect sense. He was dedicated. He sacrificed so much, and he did it for them. She would know if he was up to no good. She chided herself for even thinking that could be a possibility.

But yet... she wanted to see him. Right now. She wanted to tell him what Claire was saying, prove to her that she was wrong.

Running, staggering, stumbling into the kitchen, she opened the big blue diary next to the phone and searched back to where she'd written the details of this job when the first enquiry was made.

Hands sweating, they were sticking to the pages as she flicked through them, until...

There it was.

Yvonne McTay, 23 Stonebrae Street, Glasgow.

A slight chill. That was definitely in the same area as Claire's pal Jeanna, about four miles from where she was standing now. Before she could give it any rational thought, she'd grabbed her keys and was out of the door, jumping into the white Audi Quattro that Ray had bought her for her thirtieth birthday. It wasn't a brand new one, but she didn't care. He'd tied a huge pink bow around it and parked it out front for the whole street to see. She'd been the talk of the town for weeks. If her mother was still alive, she knew that, like every other time she rolled up with a new car, Agnes would accuse her of getting above her station. 'They're just jealous of you, Den,' Ray would tell her. 'They can't stand to see you so happy.' Would a man who loved her that much be having an affair? Of course he bloody wouldn't.

At the end of the street, she spotted Claire and Doug getting on the bus and knew immediately where they were headed. Fred's house. Of course they thought he was the big hero, but Denise knew exactly who he was – the father who had been nothing when she was growing up, because he let his caustic wife steamroller over everyone in sight. What kind of man did that?

Shrugging off the kids' desertion, she kept driving, not even seeing the streets, the lights, the people as she passed them. Fifteen minutes and a few wrong turns later, she reached the housing scheme and stopped to ask an old man walking his dog for directions.

A few more turns and she pulled up outside 23 Stonebrae Street. She knew she had the right house because Ray's van was parked right outside. There was an immediate feeling of relief as she spotted the half built extension on the left hand side of the end terrace house. See! He was exactly where he should be and…

It took her a moment to realise there were no lights on in the extension. He wasn't working in there then.

Her eyes flicked to the right, to the downstairs windows. No lights in there either.

They moved upwards. No light in the upstairs right hand window.

Left. To the final upstairs window. Curtains were closed, but there it was. A dim light, maybe a bedside lamp or perhaps a few candles.

Denise realised she was no longer breathing, her brain screaming as realisation dawned.

That had to be a bedroom. And Ray was in there.

There was no explanation that made sense. It was strange. Suspicious. Horrifying. Her lungs were sore now, making her gasp for breath.

Claire was right.

He was having an affair.

Her Ray, the love of her life, the only man she'd ever been with, was in there right now in another woman's bedroom, in another woman's arms.

Her first instinct was to run over there, to break down that fucking door and see the truth for herself, but she knew her legs wouldn't carry her. Instead she sat, for seconds, minutes. Eventually, the sobbing stopped and she slipped into an almost catatonic state.

Pupils dilated, eyes fixed on some far away point, she looked like someone who knew their end was coming and wanted to stare it in the face.

She'd been there for perhaps an hour when something flickered in her peripheral vision. A downstairs light came on, then the front door opened.

Ray, in the doorway, throwing his head back and laughing. A woman, long brunette messy curls, wearing a cream dressing gown, silk, just like the one he'd bought her last Christmas.

The scream got stuck in her throat.

She watched as he took a couple of steps down the path, then stopped as if she'd said something, then he grinned, turned back, kissed her in the doorway and started walking backwards, still facing her, their hands trailing against each other until only their fingertips touched and they paused, unwilling to let each other go. Ray made the first move, leaving her smiling like someone who had just had the best time.

Like someone in love.

Why? Why would he do this? How could he touch someone else? Was she not enough for him? Was he not happy with her? Was he leaving her? Did he actually have feelings for this woman or was this just some fling, some tart he was using for sex? Worse, had she already lost him? No. She would have known. He would have said if he was leaving her. They'd had sex only last night. She was still in this. She hadn't lost. Had she?

The searing heat of a hot poker being pressed on her heart was unbearable.

Because that's when she knew. She had two choices.

Choice one – she could go over there, confront him, make a scene, scratch that bitch's eyes out. Tell him to choose.

But then... what if he didn't choose her?

He was everything, her whole world. He was the only person in this life who made her laugh, who made every day better and who truly loved her. What did she have without him? Nothing. Just two kids to take care of. Jenny and Pete would, of course, take his side, no matter what he'd done, so she'd lose them. And God knows, Fred had never been much use to her.

Or…

Choice two – she could go home, pretend tonight never happened. She could hope that this was just a fling while this one job lasted.

She briefly wondered if it had happened before, then dismissed that thought out of hand. He wouldn't do that. He was a good man. This was a one-off mistake, no one was perfect. She could love him so much, make him so happy, that he would put an end to whatever madness this was, he'd come back to her and her alone, and she'd make sure he never felt the need to do it again.

There was absolutely no way she was giving him up, no matter how much this hurt – because nothing could be more painful than losing him.

As his van slowly passed her car, she slid down in the passenger seat so that he wouldn't see her. Only when the van was out of sight did that bitch at the door stop waving and go back inside.

No. She wasn't giving Ray to her.

Not in this lifetime.

She dried her eyes, started the engine and drove off in the same direction as the man she would follow to the ends of the earth.

Thirty-Two

Claire – 2019

'It's a bastard of a disease, that cancer,' Val said, her voice thick with compassion. 'Och, Jeanna love, I'm so sorry you went through that. I had no idea.'

Jeanna shrugged. 'It's not something I shout about,' she revealed. 'The treatment worked, I've been cancer free ever since, eight years now, and I'm just beyond grateful that it's in the past and that we got through it. I wouldn't have without Claire though.'

'Of course you would have,' Claire chided her. 'There's nothing you can't handle.'

Jeanna gave her a grateful smile. 'Anyway, it's not something I dwell on. It happened back then, we survived and I hope beyond words that it never happens again. I really do feel lucky. I also feel like life's too bloody short, which gets me into way too much trouble.' She turned to

Claire, 'But my one regret is that I've always felt that it was taking care of me that ended things with you and Sam.'

'No, you're so wrong!' Claire countered. 'You had nothing to do with it, I promise. It was absolutely down to Sam and me and the problems we already had, but if there were any external factors, it was my grief over losing my grandad, and the fact that my parents' lies and duplicity, what they'd done to Fred, sent me into a downward spiral. My dad had always been a lying prick. He'd cheated for years. We all knew it. Even my gran, Jenny, who thought he walked on water, knew in her heart that he was up to no good. But my mother just refused to see it.'

'That's right! Remember, he was shagging Yvonne McTay on our estate? That kept our whole street entertained for ages.'

Claire nodded. 'Yep, but even when I told my mother about that one she chose to ignore it. Doug and I left home that night and never went back. Moved into Fred's house. So I've no idea what happened after that with the other woman.'

'Wonder what became of her?' Jeanna mused. 'Last I heard, she upped sticks and moved to some fancy big house in the west end.'

'I've no idea, but good luck to her. She deserved more than a big house for putting up with my scumbag dad. Anyway, what was I saying?' Claire pondered a moment, finding it tough to put it into words. 'With Sam and I, what it came down to was that it was just too much at one time. It was all so overwhelming that something in me broke for a while.'

She had to stop for a moment as Suze applied lipstick, before going on, 'Sam couldn't understand it at all, but it was like the fallout with my parents brought back every fight, every sleepless night, every moment of anger from my childhood. I got so wrapped up in my disgust with what they'd done to Fred – conning him out of the house, making money out of his death – and, on top of that, the pain of losing him was unbearable. Subconsciously, something snapped and it was easier to just shut down. It made me bitter and closed off and eventually Sam and I just couldn't deal with it any longer. I was disappointing him constantly, hated the pressure of feeling that I was letting him down. I just didn't want to deal with our problems any more. It was like I was protecting myself from more loss by being in control. I just wanted to be on my own, to lick my wounds, get through all the hurt and pain and try to focus on things that made me happy. That was you getting well and my boys. That was all I cared about for a long time.'

'It wasn't all down to you though,' Jeanna defended her.

'I know.' The thought gave Claire no consolation. 'Sam had become work obsessed, fell into the habit of leaving everything to me. He made himself absent to the point where it was hardly different to live without him altogether. God, how stupid were we?'

'What a sorry state for you all, love,' Val said sympathetically. 'I feel for Sam, too.'

Claire spoke, looking upwards so Suze could continue applying mascara. 'Back then, I felt like I didn't have any choice. When I said I wanted to split, he made a token argument, but we'd been so disconnected for years that I think he knew deep down it was the right thing to do. I don't blame him. He deserved happiness. And he found it again when he met Nicola.'

'I can't stand her,' Jeanna bitched.

'You've only met her about three times, and that was just for a few seconds at drop-offs and pick-ups,' Claire pointed out patiently.

'Yeah, well. She's way too bloody perfect for my taste. And a size ten. And always so bloody cheery. And I don't think she has a bitchy bone in her body. I mean, that's just wrong.'

'Criminal,' Josie agreed solemnly. 'I don't know how she sleeps at night, the cow.'

Claire's chuckling almost smudged her newly applied mascara. 'No, she's nice. She's great with the boys and she makes Sam happy so I'm grateful for that. He deserves it.'

Suze stopped, hands on hips. 'I swear to God, if you don't stop being so nice I'm going to have to drop you as a friend. Don't you ever think that maybe you could have got back together and made it work if she hadn't come into the picture?'

'No,' Claire replied honestly. 'Because if we were meant to work out then we would have. And whether Nicola had come along or not wouldn't have changed that.'

Val started humming 'Que Sera Sera' and by the end of the first line, Josie had joined in with the words and they were swaying in their seats.

'Am I imagining it, or am I being mocked?' Claire asked Suze, feigning innocence.

Suze pulled yet another bottle of vino out of her toolbox and scrunched up her nose as far as the Botox would let her. 'Definitely mocked.'

'Thought so.'

'But the wine will help.'

While the Doris Day chorus continued, Suze started spraying stuff around Claire's head, chatting as she went.

'What is the plan for the next stage of your life then? This is a really exciting chapter, if you look at it objectively. You've got more free time than ever. The business is doing well. You're financially stable. You've got us. And you look fecking gorgeous,' she finished with a flourish, before pulling the towel from around Claire's neck and spinning the chair round so that she got a full view of her reflection.

It took a moment for it to sink in. Gone were the grey streaks and the hair that was unstyled and messy and invariably stuck up in a scrunchie. In its place was a glossy curtain of sun kissed highlights that fell to just above shoulder length and swished when she moved her head from side to side. Her skin was glowing, her eyes were wide and defined and…

'Holy shit, are those cheekbones?' she gasped. Yup, she had cheekbones. Two of them. And they *were* bloody gorgeous.

It was as if Suze had rewound the clock ten years, to a different Claire, one who hadn't yet been battered by events that changed everything. More than anything though, she realised she looked… happy. She would have burst into tears of joy if it wouldn't have wrecked her smoky eyes.

'Yer gorgeous!' Val announced. 'I mean, you always were gorgeous, but now you're shiny, too.'

Claire realised Suze was still waiting for her verdict. She had to clear her throat to shift the lump that was lodged there. 'Oh, Suze, I love it. I really do. You are beyond brilliant.'

'I am,' Suze agreed, laughing.

'And I don't know where you got these cheekbones from, but I'd like to keep them,' Claire added. Stuff the extra thirty pounds. Stuff the whole fecking ageing process. Right there, right then, she looked and felt fabulous and that was all that mattered.

'They were always there,' Suze told her. 'And far be it from me to be deep and profound… so were you. Now you've got to see that. So it's time to get out there, plan your next big adventure, find new things that you enjoy and start living life.' It was all going well until she added, 'I've been reading too many of those bloody inspirational quotes on Facebook. That's the most sense I've talked for years.'

Claire's smoky eyes were in no way affected by the fit of the giggles that ensued, or the tight, dancing hug that she delivered to her personal hair and beauty guru by way of thanks. Gratitude for the work and the words too, because Claire knew Suze was absolutely right.

For the first time since she left that campus in Tennessee after waving her youngest child off to start his new life, she felt a bubble of excitement. This was her time… She just needed to decide what the hell she wanted to do with it.

Thirty-Three

Claire – Earlier in August 2019

The FaceTime signal was fuzzy and kept dropping out, but Claire didn't care. All that mattered was that she could see her boy's gorgeous, smiley face, even if he was rolling his eyes at her.

'Mum, I swear I'm not in any danger. I'm in the mess hall on a base in Portsmouth, not trawling the waters off North Korea. The only chance I've got of dying is if I choke on this pizza,' he said, holding a slice of deep pan pepperoni up to the camera.

'Max Bradley, enough of the cheek to your mother,' Sam chided him playfully, as Claire turned the phone slightly so Sam came into shot. 'You're never too old to get grounded.'

'I'll let the navy know I'm not allowed on manoeuvres because I'm on the naughty step,' her boy fired back. 'It's so weird seeing you two together, by the way. I feel like I'm ten and getting a telling off for the state of my room.'

'That's tomorrow's lecture,' Claire told him. 'I'll give you time to tidy it before I send in the inspection team.'

Max laughed. 'Mum, this screen is about to go blank any minute, but it's because the battery is almost dead. It's not because we've suddenly been invaded by rebel forces, so don't go alerting the authorities, OK?'

'That was just the once. And I only phoned the coastguard,' she said, knowing he was referring to the time he wandered off for five minutes on holiday at a Cornish beach. 'OK son. I love you. I'll call again in a couple of days.'

'No worries. Tell Jordy I said good luck. And remind him I was always better at football, will you?' It wasn't true, but winding his brother up was one of his greatest pleasures in life – and vice versa.

'I will and...'

The screen went blank. Bugger.

'Should it worry us that he's tasked with defending the country but he can't remember to charge up his mobile?' Sam asked, lifting a piece of toast from the basket on the table in front of him and beginning to smear it with strawberry jam.

Claire decided that it looked too good to resist and followed suit. 'As long as the fleet doesn't get summoned via an app, we should be fine.'

'Morning,' Jordy greeted them, pulling out another chair at the table.

'Morning, my love. Did you sleep OK?' Her throat tightened as another wave of emotion caught her unawares. In a few hours she'd be leaving him. She pushed that thought away, refusing to fall apart over breakfast.

'Man, the jet lag is a killer,' he said in reply. 'I've been in the gym for two hours because I woke up at 6 a.m.'

'Really?' Claire shot back, innocently. 'I didn't see you there. I did ten miles on the treadmill. My buns are like steel.'

'Dad, make her stop,' he begged Sam.

'Not my job,' Sam bantered back, hands up in the air. 'Anyway, time to get going?'

'Nope,' Claire replied.

'Claire,' Sam came back, a hint of jokey reprimand in his voice. 'If we stayed here for a month, would the answer to that question be any different?'

'It would not,' she answered truthfully, realising that she knew where he was going with this. It would never be time to go, to take her youngest child to college, to wave him off, knowing she wouldn't see him again for months. Nope, she'd sit here smearing strawberry jam on her toast until the end of time if it meant she could keep Jordy with her.

They'd arrived in Nashville three days before, giving them time to get organised for Jordy moving into the dorms. They were staying in a city hotel, handy for a huge mall where they'd managed to pick up duvets, pillows, towels, crockery, a TV, USA electrical adaptors, and even a mini fridge for his room.

The trip had been on the calendar for months, since the day he'd signed the commitment letter and accepted the college scholarship that he'd been working for since he was twelve. However, she'd been surprised when Sam had called her the week before and suggested joining them.

'Really? Are you sure?' she'd asked, then realised that might have sounded offhand. 'I mean, you're very welcome!

It would be lovely to have you there. You can hold the Kleenex and prise my hands off his ankles when he tries to leave.'

His laughter had made her smile. 'That was exactly my plan. Text me the details and I'll get a flight and book a room in the same hotel.'

'No worries.' A thought. 'If you and Nicola want to use your air miles to go in business class, we won't be offended,' she'd said, knowing that he flew so often with work he always tried to use the points he'd accumulated to upgrade his holiday flights.

'Nicola can't make it – it's just me.'

'Oh. OK.' That had surprised her. 'I'll send you the text over now then.'

She'd done so and he'd met them at the airport, delighting Jordy. After they'd separated, Sam had made a conscious effort to sort out his work-life balance. He'd stopped working late every single night and had started pitching in again to help with the boys' schedules. In the years since then, Claire couldn't remember him missing a single football or rugby game. He'd stand with her on the touchline, chat away, and it was all very amicable and civilised. They'd even managed to rebuild a really good friendship. She was proud of that. All they both wanted was what was best for the kids and they'd managed to pull it off.

Once the surprise had passed, she'd been pleased he'd managed to join them. It was great to have help with all the lugging around of suitcases and boxes.

Now they were about to lug them for the last time.

The radio in the hired car played rock anthems the whole way to the campus, and she and Sam sang along, rising to the top of their voices when 'Sweet Home Alabama' came on.

'It's a wonder I turned out anywhere near normal with you two as parents,' Jordy informed them.

'It's either this or I cry the whole way and beg you not to go,' Claire told him.

'Turn that radio up, Dad,' Jordy quipped.

Claire could see the bright eyes and flushed face of excitement on her boy and once again she was determined to hold it together. She was going to stay positive, be happy for him, and smile as she waved him off on the most wonderful adventure of his life.

The hours on campus flew by with a flurry of form filling, unpacking, bed making and introductions to his roommate – Kurt from Pennsylvania, also on the soccer team.

It was getting on for 4 p.m. when Claire realised that their work was done here. Kurt from Pennsylvania was suggesting to Jordy that they hit the sports hall, and by the look on her son's face, she knew he wanted to go.

'I guess we'll get off and leave you then,' she said, trying desperately not to sound like the words were choking her. They were.

Do not cry. Do not cry. She forced the mantra to repeat itself in her head and block the tear ducts.

'Ok, Mum. I'll walk you to the car. Kurt, I'll see you over at the sports block in ten?'

Kurt, earphones in and focus on the screen of his iPhone, nodded in agreement.

The whole way back to the car, Claire repeated the pre-leaving-home warnings that she'd been drilling into her youngest son for the last fortnight – the same ones she'd given Max the year before. Don't leave drinks unattended. Make sure your phone is always charged (Max clearly missed that one). Don't try drugs of any kind. Just say no. Respect other people's boundaries. Treat girls with respect. Never, ever snog a girl who is drunk, even if you fancy her – see her home safely and then call to check on her the next morning. If she's nice, only then can you ask her out. Text your mother every night and FaceTime at least once every two days. Never go along with something if you don't think it's a good idea. Trust your instincts. Don't go in a car with anyone who has been drinking or taking drugs. Always wear a seat belt. And a condom. Always, ALWAYS wear a condom. And if you can find a pair of bubble-wrap pants, pull them on too. You can never be too careful…

'Mum, here's your car,' Jordy pointed out and she realised they were standing next to the rental. 'And don't worry. I've got this. I promise.'

Another chink fell off Claire's heart. Of course he did. He was a smart, sensible, big hearted kid. Sure, he would make mistakes, but he would always be a good guy. He took after his father.

Sam hugged his boy for way longer than their usual man code allowed. Jordy didn't complain.

'Love you, son. I'm so proud of you,' he said, and Claire was shocked to hear that his voice was choked with emotion too. Sam was always the strong, stoic type.

'Love you too, Dad,' Jordy replied, when Sam finally released him. He then turned and wrapped his mother in his big strong arms. 'Love you, Mum.'

That almost ended her. Almost. He was her baby, yet she barely passed his chest now, and he still smelled exactly the same as when he was a little guy who would climb into her bed every morning and tell her how much he loved her. Tears sprung to her eyes, but she fought them back. She would wave him off smiling if it killed her.

'I love you, son. With all my heart,' she replied. 'And I'll always be on the other end of a phone, day or night, for anything. You're never alone, you hear me?'

Jordy cleared his throat. 'I hear you.'

'Right, well go on before Kurt sends out a search party.'

They watched as their baby, all six foot three of him, walked back to his new life.

Beside her, she felt Sam taking her hand. 'You're going to crumble into a sobbing mess any minute, aren't you?'

'Absolutely,' she said, chin wobbling, the lump in her throat well and truly back in position. 'You?'

'Already there,' he answered.

She glanced up to see his tear filled eyes. The state of the two of them made her dissolve into something between a sob and a giggle.

'I'll make a deal with you,' she managed to say. 'We're going to get into that car, we're going to put the music on full blast and we're going to sing all the way back to the airport. And when we get there, we're going to go into the first bar we find and get hammered. How does that sound to you?'

'Like the best idea I've ever heard.'

They might not have made it work as a married couple, but parents, travel companions and drinking buddies? She was 100 per cent sure they had that covered.

They both climbed into the car, he started the engine and the music blared as he pulled out of the parking slot. As soon as they started to drive, his hand fell on hers. She knew it was a token of friendship. Comfort in an emotional situation. But for the first time since they'd said goodbye all those years ago, her stomach flipped at his touch.

Thirty-Four

Denise – 2019

Denise stared at the phone, waiting for a reply. It had been an hour now since she'd sent the text to that cow and she'd still heard nothing back. Nothing.

In that time, she'd read every single text they'd sent each other and they'd made her retch many times over. It was disgusting. Absolute filth.

But more than that, she just didn't understand, so many whys. Why was he texting that whore? If he had needs or he was into that kind of thing, why couldn't he have sent texts like that to Denise? She'd have answered them, even the really crude ones, and sure, it might have been a bit embarrassing at first, but if that was what he liked, she'd have gone with it. Of course she would – she'd have done anything for him.

Another why – why did he feel the need to have another woman on the side? Wasn't she enough for him? Did that bitch have something, say something, or do something that she couldn't?

And why – oh fucking why – had she not suspected that this was still going on? And for all this time?

There had been absolutely no red flags, no warning signs. Sometimes he still came home late, but that had always been an occupational hazard in the building trade. Other than that, and the fact that he was away a lot because he'd had more and more jobs in different cities, there was nothing out of the ordinary between them. He still brought her flowers almost every week, still made love to her every couple of nights, still seemed as into her as he'd always been. Right up until the end, they'd still been making plans for the future, for their next holiday, next adventure, for their retirement. Were those the actions of a man who was saying such disgusting things to another woman?

None of this made sense. None of it. Not the texts, not the financial accounts, not the fact that he was lying in a bloody mortuary, his body cold, while she lay in their bedroom alone.

The anxiety, the fury, the rage all gripped her and she snatched the phone up again, her fingers flying across the keypad as she typed out another message.

I know everything.

Send.

Before she threw the phone back on the bed, she spotted the time on the home screen. It was almost five o'clock, so even if that boot worked somewhere that gave her no access to her phone in office hours, she'd see the messages soon. Good.

That thought led to another one. She still had another call to make.

She poured more red wine into her glass, took a long drink, then searched through Ray's main phone – not the secret one he used to call his lover – and searched up the number for his lawyer. Dial.

A receptionist answered.

Denise cleared her throat and tried to sound as normal as possible. 'Can I speak to Mr Dawson please?'

'Who's calling?' she replied in a singsong voice.

Denise wanted to tell her it was none of her fucking business.

'This is Denise Harrow. My husband is… *was* Ray Harrow. He is… *was* one of Mr Dawson's clients. I need to notify him of my husband's death.'

A few minutes passed before a male voice came on the phone. Hugh Dawson was an old teammate of Ray's from back in the junior football days. A group of them still played occasionally, Dawson included, and they still enjoyed the odd night out. Denise had only ever met him in an official capacity though, several times over the years, when they were incorporating the business, drawing up contracts, writing their wills, buying her dad's house and, later, selling it. In fact, it was Hugh Dawson who had certified Fred's power of attorney, saying that he'd witnessed the old man signing it. She still had no idea how Ray had persuaded him to do that, but she knew it involved a large bill from the Gleneagles Hotel.

'Mrs Harrow,' he said, his voice deep and thick with the kind of confidence that was essential in someone like that's job.

'Mr Dawson. I'm not sure if you remember me…'

'I do, Mrs Harrow.'

Of course he did, she thought. Ray always told her that she was so gorgeous that no one could ever forget her face. Shame that he apparently did when he was texting his whore.

Back to the call. She needed to concentrate. Focus.

'Right then,' she continued. 'I'm afraid, my husband passed away this week.'

There was a gasp at the end of the sentence as she reeled from the pain of saying that out loud. It took her a moment to recover, and for him to come up with an appropriate response.

'I'm so sorry to hear that. Please pass on my deepest sympathies to the whole family.'

The whole family? It was only her. They'd all left her. Deserted her. Turned their backs, after she'd brought them up and given them everything.

Somehow, she managed to find her voice again.

'Thank you. Can you advise me on the process going forward? I'm afraid it's all been very sudden and not something we'd prepared for. I've also discovered some… irregularities in our finances today that I really don't understand. It seems my husband was in considerable debt in some of his bank accounts. I'm absolutely sure he must have transferred the funds to another account, but I can't quite locate it.'

There was another pause, a much longer one, and this time it was Denise who broke it.

'Mr Dawson?'

'Yes, er, my apologies, Mrs Harrow,' There was a hint of edge in his voice now, like he was flustered? Uncomfortable? Of course he was. It must be so difficult to discuss the lives of people who were so recently deceased. 'I'm afraid I can't discuss Mr Harrow's finances, or any other aspect of his affairs.'

The word 'affairs' jolted her, until she realised he was referring to his financial situation, not his sex on the side. It wasn't a huge surprise that he couldn't discuss this on the phone. There was all that data protection stuff now. She was probably going to have to go into the office to sort it out.

'If you could send me a copy of Mr Harrow's death certificate, I can begin the process of disposing of his estate.'

'Perhaps it would be best if I just brought it in when I come along to see you?'

'To see me?'

'Yes.' She didn't understand the way this conversation was going. Surely he had to see her to get things stamped and signed and all Ray's possessions turned over to her? 'I assume there are formalities to attend to with regards to signing over our house, our joint accounts and any assets that were in Ray's name?' She was trying desperately to be switched on and focused here, but it was like she was speaking in a language that even she didn't understand. 'When we made our wills, I believe we discussed our wishes, and our plan was that everything would go to each other.'

'Mrs Harrow, are you referring to the wills you made in 2009?'

She tried to remember, but her brain wouldn't co-operate. 'Erm, yes, that sounds about right.'

'I see.'

She could hear tapping in the background, as if he was typing on a keyboard.

'Mrs Harrow, we do still have your original will on file. However, at his request, we then worked with Mr Harrow again in 2016, on a revised version of his will. For obvious reasons, I can't discuss that with you. But what I can tell you is that I was, in that later document, named as the executor of his estate and, as such, will be actioning his wishes. Due to the fact that I will therefore be representing Mr Harrow, I would advise that you enlist the services of another lawyer, because we now clearly have a conflict of interest situation.'

A conflict of interest? What did that even mean? That couldn't be right. It couldn't be. There was no conflict here. Ray was her husband. She was his wife. His world was hers and vice versa. She took another slug of the red liquid in her glass.

'Mr Dawson, I don't understand. Why would there be a conflict of interest?'

'I'm afraid I can't divulge that information, Mrs Harrow. 'As I said, with immediate effect I would recommend that you enlist your own legal representation. If you would be as good as to let me know who that is, I will be in touch in due course.'

A terrible, chilling thought filled her mind.

'Mr Dawson, has my husband left me nothing?'

'I'm afraid I—'

'Stop bloody saying that!' she blurted, sick to the back teeth of all this formal talk and legal bullshit. 'Just tell me where I stand and—'

'I'm afraid I—'

Aaaargh! She couldn't listen to him saying that even one more frigging time.

'Really? You know what, Mr Dawson? You're a—'

Click.

He hung up. The bastard disconnected her call and left her with nothing but more stress and more worries. What the hell was going on here? It was like she'd entered some kind of nightmare where her whole world had fallen apart and she was left with nothing. Absolutely nothing.

Another slug of wine.

Actually, not completely nothing. She still had that whore's phone number.

She snatched up the secret handset again.

Don't think I'm letting this go. I'm not letting you get away with this. I thought you'd have learned the lesson last time.

Send.

She hoped with every fibre of her being that Yvonne McTay got the shock and fright of her life when she read these texts. The bitch was soon going to find out that she'd picked the wrong woman to mess with. She should have learned back then that Denise wasn't someone to give up without a fight.

Thirty-Five

Denise – 1993

He was snoring next to her. In days gone by, she'd have just fallen asleep to the rhythm of the sound, but not now. Now, more than six months later, she stared at the ceiling, night after night, unable to get rid of the image of him standing on that doorstep, kissing her, touching her hand, walking away with a regretful smile, like he couldn't bear to leave her.

It was driving Denise insane.

But of course, she couldn't tell him that. There was no way on this earth that she was going to confront him, because then she'd force his hand. It would lead to an ultimatum and, much as it eviscerated her gut to admit it, she wasn't sure he would pick her.

Instead, she'd gone with a different strategy. She'd turned up her attention to him even higher. Every evening now when he came home from work, she was wearing something she knew he loved. And something she knew he would love even more underneath. Every lingerie shop within ten miles must be wondering why their profits had shot up.

One of his favourite meals would be ready for him, or a table booked at a restaurant that she knew he liked, and she'd be sweet, and funny and flirtatious, and massage his cock with her foot under the table.

Afterwards, there would be sex and not just the basic service. There would be slow, intoxicating seductions, ferocious quickies, even sex toys and the kind of filthy talk that she knew turned him on, but she was usually too embarrassed to go along with. They didn't have to worry about making noise any more, because Claire and Doug had packed their bags after that last fight and shifted off to live with Fred. In truth, she was relieved, and so was Ray. He said it gave them the freedom to do whatever they pleased and he loved every minute of it.

'I told you this would happen, Denise,' he'd said with a devastatingly attractive smile, when he came in from work that first night and she was sitting at the kitchen table in just a robe and stockings and suspenders underneath. 'I knew that the minute those two left, things with us would be better than they'd ever been. Now come here, you sexy bitch.'

Yep, he thought this whole new and improved wife act was all down to the kids shoving off. If only he knew it was more down to where he was shoving his dick. That thought made her wince as she squeezed her eyes shut, desperate for sleep to come and make this stop.

Sex was only one part of the battle though. She knew the thing that turned him on more than anything was the prospect of more money in his bank account, and she'd come up with a way to do that.

It had all come from a report she'd read in the paper about people buying their council houses. Everyone was doing it these days. That's why you could drive along any street in any estate and see at least one house outdoing the neighbours with new windows and a fancy front door.

When Claire and Doug had buggered off to Fred's, it had given her a thought. He was in a council house and he'd never bought it. Ray had raised the idea with him a few times, then said he was an old socialist sod for sticking to his principles that it was to go back to the council when he died. What was the point of that? Her and Ray had both voted Conservative at the last election. He'd told her many times that it was the Tories that stood for the same things as they did – putting the work in and reaping the rewards. She'd come from a council scheme and now look at her, with her beautiful house and the Audi Quattro sitting in the drive. And where was Fred? Still in that damp old house she'd grown up in. That said everything about which political party was the way forward. She didn't understand Fred and his principles at all. He'd be far better to buy that house for the pennies they were asking for it and then it would be his own.

More importantly, when he was gone, it would come to them and Ray could do it up, sell it on and make a few quid. A lot more than a few, actually. Houses in Fred's street were going for fifty grand now. Who would pass up a chance to make that kind of money?

The idea had grown over a week of sleepless nights, staring at this same ceiling, until she'd decided to do something about it. She'd gone down to the council offices, found the housing department and explained that her dad wanted to buy his council house.

No problem, they'd said, handing her a pile of forms.

That night, she'd talked it over with Ray, watched as his face lit up when she finished with, 'Maybe we could buy it and he'd never have to know. I mean, what difference would it make to him?'

'Christ, Denise, you're not just a pretty face, are you?' he'd said, leaning over and kissing her. 'It's a bloody brilliant idea. I don't know why we never thought of it before. You'd do that?'

'It would be the only way. My dad would never go along with it,' she'd said.

Ray thought about it for a moment. 'Maybe he doesn't have to. There must be a way around it. Leave it with me.'

The next night he'd come home with a plan. 'Power of Attorney,' he'd said, then he'd gone on to explain it. Turned out it was a thing whereby people, especially the elderly or vulnerable, could sign over all control of their affairs to their next of kin so that they could take care of their finances and decisions.

'I don't know, Ray...' she hesitated, positive that Fred wouldn't agree to doing that. Ray had already thought it through and come up with a way to overcome the problem. That's why, the following day, she was at her father's house.

Fred had looked surprised when she'd chapped on his door, but she went with the pretence of checking on Claire and Doug. It struck her how old he seemed now, and yet he was only in his mid-fifties. He walked with a stoop, a consequence of years of hard labour at the power plant, and he'd let his beard grow so that it was long and messy. He was in a right state. Agnes would be turning in her grave if she could see him.

As soon as she'd established that the kids weren't home from school yet – she'd deliberately chosen a day that she knew they were both in afterschool activities – she'd pulled the papers out of her bag and told him he needed to sign forms for the school now that they were living with him.

He hadn't hesitated. Old fool hadn't even read them, just signed on the dotted line.

'Also, since the kids are living here, Ray and I will take over half the rent. So if you just send half the payment to this account every month…' she handed him a piece of paper with her bank details, '… we'll make up the difference and send the total to the council.' This was the risky bit. It was the only way they could think of to take over his rent payment. He didn't need to know that no rent would be due, because they'd own the house. However, Fred was a proud man and she'd anticipated his objection, so it was no surprise when it came.'

'Indeed I will not. Those bairns are welcome here and don't want a thing from you.'

'Dad, if you don't accept this deal, Ray and I will need to insist they come home. My Ray is a proud man too, and he'll not have someone else supporting his children.'

She and Ray had practised that line, and she was glad, as she could see Fred thinking it over. There was no way he wanted the kids to be forced to leave, so reluctantly he gave in.

'Aye, fine then. I'm not having you dragging them away against their will. You know, Denise, I don't know what happened to you. You were a lovely lass. You really were. God knows, yer mother was hard on you, and I blame maself for not stopping her. It was never worth ma while to get in the way of Agnes and her temper. I know you felt the brunt of it way too often, so I understood when you shifted out of here as soon as you could, but I'll never know why you've treated these bairns the way that you have. You're so busy looking at that man of yours through rose-coloured glasses that you can't see the truth in front of you. All talk and no trousers that one. Always was. Too flash and too damn arrogant for my liking.'

Denise could feel her blood beginning to boil. 'Don't you be judging me, Dad. You stayed with my mother all those years and she could whip any one of us with that tongue at a minute's notice.'

'Yer right, hen. And, like I said, I blame maself for not stepping in there. It was an easier life just to stay out of the way and leave her to it. Sure, she drove every one of you away. I don't think I've seen our Ronnie or Rachel this year, and as for Donna...' His voice had trailed off and she'd almost felt a pang of sympathy for him. Donna had gone to live with Rachel a few years before, when Agnes died. She'd convinced Fred that it was better for her to live with her sister, and he'd given in to her, not wanting to turn her against him by refusing. '... Aye, well, I don't see Donna much either,' he'd said simply. 'But I learned ma lesson and I'd like to think I've done it right this time. I was a let down as a father, but I've tried my damnedest to make up for it as a grandfather. Those two bairns of yours would be a credit to any family, so they would. I don't know why yer too wrapped up in that husband of yours to see it.'

'If they're a credit, it's because we made them that way, Da. My man is the best father any kid could have and he tells me every day what a great mother I was to them.'

She could feel her old broad accent returning, the one she grew up with, as opposed to the one that she'd rounded off when she moved to a much nicer area. 'If they can't see that just now, then that's their problem. They'll realise it soon enough and come crawling back.' She actually wasn't sure that was the case – Claire had a ferocious stubbornness on her and Doug wouldn't come back without his sister. More than that, she didn't particularly want them back. Ray might not know the full story – he had no idea that Claire had told her about his affair – but there was no denying that life was much easier when there were less distractions and no one else to cater to.

Putting the signed forms back in her bag, she decided she'd had enough of her dad's nonsense. Out the door and back in the car, she'd just switched the engine on when she spotted Claire and Doug in her rear view mirror, getting off the bus and walking towards the house. She'd slipped the handbrake off and driven away without a backward glance.

There had been a slight glitch in their plan when they'd realised that the power of attorney application had to be witnessed by a lawyer. Denise had no idea how Ray handled it, but there was a visit to his old football pal and lawyer, Hugh Dawson, and a weekend in Gleneagles, men only, and the next thing she knew, it was sorted.

She wrote a cheque for eight thousand pounds, took it down to the council offices with all the forms and handed it in. Three months later, the house was theirs, all the intervening correspondence sent to their address, because as far as the legal world was concerned, she was his official representative.

Her dad should be grateful to them, after all it was their money they'd shelled out to buy the house and Fred only paid a pittance in rent now. All they had to do was keep it quiet until the old man passed and then the house – and the profits – would be theirs.

Ray had taken her for a long weekend to London to celebrate that one. Two nights at the Hilton and front seats at *The Phantom of the Opera*.

None of that was any consolation now though, as she lay there, staring at the ceiling, night after night. She was so, so tired. And sick of being worried. If he came home late, she was frantic. If he had to work away for a few days, she'd be climbing the walls until he walked back in the door. When he was out playing five-a-side with his football mates, she paced the floor until he returned, and felt dizzy with relief when she pulled a sweat soaked kit out of his bag. When he was at the pub, she insisted on dropping him off and collecting him, and he never knew that she sat round the corner, watching the front door to make sure he didn't leave and go elsewhere. She'd never found anything that raised the slightest suspicion. Until tonight.

A woman in the west end of the city had called and booked him in to give her a quote for a new kitchen. He'd gone out in plenty of time for the seven o'clock appointment.

At eight thirty, the woman had phoned and said he'd just left but she'd forgotten to ask him something – could he call her back? Denise had told her he'd return the call as soon as he got in.

She'd watched the clock. Ten past nine. Half past nine. Ten o'clock. Ten thirty. Eleven. Twenty-five to twelve, he'd walked back in the door.

'Jesus, that woman and her man could talk,' he'd said, without the slightest hint that he was lying. 'He ended up giving me a beer and we've practically redesigned their whole house. Be a cracker of a job if it comes in.'

She hadn't challenged a word he said, because she knew... just knew.

And now, she could barely breathe because of the weight that was sitting on her chest. She'd tried everything to make him faithful again and yet still he was playing away. Sixth sense, female intuition, call it whatever, it told her that once again it was that Yvonne McTay from the Stonebrae estate.

A thought worked its way through the crevices of panic in her mind. She'd tried it one way – ignoring the affair and hoping that it would end when the whore's extension was finished. Well, months after that job was done, she was now positive it was still going on. She'd be damned if she would lose him though. It was time to come at it from a completely different direction.

His snores told her he was still asleep, and the rhythm of his breathing didn't change as she slipped out of bed and pulled on her jeans and a jumper.

Creeping downstairs, she grabbed her car keys from the hook in the kitchen and silently slipped out of the door. There was a risk that the noise of her car starting in the driveway would wake him, but it was one she was willing to take. She already had a cover story that she was popping out to the all-night garage for some paracetamol for a migraine.

It wasn't a complete lie that she was going out to get rid of a headache.

When she pulled up outside Yvonne McTay's house, it was shrouded in darkness. The clock on the dashboard said 3 a.m., so the whole scheme was deserted.

As quietly as she could, Denise opened her door, closed it behind her and walked up the path to Yvonne McTay's front door. She held her finger on the doorbell until she saw a light come on in the room directly above her, the one that her husband had been in all those months ago. That very thought made her anger swell enough to suffocate all the nerves and anxiety she'd been feeling on the way there.

Her finger was still on the bell, the buzzer piercing the air inside the house, when that whore threw open the door. Denise could see she was ready to launch holy hell on the person who was disturbing her sleep until…

There it was. That flinch of recognition. That's when she knew that she'd been absolutely right about the affair being a long-term thing as opposed to a one-off fling. This woman had no reason to know what she looked like, they'd never met and she was positive Ray wasn't the kind of man who showed his clients happy snaps of the missus. Yet this woman knew who she was. Denise immediately guessed that just as she'd been doing drive-bys and keeping tabs on her husband's mistress, curiosity and jealousy would have compelled this woman to do the same with his wife.

The whole way over, she'd rehearsed what she was going to say. A childhood with Agnes Harrow had given her a mortal fear of confrontation, but she was fighting for her life here and she wasn't going to allow her whole world to be taken away by this bitch standing in front of her, wearing the same robe she'd been wearing that night she'd had her tongue down Ray's throat on her doorstep.

'You know who I am,' Denise began. 'And I know you're sleeping with my husband.'

There was a pause as she could see her competition was deciding how to react. Deny? Apologise? Go with arrogance and disinterest?

To Denise's surprise, she went with calm acknowledgement, topped off with an edge of superiority.

'I'm not going to deny it,' McTay said.

Denise had never committed a violent act in her life but she felt an almost irrepressible urge to claw her manicured fingers down this woman's smug face. It wasn't even as if she was some kind of stunner. Yvonne McTay was older than her, heavier and those roots showed she was no natural brunette. She looked... rough. Easy. Like the kind of slapper she didn't think Ray would give a second glance to. She should be no competition for Denise and the time had come to make that clear.

'Let me ask you then – you like living around here?'

''S'okay,' came the reply, wary this time.

Denise reached into her pocket, pulled out an envelope and held it out.

Slowly, as if unsure whether it was some lethal weapon, Yvonne extended her hand and took it. 'What's this?'

'Look inside.'

Yvonne gingerly used one finger to flip up the fold of the envelope and there was a slight gasp when she saw what was inside.

'There's £2,000 there,' Denise said. She'd been squirrelling money out of her bank account for the last six months, not entirely sure why. Now she realised that she'd always thought it might come to this.

'You can't buy me off,' Yvonne challenged, but Denise could see that now the money was in her hands, there was less bravado.

'Maybe not. But here's the thing. You can take that money – call it a going away present – and you can do whatever you want with it, as long as you have nothing more to do with my man.' Denise kept her voice low and steady and just prayed that the other woman couldn't see that she was shaken to her very core. She could not show weakness. If she did, she knew she would lose this battle.

'And if I don't?' Yvonne asked tartly.

Denise still wasn't sure that she was winning here. Time to play the last card.

'That's why I asked if you liked living here. Because if I find out that you've been seeing my husband again, I'm going to put letters through all your neighbours' doors telling them what a slut you are. I'm going to spray paint "whore" on your walls for the whole world to see. I'm going to find out where you work and place a call to your boss. Then I'll stand outside every day and tell everyone who passes exactly what you've done. I'm going to shame you until you can't even remember how to hold your head up. Do you understand?'

Yvonne's face was a mask of fear and doubt now. One of those threats had clearly struck home and victory was Denise's. Slowly, almost indiscernibly, Yvonne nodded.

'You'll call him tomorrow and you'll end it. You'll say you've met someone else. Oh, and if you dare tell him about me coming here, I will carry out every single one of those threats, no matter what the outcome.'

With that, Denise turned around, walked to her car and didn't look back until she was turning the engine on. The doorway was already empty. Denise's heart was racing. There was every chance that she was in there right now, calling Ray to tell him what had just happened. It was a risk she'd been prepared to take.

When her hands had stopped shaking, and she regained the power of her legs, she slowly, cautiously, drove home, tears dripping down her face the whole way.

When she pulled back into the driveway, she felt something beyond relief that the house was still in darkness.

Upstairs, she slipped back into bed, beside her snoring husband. It was as if the last hour had never happened. Maybe, if she tried really hard, she could convince herself that it hadn't.

It was dawn before she felt her eyes closing. For once, she didn't get up to make Ray's breakfast before he went to work. The whole day she lay in bed, every nerve and muscle in her body rigid with fear and anxiety, unable to shift the duvet from over her. She was still there when she heard his key in the door, his footsteps go through to the kitchen, then climb the stairs to their bedroom.

This was it. She was about to find out if her play had worked, if that whore had called it off or if she'd contacted him, told him what had happened, set him off on a rage that she knew would come her way.

Her breathing shut down altogether as he opened the bedroom door.

Silence.

Then, just as she was about to cry, to beg him to stay, to swear her love for him, he spoke.

'Baby, are you OK?' he asked, crossing the room and perching on the side of the bed. She felt the soft touch of his fingers as he stroked her hair back off her cheek.

Tears of relief began to fall.

'Honey, what is it? What's wrong?' He sounded so worried, so alarmed, that all she wanted to do was cling to him, sob in his arms, hang on to him and never let him go.

That wasn't the way to do it though. She knew she must brazen this out, underplay it, do nothing that would arouse his suspicions.

'Just a migraine, baby. I've had it all day.'

'Oh, you poor thing. I'll go make you a tea. And don't worry about dinner, I'll call something in.'

He lifted her damp hand to his mouth and kissed it, then gently placed it back down on the duvet. Denise wanted to lift it back up and punch the air in triumph. It had paid off. She could feel it. He was totally devoted to her. His other woman had kept her side of the bargain. It was over.

That night, for the first time in months, Denise slept through the night, knowing that her husband was hers, and hers alone.

Thirty-Six

Claire – 2019

'I think that makes it mission accomplished and time to move, people,' Josie said, draining the last of her wine in one expert motion.

Claire was still staring at her reflection, like it was a portrait she recognised but couldn't quite place. 'Where are we off to?'

'We're going to Gino's. We've got a table booked for six o'clock.'

'Oh my God, is it that time already?' Claire gasped.

The day had flown by. It had been funny, sad, comforting, painful, touched almost every page on the encyclopaedia of emotions. More than anything, though, it had completely soothed her soul. It had closed one chapter and opened another. The way she felt right now was so far from the tense, devastated, pissed off person she'd been that morning. She felt... happy. Excited. Alive. And yes, a little bit drunk, but that was OK too. Oh, and ravenous. She was suddenly famished. Nothing, absolutely nothing, sounded better than a night at Gino's, the little Italian restaurant at the end of the street.

'I am so in,' she blurted. 'This hair and face deserve a public outing. I can't thank you lot enough, I really can't. I don't want to get all mushy because Josie and Jeanna will throw up and Suze will stab me with an eyeliner pencil, but I just want to say I love you all. I really do. Today has honestly been one of the best days of my life, and it was nothing to do with a guy, or my kids, or anything else – it was all down to how you've made me feel. Thank you so much.'

The last word was muffled by Val throwing her arms around Claire, tears glistening in her eyes.

'You deserve it, pet. We all love you and this next stage in your life is just going to be bloody brilliant for you. I can feel it in ma water.'

'You sure that's not a wee infection?' Josie interjected. 'That can happen at your age.'

Val released Claire, then batted Josie with her handbag. 'Shut it. Right, let's go.'

'I'm just going to leave all this kit here and I'll send someone up for it tomorrow. I'm not climbing up those stairs again,' Suze decided, touching up her lipstick in the mirror, before joining the line of them trooping to the door.

'Hang on, hang on!' Claire bellowed, as it struck her that she wanted a souvenir of this moment. She pulled her phone from her bag, positioned herself in front of the gang and took her very first selfie. For years she'd been the one taking the pics of the boys. Time for change.

With a couple of clicks, she sent it to her sons with the message, 'New me!' She wasn't sure if it was her or the wine that was typing, but it made her giggle anyway.

Claire quickly switched everything off, set the alarm and locked the door behind her. They moved downstairs like a synchronised swimming team, out the door, turned left and...

'Going somewhere, ladies?'

A male voice stopped them in their tracks. A familiar one.

Claire turned to see Doug getting out of a car parked a few feet along.

'Doug!' she bellowed, throwing her arms wide and hugging her brother. In the excitement of the moment, Jeanna's sexual revelations of the day were completely forgotten. 'What are you doing here?'

He stood back and held her at arm's length. 'I reckoned you'd be up there working out ways to hack a satellite so you could spy on the boys. Thought I'd come and cheer you up, but...' He took in all the other beaming faces. 'Clearly you've already got that covered. By the way, you look brilliant.'

'That was me,' Suze interjected. 'Nothing to do with her at all. She just sat there.'

Doug laughed, then let Claire go so that he could greet all the others with the customary kiss on the cheek. No one commented on the fact that he lingered a little longer when it came to Jeanna.

'Hi babe,' she crooned, adding a hug.

Josie cleared her throat and the moment passed.

'We're just heading to Gino's for dinner. You're very welcome to join us,' Claire offered, really hoping that he would. This day was getting more perfect by the minute. Having Doug here was the icing on the cake.

'Sure, I'd love to. Only thing is, I brought a mate, so is it OK if he tags along?'

'Of course!' Claire exclaimed. She'd met all of Doug's friends over the years and they were all lovely. She'd be delighted to have any of them join the party. 'Who is it?' she asked, peering behind him, just as his buddy got out of the driver's side door of the car.

She wasn't sure if the gasp came from her or one of the women behind her.

Either way, it was an exclamation of both surprise and delight to see him.

'Sam!'

He walked towards her, that very familiar grin in place, and she automatically reached up to hug him. He reminded her so much of the boys. Over six foot tall, Max's thick dark hair and brown eyes, Jordy's broad shoulders and contagious smile.

'What are you doing here?' she asked, for the second time in five minutes.

'That's the ex?' Josie whispered to Jeanna.

'Yup.'

'Holy crap, I'd have hung on to him with a padlock and chain.'

Thankfully, Sam didn't hear that bit, still focused on Claire's question. 'This whole empty nest stuff isn't just for the mums,' he joked, before explaining more. 'I was missing Jordy, and when Doug and I were going out for a pint, the car decided to detour to see if you needed company. That car never gets it right,' he laughed as he kissed Jeanna and then gave an introductory wave to Val, Josie and Suze. 'Good to meet you. I'm Sam. Claire's ex.'

'Really? Claire never mentioned you,' Josie teased, making him laugh.

Today was getting better and better, Claire decided. She had absolutely no idea how the stars had all aligned to make this happen, but she was thrilled that they had.

Their group now two members bigger, they all headed along the street.

'Hang on.' As they passed CAMDEN, Josie opened the door and shouted in, 'Caro, we're heading to Gino's for dinner. You two coming?'

Claire couldn't hear the reply, but Josie appeared satisfied with the answer.

'Great, they're going to come along after they've locked up,' she announced.

'Smashing,' Val chirped. 'Jen and Chrissie are going to pop along after closing too,' she said, referring to her adopted daughter and the assistant manager in Sun, Sea, Ski – the third shop in the row, next to Suze's Pluckers and CAMDEN.

Gino welcomed them with open arms, hastily added two more tables to the one he'd already reserved, then got the wine flowing without delay. It was a small bistro, maybe twenty tables in total, but it was the perfect example of an authentic Italian restaurant. The aromas were breathtaking, the decor a combination of deep wood panels and exposed brick walls, one of them almost entirely covered in a wine rack containing hundreds of bottles. The ceiling was draped in fairy lights and the tables were thick mahogany slabs, surrounded by beautifully carved wooden chairs, upholstered in red leather, on one side and, in the case of their table, a long red banquette seat on the other.

Claire ended up with Sam on her left and Doug on her right.

'We need to talk at some point,' she whispered to Doug, making sure that Jeanna, on the other side of him, couldn't hear her.

'Oh bollocks,' he whispered back, amused. 'You're using that tone that scares the crap out of me. Did I break your Barbie again?'

'Nope, you shagged my pal,' she shot back, breezily.

Doug almost choked on his wine, drawing everyone's attention – the exact opposite of what Claire had been aiming for.

'His antics with Jeanna?' Josie asked, eyebrow raised.

Doug turned to the woman on his right, the one he'd known for over twenty-five years, albeit more intimately than Claire had realised.

'You told everyone?' he asked, shocked.

Jeanna shrugged. 'Does the fact that I've got a big gob, I'm woefully indiscreet and didn't think through the consequences of my actions surprise you in any way?'

'No,' he admitted.

'Then you should have seen it coming. Do you want to share a focaccia?' she finished sweetly.

He was laughing as he accepted the offer.

The rest of the night passed in a riot of wine, laughter and conversations that had tears of mirth trailing down Claire's cheeks. Never had she felt so loved, or so content. Max was fine. Jordy was fine. Everyone else she loved was in this room and they were having a ball. It didn't get any better.

She wasn't sure when she realised that her and Sam were the only two remaining in their party, but it was just after Jeanna and Doug had insisted on paying the bill as they left together, and just before she decided she was going to have to climb over Sam to get out to the loo.

'No worries, I'm just going myself,' he said as he rose and stepped to the side to let her past, then followed behind her.

In the toilets, Claire felt the heady rush of the wine and the sheer giddy joy of the atmosphere. As she washed her hands, she danced along to the sound of Dean Martin crooning through the speakers. She was still walking with a shuffle in her step as she headed back out the door, bumping straight into Sam as he emerged from the Gents'.

'I'd dance with you, but you know how bad I am,' he joked.

'Yep, don't ever do that. It's not safe for innocent bystanders. They'd be scarred.'

It had been the running joke throughout their relationship that she was a terrible dancer, but he was even worse. He took it all in good humour.

'Exactly,' he agreed, with a self-deprecating grin. 'You know, I was worried about you today. I know how hard it was to leave Jordy, but I should have known better. You always manage to sort everything out. Look at tonight. It's been brilliant.'

'I take no credit for this,' she replied honestly. 'This was all on my friends. They did it all without me knowing and I'm so grateful, because I was a frigging mess this morning. It's hard saying goodbye, isn't it?'

He was suddenly serious. 'It really is. More than you know.'

She'd been talking about Jordy, but as their gaze met, even through the haze of way too much wine, she knew that now they were talking about something else.

This wasn't wise. And she never did things that weren't wise. Time to get this right back on track. Past is the past. Enough of the sentimentality.

'I miss you,' she blurted.

Fuck! Definitely not wise. But even as she said it, she knew it was true. When he'd first left, she'd been lost in grief, and fury, and worry about the future. Only when she'd battled through, come to terms with a world without Fred, found a way to block out her parents' betrayal and got Jeanna well again, did she realise how much she missed and wanted him, how stupid she'd been to let him go. In the years since, she'd been so closed off to a relationship because, much as she suppressed it, she'd never got over losing the only man she'd ever loved.

A tug of regret suddenly kicked in. She'd always been grateful for their friendship, figuring it was enough that they were still in each other's lives. Now she'd just blown that by being woefully inappropriate. Bugger!

'I'm sorry, I shouldn't have...' she began but didn't get any further.

His mouth was on hers, and he was kissing her, that long, slow, utterly intoxicating kiss that she'd locked in the back of her mind in a box with hazard tape and barbed wire wrapped around it.

'Shit!' she blurted suddenly, pulling away, a dart of guilt having made it through the cloud of bliss. 'Oh God, Sam, we can't. Nicola...'

'Moved out last week,' he said, then resumed his soft, tender lip lock for a few more moments, before he pulled back this time. 'But if you don't want to... Or if you think it's too soon...?'

Her arms were up around his neck and she kissed him until every last drop of Suze's lipstick was well and truly gone. Only when she finally came up for air did she reply to his question. 'Hell no.'

'No?' he said sexily, kissing her again.

'Nope.'

'So what's next?'

This time she didn't even reply. She just took the love of her life by the hand and led him out of the door.

Thirty-Seven

Denise – 2019

The only light in the room came from the bedside lamp that she'd switched on before she became too drunk to find the plug. She was way past that now. Her legs were heavy, her head was woozy and her fingers were now struggling to work the remote control that was operating the music system, so Adele had sung 'Make You Feel My Love' so many times that Denise had lost count. The minute she had heard that song she'd known that it perfectly summed up her feelings for Ray. There was nothing she wouldn't do for him. She just hadn't realised the line about not making his mind up applied too.

Lifting the phone from the bed beside her, Denise squinted at the screen. Nothing. Still no text back from that woman.

The irony was that she was now two bottles of wine in, trying to numb the pain, but all that had happened was that it was making her stomach churn and her mind run riot. She'd thrown up again – this time without making it to the bathroom. She'd grabbed a bowl that was on her bedside table, but it had still splattered across the carpet too. She didn't even care any more. Fuck it. Who'd see it anyway?

And lying here next to a pool of the liquid contents of her stomach was so much less offensive than the scenarios thundering around in her head and her desperate grasping for thoughts that could make sense of all this.

She had to accept the inevitable. The messages on the phone proved that Ray had been having a relationship with Yvonne McTay again, going back at least a couple of years, since he'd upgraded his iPhone and put a different SIM card in this one.

So what had happened? Had they met again, after more than twenty-five years, and rekindled their affair? Had she tracked him down? Or had he gone looking for her?

He wasn't on Facebook, but his mobile phone number was on his website, so he wasn't hard to find. One call would have been all it took. Was that it? She'd phoned him and he'd gone running to her?

Or – and this thought made her pause, swallow, force herself not to throw up again – had the affair never stopped? Had Denise been living a lie for more than two decades, with a man who had never been faithful to her?

But if that was the case, why would he stay? Why wouldn't he just leave and go to her, start a new life there?

It didn't make sense.

Neither did the money situation.

Where had it all gone? There had to be a simple explanation, but she'd be a fool not to be concerned that the best part of £200K had been drained from their accounts. Had he really done that?

Her first instinct would have been to brush that suggestion off as nonsense, but then how could she explain the call with the lawyer? Conflict of interest, he'd said. Did that mean Ray had done something that was going to be detrimental to her? This whole fucking day had been a conflict of interest.

Maybe her whole life had been too.

They'd been so young when they'd met and she'd been completely in awe of him from the first moment he'd asked her to dance. That had never diminished, not by a heartbeat. Later, when she'd realised that he expected to come before her family, her friends, her own children, she'd been more than willing to put him on that pedestal because he took her up there with him.

He'd loved her. She knew he had. There was no way he could have faked it for almost forty years.

But had he loved someone else too?

The room suddenly turned cold, causing her to shiver.

In her head, she heard Claire's voice, that angry, indignant teenager who was determined to make her face what was happening. She could still remember every word. *'Let me do you a favour and be the one person who tells you the truth for a change. He isn't out working to support us. He's out shagging that woman whose house he's working on. She lives round the corner from Jeanna and it's the talk of the scheme. So next time you're worried about my pals being the wrong kind of people, maybe you should think about the fact that the real scumbag here is your lying bastard of a husband.'*

Maybe she should have cut her losses right there, when she was still young enough to start again. Now she was fifty-five. Who would want her? More importantly, despite what he'd put her through and the challenges they'd faced, who could possibly match up to Ray?

No, another love wasn't an option.

There weren't going to be any second chances.

A memory of Fred floated in now. Standing in his kitchen, he was telling her that he'd messed up as a dad but he'd made amends by being a good grandfather. He'd made a conscious change and it had brought him a family and love until the day he died.

That wasn't going to be an option for her either. Her grandchildren were what? She tried to calculate their ages, but the alcohol wouldn't let her. She went for a guess. They must be about eighteen or nineteen now. Two boys. She hadn't seen them since they were kids and now they were practically men. She'd never been a part of their lives because Ray wouldn't hear of it. 'You've given so much of yourself to our kids,' he'd told her. 'Now it's their turn to look after their own children. This time is for you and me and we're going to enjoy every minute of it.'

No, there would be no second chances there, no opportunity to suddenly turn into a doting grandmother for Claire's kids.

Or Doug's for that matter. If he had any. Last she knew he was married to a lawyer, so perhaps they did have children by now.

She picked up the phone again. Squinted. Still nothing. That bitch was ignoring her. How fucking dare she?

Something tugged her mind back to the previous train of thought.

A lawyer.

Hadn't Hugh Dawson told her today that she had to hire her own representation? And how was she supposed to do that with no money?

Doug's wife. She was family. If her husband's mother needed help, surely she wouldn't refuse her?

Claire's voice again, an adult this time, back in Fred's kitchen on the last day she'd seen her son and daughter. *'You two are scum. And Doug and I don't associate with scum. We're done. Not that you ever cared, but don't call us, don't text us, don't contact us ever again. And good luck with the profits from this sale – I hope they choke you.'*

She didn't want to give either of them the satisfaction of seeing her reduced to this, to a woman without a husband, only a life of lies and betrayal and an empty bank account.

But what choice did she have?

Her children had become the only options she had left.

Before she could dwell on that pathetic truth, the phone in her hand suddenly buzzed into life, making her scream. Her heart started racing, her head started spinning. There was a long moment before she could focus her eyes well enough to read the words that had flashed up.

You have one new text... From Y.

With trembling hands, she pressed the box to open it.

I am blocking this number. Do not contact me again.

The sound of smashing glass as she launched the handset at the wall was drowned out by her screams, curdling howls of pain that went on until she buckled over in torrential sobs.

The conclusion from a few moments before returned and ricocheted through her mind.

Her children were her only options.

Leaning over to her bedside cabinet, she grappled for her own phone, knocking over the half full bottle of red that she'd left there. She didn't care.

Her fingers finally located the handset and she brought it up to a few inches from her face.

She started typing with her thumbs.

Message complete, she deliberated who to send it to. In the end, she went for the one who could deliver practical help, thanks to a wife with a law degree.

Your dad died last week. Funeral on Friday.

Contacts.
Doug.
Send.

Thirty-Eight

Claire – 2019

Claire felt the sun heating up her face, and she instinctively shrivelled back from it, clenching her eyes tight shut. Bugger. She must have forgotten to close the blinds last night. As she moved, she realised she was completely naked. Bugger, she must have forgotten to put her pyjamas on last night. And ouch, there appeared to be a train going at full speed, banging against the inside of her head. Damn, she must have drunk too much last…

'Morning, gorgeous,' the voice murmured, as a body, also naked, pressed against her back, spooning into her.

Bugger. She must have forgotten she slept with her ex-husband last night.

She'd had sex! Real sex! With Sam! In her house. The same one they'd shared when they were married. It was like some kind of sexed-up time warp.

Her first instinct was to panic. He lived with someone. He was an attached man. And never, ever, not even if it was George bloody Clooney, would she sleep with someone else's partner.

A flashing memory from the night before of Sam telling her he wasn't with Nicola any more brought her heart rate back down from borderline hysteria to 'generally freaking out'.

Ignoring the pain in her head, she managed to push herself up on her elbows, not even caring that this gave him full view of her boobs, which slid to each side of her chest. She was fairly sure that last time she'd slept with him, they'd have remained upright and facing forward. She was naked. She'd done many intimate things last night. It was a tad late for modesty.

'Sorry, but I need to check... I didn't just have sex with someone else's partner last night?'

Opening one eye, Sam gazed up at her, grinning.

'Could we go with "absolutely amazing, mind-blowing sex"? It would be so much better for my ego.'

Despite swimming in a massive vat of fear, she chuckled. 'OK, did I have absolutely amazing, mind-blowing sex with someone else's partner last night?'

Now he pushed himself up so that he was on one elbow, facing her.

'No,' he said gently, using his index finger to trail a line from her neck down to her belly button. The thrill made its way through the panic. Oh, dear God, that felt good. And sexy. And so, so horny. And she wanted to...

She stopped herself. She'd gone without sex for the best part of ten years, she could go without it for the next ten minutes, until she got some details straight.

'We split up. I told you that last night,' Sam reminded her gently.

'I thought so, but I just wanted to check.'

She rolled over onto her side, replicating his position, so that they were facing each other now, heads on pillows, their faces just a few inches apart. The freak-out was replaced by a warm, glorious feeling of happiness. Sam was here. She'd never been able to admit to herself how much she missed him until he was right here, lying next to her, where he should have been all along.

'What happened?' she asked softly. She wasn't sure why it was important for her to know, but she had to. If this was some temporary blip in Sam's relationship with Nicola, she wasn't going to keep him amused until he toddled off back to her. Her heart couldn't take it.

'We decided to call it a day. There were no hard feelings. If we'd been honest with ourselves, we'd have seen it had been coming for a while. We've been together for five years and things change over time and we just want different things now.'

'Like?'

'She wants children. She's thirty-five now and she's decided that it's time to have a family.' He reached over and touched her cheek. 'I already have one.'

Wow, the tenderness of his touch and his words sent a lump right to her throat. It took her a moment to recover.

'And you? What do you want?' she asked.

'I want to be here,' he said simply, before reaching out, sliding his hand around her face and gently pulling her to him.

This time they made love in a whole different way from the night before. In the darkness, it had been heated, frantic, urgent, but now, their gaze locked the whole time, it was gentle and... it was love. Pure love.

Afterwards, they sank back in the pillows, facing each other again.

A sudden urge to giggle consumed her. 'How many lectures have I given our boys about getting drunk and having sex with someone you just hooked up with that night?'

'Yep, we're completely irresponsible. We should be deeply ashamed,' he countered, in a tone that made it clear he wasn't ashamed at all. Neither was she.

'Hang on, don't move...' She jumped up, pulled on his shirt from last night, then nipped downstairs to make a couple of coffees, picking up a trail of discarded clothes as she went. On the way back up, she stopped in the bathroom to brush her teeth and... Shit. She caught her reflection in the mirror. She'd been under the misapprehension that she still looked like the woman whom Suze had spun round in the chair after the makeover yesterday. Apparently not. Hair like stuffing exploding from a burst couch, mascara tracks down her cheeks, her skin a subtle shade of grey. He'd gazed into her smudged eyes for the last half an hour as they'd made love. The poor guy must be traumatised.

She did a hasty repair job, washing her face and giving her hair a quick brush, but she wasn't sure there was much of an improvement.

Picking up the cups, she marched back into the room. 'Seriously? This was all straight from some romantic movie until I just caught a look at myself. It's a fricking horror show. You might have warned me I looked like an extra from The Walking Dead.'

'Yeah, I was wondering what look you were going for with that,' he teased, sitting up and reaching for the coffee.

As the sheet slid down beside him, she could see his wide shoulders, the chest muscles, the defined abs... 'I can't have sex with you ever again looking like that. I'd spend the whole time breathing in and trying to clench my arse so it looks better. Why couldn't you have let yourself go to ruin like I did?'

He put the two coffees on the bedside table and tugged her down on top of him. 'You're still the sexiest thing I've ever seen.'

She shrieked, laughing as she fell on him. 'I'm like a before advert for Slimming World! I'm not getting my kit off again until I've lost three stones.'

'Enough,' he chided her. 'You're fricking gorgeous and you're perfect the way you are. Now come here and I'll prove it.'

'Sooooo corny, Mr Bradley,' she teased.

'Shit – that was my best line,' he shot back.

The coffee was cool by the time they got to it. They were back under the duvet, on their sides facing each other again, both of them grinning like teenagers.

Shouldn't you be heading off to work?' she asked.

He shook his head. 'I'm still on holiday. I took some extra time in case I wanted to stay in the USA after we dropped Jordy off but didn't get round to arranging anything. Shouldn't you be heading to work?' he repeated her question.

'I don't have any clients today, so I think I can officially skive. God, this being irresponsible definitely has some plus points.' She stretched, then faced him again for the next question. 'I want to know. When did you decide you wanted this?'

'When I touched your hand in the car after we dropped Jordy off at college, I knew I didn't want to let it go again,' he said sincerely. He then slightly spoiled the moment with a cheeky, 'I also realised that I wanted to scoop you up, take you to a hotel and do all the things we just did.'

Her laughter was hoarse thanks to the hangover. 'You had me floating in sentimentality there until you added that last bit. You should have stopped at the hand holding.'

'I am so out of practice at this stuff,' he said, his smile adorably self-deprecating. His turn for a question. 'So what now?'

'What do you mean?'

'Do you think we can try again? See how it works out this time?'

'I think…' She paused, not really knowing what she thought, other than this was the happiest moment she'd had in a long time. But there were considerations, mainly involving the boys. Would it be fair for them to see their parents back together and then have to go through another split if it didn't work out? Was that a chance they'd want to take? Their family had a great dynamic, they were all happy, there were no conflicts or lingering tensions. Did she really want to change that? 'I think…' she repeated.

'Claire!' bellowed a voice from downstairs, startling her.

'Jeanna?' she replied.

Oh bloody hell. Jeanna downstairs. Sam upstairs. It was only 8 a.m. and already this morning had all the signs of turning into a dramafest. Jeanna was sure to make a big deal of this, and she'd been hoping to keep the fact that she'd just slept with her ex-husband of many years to herself for just a little bit longer. Maybe until lunchtime.

Jeanna's answer was the sound of footsteps thundering upstairs. Damn. No time to flee, hide or cover up Sam. Her pal burst into the room with her customary impact.

'Holy shit!' was the first thing out of her mouth, followed by an uproarious cackle. 'About bloody time.'

She really needed to take Jeanna's key off her.

It was only then that Claire noticed another head behind her friend's messy mane of hair. Great. Her brother had just seen her in bed with her ex too.

All dignity was officially out of the window.

'All right, Sam,' Doug said as if he'd just bumped into him in the pub.

Sam nodded with admirable nonchalance. 'All good, bud.'

'What are you two doing here?' Claire asked.

Jeanna plonked herself down on the edge of the bed. Claire had no time to think too deeply about the fact that her brother and best friend were together at 8 a.m. on a morning after a night out, and for the first time in history Jeanna McCallan was out of the house without a full face of flawless make-up. Although she did, of course, still look spectacular in her black skinny jeans and a Nashville sweatshirt Claire had brought her from the trip last week.

'We have news, sis,' Doug said tentatively. His expression was dark and his tone almost fatalistic, so Claire immediately sensed something had happened that wasn't good. Of course, her mind went to the obvious place.

'Is it my boys? Has something happened? Are they hurt? Are they OK?'

Doug put his hands up. 'No, no, no, they're fine. It's nothing to do with them.'

The relief made her sag back onto the pillow and she tried to get her breathing under control. The boys were fine. That was all that mattered.

Doug got straight to the point. 'Our mother sent me a text during the night, but I only saw it when I woke up this morning.'

Irritation was instant. Anything to do with her parents put her back right up. Didn't it say everything that they never called Denise 'mum'. That was too informal, endearing. The fact that she gave birth to them was just a biological detail that made her their mother. The rest of the maternal role didn't apply, not when they were growing up, not when they were still in contact and definitely not now.

More than the reality that they'd been crap parents and pretty twisted human beings with a completely dysfunctional relationship, she would never, ever get past what they'd done to Fred.

'Saying what?' Claire asked, with an overtone of disgust in her voice. In truth, she didn't really care. There was nothing that Denise or Ray Harrow could say to her that would make her change how she felt about them. Nothing at all.

'Saying that our father died. She wants us to go to the funeral.'

Thirty-Nine

Denise – 2019

The fog was dense and chilling, but it was on the inside of Denise's skull. The sun shone through the window, reflecting against the mirror in front of her, but the heat couldn't permeate her body or her mind. Her movements were slow, fumbling, frustrating. The buttons on the black jacket that she couldn't make fasten. The hairbrush that she could barely raise to her head. The eyelids that she could hardly lift because she didn't want to view a world without him.

Ray was gone.

A visceral reaction to that thought forced the air out of her chest, causing her to buckle forward.

He was gone.

Her whole life wiped out in the seconds it took for his brain to stop functioning, then his heart to fail and stop. No warning. No second chances. No hope. Fifty-six years old and he was just gone, leaving a soulless vacuum, an empty bank account and a million questions behind.

She'd given up everything for him, willingly and without question. Now waves of grief were dragging the shifting sands of her life back into the water, sucking her down with them.

But she had to do this last thing for him today.

The crematorium was only a few miles away, on the south side of Glasgow. He was there already. Waiting for her. She was wearing the gorgeous Gina Bacconi black dress and jacket he'd bought her from House of Fraser last year, she'd done her make-up just how he liked it, and she was going to walk into that crematorium with her head held high.

Today she would say a last goodbye to the man who had been her world and she knew, without hesitation that, despite everything, she would love him until the end of time.

At the crematorium, she walked to the front of the aisle, touched his coffin. 'Always yours, my love,' she whispered. For it was true. No matter what he'd done, no matter what would come to light in the future, they'd had a wonderful life together and she wouldn't change a single minute of it – obviously with the exception of his dalliance, but she wasn't going to think about that. Over the last couple of days, since the morning she woke up surrounded by chaos and vomit, she'd pulled herself together, got some perspective. The money situation had to be a glitch, she'd convinced herself. Of course it was. She'd recruited a lawyer – not Doug's wife, as it turned out they'd divorced years ago – and he was going to look into the situation. She was confident it would all be resolved.

As for the affair? Sure, it had hurt, but at the end of the day, so what? Countless men had done it. What was important was that he'd never left her. The affair was just sex. What they'd had together was love. Real love that had lasted their lifetime.

As she looked around her, Denise saw a few faces that she recognised. A couple of blokes from the football team. Christ, they were looking old. They obviously hadn't taken care of themselves the way her Ray had done. Behind them, there were a few sub-contractors that had been brought in for the construction jobs. A couple of neighbours from their street. God knows how they'd found out, but news travelled fast around here. They'd probably only come for a nosy and a sausage roll from the buffet afterwards.

With Ray's parents long gone, she sat in the front row alone. In some ways, she was glad they weren't there. They'd never had the kind of class that she and Ray had developed over the years. Even now, she still found it hard to believe that they'd come from such basic roots.

She scanned the room again, searching for two faces. Nothing. They hadn't come. Her own children hadn't had the decency to show up and pay their respects to the man who had given them everything. Ray was right in every single thing he'd ever said about them. They were ungrateful, spoiled brats, who had no appreciation for anything.

She could hear Ray's voice telling her not to care. Again and again he had told her that all that really mattered was him and her, Ray and Denise against the world. Just the two of them. He was right. But now she sat alone, and he was in a coffin in front of her.

The funeral director showed an elderly man to the stage, a humanist celebrant recommended by the undertaker. She'd decided against a religious ceremony, because neither of them gave a jot about church, but it still seemed right to have someone speak about him. Really, though, what did it matter? Ray was dead. Whether they cremated him without words, listening to a vicar rambling about God, or after some non-denominational stranger wittered about what a lovely man he was, he was still going to be dead.

His words blurred into each other and the room became hazy, as she detached herself from what was going on around her. Despite her earlier gesture at the coffin, she did not accept that her love was lying in that box, only feet away. She did not watch as the coffin slid forward and a black velvet curtain closed behind it. She did not shed a tear, because he would have wanted her to be strong and because, if she let herself feel just one glimmer of the pain that she was holding inside, she would collapse on this floor and she wasn't sure she would ever get up again.

She chose to believe that there was a different reality and, in it, he was with her. He was in the room. He was watching her, loving her, caring for her even now. She had to believe that because the alternative was unbearable.

As the man's voice droned on, she rewound their lives together, choosing to live in the past, rather than the present. The night they met. Only a boy then, but he still had the most beautiful face she'd ever seen. The incredible feeling the first time they'd made love. Followed not long after by the mortification of the day Agnes had dragged her round to Jenny and Pete's house to confess that she was pregnant. Their wedding. The day they had promised that they would love each other until death parted them. And they had. Although she could still hear her father-in-law Pete's voice, in the alley beside the reception hall, saying they had to 'make the best of a bad lot'. All these years and she'd never forgotten that.

She pressed fast forward. The birth of their children – her irritation at the fact they weren't there threatened to snap her out of that long gone place, but she forced herself to let it go. Their exquisite holidays, their romantic dinners, the nights he'd made love to her and the countless times that he would tell her how incredible she was and that she made him the happiest man alive. That was all that mattered here, not this old man's words or this crowd of strangers, mourning something they never had.

Only the silence and the expectant glance of the celebrant told her that the service was over.

Slowly, eyes straight ahead, oblivious to the nods of the other mourners, she rose and walked back down the aisle and out of the huge dark oak double doors.

She squinted for a moment in the daylight, turned her head, and…

That's when she saw her.

She was about ten feet away, heading across the car park, walking quickly, obviously having darted out of the door right before her.

Denise's decision was instinctive. No, she wasn't going to let this happen.

Ignoring the shocked glances of those around her, she crossed the distance in seconds, put her hand on the fur on the woman's shoulder, spun her around.

It was her.

The same tall frame, the same repulsive, heaving chest, the same long brunette wavy hair, still out of a bottle.

Yvonne McTay had the audacity to show up here today. The whore.

'How dare you...' Denise hissed. They were about twenty feet away from everyone else now, out of earshot but within sight. Denise didn't care if they had an audience. None of these people mattered to her.

If she expected the other woman to back down, to apologise, to be afraid, she was very, very wrong.

Yvonne McTay lifted her chin, then spoke with quiet firmness and unequivocal resolve. 'I have every right to be here. I'm more than entitled to say goodbye to him.'

Denise snorted. 'You have no right,' she spat, her face a twisted veil of disgust.

Her husband's mistress came right back at her. 'Of course I do. Twenty-five years we loved each other. That gives me every right.'

The pain was like the most ferocious slap across the face, followed by an excruciating body blow that made her fold at the waist. There was screaming in her ears, explosions in her head, no breath whatsoever getting to her lungs.

She desperately wanted to run, but her legs wouldn't move. They could barely hold her up. She felt like she was falling... falling...

'Mother.'

The voice sliced right through the white noise screeching in her brain. She managed to lift her head, to focus her eyes, to register the person in front of her.

Claire.

Her daughter had come.

Forty

Claire – Two Hours Earlier

Claire sat on the end of her bed, back straight so as not to put creases in the black dress she'd just peeled from the dry-cleaning bag. A loose strand escaped from the chignon at the nape of her neck and she pushed it back behind her ear with shaking hands, her fingertips gliding over the jaw that was set in defiance of her emotions. She wouldn't crumble. She wouldn't falter.

Her father was gone.

She exhaled, trying desperately to banish the knot that was twisting her gut.

He was gone.

For thirty-nine years, he'd been an undeniable force in her life, his actions and her reactions determining so much of who she was and what she'd become.

A vision of her mother flashed before her. Losing the love of her life would have left her heartbroken, but Claire was sure to her core that Denise would hold it together, put on one last show for her man. She had never let him down, never faltered in her adoration for a man who was so much more than flawed.

It went against the laws of nature, the ways of humanity, but all she felt for her parents was disgust.

And that's why she was going to walk into that crematorium with her head held high.

Today she would say a last goodbye to the man who had treated her like she was nothing and she knew, without hesitation, that she would despise him until the end of time.

'Are you sure you want to do this?' Sam asked her, clipping his cufflinks into the cuffs of his white shirt. He was coming with her, said he didn't want her to do it alone. Almost a decade apart, and every heartbeat of her love for this man had come right back. And more.

'I do. But I still can't tell you why,' she said, replaying the conversation they'd had so many times since Doug had told her about the text. It was like a feral, irrepressible need to see that it was over. That he was gone. The overriding negative emotion in her life for so long had been her hatred of her parents. Now she was going to say goodbye to half of that. Maybe all of it. To draw a line and move on with nothing but love and decency in her life.

A car horn sounded and Sam held his hand out. 'They're here.'

Claire stood, inhaled, exhaled. She could do this.

By the time she'd made it out of the house, Doug had climbed out of the car and was holding the door open for her. She hugged him, squeezing him tight.

'You sure you want to come?' she asked him for the umpteenth time.

He nodded. 'You go, I go. It's how we roll,' he said softly, hugging her again.

It was true. They'd stuck together through everything. Through Denise's indifference to them, Ray's undisguised resentment and dislike for them, through marriages and divorces, and through a secret affair with a best friend that Claire was definitely going to discuss with them when this was all over.

Right on cue, Jeanna leaned forward in the passenger seat so she could catch her eye. 'Would you hurry up and get in? This is like a scene from the fricking *Godfather* out there with you two.'

Despite the black clothes and the dread of what was ahead, Claire couldn't help but laugh. When this day was over, she would still have these people with her. That thought was enough to get her through anything.

They'd left with an hour to spare, because they'd planned to make a detour on the way. Ten minutes later, they turned off a winding road, through a huge set of black iron gates and wove their way through a sea of headstones, eventually stopping at a simple black granite stone with silver writing.

FRED MCALEE
1935–2011
BELOVED HUSBAND, FATHER, GRANDFATHER AND
GREAT-GRANDFATHER
A PIECE OF OUR HEARTS HELD CLOSE FOR EVER

Claire and Doug had designed the stone and had it installed after Fred passed away. She knew he'd love it, just as he'd love the bench that they'd had placed on the edge of the grass in front of it.

Sam and Jeanna stayed in the car, while Claire and Doug climbed out and sat down, her hand reaching for his.

'I come here and feel loss,' Doug said. 'Yet I'm going to our father's funeral and I feel nothing.'

He couldn't have summed it up any better.

'We're going to close a book,' she told him, before turning to stare at the stone. 'I feel Grandad showed us what it was to care for someone, to love them, be there for them. We were lucky to have him.'

She stood, crossed the grass, laid her fingers on the stone, spoke softly, tears running down her face.

'See you later, Grandad. We'll always be grateful for you.'

Doug's arm came around her as she took the first step back towards the car, before he stopped, turned... 'And, Grandad, if there's an afterlife, you might want to go and barricade the doors, because you're not going to like who's on the way.'

Five minutes before the ceremony was about to start, they pulled into the car park. They only knew the details because Doug had called his mother that morning at Claire's house when he'd stormed in with Jeanna and told Claire the news. They'd moved down to the kitchen, sat around the table, drank tea and discussed what to do.

In the end, Doug had bitten the bullet and called her, with Claire, Jeanna and Sam listening beside him.

'I got your text,' he'd said.

There was a pause. 'Well, I suppose phoning back is the least you can do.'

'Hang up,' Jeanna had whispered, face flushing, and Claire could see her friend's protective instinct flaring. There was definitely more than a casual thing going on between those two.

Doug had ignored her, focused on the call and on Denise's voice coming from the speaker.

'I need a lawyer. Your wife. Can I speak to her?'

Claire's jaw had fallen. So she hadn't even texted or phoned out of some misplaced parental duty. Nope, she contacted him because she needed something – legal advice from the woman Denise thought was still Doug's wife.

'It's the least you can do,' she'd told him haughtily.

Claire had wanted to grab the phone, tell her mother exactly what she deserved, but she'd stopped herself, because even in the midst of this emotional maelstrom, she knew that Denise must be destroyed by this loss. Ray Harrow hadn't just been her husband, he'd been her reason for living, the very purpose of her being, the focus of every single day of her life. Putting her own resentments and feelings to one side, on a purely humane level, she knew this woman on the other end of the phone must be in hell. Now wasn't the time for castigation or reproach.

'Fiona and I divorced many years ago,' Doug had said simply.

There was a pause. 'Fine. The funeral is at 11 a.m. on Friday if you want to pay your respects.'

Then she'd hung up. That was it. Conversation over.

Now it was 10.55 a.m. and the four of them were in the car, watching people dressed all in black enter the building.

'Are we going to do this?' Jeanna asked. 'Because, to be honest, I'd be happy to swerve it altogether and just go and have our own wake in the nearest bar.'

'No, we're doing it,' Claire said, firmly. 'But you don't have to come with us, Jeanna. We can meet you later. There's honestly no need to subject yourself to this.'

Only when Jeanna didn't immediately answer did Claire lean forward so that she could see her friend's face. Jeanna's eyes were fixed on the door of the crematorium, at the last of the mourners going through the thick wooden doors.

'Oh bloody hell… I don't believe it,' she whistled. 'Would you look at that?'

Claire turned her gaze to see what Jeanna was looking at. She could see nothing out of the ordinary, just a man holding the door open for a woman in a long black fur coat and black high heels, her brunette hair falling in waves down her back.

'That's Yvonne McTay from our scheme.'

'What?' Claire gasped, just as Doug reacted with a 'Nooooooo.'

'Who's Yvonne McTay?' Sam asked, puzzled.

'I grew up in the Stonebrae scheme, and when we were about fourteen, the bold Ray Harrow was screwing the woman across the road. It kept the garden fence gossips buzzing for months. Her name was Yvonne McTay. And she just walked in there.' Jeanna reached for the handle. 'Oh, I'm coming in now.'

Claire's shock turned to a strange numbness. A bizarre disbelief about where she was and what she was doing there. It allowed her to be led out, to link arms with Sam, to walk towards the building containing the body of a man she'd avoided for most of her life.

The celebrant had just started speaking as they slipped into the back row, on the opposite side of the aisle from her father's mistress.

She could see the back of her mother's head, alone in the front pew. She thought for a moment about her paternal grandparents. She knew they'd passed away, but she hadn't spoken to them since she was a teenager, not since Jenny had reprimanded her and Doug for moving in with Fred, spinning the same line as Denise about how her father was a wonderful man who deserved respect. Jenny had refused to hear different, so Claire had nothing more to say. They'd never met again.

The coffin slid forward, the black curtain closed and Claire realised that she felt nothing. No sadness, no pain, nothing. Just closure. It was done.

As the celebrant wound up the service, the mourners at the front rose and began to walk towards the doors. Her mother looked straight ahead, eyes never veering from the doors in front of her, seeing none of them. Claire couldn't believe how little she'd changed. Yes, her expression was stony, her lips a thin line of suppressed emotion, but Denise Harrow was still a stunning woman who looked like she was in her early forties. Clearly that's what money and self-indulgence bought these days.

As was customary, everyone waited until the chief mourners passed before vacating their seats, except... she just caught a glimpse of the fur coated woman to her left slipping out of a side door.

Her mother passed, but it was a few more moments before those sitting in her row could follow. When they eventually made it into the daylight, Denise was nowhere to be seen.

Claire put her hand above her eyes to block the sun as she scanned the car park. 'Where is she?'

'There!' Doug said, pointing to the left, to where their mother was standing, face like fury, confronting one very glamorous, very composed mourner.

'I'd buy tickets for this,' Jeanna blurted, inappropriate as always.

Claire rapidly ran through the options. Leave. This was nothing to do with her. She didn't care. Her reason for being here was done. Chapter closed. Or go over there. Intervene. Because it was more than probably the right thing to do.

'Damn it,' she blurted, before taking off, walking swiftly towards the two women fronting up to each other in a crematorium car park.

Her interruption was forceful and invited no argument. 'Mother! What the hell is going on?'

Denise immediately clamped her mouth shut, her face a mask of pure arrogance. The other woman didn't say anything either, just stood there, chin jutting forward in defiance.

Claire decided to tackle her first. 'I'm Ray's daughter,' she said, not unkindly.

'I know who you are,' Yvonne answered in the same conciliatory tone.

'OK,' Claire said, exhaling, no idea where to go next. She decided on honesty. 'I know who you are too, Ms McTay,' she managed a weak smile, trying her best to de-escalate the situation and restore some kind of civility. 'And I'm sure you and my mother must have a lot to talk about, but I'm thinking this probably isn't the best time and place.'

'I don't give a damn,' Denise blurted. 'I want answers.'

Yvonne immediately narrowed her eyes at her again.

Claire could feel her old aversion to confrontation rising. Oh, crap, this wasn't going well.

'OK, OK. Look there's a conservatory over there...' she said, pointing to a glass structure that sat beside the garden of remembrance. There were chairs in it, somewhere family members could go to feel close to the loved ones whose ashes were scattered there. It wasn't exactly meant to be the venue for two furious women to have a showdown, but it was the only port in this storm.

Denise went first, walking with determination and a face like thunder, while Claire and the mistress followed behind. Claire was panicking inside, no clue whatsoever on how to mediate this, but knowing she had to. Bloody hell, this day had definitely taken a turn for the unexpected.

Thankfully, the conservatory door was open and they marched in. Yvonne sat on a dark grey seat, while Denise stayed upright, pacing. Just as Claire was about to close the door behind them, Doug slipped in too, making Yvonne gasp. Claire wasn't surprised. She always forgot how much Doug resembled their father. He sat beside her on a bench seat attached to the wall just inside the door.

'I've told everyone else to go on to the wake,' he said.

That was a small consolation. At least they were no longer going to have an audience.

'Sam and Jeanna?'

'Waiting in the car.'

Claire glanced outside and could see the two of them sitting in the front seat of the jeep, staring in at the action. Forget that thought about the lack of audience, there was one right there, watching from afar. And they'd better crack on before Jeanna's frustration at not being able to hear the conversation got the better of her and she came crashing in here.

'So who needs to start?' Claire asked.

'I do,' her mother said, leaving no room for argument. 'Were you still screwing my husband?'

Claire's gaze caught Doug's with a helpless look. Nothing like getting straight to the point.

'Yes.' Yvonne's reply was equally frank and contained absolutely no hint of repentance or regret.

They could all see that Denise was so enraged she could barely get the words out. 'For how long?'

'Always.'

'But I warned you...'

Yvonne snorted. 'And I took no heed.'

Claire could see her mother's confusion. It matched her own and she couldn't help ask for clarification. 'I don't understand...'

Yvonne seemed fine with enlightening her. 'Years ago, your mother found out I was seeing your father...'

Claire felt a pang of guilt as she remembered who'd broke that little nugget of truth to Denise.

'And she came to my door in the middle of the night, gave me money, tried to pay me off.'

'Really?' Claire exclaimed. Wow. She didn't know that. But then, her and Doug had moved to Fred's house by then. 'And what happened?'

Yvonne's expression oozed smugness. 'I told your father. We used the money to go on a weekend break to Paris.'

There was a whimper of utter agony from Denise and she went so pale, Claire wondered if she was about to faint.

'No, that couldn't... Why? Why didn't he say anything to me?'

'The timing wasn't right,' Yvonne answered truthfully.

Claire decided to step in. 'Hang on. So you've been seeing him all these years? Yet he stayed with my mother? Why didn't he just leave her for you? Why stay? What do you mean about the timing?'

Yvonne sighed. 'When I met him, I'd just had a baby. My daughter.'

Claire understood immediately. Denise's gasp told her she'd cottoned on pretty quickly too. Ray Harrow needed to be 100 per cent centre of attention at all times. He'd resented her and Doug's very existence because he couldn't bear to share Denise's time or affection. There was absolutely no way he would enter into another full time relationship with someone who had a child.

'Ray didn't want to live with someone else's kid in the house. Said he'd already done the family thing and he had no desire to do it again. So we came to terms with living a different life. He decided to stay with her, but we continued our relationship.'

'Why? Why would you agree to that?' Claire wanted to know. What was wrong with these women? Why would they demean themselves like that? And why would they do it for a despicable man like Ray?

'Because I loved him.'

Claire wanted to slap her hand to her forehead. Fuck. Here we go again.

Yvonne shifted in her seat. 'I tried to break it off a few times, to see other people, but no one ever made me feel like he did, no one ever took care of me the way he did, so I learned to live with it. He supported us, he gave us a good life, a home...'

Claire remembered something Jeanna had said about Yvonne moving to another area. 'He bought you a house?'

'At first,' she conceded. 'Then he built us one,' she replied.

A low, anguished howl came from her mother, followed by a whisper, steeped in pain. 'That's where all the money has gone.'

'What?' Claire asked. 'What money?'

'All his bank accounts are empty.'

'Shiiiiiiiit.' That prolonged whistle of surprise came from Doug.

Claire, however, was busy doing the maths. 'What I don't understand though... I was about fourteen when all this happened. If you already had a child, she must be about twenty-five by now. Why didn't he move in with you when your daughter became an adult?'

She was so intent on waiting for Yvonne's answer that she didn't even hear the door opening beside her. She only realised they'd been joined by someone new when the new arrival spoke.

'Mum, what's going on?'

The look of panic on Yvonne's face was unmistakable. 'I told you to go straight to the car, son.'

Claire glanced up, gasped. A dark haired guy stood there. Maybe seventeen years old.

Claire could barely believe what she was seeing.

Yet another younger, taller, but unmistakable version of Ray Harrow had just walked into the room.

Forty-One

Denise – One month later

Denise walked out of her lawyer's office, held her face up to the sunlight and then she screamed at the top of her lungs. Passers-by glanced at her warily, but she could honestly say she did not give a fuck what anyone thought. Nobody mattered any more. Not even herself.

Thanks to her lawyer's digging, information spilled by that bitch Yvonne, and endless communications with bank managers and insurance companies, she had a full picture of the decimation of her life now.

Ray had transferred all their cash into an account he shared with that woman. They'd been planning to start a new life together, in the home he'd spent the last few years building for them. Oh yes. All those jobs in different cities that she thought he was working on? He was ten miles away, building the house of his dreams for him and that tart to live in. Not that she'd been slumming it before that.

For twelve years previously, she'd been living in a house he paid for. Not much more than prostitution, as far as Denise was concerned.

Anyway, the cash was all gone, either into the house or his joint account with her. He'd even put the house in Yvonne's name so that Denise couldn't claim on it when he divorced her, as it had become clear he intended to do. His life insurance policy that had named Denise as the beneficiary had been cancelled and he'd written a new will, leaving everything he had to the other family.

Despite his wishes, under Scottish law, as his legal wife, she was entitled to half his moveable estate, which encompassed the cash that was left over after all his debts were paid. It had taken her several sessions with the lawyer to work how much that would be. Nothing.

If there was a consolation, it was that Scottish law also awarded a percentage of the moveable estate to his children, but given there was nothing left, Claire, Doug and Yvonne McTay's son would be getting nothing either.

The only glimmer of reprieve for her was that the house she was living in now was still in their joint names. She'd be able to sell it and keep half the proceeds.

She would never, ever understand why he'd done this to her. How could he even think of leaving her? Yvonne McTay insisted that it came down to a simple choice. She'd given him an ultimatum, she said, that when their boy went to university, Ray would finally choose who he wanted to be with or they were done. All those years, he was just playing both sides, hedging his bets, taking his time to make up his mind. In the end, he'd picked Yvonne. Denise would never accept that though. After meeting McTay, she'd decided that it hadn't been Ray's fault. He'd been corrupted by that devious cow who had tried to steal him. She might think she'd won, but Denise had convinced herself that he'd have come back to her if he hadn't died when he did. They'd have made it. She was sure of it.

Meanwhile, the proceeds of the house sale were going to be enough for Denise to buy a small flat, and – if she was frugal – to live on the rest of it for a considerable time. Not that she'd planned to do it that way. Nope, she was going to get a job, get back out in the workplace. Her lawyer had already mentioned that when her case was resolved, she might want to apply for a position that was coming up on reception in his firm.

He was older than her, maybe sixty. Overweight. Crumpled suit. Didn't look like anyone was taking care of him at all. Not like she'd done with her Ray. Anyway, she would apply for the job and she would make sure that she made herself completely indispensable. Hadn't she and Ray clawed their way up from nothing? If she had to do it again, then she had absolutely no doubt that she could. Wasn't Ray always telling her how strong she was?

Her scream subsided, tension released. Time to move on.

She jumped into the car – it was in his name, but she'd set it on fire before she gave it to Yvonne McTay – and drove home. As she pulled into the street, she saw a woman with two teenagers get out of a car near her house. At first she thought… No, it wasn't Claire. Couldn't be. Her boys had gone now anyway. As she got closer, she saw that the woman was older, maybe her age. Probably her neighbour and her grandsons. For a second, Denise paused, a thought coming to her. Did she regret having nothing to do with her grandsons? Or with her own children's lives, for that matter?

She let that settle, until her gut told her the answer.

No.

There wasn't a single regret about the way she'd lived her life. She hadn't even seen sight of Claire or Doug since the funeral and that suited her just fine. Nothing they could say or do would change how she felt. The only person who could ever light up her room, make her laugh, make her feel complete, wasn't here.

Everyone else was just a poor substitution.

That's why she'd trained her mind to focus on her Ray. Not the one who'd done all those terrible things. No, she chose only to think about the man who had been with her for almost forty years, the one who'd given her a wonderful life and the kind of love that most people never found in a lifetime. That was the man whom she thought about now, every day and every night.

She let herself in and went straight upstairs, second nature to her now. In her room, she pulled off her clothes, and grabbed his robe from the back of the door.

She poured a glass of wine from the minibar and padded across the carpet to the bed. A rug covered the vomit splash stains from that unfortunate night. She'd wanted to replace the whole carpet, but she wasn't wasting the money, not when she'd be moving soon anyway.

'Hi, honey,' she said, as she always did when she lay down on the bed. Her fingers reached over to his bedside table and gently touched the brass urn that sat there.

His ashes.

This was her Ray. Right there. The love of her life. All of him. And she didn't need to share him with anyone.

Epilogue

Claire – 2019

'Are you ready to do this tonight?' Sam asked her, and she responded by going up on her tiptoes and kissing his face off.

'Absolutely,' she murmured.

'Will you two stop bloody doing that!' Jeanna wailed. 'I swear to God, it's making me want to heave.'

Claire tossed an oven glove at her, ignoring her indignant 'Ouch!'

'Doug, are you going to let her do that to me?'

'Absolutely,' he said, aping Claire's earlier response to Sam.

Claire giggled and high-fived her brother.

'You two are so immature,' Jeanna drawled.

'I'm not the one who kept my relationship secret for years like some naughty teenager,' Claire bit back, teasing her. In truth, she loved that Jeanna and Doug had finally, after all these years, come clean about their love and made it official. It made so much sense that she found it difficult to believe that she hadn't thought of it before.

Only one thing had bothered her when she'd finally spoken to Doug about their relationship, late on the night of their father's funeral. They were back at her house and Sam had already gone to bed. Jeanna was conked out on the couch and they'd thrown a blanket over her. Sitting at the kitchen table, they were several gins down and she felt completely comfortable probing into his love life and invading his privacy.

'Years ago, when Jeanna got sick, she told me she'd been seeing someone other than Giles. That was you?'

He nodded. 'Yeah.'

'And yet, you didn't admit your relationship even then?'

He shook his head, his shoulders slumped with regret. 'She told me she wanted to call the whole thing off. That it had been a mistake. That she'd only been having the odd one night stand with me for all those years because it was a bit of fun, a distraction.' He was a couple of drinks too far in to say 'distraction' properly, so it came out as a bit of slur. Luckily, Claire was just on the right side of drunk to understand him. 'It was only a couple of years later, when we got together at your thirty-fifth birthday party…'

'You slept together at my thirty-fifth birthday party?!'

'Yeah, sorry about that. We weren't actually checking out the tilework in the toilets.'

'I don't even recognise you any more,' she told him, feigning outrage and pursing her lips to stop them smiling.

'It was only then that she admitted if she'd let me take care of her when she was sick, she'd never have known if I was there for her, or out of sympathy and the need to do the right thing. She's so stubborn.'

'You think?' Claire asked, sarcasm dripping.

'Thing is,' Doug admitted, 'I'd have been there in a heartbeat. She's stubborn and bitchy and difficult and a train wreck of unpredictability… but I've never loved anyone like I love her. God help me.'

Claire knew he was definitely way past his normal levels of drunk to admit that. And she adored him for it.

The two of them had sat with that for a moment, before Claire's mind had gone in a different direction.

'Our mother only ever loved our father,' she said, not sure what point she was making.

Doug nodded. 'But that was a twisted love. It's different.'

Claire took a minute to process that. 'Do you think she'll want to be back in our lives now that he's gone?'

Doug shook his head. 'Nope. And we can't get back in her life because we were never truly there to begin with.'

Claire knew he was right, but she needed to bare her soul a little further and he was the only person she could do it with.

'I agree. Even if she turned up at my door tomorrow and asked to be part of our family, I wouldn't let her. Not because of the way she treated me – I learned to deal with that a long time ago – but because of the way she treated Fred and my kids. It was like they were completely unimportant, didn't matter. She barely spoke to the boys their whole lives, had no interest in them whatsoever. As a mother, defending my own kids, I'll never forgive her for that.'

'And you shouldn't,' Doug agreed, reinforcing her feelings.

'I pity her,' Claire went on. 'Because she never learned that all that really matters in life is family, and if someone wants you all to themselves it's because they want to control you, not because they adore you. She never grasped that. Or maybe she did, but she still chose to live that way because it genuinely made her happy. But where's it got her? She wouldn't give love to anyone but him and it's left her a sad, lonely woman. What a waste.'

Doug was nodding as she spoke. 'Forget her. Don't let her take a single minute more of your time. You have an incredible family, great boys, a good man and a world of people who love you. What was it that Grandad told us Gran used to say? She made her bed so she could lie in it. Well, our mother made her bed and the result is a pathetic life. Her choice.'

A pause while Claire digested that. 'At least we got a brother out of it.'

Doug grinned. They'd met up with Ryan, their half brother, the week before. Yvonne had dropped him off at Gino's and come back for him a couple of hours later. It had been a bit awkward at first, but by the end of it, they'd started to form the kind of bonds that she hoped would become much stronger over time. She always had room in her life for someone else to love, and thankfully, despite the physical resemblance, he'd turned out to be a decent, caring guy who was nothing like his father.

'Just don't decide you like him better than me,' Doug joked.

'Depends whether he keeps lifelong secrets about his relationships,' Claire jibed back. He was still laughing when she'd leaned over, wrapped her arms around him, and stayed like that, feeling safe and loved... at least until she'd realised that he'd fallen asleep, at which point she'd slid out, let him slump forward on to the table, and gone off to bed. In the morning, she'd found him wrapped around Jeanna on the couch. It was one of the most heart warming things she'd ever seen.

Until tonight.

She answered the doorbell and in trooped Val and her husband, Don, Josie and Suze, and Cammy and Caro. They were all holding large bags with tantalising aromas wafting out of them.

'Christ on a bike, we're lucky to make it here alive,' Val blurted. 'Ma nerves are shattered. Have you ever seen six people, an Indian feast for ten, and four extra portions of pakora fit into a Hyundai? If the police had caught us, we'd be sucking our samosas in a cell right now.'

'I didn't mind it, to be honest. It's the closest thing to an intimate moment I've had in months,' Josie cackled, making Sam howl with laughter. He'd absolutely fallen in love with these women, which was just as well, given the change in status that was about to affect their relationship.

They ate first, drinks flowing as freely as the laughs. It was five minutes before ten o'clock when an alarm sounded on Claire's phone.

'It's time! Right, Doug, make it happen.'

Doug slid over to a laptop that had already been set up on the shelf underneath the TV that was fixed to the kitchen wall. It was a large flat-screen, fitted there so that the boys could have all their mates round and hang out in the kitchen to watch sport. Claire had barely switched it on since they'd left, but she cheered now as it sprung to life, thanks to some wire that was connected to it from the laptop. A few clicks of buttons later and Jordy's face filled one half of the screen, Max's face the other. The sight of them sent another cheer around the room and made both boys laugh. Setting up this joint call had taken over a week of planning and they had both boys together for exactly ten minutes before Max had to go off to... actually, she had no idea what he was going to do, but it was something to do with a submarine and the Official Secrets Act.

'Eh, looks like you've got a party going on there, Mum,' Jordy laughed, and she knew he'd be gutted he was missing it. That shy little guy on the first day of school had turned out to be as much of a party animal as his brother.

'We do! Only people missing are you two,' she said truthfully, mortified that tears shot to her bottom lids. She blinked them back. Bloody hell, she thought she'd got over that.

'Hi, Uncle Doug, hi, Aunt Jeanna, Hi... Dad?' Max said, shocked, peering closer to the screen at his end, to make sure he was seeing it right.

'Hi, guys,' Sam greeted them, stepping fully into the frame.

Jordy's grin became even wider, although there was a quizzical look there too.

'Dad! What are you doing there? And where's Nic—'

'Stop right there, young man,' Jeanna interrupted him. 'You always did ask too many questions.'

Jordy nodded, giving a rueful shrug of admission. He adored his Aunt Jeanna and they'd always had that banter that was based on love dressed up as mutual insults and brutal honesty.

Claire decided to step in. 'OK, so the thing is, we've got something to ask you guys. And there's an audience here, so think very carefully about how you answer.'

When she'd suggested this, she'd known it was a risk, but she'd talked it over with Sam and they'd decided to go for it. What it all came down to was that she wanted everyone she loved in the same room, to hear the news at the same time.

Doug and Jeanna were the only ones who knew what was about to happen, so the others had the same puzzled faces as the boys.

'We wanted to know how you'd feel about your dad and I getting married again.'

Jordy yelled and punched the air. Max shouted an ecstatic 'Yasssssss!!!' Everyone at the table jumped up, cheering and hugging them, except Val, who was in floods of happy tears and bustling over to the worktop for some kitchen roll.

They cheered, they laughed, they cried, and long after the boys reluctantly disconnected the calls, they hugged again as they said goodbye to everyone, leaving Claire and Sam wrapped in each other's arms, their faces beaming.

'Do I have to get you a ring this time?' Sam asked, grinning. 'Or do we do the same as last time and go straight to the wedding bit, without bothering to get engaged first.'

'Let's do engagement without the ring, then straight to wedding again,' she told him. Expensive jewellery meant nothing to her. All she cared about was that they were together.

'God, you're perfect. And cheap. I think I'd like to take my fiancée to bed and show my appreciation for these qualities,' Sam murmured, kissing her neck.

'I think I'll let you,' she replied.

Upstairs, as always, they both went to the en suite to brush their teeth, before he headed into the bedroom to undress. She finished brushing, put her toothbrush back in the cabinet on the wall, paused, made a decision… There was something she had to do, something she'd been thinking about for days, wondering, contemplating an answer that she needed to know. She removed a box from the bathroom cabinet.

'I was about to send in a search party,' Sam said, when she finally made it into the bedroom, wrapped in her favourite white fluffy dressing gown.

He leaned up, grabbed the belt that tied her robe together and tugged it playfully.

'You know, this empty nest thing isn't so bad after all,' he said, his voice oozing lust and love for her.

There was a pause, before he realised that she was still standing there, in some kind of stunned, catatonic trance.

'Babe, what's up?' he asked, alarmed now.

'Do you love me, Sam?' she whispered.

'Until forever this time,' he promised.

'No matter what?'

'Absolutely.'

A smile took over her lips as she pulled a long white stick out of her robe pocket.

'Then we might have to rethink this empty nest thing after all.'

Slowly, he turned the stick over to reveal two boxes, with two perfectly formed blue lines.

Acknowledgement

Once again it was a joy to work with the fabulous team at Aria – thank you to each and every one of you for the work that you do to make my novels come to life.

Special thanks to my brilliant editor Caroline Ridding, who has guided each of my Aria books from conception to the finished article with boundless wisdom, support, inspiration and enthusiasm. Working with you has been one of the greatest joys of my career.

To all my gal pals, who are never far from my kitchen and come armed with endless laughter, great chat, buckets of moral support and barrels of biscuits. I love you all.

And finally, as always, to my guys, J, C & B – I never forget how lucky I am.

Love,
Shari xx

About Shari Low

SHARI LOW is the No. 1 best-selling author of over 20 novels, including *One Day In Winter, A Life Without You, The Story Of Our Life, With Or Without You* and her latest release, *Another Day In Winter*.

And because she likes to over-share toe-curling moments and hapless disasters, she is also the shameless mother behind a collection of parenthood memories called *Because Mummy Said So*.

Once upon a time she met a guy, got engaged after a week, and twenty-something years later she lives near Glasgow with her husband, a labradoodle, and two teenagers who think she's fairly embarrassing except when they need a lift.

For all the latest news, visit her on Facebook, twitter, or at www.sharilow.com

Hello from Aria

We hope you enjoyed this book! Let us know, we'd love to hear from you.

We are Aria, a dynamic digital-first fiction imprint from award-winning independent publishers Head of Zeus. At heart, we're avid readers committed to publishing exactly the kind of books we love to read – from romance and sagas to crime, thrillers and historical adventures. Visit us online and discover a community of like-minded fiction fans!

We're also on the look out for tomorrow's superstar authors. So, if you're a budding writer looking for a publisher, we'd love to hear from you. You can submit your book online at ariafiction.com/we-want-read-your-book

You can find us at:
Email: aria@headofzeus.com
Website: www.ariafiction.com
Submissions: www.ariafiction.com/we-want-read-your-book
Facebook: @ariafiction
Twitter: @Aria_Fiction
Instagram: @ariafiction

Printed in Great Britain
by Amazon